FALLER

WILL McINTOSH

FALLER

A TOM DOHERTY ASSOCIATES BOOK · NEW YORK

FALLER

A Tor Book
Published by Tom Doherty Associates, LLC
175 Fifth Avenue
New York, NY 10010

www.tor-forge.com

Tor® is a registered trademark of Tom Doherty Associates, LLC.

The Library of Congress Cataloging-in-Publication Data is available upon request.

ISBN 978-0-7653-8355-6 (hardcover)
ISBN 978-1-4668-9246-0 (e-book)

Our books may be purchased in bulk for promotional, educational, or business use. Please contact your local bookseller or the Macmillan Corporate and Premium Sales Department at 1-800-221-7945, extension 5442, or by e-mail at MacmillanSpecialMarkets@macmillan.com.

First Edition: October 2016

Printed in the United States of America

0 9 8 7 6 5 4 3 2 1

TO MY FRIEND COLIN CROTHERS

ACKNOWLEDGMENTS

Faller was a challenging novel for me to write. I went through more drafts than usual, and at each stage a fellow writer jumped in and provided invaluable feedback. First it was Joy Marchand, then my agent, Seth Fishman (who is not only an agent but a talented writer himself), then Sara King, then Ian Creasey, Kenneth Tagher, and Laura Valeri. I am so very grateful to each of them for their assistance and insight.

My friend James Pugh was always a phone call away to help me brainstorm when I got stuck, as he has been since the beginning. I've never met anyone who can come up with plot ideas and solutions to problems as quickly and brilliantly as he.

Because I know very little about physics, this book would not have been possible without the help of astrophysicist Marc Sher, who is a professor at the College of William and Mary. I showed up at his office door with a very strange world, one that would make a lesser astrophysicist pull out his hair and then banish me from the physics department forever, but Marc was up for the challenge, and I am sincerely grateful for his time and expertise.

Although this is my sixth novel, it is based on the first story I ever wrote, the one that started me on the path to becoming a writer, and as such it is very close to my heart. The original story (which is very different from this one) eventually found a home in a science fiction magazine called *Challenging Destiny,* and I thank its editor, David M. Switzer, for publishing it.

As always, thanks to my agent, Seth Fishman, for his guidance and support. I doubt I'd be writing full-time if it wasn't for him. One of these days we're actually going to meet in person.

Love and thanks to my wife, Alison Scott McIntosh, for her support, and to Miles and Hannah, just for being Miles and Hannah.

Thanks to Jennifer Gunnels at Tor Books for her insightful feedback.

Finally, a special thank-you to my editor at Tor, David G. Hartwell, for believing in this book.

FALLER

1

HE TRIED to open his eyes, but they felt glued shut, so he just lay there, exhausted, listening to the screams. His cheek was against a hard surface, pebbles pressed into his skin. A dog barked nearby.

Dog. The word burst in his mind, fresh, like he was giving birth to it. Yet, he knew what a dog was. When he thought the word, a picture formed. Four-legged animal, fur, wagging tail.

His mind felt slightly clearer, his energy returning.

He dragged his eyes open.

The world was incredibly bright, remarkably colorful. Someone ran by in green and white sneakers, sideways, as if running on a wall. Except he was the one who was sideways.

As he managed to sit upright, the world tilted and spun for a moment before settling into crisp focus. He was surrounded by tall buildings; cars and trucks were scattered on a street. None were moving. Thick black smoke rose from behind the closest buildings.

A few feet away a pink-haired woman was doubled over, clutching her head in her hands. There were colorful tattoos of flowers on her forearms.

"What is *happening*?" she wailed.

"I don't know."

The woman looked up, startled. "Do you know me? Do you know who I am?"

"No. Do you know who *I* am?"

The woman shook her head.

Something had happened. The confusion he felt, the screaming, this wasn't normal. He needed to figure out what was going on. Maybe he could find help. *Police.*

When he pressed his palm to the pavement to try to stand, lancing pain shot down his thumb and into his wrist. There was a deep slash across the pad of the thumb, caked with dried blood. There was more dried blood on the tip of his index finger and under the fingernail. This must have happened *before,* he realized.

Still shaky, he stood, looked around. There was a little silver cart with a yellow umbrella nearby. The word for it sprang to mind: *hot-dog stand.* A red and white bus sat parked along the curb. A few blocks away, a cluster of people stood with their backs to him.

He went to see what they were doing.

There were no buildings beyond the place where the crowd was standing. The sky grew wider as he approached, until he merged into the crowd and saw that the world simply ended a few feet from where they stood.

There was nothing beyond but sky.

Ragged asphalt and concrete marked the edge of the world. A concrete sewer pipe jutted from the dark earth below, spewing water.

He couldn't say how, but he sensed this, too, was wrong. The sky felt too *big,* although he knew skies were enormous.

A white-haired man knelt off to one side of the crowd on a stoop that led up to thin air. He was studying a small photograph, the contents of a wallet spread beside him. The old man looked up as he approached, held the photo up for him to see. It showed the man in a black suit, smiling, clutching an old woman's hand.

"I found this in my pocket. They must be people I know."

It took him a moment to realize the old guy didn't know he was one of the people in the photo.

"That's you," he said, pointing.

"That's me?" The old man held the photo closer, studied it. "That's me." He sounded surprised.

He wondered if there was anything in his own pockets. Checking the front ones first, he pulled out a folded food wrapper and a toy soldier.

There was a photo in one of his back pockets: a dark-haired woman with freckles, grinning, hugging a round-faced, sandy-haired man. They looked happier than anyone could possibly look.

He showed the picture to the old man, who pointed. "That's you."

He studied the man in the picture. How could that face be his? It was a stranger's face. He preferred looking at the woman. She had bright, intelligent green eyes that looked ever so slightly crossed, arms like flamingo legs.

He scanned the faces in the nearby crowd, hoping to spot the woman among them. His gaze paused on an old woman, hands buried in the pockets of a black sweater, standing at the edge of the crowd. He glanced at the picture in the old man's lap.

"Hey, there she is."

The old man stood, squinted into the crowd. "Where?"

"There." He grasped the man by the elbow, led him to the woman. She turned as they approached, her eyebrows pinched.

The old man studied the photo, looked at the woman, studied the photo again. He held the photo up so the woman could see it. "I think that's you in the photo. With me."

Relief spread across the woman's face. "Do you know me?"

"I don't," the old man admitted. "But we must be something to each other, don't you think? In the picture we're holding hands."

"I don't understand what's happening." She touched her face. "Am I dead? Is that it?"

"I don't think we're dead. No," the old guy said.

He was glad these people had found each other. He wished he could find the woman in his photo, so they could face whatever was happening together.

"I'm going to look for this woman." He held up his photo.

The old man nodded. "Thank you. I won't forget the kindness you showed a total stranger."

As he set off along the edge, he took a closer look at the other things in his pocket. The thumb-sized green toy soldier was connected to a toy parachute by a half-dozen threads.

As he opened the folded-up food wrapper, he stopped walking. There was something drawn on the back in rusty brown, the crude shapes smeared and splotched. A series of ovals ran down the length of the page, with an *X* over the bottom one. He moved his thumb, which was obscuring a second image in the bottom right-hand corner of the page: a triangle with two numerals in it—a one, followed by a three.

He studied the dried blood caking his thumb, set it beside one of the ovals. It was the same rust color as the writing. He'd cut his thumb and scrawled those ovals on the food wrapper with his own blood, then put it in his pocket. He'd left a message to himself. If he'd sliced open his thumb to write it, he must have known something was about to happen, and the message must be important.

He studied the ovals, the triangle with the numerals inside, and tried to make sense of them, but it meant nothing to him. Carefully folding the wrapper, he put it back in his pocket and walked on.

Crowds were gathered along the edge on every street. He searched the faces, seeking the dark-haired woman.

The crowds thinned with each block, and eventually he came upon a deserted, ruined part of the world. Only a few buildings stood; the rest had been reduced to piles of steel and concrete. Wading through the wreckage, he picked up blackened bricks, melted electronics. Vehicles had been crushed flat, fires had raged. There were no bodies, at least none he could see, and no smoke, so the destruction wasn't recent.

Feeling exhausted and overwhelmed, he squatted, closed his eyes. He was in serious trouble. All of them were. But he didn't understand the trouble; nothing made sense, none of it fit together.

What was there to do but keep looking, both for the woman in the picture and for answers? He moved on, staying close to the edge.

· · · ·

HUNGRY, HIS throat dry, he found himself back where he'd started.

The world was a circle, and smaller than he'd imagined.

Most of the crowd was gone, including the man and woman he'd reunited. They'd all no doubt gone to find food and a place to sleep. He decided he'd better do the same.

2

Two BIG-EYED children sitting on the steps outside an apartment building gazed up as he approached.

"Have you seen this woman?" He held up the photo.

They shook their heads in unison.

"Okay. Well, thank you anyway." He felt guilty leaving the children on their own, but there were so many children on their own. He'd met most of them over the past few days as he walked to every corner of the world, asking everyone he met if they'd seen the woman in the photo.

His hope of finding her was fading, and as it did, looking at the photo became painful. He longed to see her, even though he had no idea who she was.

An orange sheet of paper rolling on the breeze blew up against his shin. He peeled it off.

It pictured four men, three holding musical instruments. *Guitar. Saxophone. Trumpet.* Above the picture of the men were boldly printed letters. He squinted, trying to make the letters speak. He knew the letters, knew which was *A*, which was *Q*, and he knew they said something, but no matter how hard he tried he couldn't make them speak.

Some words came so easily. Why wouldn't the name of the woman in the photo come to him? Why wouldn't his own?

Maybe he should pick a name, for now. He was tired of feeling nameless. He folded the paper and added it to the day's collection of clues, stuffed in his pockets.

As he headed home he considered names, finally settling on Clue, because as far as he could tell he was the only person looking for them. Everyone else was focused on finding food and clothes. And weapons.

. . . .

CLUE STOOD muttering to himself, surrounded by things he'd amassed. He should be out searching for food, because the howling emptiness in his stomach made it difficult to think, but first he wanted to study everything at once, see if it sparked an insight.

The best clue was still the blood drawing, which he knew so well by now it was all but etched on his eyeballs.

The triangle with the numbers in it might have been a flag, because its shortest side—the vertical side—extended downward an inch or so. It was hard to tell, though, because the drawing was so poorly executed. There was a thumbprint smearing the top circle. He couldn't imagine what was so important about these circles that he would use his own blood to draw them.

Beside the indecipherable drawing was a length of pipe, one end ragged and twisted, as if it had been torn by a giant, the other end neatly sawed using a hacksaw from the tool box Clue had found. Sundry papers, magazines, and books filled out his collection.

One book, in particular, had photos of the world that included streets and buildings that didn't exist, set out beyond the edge of the world. It was possible these streets were only make-believe, like the images of endless bodies of water and fantastic animals he'd found, but there was another possibility: maybe the world had once been bigger, and something happened to make it smaller. The pipe was torn as if it had been ripped in half with incredible force.

Shouting outside broke his concentration. He went to the window of the apartment he'd claimed. Men carrying rifles, axes, pieces of wood were leading a dozen or more children down the street. He'd seen these men before, or others like them, stockpiling tons of food and supplies in a building with heavy steel doors and bars on the lower windows. Clue didn't understand what they'd want with children, though.

Grabbing a jacket he'd found in the front closet, he hurried down the seven flights of stairs.

By the time he got to street level, the gathering was out of sight. Hands in his pockets, he turned in the direction they'd been heading.

He should be searching for food. The stores were empty; people were going door to door through every building, smashing vending machines, emptying cupboards in unoccupied apartments, and sometimes in occupied ones.

The food must have come from somewhere. Clue had yet to find any place where cans of food could be produced, or fresh food was growing. Food grew—that much he knew. Apples grew on trees and carrots grew underground. But where? If he could figure out what had happened, maybe he could solve the food problem. If not, this was going to become a nightmare before much longer.

Clue thought he heard gunshots. He stopped, listened. In the silence he heard the gunshots clearly, along with screams. Shrill, terrified children's screams.

Taking off at a sprint, he tried to imagine what would terrify children like that. The screams grew louder as he turned a corner around a brown brick building.

He stopped short.

Men were pointing weapons at a crowd of onlookers. Other men were pushing children off the edge.

"What are you doing?" Clue ran toward the edge as a screaming little boy clung to a fat man's leg. The man pried the boy's little fingers until the boy lost his grip and fell onto his back. The man kicked the flailing boy over the edge.

Clue reached the onlookers, who were shouting and crying for the men to stop. Seven or eight onlookers lay dead at the feet of the men wielding the weapons.

"What are you doing? What are you doing?" Clue shouted, pushing through the crowd.

"They're saying there's not enough food for everyone," an Asian woman said. "We have to stop them."

It was too late, though. The children were gone. The men stood where they were, the front line with weapons at the ready, the ones near the edge—the ones who'd done the pushing—simply standing, hands hanging at their sides. The faces of a few were streaked with tears; others were grimacing, as if they'd just eaten something rotten.

A commotion rose behind Clue. He turned, craned his neck.

More men, leading more children.

"Out of the way," one of them shouted. "Move, or we'll shoot."

Shouting at the men, the crowd moved aside until Clue, the Asian woman, and two other men stood alone blocking their path. The children looked terrified and confused, but clearly had no idea what these men planned to do to them.

Two shots rang out; the man to Clue's left jerked and dropped to the asphalt, a bloody hole in his sternum. Gasping and writhing, he clutched the hole, grimacing in pain.

Clue pressed his hand to the Asian woman's shoulder, urged her toward the crowd. They merged into the crowd as the children were led past.

Clue sank to his knees as children were thrown off. He covered his ears. Their screams were intolerable; they were going to kill him just as surely as the men's bullets.

"Please don't. Please don't," he said, his palms clapped over his ears. He had to stop this. He'd rather die than live through what was happening. He struggled to his feet, woozy with shock, and pushed through the crowd.

Once again, it was too late. They were gone; the only sounds were people sobbing.

"This is for your good as well as ours," one of the men by the edge shouted. "Someone has to do it or we all starve." He was tall, young, with black circles below his hungry eyes.

A hundred shouted replies, curses, entreaties blended into an incoherent howl from the onlookers. The man folded his arms across his chest, turned his back on the crowd, shaking his head as if to say they were all fools.

The men with the weapons stood their ground, which Clue was certain meant more children were coming. What were they going to do, round up every child and throw them over the edge? Would they move to the weakest adults after that? Probably.

He heard a child crying; a moment later more children came around the corner led by more armed men.

"No. Oh, no." Clue put his hands on his knees and leaned over to throw up. Nothing came, though his stomach roiled violently. If he charged the men they would shoot him down, and that would be the end of it. He could commit suicide in that way, or he could watch, or he could run away. Those were his choices.

He decided to run. If there was a way he could save even one child, he would stay and suffer through this horror, but why witness it if he couldn't save even one?

Clue froze. He straightened, eyed the advancing line of kids. *Could* he save one? Just one?

He thought of the old man on that first day, showing the old woman the photo from his wallet. Clue pulled his photo from his pocket and marched toward the children. Three rifles spun to point at him.

"She's with me." He waved the photo, pointed at the closest child, a young girl. "I found this photo of the two of us in my pocket." He went right up to the girl, who had brown skin and came up to his armpit. "I found you. I finally found you." He gripped her elbow and led her toward the crowd.

"Get back," a grey-haired, bearded man shouted, rifle raised to his cheek.

"She's *mine,* you idiot," Clue shouted back, waving the photo. His heart was hammering, his eardrums throbbing. "If we're in a photo together she must be my daughter, or *something.*" As he led the girl toward the crowd, the man with the rifle tensed. Clue grimaced, anticipating the gunshot.

He reached the crowd. The Asian woman gripped the young girl's other hand. "Let's get her out of here before they change their minds."

"Wait." The girl tugged to free her hand from Clue's. "We have to get Violet."

"We can't," Clue said. "I'm sorry. It won't work a second time."

The girl stood her ground, eyes defiant. "Violet's my best friend."

Clue swept her up in his arms and took off.

"What are they doing?" the girl asked, looking back, as the screaming began. "Why are they crying? *Violet?*"

"Don't look," Clue said. "Close your eyes."

The Asian woman led the way, turning left and right, making it difficult for anyone to follow. Finally she led them through a smashed-out display window, into a large clothing store. She wound between display racks.

When they were near the back she motioned them to sit among jackets scattered on the floor. Clue set the girl down, his legs rubbery.

The screams still rang in his ears. His chest hitched as he took a deep, rattling breath, trying to get hold of himself.

"What did they do to Violet?" the girl asked.

"They're terrible men," Clue said.

"I know *that*," she said. "What did they do to her? Did they—" Her voice dropped to a whisper. "Did they push her?"

"Yes."

The girl nodded.

"They're going after anyone who can't defend themselves," the woman said. "They emptied out a retirement home on the other side."

"What is going on?" Clue asked. "There must be a reason this is happening."

"How do we find it, though? No one remembers."

He emptied his pocket, unfolded the food wrapper and handed it to the woman. "I drew this with my own blood right before—" He cast about for the right words. Before what? "Before. Can you make any sense of it?"

While the woman examined the drawing, Clue showed the toy soldier to the girl. "Watch this." He bunched the soldier's parachute in his fist and underhanded it toward the store's high ceiling. It floated placidly to the ground.

It made the girl smile, so he held it out to her. "Want to try?"

She tossed it in the air, then scampered to catch it. He wondered why he'd had a toy in his pocket. Did he have a child somewhere? Was he or she being pushed off the edge at this very moment?

Or was it the *parachute* he was supposed to pay attention to?

"Do you have something you call yourself?" Clue asked the girl. She'd called her friend Violet; maybe she had a name, too.

"All the girls picked flower names," she said. "I'm Daisy. The boys picked animals."

"Hello, Daisy. I call myself Clue." He'd saved this girl, this one delightful little girl with a leaf tangled in her curly hair and the eyes of a fighter. It was enough; it had to be. He had to put the others out of his mind.

The woman handed the drawing to him, shaking her head. "I don't understand it, either."

"What should I call you?" It felt good to have people to talk to. Clue had been too busy to realize how lonely he was.

"I don't know. Let's see." She looked at the ceiling. "If the girls are picking flower names, why don't you call me Orchid?"

"Orchid it is."

"I'm so hungry," Daisy said.

Clue looked at Orchid. "I have two cans of tuna left. That's all. I'm willing to share."

Orchid nodded. "I have some. Come on." Clue followed her out to the street, where she pointed at the building that towered over the rest. "We have to climb, though. I'm on the forty-first floor."

Clue nodded, gazing at the tower. It was grey, and came to a needle point at the top. "Smart move. Higher would be safer. Who would climb forty-one flights if they didn't have to?"

"I have about two dozen cans and packages. I'm willing to share it with a man who'd risk his life to save a child." She raised her eyebrows, which were nothing but thin lines. "Why don't we pick up your tuna and pool our resources?"

The thought of having a companion, an ally, to navigate this hell sent a flood of gratitude through him. "Sounds good to me. I need to bring some other things, too. I'm collecting clues, to try to figure this out."

"Fair enough, Mister Clue," Orchid said. "There's plenty of room on the forty-first floor. It's an office complex, not an apartment. No need to worry about noisy neighbors."

They did have to worry about what to do when their food ran out, though. Maybe there were vending machines higher up in Orchid's tower. Whatever they did, though, the food was going to run out before long. Then things were going to get very bad. They were going to get terrible.

3

TRYING TO stay out of sight, Clue looked out through the shattered revolving doors, at the street. Eight people were standing around, or sitting on cars. At least three had guns, the rest carried pipes or knives.

Night or day, there were always people on the street. Now was as good a time as any to go out. He turned to Orchid and Daisy.

"Don't look straight at anyone, but don't let them think you're afraid. Act like you know just where you're going."

Clue wiped his palm on his shirt, got a better grip on the butcher knife. Orchid was clutching hers so hard her knuckles were white.

"Here we go."

They stepped through the door frame and walked single file, Daisy in the middle. A tall, sunburned man noticed them, pointed them out. The group stopped talking. They turned to look at Clue, Daisy, and Orchid, who were all wearing tight-fitting clothes to make it obvious they had no food, and carried nothing except the knives. After conferring for a moment, the group turned away.

The tightness in Clue's shoulders relaxed. They weren't worth the bullets. He didn't think it would be much longer before everyone would be worth the bullets for the meat on their bones, but for now, if you could avoid being rounded up and thrown off the edge by Steel's gang, you weren't worth the bullets if you had no food.

Just thinking the word *food* made Clue's stomach clench, his mouth water. Hunger was nothing like he thought it would be. He expected to feel bad, but was unprepared for the terrible, maddening yearning. No matter how hard he tried to think of other things, his thoughts returned to savory gravy, hamburgers on soft buns, chocolate chip cookies, buttery crackers, chicken noodle soup. His head pounded from hunger.

He stepped over a body—a woman with red hair, her arms and shoulders covered in freckles. She had no visible wounds; she'd probably died of the diarrhea sickness. Orchid insisted they could avoid it if they boiled the water they got from the lake in the park. Clue didn't see how she could know that, but then again he didn't know how anyone knew anything. So they boiled their water.

"This way." Orchid pointed down a narrow street partially blocked by a delivery truck. In the distance, someone was screaming. It was one of the bad screams—not someone hungry or sick, but someone who was being hurt.

They squeezed past the delivery truck. Beyond it thirty or forty bodies hung from light poles and power lines by lengths of white plastic-coated wire. Clue reached out to cover Daisy's eyes, but she pushed his hand away. He led the way, his head down, passing through the shadows cast by the bodies.

A flash of movement caught his eye: four people, men and women, coming out of a tenement building to their right. The grey-haired man in front was carrying a rifle. Clue froze as the man noticed him, half raised the rifle.

"You." The man lowered the rifle.

Clue squinted, studying him. It was the old man he'd met at the edge on Day One. He laughed with relief, gave the man a little salute. "Good to see you again."

"Who is that?" Orchid asked.

Clue explained as they met under the feet of some of the people who'd been hanged.

"What a lovely day, eh?" Clue said after introductions were made.

The old man, who called himself Poppy, smiled tightly at Clue's attempt at humor. "You searching for food?"

Clue nodded. "We're down to two cans of beans."

Poppy folded his arms, looked up at the bodies hanging above the street. "The trouble is, you never know if somewhere has already been searched, until you see the door's been kicked in. We're all searching the same places over and over."

What scared Clue was the possibility that everywhere had been searched, and there was no more food.

"The woman with you in the picture? Is she . . . ?" *Still alive,* he meant to say, but he couldn't.

Poppy shook his head. "Disease. Ten days ago."

"I'm sorry for your loss," Orchid said. Clue nodded. At least she hadn't been hung, or stabbed, or tossed off the edge. He wondered how Poppy had met up with these other people. One was young, somewhere between a man and a boy. The two women had some grey hair.

"Will you excuse us for a second?" Poppy drew his comrades out of earshot, and a brief exchange ensued in low, urgent tones. Clue wondered what they were talking about.

Poppy turned. "There are nine of us. We share what we find and we defend each other. Do you want to join us?"

"Yes," Clue said, before the last words were out of Poppy's mouth. He looked to Orchid, raised his eyebrows.

"*Yes.* Thank you so much. All of you."

"Don't thank us, it's mostly self-interest," Poppy said. "No one bothers us if we move in bands and we're armed." He patted the shoulder of the young, pimple-faced man standing beside him. "There's strength in numbers."

4

Eight big, multicolored balls hung from the high museum ceiling. One was orange-red, one a mottled blue and white. One had a ring around it—like a halo, except around the middle.

They meant something, these balls. They were important.

Clue went back to working on his parachute. The seam was crooked, the stitches not as evenly spaced as on the toy soldier's parachute.

"There you are," a voice behind Clue said. Poppy was standing in the doorway, hands on his hips. "I thought you were going on the foraging run."

The muscles in Clue's neck tensed. "They had more than enough people. I decided to work on the chute instead."

Poppy eyed the chute. "Don't waste too much time fooling around with that thing. We need to stay focused on not starving."

There was an awkward silence, during which Clue vacillated between anger and shame. He resented being chided; he didn't need Poppy telling him what his priorities should be. At the same time, he wasn't bringing in as much food as most of the others.

"I've been thinking about the things in my pocket on Day One. Every man I speak to found a wallet in his pocket, with one of those laminated cards with their picture on it. I didn't."

Poppy shrugged. "So?"

"I think I got rid of mine on purpose. I think I wanted to make sure I only found three things in my pocket." Clue picked up the toy soldier. "There's a reason I put this in my pocket. I think it has to do with the parachute."

"What the hell are you going to do with a parachute?" Poppy threw his hands in the air. "Jump off a roof?"

Clue looked at his hands. "I don't know yet."

"Because we can't eat it," Poppy went on. "And I don't know if you've noticed, but we've got eighty-seven cans and packages of food in the lockup, and after that . . ." He folded his arms and huffed. "I vouched for you. Please don't make me regret that."

It was true, he had. Clue would be dead by now if not for Poppy. So would Orchid and Daisy. Clue set down the parachute. "*Fine.* What can I do?"

Poppy thought for a moment. "Boil some drinking water, then choose five cans out of the pantry for tonight's meal and divide it up."

"Absolutely." Clue rolled up the chute, tucked it under his arm.

As he passed, Poppy clapped him on the arm. "Thank you."

Clue paused. "I'm not loafing. We need to figure out what happened. Until we understand the problem, we won't know where to look for a solution, and if we don't find a solution most of us are going to die. No matter how hard we look, there's only so much food out there. Once it's gone, there aren't enough rats, pigeons, and bugs to keep more than a hundred people alive, and you know the Steels are going to make damned sure those hundred people come from among their numbers."

Poppy rested a hand on Clue's shoulder. "How does making a parachute bring us any closer to understanding what happened?"

Clue squeezed his eyes closed. "I sliced my thumb open and made a drawing with my blood. I put it in my pocket, along with a parachute and a photo. I must have had a reason." Without waiting for an answer, Clue headed for the pantry.

· · · ·

First making sure no strangers were watching through the enormous front window of the museum's ground floor, Clue retrieved the stepladder from against the high marble wall. He set it up in front of the massive elephant, posed with its trunk raised in the air as if charging, and climbed to the elephant's open mouth to retrieve the key to the pantry.

Lighting a torch from a pile set on the floor, he passed through a corridor filled with smaller animals, into a cavernous space filled with dinosaur skeletons. Beyond was a staircase leading to the lockup.

Clue unlocked the massive padlock, set it on a shelf, and slid the key into his back pocket. When the tribe moved into the museum, they'd found the padlock already on the huge steel door, and the key on a ring of keys in a desk. It had been the most imposing padlock Clue had ever seen.

The cans and packages were spread along the shelves. Eighty-seven of them. It wasn't much, but to people starving on the streets it was a treasure. He hated going outside, seeing the people lying in the streets, too weak to do anything but beg.

With his arms full of cans, Clue went around the corner to set them down on the table that served as their makeshift kitchen so he could relock the pantry.

Down the hall from the table, Clue noticed a painting he hadn't before. Colored balls in the night sky, surrounded by a gorgeous swath of bright stars. They were the exact same colors as the balls hanging from the ceiling in the other room. Maybe these balls belonged in the sky? The thing was, he'd looked into the night sky a dozen times, and never seen anything but stars and the moon. Had they disappeared as part of whatever had happened?

And what about all these animals? He knew they were supposed to be alive, walking around. Why were there no elephants or tigers in the world?

So many questions. Clue sat, picked up the can opener, and began preparing plates to bring down to the whale room, where they ate their meals. He hoped like hell they'd found more food.

5

ORCHID WENT to salvage more wood for the fire, which was down to crackling embers. The light in the museum's cavernous room had grown so dim Clue could barely see the giant whale hanging over them.

Daisy was curled against him, face buried in the crook of his elbow, crying softly.

"I know," he whispered. For some reason the hunger was worst just after they ate. There was something about getting just a taste that set off a terrible, terrible yearning for more.

"What if we opened one more can?" Clue asked. "There's a can of peaches in the pantry."

"Peaches!" Daisy cried, raising her head.

Poppy gave him a withering look.

"What's one can?" Clue asked.

"Why not?" Fish said. He looked far too young to have such a dark beard. "We had a good day. We killed four rats."

The other five members of the tribe chimed in.

Shaking his head, Poppy said, "All right. If that's what everyone wants. Who am I to argue?"

They headed toward the pantry, led by Poppy, who'd pulled a board out of the fire to serve as a torch.

Orchid fell into step beside Clue. "You know, I've been thinking about your drawing. What if it means nothing?"

Clue gave her a puzzled look.

"What if it was just a final offering to some gods you believed in back then? Or maybe we were all delirious."

Clue smiled. He wondered if Orchid's words were directed at the photograph as much as the drawing. "Maybe the Believers are right, and there was nothing before Day One. Maybe the gods drew the picture and cut my finger, as a test of my faith."

Orchid huffed impatiently. "The thing is, we have no idea *what* was going on, so why worry about the drawing?"

Or the photo. Orchid was bright and beautiful, and hadn't been shy in suggesting they become more than friends. But, strange as it was, he pined for a woman he didn't remember, who, as far as the evidence was concerned, was as mythical as living elephants and the ocean. He couldn't love Orchid, because he still loved that woman.

"Wait," Orchid said, sounding exasperated, as they reached the door to the next room. He waited patiently while Orchid backtracked to the other end of the room, then retraced her steps, counting quietly. Evidently Orchid had broken one of her rules. She had to take an even number of steps crossing a room. Clue had no idea why she insisted on following so many arbitrary rules, but there was no harm in it.

A shout up ahead sent Clue and Orchid racing through the doorway, down the narrow hall leading to the pantry.

Fish was squatting in front of the locker's open door. Butter was on her knees, sobbing.

The locker was empty. Completely cleaned out.

"It was Steel's tribe. I'll bet anything," Fish said. He was standing in the empty locker, arms folded.

"Then we're not getting it back," Poppy said. "There are at least two hundred of them."

The weight of what had happened began to penetrate Clue's shock. It was a death sentence. Scavengers had picked over just about every nook and cranny in the world; there were no big undiscovered caches left in the wild, and they couldn't get by on rats, cats, pigeons, and bugs alone.

"We can steal it back, at night, just like they did to us . . ." Fish said.

"They'd know it was us, and they'd kill us," Orchid said, her voice a monotone, drained of hope.

"Where's the padlock?" Poppy asked, looking around.

"What do you mean?" Rex asked. "They broke it off somehow."

Holding the torch close, Poppy examined the brackets the padlock had been threaded through on the door and wall. "But where is it? Why would they carry off a broken padlock?" He looked up. "Who was last to go in here?"

"I pulled out the day's rations this afternoon," Clue said. "But I locked it afterward, if that's what you're—" Clue hesitated. He remembered pulling out the cans and pushing the door most of the way closed with his foot until he could set the cans down on the table and return . . .

Clue squeezed his eyes closed. "Oh, no. *Oh, no.*"

Poppy reached over to the shelf, held up the open padlock.

He'd noticed that picture, and got to wondering. He'd never gone back to lock the door.

Clue looked at Daisy, standing with her forehead pressed against the doorway, and clenched his eyes shut again. "Oh, God. I've killed us all."

No one disagreed.

This couldn't happen; he couldn't watch Daisy starve knowing it was his fault. And Orchid, and the rest of his tribe.

"I'm so sorry."

He had to figure out a way to get their food back. But how could he? How could anyone?

6

CLUE LIMPED up the dark stairwell, feeling his way along. His ankle was throbbing. His sneaker felt too tight, which meant the ankle was swelling. He didn't want to stop and see how bad it was. It didn't matter how bad it was; he had to keep at it until he got it right.

The toy paratrooper's chute opened every time without fail if he folded it the right way, while his hadn't inflated once. It might have to do with his weight versus the toy, but he didn't think so; he suspected he wasn't traveling fast enough when he opened the chute. It made sense—he could get the chute to open by dragging it along the ground, but only if he ran very fast, or there was a strong breeze. The air was what pulled the chute open.

Pushing open the heavy door, he raised his hand to shield his eyes from the bright midday sun. The black tar roof was steaming hot, and sticky underfoot. His head down to avoid the sun, Clue went right to the edge.

When he saw how much higher he was, he took a half-step back. He eyed the pile of mattresses in the lot, now *five* stories below instead of three. From ground level the pile looked huge, but from up here it seemed like a very small target surrounded by a lot of very hard ground. Daisy, who was standing beside the mattresses, waved up at him. Clue waved back, somewhat less enthusiastically.

This had to work, or he was going to get badly hurt, even if he hit the mattresses.

Three figures appeared around the corner of the building next door and strolled into the lot. Their bodies looked strange—flattened and foreshortened by Clue's bird's-eye view.

He was wasting time. He tilted his head left and right, loosening the tense muscles in his neck, shook both hands at the wrist, then stepped onto the low ledge, which was two bricks wide. One final time he studied the pile of mattresses, mentally rehearsed the procedure.

Leap out, let yourself fall at least two stories to build up speed, then pull the rip cord. If the chute doesn't open, curl up into a ball.

Laughter drifted from below. The three figures were watching him.

Let them watch. Let them laugh. Clue took a deep breath and leaped. For an instant he hung in the air, then he plummeted, the whistling of the air growing louder. He delayed as long as he could bear, then pulled the cord.

He felt the chute *jump* out of the pack, heard it *whoosh*. The harness jerked, sending pain shooting across his ribs to his armpits. He looked up: the parachute was partially inflated, rotating slowly as the lines twisted around each other.

He was looking up when he hit the mattresses; he hit awkwardly and spun off, slammed chest-first into the dirt with an *oof*.

The parachute floated down over him as the onlookers roared with laughter.

Clue jumped up, whooping with joy. He dug himself out from under the parachute, limped to Daisy, lifted her in the air. *"Did you see that?"*

"I did, I did." Daisy laughed. She was far too thin, her jutting cheeks nothing but bones lying under a thin sheaf of skin, her eyes sunken. He was going to fix that. It had taken a catastrophe for Clue to realize the point of the parachute, but now he understood.

Clue set Daisy down, spun to face their visitors, whom he now recognized as Shoeless, Red, and Runner, part of the relatively harmless Subway tribe. "Get your cans ready, gentlemen; it won't be long now."

"You've got to be joking," Red said, pointing at the sky. "You might as well have filled that pack with bricks for all the good it did you."

Red's companions laughed appreciatively.

"Go ahead and laugh," Clue said, unable to stop grinning. "As long as you spread the word. I *will* jump, but there has to be a crowd of at least two hundred, paying a can apiece."

"Oh, sure, you bet," Red said, his tone making it clear he thought Clue was a self-deluded idiot. That only made Clue want it more. He would do this. He would save his people. The parachute still needed work, and he had to figure out how to keep the harness from digging into his armpits. All he had to go on there was the toy's painted-on harness, but he'd figure it out.

"*Clue,*" Runner said, laughing. "More like No Clue. Clueless. Haven't a Clue."

"More like *Faller,*" Red said.

Red's friends burst out laughing as if it were the most hilarious thing they'd ever heard. Clue liked the name, though. He liked it better than Clue. *Faller.* It felt right; it suited him. From now on he would be Faller.

7

THE QUICKEST route to the Tower was straight through the heart of the city, but with so many people following it was easier to wind along the edge of the world, where there were fewer rusting cars blocking their path, less trash underfoot.

Faller walked close to the edge, just shy of the point where tripping on a brick might send him tumbling into eternity. He had two reasons for walking so close. First, it unnerved the people following him. Second, the vastness of the sky soothed him, and Faller needed soothing. Doubt and anxiety were growing with each step.

"Don't do this," Orchid said. "We'll find another way." She carried on tracking her steps as she spoke, poking out thumb, forefinger, thumb, forefinger, so she knew if she was on an odd step or even.

"People are going to remember this day, like they remember Day One," Daisy said, taking twice as many steps to keep up with Faller and Orchid.

Orchid threw back her head and laughed a bit more heartily than Faller thought necessary. "I don't think Faller plunging to his death is in quite the same category as Day One."

"*I* think it is," Daisy said, splitting off momentarily to move around a lamppost canted at an angle. "Everyone will talk about this for years."

"This will be remembered about as well as when old Crabby got pushed out a fifth-story window by a dog trying to get the beans Crabby was eating."

"Can we stay on topic? We're talking about how people will sing songs about me." Faller looked pointedly at Orchid. "And can you please stop referring to this as me plunging to my death?"

Orchid grabbed his arms, yanked him to a stop. "I'm trying to paint an image for you, to bring you to your senses." Her dark eyes, shaped like two slivers of moon, searched his. "Because I care about you. More than you know. Please, *don't do this*." She squeezed his arm.

"I'll be *fine*." He tried to sound reassuring despite his own doubts. And if he wasn't fine, at least he will have died making amends for the terrible mess he'd created. "Come on, everyone's waiting."

They came to an inlet where a ledge of jagged asphalt dropped off, revealing blue sky and pink-white clouds below. Faller veered around it, eyeing the broken ends of huge pipes jutting out into space from the rock face, the gaping hole even farther down that was the abrupt end of one of the subway tunnels crisscrossing the world.

With the Tower looming, they cut toward the heart of the city, away from the edge. Weeds plucked at Faller's pants as they cut along a shattered sidewalk, past red-brick apartments atop plundered stores. They passed under the legs of a giant billboard that pictured beautiful people no one ever remembered seeing, not even in the early days before the die-off. The beautiful people on the billboard were smoking cigarettes.

He wiped his sweaty palms on his jumpsuit.

They cut down a narrow cobblestoned street, the red- and brown-bricked buildings hugging the street.

"There he is," someone called from above. Three young girls were on the roof of one of the tenements, probably a vantage point from which to watch his jump without having to pay. He raised his hand and waved to his fans. *Fans* was the only way Faller could think to describe them. It was one of those words that sat unused in that place in the back of his head, because it never applied to anything. And now, here, suddenly it did. Faller liked having fans; it put a swing in his step.

"Watch," Orchid said, pulling his hand.

Faller looked down just in time to sidestep a jutting femur someone had tried to stuff down a sewer. There was a skull as well, wedged into the too-small sewer opening. Probably someone had found the bones in an apartment they wanted to live in.

Still two blocks away, they reached the roadblocks the Steel tribe had erected all around the Tower, to ensure everyone paid. It stuck in Faller's craw that the Steels would get ten percent of the gate and free admission, given that they were the bastards who'd stolen the food in the first place, but a tribe as small as Faller's could never pull off this sort of event without an alliance. At least it ensured there wouldn't be many gate-jumpers; few people thought saving one can of food was worth risking a trip off the edge.

A block ahead, the crowd grew thicker and more boisterous. Faller picked up his pace.

There were more people packed in the street along the edge side of the Tower than Faller had ever seen together in one place. Many had dressed for the occasion in whatever passed for their finest—skirts, suits, colorful bandanas, cowboy boots. Most of it was worn, soiled, and wrinkled almost beyond recognition. It was depressing, how the colors so vivid on Day One were draining out of the world, replaced by the browns of dirt and rust.

A roar went up as Faller approached. He held up his hand, then noticed a strange mound in the weeds by the crumbling fountain. It took him a moment to recognize it as a pile of pillows and mattresses. He stopped short, pointed at the mound. A roar of laughter filled the air.

"Just in case," shouted Fish, who was standing close to the mound. It set off another round of laughter.

"It'll have to be a lot bigger than that if my chute doesn't open," Faller shouted. His stomach was in knots; he wasn't in the mood for banter, but this jump was an excuse for people to gather and celebrate. That was at least part of the reason they were paying a can of food none of them could afford to pay.

Many were probably hoping the parachute collapsed into a fat spinning tail and he plummeted one hundred seven stories (he'd counted) to his death. But he was going to disappoint them. He was going to fly, not five stories off the roof of an apartment building this time, but on and on like a bird over the tops of buildings, until he drifted softly back to earth amid a cheering crowd.

Faller squatted beside Daisy so he would be eye level with her. "Why don't you wait here, with Butter?" He pointed Butter out, sitting with Speedy on a blanket spread on the sidewalk. Daisy wrapped her arms around him; Faller hugged her in return, fighting back tears. If things went wrong, he hated that Daisy would be here to witness it.

Giving him one last squeeze, Daisy said, "Please don't screw up." Having given him her vote of confidence, she joined Butter and Speedy on the blanket.

Faller and Orchid continued to the Tower. Biter, the Steel gang leader, was waiting at the foot of the steps outside. He was a remarkably handsome man, tall and muscular, like one of the men on the billboards, only less clean, and wearing a dirty neon-orange T-shirt instead of a suit.

"Word is, we've got close to three hundred cans," Biter said, grinning.

"That many? Terrific. Worth risking my life over. No doubt about it."

Biter nodded. "Good. Hang on to that thought as you're climbing. We don't want to issue refunds."

"I won't be taking the stairs down. I guarantee you that." Faller's voice was shaking.

While he and Orchid strode toward the Tower, Faller looked up. It was impossibly tall. He was afraid to think how he'd feel when he was at the top, looking down.

He pushed open a squealing door and stepped into the dark lobby. They skirted broken glass sprayed from broken windows, and stopped at the stairwell.

"There's no point in you walking up all these steps with me." He waved toward the doors. "Go on out and wait for the show. I'll see you in a couple of hours."

Orchid looked so terribly sad. It broke Faller's heart. "Is there anything I can say that will change your mind?"

Even if he wanted to, there was no way to back down now. If he did, in all likelihood the Steels would drag him up the steps and toss him off.

But even if the Steels weren't involved, he would still jump. They needed food. Daisy needed food.

"No."

Orchid's eyes filled with tears. "If you're really going to do this, I want to be there with you." She held out her hand. "I'll carry your gear. You'll need all of your strength for the jump."

"No, no, that's all right," Faller said. "I've got it."

Orchid tugged the pack out of his hand. "Give me that. It's a hundred flights; you're going to be so exhausted you won't know which way is down."

Faller let go of the pack. She was probably right, and in any case arguing with Orchid was futile.

They headed up the first flight. Faller's heart was thumping, his fingers tingling with anticipation. Orchid counted steps under her breath.

8

By the fiftieth floor he was entirely spent and ready to give up. To celebrate reaching the halfway point, they rested.

Faller's head was pounding in time with his heart, his calves quivering.

Orchid pulled his canteen from the pack, took a drink, then offered it to Faller. He accepted it, took a long drink.

"Promise me you'll take care of Daisy if anything happens to me."

"Mm." Orchid didn't look at him.

He put a hand on her shoulder. "I need to know you'll take care of Daisy."

Orchid stood, Faller's pack still slung over her shoulders. "You know I'll do my best. But it's you she counts on."

"I know." He took a swig of water; his throat stayed dry no matter how much he drank. "That's why I have to do this."

. . . .

By the eightieth floor he was numb, staggering like a drunk. He waited for Orchid, who was walking a half-flight behind him, counting her steps aloud.

"You should turn back. You have to climb down as many steps as you've climbed up. I'm afraid you're going to take a tumble and hurt yourself, and there'll be no one around to help you."

Orchid laughed dryly. "You're afraid *I'm* going to hurt myself?"

"Yes." He wrapped one arm around Orchid. "I'll wait for you in the street. If all goes well, I'll get there before you."

She shook her head. "I don't want to be on the stairs, inside, when you jump." She gestured toward the next flight, whispered something under her breath meant only for her. "Let's go."

Sighing, Faller headed up the steps.

. . . .

WHEN HE reached the top, he collapsed, gasping. He was nauseous. His legs were quivering and the edges of his vision were grey. Orchid dropped beside him.

When the worst of the nausea had passed Faller lurched to his feet, spat a few times onto the concrete to clear the phlegm from his mouth, and went to the edge. Most of it was ringed by a wall of transparent plastic, but two sections had broken off, leaving nothing but a waist-high wall.

He changed his mind about jumping as soon as he looked down.

The street was far, far, far below. Just three blocks beyond was the edge. The endless blue sky was staggering from this vantage point.

He walked all around the perimeter, marveling at the breathtaking view, with Orchid trailing a few paces behind him, hands on her hips. The world seemed even smaller from up there, its cigar shape evident. He could trace the edge all the way around, could see every building, their heights flattened by the perspective. Even the scorched field of rubble at the far end of the world looked beautiful, somehow. It wasn't often one was high enough to truly appreciate how small the world was, hanging there in the enormous blue sky. It made you feel tiny—a speck on an insignificant speck.

When he was finished enjoying the view, Faller looked down again.

What had he been thinking? He couldn't jump from here.

He'd considered working his way up to the Tower slowly—jumping from the roof of a six-story building, then ten, then fifty. But he hadn't seen any point. Once he got much above eight stories, all the mattresses in the world wouldn't save him if the parachute failed.

In theory, jumping from this height wasn't much more complicated than jumping from a five-story building. But he realized now that the technical aspect was only part of the jump; there was also the psychological to consider.

"Can we go home now?" Orchid asked.

Faller pulled the toy paratrooper out of his pack and set it on the ledge.

"You little fucker. What have you gotten me into?" It was apropos that a toy had inspired this entire endeavor.

The webbing that ran from elbow to waist on the paratrooper puffed out, blown by a heavy gust, and it fell over.

If he didn't jump, he'd have to look Daisy in the eye and tell her she'd have to go ahead and starve, because he was afraid.

He turned to look at Orchid. "I have to do it."

"I understand. I love you. I always have." The wind muffled her words.

"You're acting as if I'm already gone. Jelly on the pavement. Have a little faith." He lifted his arms, flapped them, trying to lighten the mood, maybe give himself some courage.

Orchid didn't laugh. She stepped close and gave him a fierce hug.

"See you soon," he said.

He could see the people below—speckles mottling the street and sidewalk, waiting, watching.

Experimentally, he sat on the low ledge, swung his feet out over empty space. It took all of his willpower to keep from throwing himself back to the safety of the roof.

The wind was hard, gusting on and off unpredictably. Could a gust blow him into the side of the building before he got his chute open? He'd have to open it very quickly, then use the webbing on his jumpsuit to coax himself away from the wall.

The image calmed his pounding heart. He could drift on the breeze, the parachute a protective canopy above his head. He took a deep breath, looked out at the clouds passing, so impossibly huge and bright. Willing himself to keep his gaze *out* instead of *down,* he stuffed the paratrooper into his pocket, then drew his feet under him until he was squatting on the wall.

A few deep breaths, then, arms outstretched for balance, he stood.

The wind nudged him backward; he leaned into it to regain his footing. It stopped suddenly and he lurched forward, almost falling, his heart tripping madly. He grinned at his terror. Falling was the whole point.

"Jump," he said aloud. "Go ahead, goddammit. Just jump."

Faller coiled, tensed, glanced down at the street.

This was madness. It was too high; the restraints of his own sanity would never allow him to leap from this height.

He climbed off the wall. Orchid, who'd been squatting a dozen feet behind him, stood, her eyebrows raised.

Any way he looked at it, he was a dead man. There was no way he could survive that jump, and if Biter didn't kill him, starvation would.

"Fuck it," he said. He climbed back onto the wall. If he was going to die anyway, why not die in style?

Without allowing himself time to think, he jumped.

Everything inside him clenched. His hands in fists, his jaw clamped, Faller tumbled forward. It gave him a terrible full-on view of the street so far below. He kept rolling until he was plummeting headfirst, the glass exterior of the Tower passing upside down in a blur. He was falling way too fast, faster than he'd imagined possible. His jumpsuit flapped so hard it was like being slapped.

As he tumbled back upright he remembered the chute. He reached back and yanked open the Velcro-fastened flap of the backpack in one swift, well-practiced motion. The chute flew out, followed by the six suspension lines. He squeezed his eyes shut, braced for a yank on his harness so jarring it might break his neck.

He felt a jerk that slowed him momentarily, then he kept falling. Above him, the chute snapped frantically in the wind. He opened one eye, peered up at the chute, and screamed.

Only four of the suspension lines were attached. Two others were twisting around each other uselessly. The collapsed chute was doing nothing to slow his fall.

Frantically, he began pulling everything toward him, to try to reconnect it before he hit the ground, although the tiny sliver of his mind that was still rational knew it was hopeless. It was over; he was dead. He was going to slam to the pavement, then everything would go black. They would have a funeral and roll him off the edge and his body would fall forever.

His fingers froze on the lines as a glimmer of hope broke through his terror. Unless he went off the edge. He'd seen birds gliding on the wind with their wings spread. Could he do the same? He released the suspension lines, gauged the distance to the edge as he stretched his arms and legs into an X.

It worked; he drifted away from the Tower. But what was the point? If he made it, he would still die. Maybe it was best to get it over with quickly.

Arms and legs still spread, he coaxed his body to glide horizontally on the buffeting wind. The force of it nearly flipped him; he tipped left, then right, struggling to keep his arms from being thrown out of place. The fabric of his jumpsuit flapped wildly as the city glided by beneath him even as it rose toward him, growing larger and better defined by the second. The wind was deafening—a vertical hurricane that jerked and bounced him.

This was madness. Dying would be easier than hurtling into the void. He'd lose his mind long before he died of thirst. Yet he couldn't bring himself to give up, to draw his limbs into a cannonball and let the pavement have him.

His shoulders were burning from the strain as he reached out toward the edge of the world, his arms wide, his fingers splayed as if he could claw his way to it.

In the streets below, some of the tiny figures had broken from the crowd and were headed toward the edge, following his trajectory. Too late, he realized another skyscraper was between him and the edge. Faller twisted as he hurtled toward the glass face of it, changing his trajectory. He glided at an angle to the skyscraper, missed slamming into it by a matter of a dozen feet as he dropped toward a strip of black rooftops—a row of tenements that hung over the edge.

For the briefest instant he caught sight of people sprinting into the open, their heads craned upward, tracking him.

He strained, trying to squeeze every last inch of vertical movement out of the webbing as the roof expanded. He could see detail—satellite dishes set along the roof, a wooden water tower. At the last instant he threw his arms over his face and squawked in terror, his whole body flinching as he hurtled toward one last lousy span of roof.

A bright burst of pain lanced his foot as it caught the edge of the roof and sent him spinning end over end, his field of vision filled alternately by red brick, blue sky, then black rock until, pinwheeling his arms wildly, he stopped flipping.

He kept falling, though.

The world slid past as his heart hammered, his mouth cranked wide in a silent, breathless scream.

I

PETER DRAGGED his hand through his hair as he studied the tissue sections and sequences. His hair was oily as hell, because he hadn't showered in three days. The data, however, were clean and beautiful. The tuberculosis-riddled human lung had come through the duplicator unaltered; the duplicate lung was genetically identical to the original, right down to epigenetic mutation, only it was free of Tuberculosis-8.

"Beautiful," he said.

"I know, isn't it?" Harry Wong said, grinning.

Someone had a radio on nearby, tuned to an oldies station playing "Open Arms," by Journey. It seemed unlikely background music for a monumental scientific breakthrough.

As techs and colleagues passed, some brushing against Peter in the tight maze of lab islands, Peter scrolled to the last page of the printout, which summarized the results.

"It's all good, Doc. Right down to the fine print," Harry said.

Peter looked up. "Did you just call me Doc?"

Harry gave Peter a big, toothy, semisarcastic grin. "Yes, I did."

"No. Don't even think about it." Peter pointed his pen at Harry's face. "In grad school you had just about everyone calling me Sandy." Lowering the pen, he closed the printout. "We're *weeks* away from being able to provide workable replacement organs. Can you believe this?"

"It's pretty damned unbelievable," Harry said.

Peter held out his hand to Harry, palm up. Harry gave him a quizzical look.

"Will you dance with me?" Peter took Harry's hands and danced him between the lab stations.

"You drink too much Zing again?" Harry asked, somewhat reluctantly moving his hips to the music.

"Yeah. Probably." Peter did feel awfully full of pep and verve.

"Don't you dare twirl me," Harry said, as people began to notice, and laughter rose around the lab.

The thing was, when would Ugo's team be ready with the radical transplant procedure? If they couldn't get infected organs out and clean duplicate organs back in quickly and economically, not enough of the infected would benefit from this breakthrough.

"Have you seen an update on infection rates today?" he asked Harry.

Harry stopped dancing. "You don't want to see them. The Peterson-Jantz prion is out of control in the Ukraine and Romania. TB-8 has crossed into Nepal and Bangladesh."

"Shit." A now familiar jangling dread hit Peter, dampening his high spirits. "Damn Saudi Arabia's lying ass."

And Saudi Arabia wasn't even one of the combatants. They'd lied and lied about the extent of their oil reserves, and finally left India high and dry. If not for them India wouldn't have thrown trillions of rupees at Mozambique to effectively steal Russia's stake in Mozambique's natural gas production.

Everyone had been afraid Russia would respond with military force. Instead, *surprise*—they released a deadly disease on India. Insanity had reached a new height.

"Harry? Can I borrow you?" Jill Sanders called from four or five stations away.

Harry patted Peter's back. "Nice work, Doc. Want to celebrate tonight?"

"Sounds good. I'll see if Melissa's free. And if you call me Doc again I'm going to cut your salary in half."

"It's never just the guys anymore," Harry said, raising his voice over the din of the lab as he walked away. "You always have to bring the wife along."

"What are you talking about? You like her more than you like me."

"You got that right," Harry shouted.

Navigating islands of equipment, Peter headed back to his workspace, sectioned off from the rest of the vast floor by three semitransparent walls that began at knee level and ended a foot above Peter's head, the fourth wall a window that faced a fifty-foot-wide swatch of lawn sitting between their lab and a crumbling factory building. The light was fading, lending an ominous tinge to the aged and broken building. The plan had been to eventually convert all of the old factory buildings to labs as part of the Cross-pollination Project, but only four had been completed.

Squatting, Peter opened his minifridge, pulled another bottle of Zing energy drink from row upon row that filled the fridge. He was about to slam the fridge door closed when he noticed interlopers.

Three squareish plastic bottles were tucked toward the back of the far right row of roundish Zing bottles. Peter pulled one out and examined it. It was a seaweed-colored liquid called Green Goodness, a "drinkable army of fruits and vegetables, packed with antioxidants, vitamins A and C."

Chuckling, Peter set it back in the fridge. *Melissa strikes again.* All she ever drank was diet Sprite, yet she worried about Peter getting enough nourishment.

Over the general din of the lab, Peter heard burbling near the ceiling, among the rusted steel beams that were part of the original World War II artillery factory. *Pigeons in the rafters again.* He didn't mind them, but they drove Ugo nuts. The guy hated animals. He would deny it to the end, especially if Izabella—his animal-loving wife, sister of the provider of Green Goodness—was with him, but you could see him growing irritable when an animal was nearby, except when it was being served to him on a bed of rice.

"Dr. Sandoval?"

Peter went to his door, smiled at the tech standing near the duplicator with a screen open, data flashing across it. "Hey, Arthur. What's up?"

"It didn't work," Arthur said.

Peter only glanced at the two identical human livers laid out on a wheeled medical cart near the delivery ducts before diving into the numbers. He was a theoretical physicist; it would be Ugo's job to examine the livers themselves.

"Wasn't fooled, eh?" Peter asked, scanning the data. No matter how cleverly they tried to disguise foreign bodies as part of a biological entity, or make cells in a biological entity appear to be foreign bodies, they couldn't fool the duplicator. The results provided fascinating clues about the nature of his duplicator, about what was going on when they sent something through the miniature wormhole, but in terms of being able to produce a cancer-free, rejectionproof replacement liver for people suffering from liver cancer, the experiment was a bust.

The big double doors leading into their lab swung open. Ugo breezed in wearing his inevitable Panama hat and a black blazer.

Peter waved to get his attention.

"Which experiment is this?" Ugo asked, bending over to examine one of the livers, breathing heavily through his nose.

"Part of the masking series. It didn't work." He led Ugo away, toward Harry's station. "More importantly, though"—Peter paused for dramatic effect—"we've got a duplicate lung completely clear of TB-8."

Ugo let out an uncharacteristic bark of laughter. "It's clear?"

"Completely."

Ugo examined the lung, then looked at a cross section under a microscope. When he was satisfied, he lifted his head and breathed, "We did it."

Peter held up his hand for a high five; Ugo eyed it with impatience, then stuck out his hand, offering to shake.

Relenting, Peter shook. "Harry and I were talking about a celebration dinner tonight. Are you and Izabella free?"

Ugo tilted his head. "As far as I know. I'll check with Izabella." He clapped Peter on the shoulder. "Shall we walk?"

Without waiting for an answer, Ugo bounded toward his office to retrieve the flashlights. Peter followed less buoyantly. Walking was a major pastime in Serbia, evidently, but Peter would just as soon take a morning drive.

Handing Peter a flashlight, Ugo led the way down the long hall, as Peter struggled to match the man's long, sweeping strides. Peter wondered if the techs joked that he and Ugo looked more like a comedy team than a pair of scientists, with Ugo so tall and beefy, Peter short and slim.

Honestly, they didn't have much more in common on the inside. Ugo's adopted father was a retired general, while Peter's father had driven a school bus and cooked meth, at least until he blew their home up during a cook. Ugo collected rare wine, golfed, was a connoisseur of gourmet chocolate, listened to string quartets, and wore Panama hats and burgundy cravats. Peter listened to death metal, wore T-shirts, and was an avid cloud watcher.

They switched on their flashlights as they pushed past the steel door that led down into the darkness—into the seemingly endless, twisting bowels of the old factory, mostly built below ground to repel an air attack.

It was the compromise that made the daily walk palatable to Peter: if he was going to walk, he wanted to explore the dark corridors of the factory, rather than circle the walking trail that ringed the facility outside. The factory never ceased to surprise, with another cellar, a stairway you hadn't noticed before. A few floors below them was the main factory floor: iron machines as big as locomotives, great wheels coming out of the floor, silver pipes snaking up the walls and disappearing into the ceiling. It was beautiful in the way forgotten, obsolete things could be.

"Now we have to get a handle on Peterson-Jantz," Ugo said as they whisked along the familiar corridor that led out of the locker room at the bottom of the stairwell, into the factory proper. "I think I'm close to understanding why the Woolcoff Virus's prion-suppressing properties affect memory as well."

Peter made an encouraging sound. *Affect memory as well?* The virus completely obliterated subjects' biographical memory, and damaged semantic memory as well, leaving them barely able to function. The Peterson-Jantz prion was forced into stasis, yes, but at an outrageous cost. Prions were disease-causing versions of proteins that were found in nervous system cells, so they targeted the brain, making Peter's duplicator no help. You couldn't transplant a brain.

"I think I can isolate the problem in another six months," Ugo continued.

The corridor opened onto the factory floor: a maze of conveyor belts, hooks, oil stains, catwalks. Stacks of cardboard boxes lined one wall, emergency supplies in case they were ever forced into emergency lockdown.

There was a howling sense of loss in this place that used to be packed with rough-handed workers, sweating on the night shift, carrying out vein-bulging work to the deafening rhythm of machines. Peter loved the gritty feel of it. With everything he'd accomplished, he could easily get funding for his own shiny new facility, but he'd grown fond of this place. He liked being around the best and brightest minds from a cross section of fields.

A muffled whisper caught his attention. "What was that?" Peter pointed his flashlight toward the wall. Two nervous faces peered out from beneath a blanket between rows of boxes.

"I'm sorry, you really shouldn't be in here—" Peter began, guessing they were homeless people who'd somehow gotten inside. He stopped short as he realized it was Jack Raga, their janitor, and Victoria Rivera, one of the facility's security guards. "Oh, jeez. Sorry." Peter raised his arms in front of his face, turned to beat a hasty exit, trying to stifle laughter.

Ugo stormed right up to them. "Get dressed," he snapped, hands on hips. "You're both fired."

"No, they're not *fired*." Peter tried to keep from bursting into laughter at the thought of these two sixty-somethings sneaking off for a quickie. Jack was divorced ten years, Vicky a widow, so no one was getting hurt. "Come on, Ugo, I'm turning all shades of red here, and I know I'm not the only one."

"No, this is completely unacceptable," Ugo said. "They're fired."

"Don't be a dick. These are good people. They work hard for us."

Ugo stormed toward him. "A *dick*? Did you just call me a dick?"

"No. I didn't call you a dick, I was imploring you not to be one. There's a big difference." Peter was still feeling giggly. Definitely too much Zing, too little sleep.

Ugo got so close Peter could smell the sausage he'd eaten for breakfast. "I am a senior fellow at MIT, the youngest recipient ever of the Heritage Award in Biotechnology. Don't you ever speak to me like that again."

Peter raised his hands in surrender. "I'm sorry. I meant it as a joke. Just trying to lighten an awkward situation." He turned toward their amorous employees. "We're going to give you some privacy now."

"We're very sorry, Dr. Sandoval," Vicky called from under the blanket, sounding so like a teenaged girl caught in the backseat of her boyfriend's car that Peter had to clap his hand over his mouth.

"Vicky, did you forget my first name again?" Peter called when he had himself under control. "I have to keep reintroducing myself to you."

"Sorry, Peter. This won't happen again."

"No, no, I think it should happen as often as you guys want it to, just not during work hours. Okay?"

"You got it," Jack said. "Thank you, sir."

They headed back, the only sound the scuffing of their shoes on dirty concrete.

No way was Peter going to apologize for the dick comment. He and Melissa had both worked a million crappy jobs in high school and college. He knew exactly what it felt like to be treated like shit because you were wearing a white apron, or a Wendy's name tag with that little orange-haired girl on it. He'd never forget.

He wondered, not for the first time, how he'd become friends with Ugo in the first place. About the only thing they had in common was a bad childhood. Ugo's had ended when he was adopted out of a Bosnian orphanage that had done a good impression of a concentration camp. He'd been adopted by Serbians after the war ended, into a life of privilege, evidently as their way of making a point about reconciliation. Peter's bad childhood hadn't been nearly as awful as Ugo's, but the bad part had lasted longer.

It had been Ugo, not him, who cultivated the friendship at Stanford, introducing himself at a brown bag seminar and suggesting they meet for a drink. Peter couldn't help suspecting Ugo had been drawn to him because of his rising-star status. Then Ugo had met Izabella, who'd been in town visiting Melissa. Ugo had become family, and Peter stopped having a choice about whether to be friends with him.

9

THE ENTIRE world hung above him, blotting out the sky like the underside of a giant plucked weed, spinning into view and then out again as he tumbled. It was a sight reserved for the dead and the doomed, people who had jumped in the early days because they couldn't stand another day of hunger, and the thousands who'd been thrown. And now for Faller.

His arms flailed instinctively, seeking something to grab onto to stop his plummet. His screams were whipped away by wind that buffeted him like fists. Some ancient part of him kept expecting to slam against solid ground, even though his eyes told him there wasn't any.

· · · · ·

EVENTUALLY, COHERENT thoughts began to break through the howling panic.

Daisy must be inconsolable. Had she been peering over the edge, watched him fall, a speck growing smaller by the second? He hated the idea of that. She'd had enough misery since Day One.

Faller shouted in frustration and slapped his hands to his cheeks. What had happened to the parachute? He'd checked the lines before he packed the chute and left the museum.

He had all the time in the world to figure it out. Grasping one of the suspension lines still attached to the parachute, he reeled it in and examined the steel hooks where the clamps on the end of the loose lines should have been attached. Then he reeled in the loose lines and studied them.

They'd torn loose from the clamps. He'd been falling too fast for the knots to hold. How could he have been so stupid? He should have tested the parachute more thoroughly before he jumped. He could have attached something heavy to it and tossed it off the Tower with a long string attached to open the chute from the roof. He'd been so eager to fix the mess he'd made.

He opened his mouth to curse, immediately closed it. The wind was relentless. When he opened his mouth, it blew his cheeks open wide, made them flap and vibrate uncomfortably.

Faller craned his neck to look up. The world was the size of an ant.

He watched it shrink, not wanting to look away, because in every other direction there was absolutely nothing to see. The sky he'd loved so much when his feet were on solid ground terrified him.

The irony of the name he'd chosen suddenly hit him: it was also the means of his death. Like naming yourself Starver, or Bleed to Death.

Unzipping his pack barely two inches and fishing around, he took inventory of his meager possessions by feel, not because any of it could save him, but because they were a link to the world. He longed to feel anything solid, anything that belied the emptiness.

There was an eighth of a canteen of water left from his hike to the top of the Tower. It could have been a barrelful for all it mattered. He also had two clumps of dried dog meat, the toy paratrooper that had started this whole mess, the map, and in his back pocket, the photo.

Making sure to grip it tightly, he withdrew the photo from his pocket and cupped it in his hands, the howling wind whipping its corners. He studied the woman he'd known before the beginning of time. She was pressing her cheek against his shoulder, looking so shockingly clean her pale skin glowed. She had shoulder-length black hair, freckles splashed across sharp cheekbones, a hard, square jaw, which would be too masculine if not offset by those expressive green eyes. Looking at her face, her bright smile, never failed to fill him with a complex cocktail of emotions he couldn't begin to decipher.

How many days had he spent early on, walking the streets, searching for that woman? Enough to know the world was nineteen thousand steps long and ten thousand steps wide.

The world was a spot, a freckle on the sky. Faller fell through a cloud, and could see nothing for a moment. After he passed through the cloud it obscured his view of the world. He kept his eyes glued to the place where it had been until the cloud drifted by and he could see it again.

His world had shrunk to the size of a fleck he could only see if he looked to the side of it.

Then it was gone. No matter how hard he looked, how much he strained, he couldn't see it. Blue nothing, broken only by clouds, stretched in every direction, and Faller hung at the center. He looked at the photo and tried to banish the cold despair tearing at his guts with the sight of a human face.

II

"I THOUGHT we were going to Le Yaca," Ugo called from the backseat of Melissa's van.

"Change of plans," Melissa said.

"Change of plans?" Ugo sighed theatrically. "I *like* Le Yaca. I was looking forward to the beef tenderloin."

"We're having a murder-free dinner, sweetie," Izabella said, patting Ugo's shoulder. "No animals will be harmed in the making of this evening. You're going to love it."

Ugo groaned, planted his chin on his fist. "Wonderful."

Peter reached over and squeezed Melissa's knee. "You've got something up your sleeve."

She stretched one corner of her mouth, made a clicking sound—a classic Melissa gesture. "Maybe."

"Wait a minute, secret surprise plans were made, and I wasn't in the loop?" Kathleen said from way in the back.

"It was a last-minute thing," Izabella said.

"I don't care. From now on, unless I'm the one being surprised, I want to be in the loop."

Peter glanced back at Kathleen. She sounded semiserious, like she was really hurt that she wasn't in on whatever Melissa and Izabella had planned. Reaching up, she tapped the ceiling twice, completing some OCD ritual only she would comprehend. "So where are we going?"

"Kathleen, it's a *surprise*," Izabella said. She looked tired.

"When did you get back from Mumbai?" Peter asked.

"Yesterday. I'll never get used to the breakneck time changes in this job."

"I doubt anyone could," Harry said from the back. "I doubt it's physically possible. Unless Ugo develops a designer virus that rewires our internal clocks."

"Not high on my list of priorities right now," Ugo said.

Melissa turned onto Colonial Parkway, heading toward Jamestown.

· · · ·

MELISSA AND Izabella led the way along the dock. Walking in the moonlight together, the two sisters looked so strikingly different: Melissa, skinny, knock-kneed, pale, and freckled like her Scottish father; Izabella small, duck-footed, and bronze like her Mediterranean mother.

It was so hard, looking at them, to see any vestige of the girls who'd lived in a trailer half a mile from Peter in Gaskill, New York. He and Melissa had discovered each other in chemistry class, both of them out of place, geeks in a redneck world. Senior year they'd practiced together to eradicate every trace of where they'd come from. They stopped saying *ain't*, worked on saying *milk* instead of *melk*. "I ain't goin' nowhere" became "I'm not going anywhere." They'd laughed so hard at first, because it sounded so weird, so artificial, to speak like the news anchors on CNN. Somewhere along the way, they'd passed an inflection point, and it began to sound weird to say things the way they used to. They could still crack each other up saying something the way they used to say it. They got married and moved to New York City the day they graduated from high school. Melissa wanted to be an actress, and was as surprised as anyone when the weird sculptures she'd been making in high school in her backyard turned out to be her real talent.

Three triple-masted ships rocked on gentle waves to their left. Peter knew them well from previous visits—replicas of the *Susan Constant, Godspeed,* and *Discovery,* all of which had crossed the Atlantic packed with Jamestown's settlers in the early 1600s. Each had a spider's web of riggings crossing their decks. The third in line—*Discovery*—had her white sails out. Melissa and Izabella stopped at *Discovery's* gangplank.

A red-bearded man wearing period military garb and a long, striking red cape appeared on deck.

"Welcome aboard," he called, striding down to unhook the chain running across the gangplank.

They crossed single file, as six crew members came out from belowdecks, wearing billowing shirts and high socks. They swarmed across the deck, taking their positions as Peter and his companions were led down the ladder belowdecks. Fifty or sixty people had once shared the space, which was about the size of someone's living room, for a four-month voyage. Now it contained only a table set with antique china and utensils. The rough reddish wood walls and blond planked floor glowed with a cozy hue in the candlelight.

Tuxedoed waitresses were waiting with wine and scotch. Peter introduced himself to each of them before sitting.

"Isn't this better than Le Yaca?" Izabella asked Ugo.

Ugo waggled his hand, but his smirk gave him away. "All right, maybe it is."

"This is incredible. Thank you." Peter squeezed Melissa's knee. Above deck, orders were shouted as the ship prepared to set sail on the James River.

"Scotch?" one of the waitresses asked, holding a bottle for Peter to examine.

"Absolutely." He held out his glass. "Thanks, Jamie."

Peter looked around the table, warmed by the faces of his friends, so animated, already deep in conversation.

Despite the remarkable, anachronistic surroundings, it reminded Peter of Stanford, of grad school. How many nights had the six of them spent eating and drinking and bullshitting? It happened so rarely now, with Izabella out of the country so often, and Melissa working odd hours on her sculptures.

Who would have guessed they'd be here, just four years later? Izabella, a diplomat; Kathleen working in PR for the president, Ugo the biotech whiz kid, and Peter, turning theoretical physics on its ear.

He watched Harry throw back his head and laugh at something Melissa said. Only Harry had stumbled, when measured against his potential. He seemed happy, though. What was it Kurt Vonnegut's sister had said, when Kurt pointed out that she was a better writer than he, and was doing nothing with her talent? There's no cosmic rule that says you're obligated to fulfill your potential. Something like that. Although in Harry's case, it had been a nervous breakdown that stopped him from finishing his degree, not a conscious decision.

Harry saw Peter looking at him. "This place is no good. I can't bask in reflected glory if there's no one around to recognize you and consequently be impressed with me."

Melissa turned. "What was that?"

"Harry said he can't bask in reflected glory here, because there's no one here to notice."

"'Bask in reflected glory'?" Melissa laughed. "What the hell does that mean?"

"Building your own self-esteem by connecting yourself to someone famous or important," Peter explained. "Like, if you went to high school with Beyoncé twenty years ago, and that's the first thing you tell people when you meet them."

"About seventy percent of the self-esteem I manage to possess is because I work with Peter," Harry said. He stuck out his hand for Melissa to shake. "Hi, I'm Harry Wong. I'm a senior assistant in Peter Sandoval's lab. You know—the world-renowned physicist? We're friends." He let go of her hand. "That's how I introduce myself."

"I'll bet that's not particularly effective in getting you laid," Melissa said. "The words *assistant* and *physics* are both in that sentence."

"It's not effective for anything, but it's all I've got."

Jamie, their waitress, slid a salad in front of Peter. He thanked her, picked up his fork.

Melissa picked up her dinner fork instead of her salad fork and went to work on her salad. Smiling, Peter switched to his dinner fork as well. When had he gotten all civilized? Where they grew up you were happy if the fork was clean, the tines all pointing in the same direction, rather than melted from a meth cook.

An image came, unbidden: flashing lights, his father on a stretcher, screaming in agony from chemical burns to his face and hands that made him look like he was melting. In the background, their home, burning.

At the other end of the table, he heard Ugo holding forth, his drink palmed in one hand. "Freud said it was sex that drove people at the most fundamental level, but he was wrong. It's power."

Peter rolled his eyes. *Here we go—the world according to Ugo.*

Izabella tsked, crossed her arms. "Oh, Ugo, you don't really believe that." She looked at Kathleen. "He loves to say outrageous things just to shock people."

Smiling, Ugo said, "That's true, I do. But in this case the outrageous thing also happens to be true." He took a swig of scotch. "Most people don't want to admit they crave power, even to themselves, because it makes them feel ashamed. So they mask it as a desire for respect, success, admiration, sometimes even love. But if you dig down into the psyche, you'll find it's all the same: a desire for power."

"Love is *not* a desire for power," Izabella said.

Ugo reached out, took her hand. "Not *all* love. Sometimes love is just love, just as Freud said a cigar is sometimes just a cigar."

Peter leaned forward in his seat, began to speak, but Ugo pushed on, not giving Peter an opportunity to interrupt his grand discourse.

"Freud got one thing correct, though; he said, left to their own devices, people are innately evil. Fear of being rejected or punished by a civilized society is what keeps us in line."

Melissa made a face. "I don't buy that. Most people wouldn't kill or steal even if they knew they could get away with it."

"That's why when there's a blackout, everyone is out looting stores," Ugo said.

"Not *everyone*. Most people are home caring for their families, checking on their neighbors to make sure they're safe."

Ugo grunted, shook his head. "In the movies, maybe."

"All right, that's enough nihilist philosophy for one night," Kathleen said.

"Yes." Izabella held up her wineglass. "Peter." She turned, looked at her husband. "Ugo. Even when I'm sober I can't follow much of what you do, but I do understand that you've jumped way ahead of everyone else, and the world will never be the same." She turned to Peter. "One day soon the two of you arc going to save millions of lives, and I'm proud of you both."

They raised their glasses.

Melissa tapped Peter's hand. "Have you heard Kathleen's idea?"

"I don't know. I've heard plenty of great ideas from Kathleen." He poured himself another dram of scotch.

"Have you ever considered using your duplicator to end hunger?" Kathleen said. "Instead of flying in planeloads of grain, we fly in a chicken and a duplicator."

"The bioterrorism-driven epidemics take precedence," Ugo said. "We can't take our eye off that target."

"Beyond that, a duplicator wouldn't be the panacea for world hunger you'd think it would," Izabella said from the other end of the table. "A lot of the duplicators would be seized by dictators and warlords in those countries, unless you had an army guarding each one."

Under the table, Kathleen's fingers were counting, her thumb and index finger opening and closing, probably keeping track of whether Izabella spoke an odd or even number of words. Peter looked away from her hand, hoping Kathleen hadn't noticed him noticing.

"From what Peter's said," Izabella went on, "manufacturing a duplicator is outrageously expensive. For that money you could set up agricultural programs, if the local governments would go along." She took a sip of water, shaking her head. "At this point hunger is mostly political. It's not about a food shortage."

Kathleen lifted and set down her wineglass twice, then took a big swallow. She looked hurt to have her idea stepped on. "What about famines, where countries fly in planeloads of food? That's incredibly expensive."

Izabella shrugged. "It might be viable for famine relief, just not large-scale hunger relief."

"Fine." She turned to Peter, set her chin on her hand. "Famine relief, then."

Peter sipped his Glenfiddich, relishing the oaky burn. "I'm all for it. Let's look into raising funds. I think—"

His phone rang: an international number. "Excuse me." He hopped up the ladder to the deck.

"Hello?"

"Dr. Sandoval?" It was a man with an accent. European, maybe.

"Yes?" Peter crossed the small deck, looked out over the dark water, spotted here and there with lights from boats.

"This is Gunnar Oquist, secretary of the Royal Swedish Academy of Sciences. I apologize for calling so late in the evening."

Peter tried to say, "That's all right," but nothing came out but an incoherent yawp. Was there any other reason the Royal Swedish Academy called someone? But he was too young . . .

"I'm calling to inform you that the Royal Swedish Academy of Sciences has decided to award you the Nobel Prize in physics for your work on quantum cloning. I'd like to congratulate you on behalf of myself, and the academy."

Peter gripped the railing. A Nobel Prize. He'd won a fucking Nobel Prize.

Gunnar Oquist chuckled on the other end of the line. "Dr. Sandoval? Are you still there?"

"You're serious. I won a Nobel Prize?" Dark speckles spotted his vision; he'd come this close to passing out, he realized.

"Indeed. A Nobel Prize. The announcement will be made in the morning. If there were other recipients I would typically inform you of who they are, but this year you're the sole recipient in physics."

"That's wonderful. I'm bursting. I have to tell my wife and friends."

"Of course. It's been a pleasure, Dr. Sandoval. I look forward to meeting you at the ceremony."

"Thank you." Peter signed off. Still feeling woozy, he leaned his elbows on the railing and stared out at the river, the only sound the slosh of water against the ship.

He'd won a Nobel Prize. Him—the dirt-poor kid whose father had blown up their home cooking methamphetamine. He'd won a Nobel Prize.

He couldn't wait to tell Melissa and his friends. Although, maybe this wasn't the right time. This was Ugo's night as well as his, and Peter had no doubt Ugo was going to be devastated by the news. Ugo couched his competitive comments in laughter, but beneath the laughter, Peter was sure Ugo saw him as a measuring stick.

"Who was it?" Melissa put an arm on his shoulder. "You okay? You're shaking."

Peter couldn't keep from grinning. "I'll tell you after the party. It's good news."

Melissa raised her eyebrows. "Oh?"

Peter wrapped his arm around her and led her back belowdecks.

10

NIGHT FELL. Faller was relieved to have the company of a half-moon and a million pinpricks of starlight, but the wind turned to ice. Through trial and error he'd figured out how to stop tumbling, and he'd fallen feetfirst for most of the day because it minimized the buffeting gale. Now he shifted so he was falling back first. He pressed his forearm over the neck of his jumpsuit, trying to cut off the flow of air. The wind still cut like a knife. His muscles ached from its relentless tug; his skin was chafed and burned, his ears ringing.

What an utterly pointless existence he'd led. A few hundred days of wondering what it meant, to suddenly pop into a world and a life that he couldn't remember, now he was going to pop back out, understanding no more than when he'd arrived. What he wouldn't give to know what had happened. Besides leaving Daisy and Orchid, dying in ignorance was his greatest regret.

· · · ·

HE MUST have fallen asleep, because he had one of his nightmares. His dreams had once been random things, the topics pulled from the hat of his daily life, but more and more they were dark and bizarre messes that had absolutely nothing to do with his life. They repeated, and each time the curtain was drawn back a bit further, more awful details were revealed.

In this latest (and perhaps last) nightmare, it was raining, only the raindrops were red. Faller was on a street packed with people who were shouting, running blindly in every direction, crashing into each other. They were terrified, soaked in thick rain the precise color and texture of blood. He'd had this dream before, only this time besides the blood rain, airplanes filled the sky. They were rumbling in neat rows, staying up there when all logic screamed that they should fall, and they were shitting bombs, and when the bombs landed whatever was under them was thrown into the air, and bricks and glass and splintered wood rained down along with the blood.

He'd never had a dream before where machines worked, and he hoped he died before he had another. It reminded him of the very early days, when some persistent tinkerers managed to get a car or truck—and in one case even a crane—operating. Faller had a vivid memory of a guy plowing into the side of a building in a little red car. He'd gone right through the windshield, headfirst into the brick wall. One by one the vehicles had stopped working, and they never worked again.

11

FALLER THOUGHT he'd been falling for three or four days, although there was no way to tell for sure. He no longer felt like he was falling. He hung upright and motionless while a tremendous wind blew up from below. Even if he tried, he couldn't regain the sensation of falling. He was going nowhere; he was the center of this blank universe, standing on nothing.

His mouth had dried out the previous day, giving him no need to swallow, but hunger and thirst tormented him. Unless he made a point of looking around—and there was really no point in that—he often couldn't tell whether his eyes were open or closed. The featureless landscape had a way of robbing him of his sight.

Since those first awful minutes, Faller hadn't spent much time wondering about his failed parachute. Wondering required effort, and as Faller fell into a numb, confused stupor, he didn't have the energy for it.

Regrets, on the other hand, seemed to roll out effortlessly.

Besides jumping off the Tower, Faller's biggest regret was that he hadn't been able to do more to stop the killing in the early days. He had saved Daisy, though. That was something, and not something small. Daisy's wry, too grown-up voice often kept him company as he drifted in and out of consciousness.

Faller also regretted that he never found the woman in the picture, or at least figured out who she was. Likely she had died in the early days. So many had died in the early days. So many. While Daisy's voice comforted him in these final hours, the screams of those terrified children haunted him. There had been days afterward when he would have done anything to forget those faces, to blot them from his mind.

Maybe that's what had happened to all of them. Maybe they'd done something so awful, they would do anything to forget. So they'd used their machines to make themselves forget. From all the pictures and paintings of places that didn't exist, Faller was sure the world had once been much bigger—maybe ten times bigger—and he suspected the awful thing they'd done had had something to do with making the world smaller.

If that was the answer, if they'd done all this to forget, then it was a great irony that all he wanted was to remember.

III

THROUGH THE French doors of his study, Peter watched Melissa strain to lift a slab of granite, setting it atop two other vertical slabs to form an inverted *U*. She'd been working on the thirteenth hole—the Stonehenge hole—of her miniature golf course/sculpture garden for a week straight.

Grinning, he surveyed the other twelve: Graceland, with its canted roof and velvet curtains; Area 51, complete with spaceship and alien; Venice, with its harrowing waterways; Fenway Park, where balls rolled partway up a velvet green monster on their approach. From Peter's vantage point the course was framed by a skyful of stratocumulus undulatus, set in vertical rows, a blue sky peeking between them.

Peter watched the clouds drift, like frozen white breakers on the beach. When he was young and his parents were dragging him from one trash-strewn neighborhood to another, he'd discovered the sky, always bright and clean and beautiful. The uglier the landscape, the more time he'd spend with his face upturned. In grad school, when his ideas felt splintered in a million directions, they clicked into place most easily when he was watching clouds. While searching for cloud books online, he'd stumbled upon the Cloud Appreciation Society. Their Web site had been his home page ever since.

His phone rang just as he was turning back to his computer. It was Harry.

"Are you watching the news?"

Peter grabbed the remote on the desk. "You never want to hear someone open a conversation with that. What's happening?"

"They're bombing the Trans-Alaskan Pipeline."

"*What?* Who is?" The TV's picture came on, showing thick black smoke billowing from an oil refinery.

"The Russians. We're at war, Peter. I think World War Three just began."

Peter turned and saw Melissa squatting in her miniature Stonehenge, phone to her ear, head down. He thought she might be crying.

"I have to go. I'll call you back." He tossed his phone on the sofa and rushed outside.

She was crying so hard she seemed to be having trouble breathing. Peter squatted beside her, wrapped his arms around her. "We'll get through this. The country's been through wars before."

Melissa lifted her head. "What are you talking about?"

"The war. Isn't that—"

"Izabella has Peterson-Jantz."

Peter fought an urge to clap his hands over his ears, to curl up into a ball. *Bella?* Bella was dying? "How could she have contracted it?"

Melissa wiped her nose with her fist. "Everyone who took the trip to Mumbai got it. They think Pakistani agents sabotaged their food." She wrapped her arms around Peter's neck, pressed her face into his chest. "I can't do this. I can't watch her die. I just can't."

Peter hugged Melissa tight, his thoughts a howling storm. He wanted to say something comforting, but what could comfort her at this moment?

"I'm so sorry. I'm here for you. We'll face it together." It sounded so inadequate; a handful of sand to stop a tidal wave. "Ugo's been working night and day on his cure. He'll come through."

Melissa nodded, sniffed. "He will. We can't lose Bella. We just can't." She relaxed her grip on him, leaned back, looking at the ground. "What were you talking about, that we'll get through the war?"

Peter had completely forgotten Harry's call in the wake of Melissa's news. "Russia just dragged us into the war."

Melissa squeezed her eyes shut. "Oh, shit."

The two worst pieces of news they'd ever received, and they'd come at the same time. "Where's Bella now?"

"Home, I think," Melissa said.

"I'll get my keys."

12

A SPASM of terror pulled Faller from a semidream. It had been an image more than a dream: his lifeless body, plunging like a sack of meat in the endless sky. He tried to banish the image, but it hung there, tormenting him.

Would his body rot? Did you have to be on the ground, or under it, to rot? He saw himself as a skeleton, his jumpsuit flapping loosely.

His throat hurt. He had sores from the constant rubbing of his jumpsuit. There was nothing to do about any of it. In that one important respect dying was easier than staying alive had been.

There was a blot on his eye, one of those visual mosquitoes that sometimes danced in his vision. Only this one wasn't dancing. It was stationary, planted in the steel-blue dawn beneath his feet.

Faller touched his eyelids, to make sure they were open. They were. He looked again.

It was a pea-sized blot, slightly darker than the early morning sky. Faller rubbed his eyes, lightly slapped his face to make sure he was awake, and looked a third time.

He let out a croak that rose at the end, taking the form of a question.

A cloud passed in front of the blot. He waited, heart hammering.

When it reappeared, it was larger, its edges more distinct.

It grew larger. Faller tried to guess what it could be. A bird that had strayed far, far from the world? Birds moved, though. This wasn't moving; it just hung there in the sky. Maybe it was something light dropped from the world that he was catching up to?

When it was so large he couldn't block it out with his thumb, he knew what it was.

It was a place—a world.

His heart was too weak to pound, but it fluttered as his dried-out mind tried to grasp the notion of another world. His lip split in two places as he smiled, then laughed, although the laugh sounded like little more than a dry croak to his ears. The universe had saved a stunning surprise for his final hours.

Maybe the universe was nothing but a giant circle, and if you fell long enough you ended up back at the world?

The place kept growing until it was bigger than his fist, then a big round-ish plate like a manhole cover in the sky. His vision was blurry, but eventually he made out some details. Clumps of rectangles all over that he guessed were roofs. Patches of green here and there. A bluish stripe and a few sundry bluish circles that must have been water.

The closer he fell, the surer he became that it wasn't his world. It was another place.

It was divided into sections. Two lines running roughly parallel from one end of the world to the other created a band down the center. The two remaining sides were further divided into uneven parts.

He wondered if he should get the world under him and slam into it to end this. Maybe that was best. What would the people down there make of him and his parachute when they found his body? He glanced up at the chute, that traitor, that faulty bastard that had been snapping impotently above him for days.

As he was silently cursing it, it occurred to him that he could try to fix it.

Faller reached up and grabbed the lines. It felt as if he were trying to reel in a whale instead of a chute, a task that wouldn't have even winded him a few days ago. When he got the chute in his hands he rested, periodically glancing at the world he was fast approaching.

With trembling fingers, squinting eyes dried from dehydration, he struggled to tie off each of the broken suspension lines—doubling, tripling, quadrupling the knots, hoping they'd hold this time. Then he reattached the clamps. He kept snapping the clamps into thin air, his vision doubled. Finally he shut his eyes and clamped them by feel.

He couldn't get the chute into the backpack. Reaching behind him with the wind tearing at the chute quickly turned his arms to jelly. Unstrapping the pack from his back was out of the question—the wind would yank it from his hands. He twisted onto his stomach and clutched the bunched chute to his chest. Stretching one arm and his legs and holding them stiff against the battering wind was agony. He inched toward the world with a drunken wobble, gasping at the effort.

By the time he was over it, he was close enough to see vehicles in the roads. He swung the parachute clear and let it go.

The parachute crept out tentatively, flapping like a wounded bird. Too exhausted to be afraid, Faller wondered if there was some top velocity beyond which parachutes just didn't work.

The chute surged upward and opened with a *pop*. Faller's head snapped back, sending shooting pain down his neck and shoulders; his vision burst with pinwheels and the harness bit into his chest and back.

The world went utterly silent. The wind, which had been with him so long it seemed a part of him, was gone. Faller looked down. Here and there he could see the outline of buildings, roads, vehicles in the creeping dawn. The buildings were squat, the streets narrower, but it didn't seem too different from home.

He was dropping toward them surprisingly fast. Faller looked up, saw that one of his knots had failed. One section of the parachute was flapping, spilling air.

Spinning in a tight circle, Faller plunged onto the roof of a long building. His legs crumpled when he hit; he landed hard on his ass. For a moment he was able to see the roof, then the chute settled over him, blotting out everything. He tried to pull it off, but it seemed to go on and on, a mile of fabric. He gave up and collapsed onto his back.

A door creaked open.

"There he is." A child's hushed but urgent voice, and it was followed by fierce whispering that edged closer.

"Water," Faller rasped. "Please get me water."

"Where did you come from?" a second child's voice called, this one a girl.

How could he possibly answer that? "I don't know. I'm dying. Water. Please."

"Get Dad," the boy said. They ran off.

Faller ran his hand over gritty plaster. He was on another world. It was too much to wrap his exhausted mind around, so he lay there waiting for the children to fetch their dad, thinking of nothing.

Eventually he heard the children approach again, chattering excitedly. An adult male voice shushed them.

"What are you doing hiding in there? Come on out."

Faller was too exhausted to move. "Water," he said. He pursed his lips to add *please*, but it was too much effort.

The parachute slid across his face with a soft zipping sound until it came completely off and he was squinting into an overcast sky. A man's scowling face, thick-bearded and weather-beaten, appeared over him, appraising him like a stinking dead fish.

"I've never seen you before. Which borough are you from?"

Another voice cut in, from a distance. "Who is it?"

"I've never seen him before," the scowling man said over his shoulder.

"He fell out of the sky," one of the children offered, a red-haired girl with a big bald spot above one temple. Three adults pushed in close to stand over Faller. Their faces were gaunt, their eyes too deep in the sockets, their cheeks hollow.

"He's definitely not from this borough," a man with no front teeth said, before turning to spit on the ground.

The ground felt unsteady under him, as if he, these people, and the ground itself were still falling. It was hard to grasp that he was going to live. If he could get some goddamned water he was going to live.

"What do you think happened to him?" a bucktoothed woman asked. She was wearing two strands of brown-stained pearls around her wrist. She raised her voice. "What happened to you? Who are you?"

"I—I fell." When no one seemed to understand, Faller pointed at the sky.

The people looked at each other, frowning.

"We saw him fall," the other child, a boy, insisted.

"He's from another borough. Uptown would be my guess," Dad said, ignoring the kids. He turned away. "I'll be right back."

"Water?" Faller croaked. No one moved.

The kids' dad returned carrying a dirty half-brick. "Simplest thing to do is bash in his skull and drag him to a sewer."

"No!" Faller said, lifting his hands.

Dad pointed. "You kids go on home. You're too young to see this sort of thing."

"Hold on, Bo. Maybe we should take him to Moonlark's people," a balding man with a grey beard hovering near the edge of the little circle said. "If he's from Uptown he might know useful things."

"Moonlark," Faller agreed, his heart hammering.

"Christ, it'll be two hours getting there and back," Bo said, ignoring Faller.

"And you're saying, what, that's not worth getting in good with Moonlark? We're bringing him a *spy*—he'll remember that."

"I'm not a spy," Faller managed.

"Yeah." The bald man laughed. "You fell out of the sky." He bent and pulled Faller into a sitting position. "Come on, fella."

They spoke strangely. *Accent* was the word that popped into Faller's mind. The man tried to pull Faller to his feet, but Faller's knees refused to lock.

"Stand up," Bo said, shaking him, which caused Faller to collapse into the guy's arms. "Christ. Help me with him, will you?"

The balding guy took one of Faller's arms. They pulled the parachute harness off him and tossed it aside, then let Faller sag and dragged him.

"Dad, what about this?" one of the kids called.

They paused in their dragging. The boy was holding one handle of a red wheelbarrow leaned up against the low wall. "That's not a bad idea. Bring it over."

Faller was loaded into the wheelbarrow like a sack of flour, his head propped against the base of one of the handles because he didn't have the strength to hold it up.

IV

"Hey, it's the boy wonder," Izabella said brightly, her words garbled. She was sitting up in bed, her hands lying palms up in her lap, her fingers alternately curling into fists and hyperflexing open.

What was it, eight days since her diagnosis? The prion worked so fast. Soon her whole body would be doing that. The prion was gradually disconnecting Izabella from her nervous system; in another month it would be completely outside her control.

Tears came to Peter's eyes, but he went on smiling. "Hi, Red Sonja. How are you feeling?"

"Like shit, if you really want to know. Like a big old sack of shit."

Peter laughed. "I'm sorry. It's not funny. I'm just laughing at how you put it."

"Go ahead, laugh at the invalid, you sick bastard." Izabella held out her hand; it took Peter a moment to realize she wanted him to take it.

"It's interesting, how much dying changes you." It was an effort for her to form the words. "I was never one of those touchy-huggy people. I didn't like to be touched. Now, I can't get enough."

Peter gave her hand a squeeze. "Maybe it's because everything else falls away, except for the people in your life." Under the sheets, her toes were curling and uncurling. He couldn't bear the thought of what she was facing a week from now, a month.

"You see, that's why I look forward to your visits. Anyone else would have said, 'You're not dying, don't talk like that.' Not you, though." Her hand squeezed and released, squeezed and released, like a heartbeat. "Even Melissa does that. She was here most of the afternoon. It's like they're embarrassed by me talking about something I can't help but think about every minute."

"They don't want to think about life without you in it. Plus, talking about death terrifies people."

"Doesn't it terrify you?" she asked.

"Hell, yes," Peter said. "I've just never been good at suppressing my fears. Or anything else, for that matter."

Izabella laughed, and to Peter, it felt like a small victory. All he had to offer, besides a hand to hold, was to make some of these moments more bearable.

"I see it's not enough to take my Nobel. You want my wife, too," Ugo said behind him.

Peter hadn't heard him come in. He opened his fingers to let go of Izabella's hand, but Izabella only drew his hand closer. She raised her other hand, held it out until Ugo grasped it. He let out a sigh like a deflating cushion as he sat on the opposite side of the bed from Peter.

"What would you do with a Nobel for physics?" Peter strained to keep his tone playful. "You need to talk to the people who give them out for medicine and physiology."

"You're saying I didn't make a significant contribution toward the work?"

"No. Of course I'm not." Peter licked his lips; his mouth had gone dry. They'd been dancing around this conversation for two weeks, the tension in the lab growing tighter by the day. "I'm not on the committee, Ugo. I would have been honored to share the award with you, but I don't get a say."

Ugo stuck out his bottom lip, considered. "Then you're saying I *did* make a significant enough contribution to merit inclusion, and the committee made a mistake?"

That's not what he'd said. Ugo was trying to back him into a corner.

"Guys? I'm dying here. Can we drop the shop talk?" Izabella said.

"Sorry." Ugo reached out and brushed Izabella's hair.

She closed her eyes. "And please, don't talk about the goddamned war."

"All right." Ugo leaned over and gave her a kiss on the cheek. "How are you feeling?"

"As I was telling Peter, I feel like shit." She gave Ugo an unreadable look, then turned to look at Peter, started to say something, then stopped.

"What is it?" Peter asked, speaking softly.

"I was wondering how the work on the duplicator was going."

"Didn't you just chastise us for talking shop?" Ugo asked.

"I was chastising you for arguing, but I was trying to be polite about it." Her jaw quivered violently, then her throat contracted in a sharp spasm. She was swallowing, Peter realized—all of that effort just to swallow. "How is the work coming?"

Peter shrugged. "Fine."

"You said the mice came through just fine."

"That's right."

A goldfinch landed on the bird feeder Ugo had hung outside her window. Izabella watched it peck seeds from the feeder. "They came out remembering exactly the same things?"

"The duplicates run mazes the originals memorized, so it sure looks that way. It'd be surprising if they didn't, given that they're the same down to the cellular level."

"Explain to me how it works again? I know you've explained it before."

Peter gave her a quizzical look, not sure why she'd suddenly taken such an interest in his work. Maybe she was just trying to steer the conversation onto safe ground, away from the argument he and Ugo had been having.

"The duplicate is an echo of the original. The original travels a millisecond back in time through a miniwormhole."

Izabella nodded, the nod jerky, tremulous.

Ugo cleared his throat. "Bella, I have a . . ."

"I want you to duplicate me," Bella said.

". . . surprise," Ugo finished. He sputtered. "I'm sorry, what did you just say?"

"The duplicate wouldn't have Peterson-Jantz, right?" Izabella said.

Her words had caught Peter completely off guard. He thought Izabella must be joking, but there was no mischievous glint in her eyes; she seemed completely earnest as she looked from Ugo to Peter.

"It wouldn't, right?"

"Right," Peter said, "it wouldn't. A prion is a foreign body." He squeezed her hand. "But Bella, *you'd* still have it."

"I understand that. But short of being cured, the most comforting thing I can imagine is knowing everything I've been, my body, all of my memories, will carry on. That in some sense I'll still live out my life with Ugo."

The thought of actually dropping Izabella through that aperture made Peter shudder.

"You're joking, aren't you?" Ugo asked.

Izabella's hands went on squeezing and releasing, squeezing and releasing. "If you were lying here, you wouldn't need to ask that question."

Ugo grasped the bed rail, leaned close to her. "Bella, I love *you*. I don't want a replacement, I want you. I'm going to get my virus to isolate the prions without damaging memory."

"There isn't time," Izabella almost shouted. More quietly, she added, "We all know that. Stop bullshitting me."

A nurse breezed in, took in the tense, silent faces and stopped short. "I'll come back later."

When she was gone, Ugo said, "Izabella, we can't possibly do what you're asking. It's unthinkable. You understand that, don't you?"

"It may be unthinkable for you. For me it feels like my last chance."

Ugo shushed her gently. "Don't talk like that. I'm going to figure this out. We're going to live a long life together."

Izabella didn't look convinced.

"I've been trying to tell you," Ugo said, changing the subject. "I have a surprise for you."

Izabella raised her eyebrows, her smile stiff, quivering.

"I know how disappointed you were that you couldn't make it to see the Brentano String Quartet perform. So . . ."

Ugo disappeared into the hall.

He returned followed by a woman carrying a cello, then a silver-haired man with a violin. The viola and second violin followed.

Izabella laughed with delight, sounding more energetic than she had since she was diagnosed. "Oh, my God. You're kidding me."

When their seats were in place, the quartet began. In the small room, the music was exquisite; absolutely, perfectly glorious.

Peter listened to the first piece with tears in his eyes, then excused himself so Ugo and Izabella could enjoy some time alone together.

Izabella's request had rattled him. They'd talked in theory about duplicating a human being, but the idea of a flesh-and-blood Izabella sitting at her own deathbed, holding her own hand, was something out of a horror movie.

On the way home, Peter got caught in a traffic jam on Richmond Road. It took him forty minutes to get past the choke point, which turned out, not surprisingly, to be a gas station. He only had a quarter of a tank left himself, but he couldn't afford to spend three hours waiting in line. Not with a new bioengineered plague breaking out in Japan.

13

IF HE hadn't been so close to death, it would have been humiliating to be pushed rattling and bumping through the broken streets while people stared. The men took turns pushing, the bucktoothed woman holding Faller's shoulder to keep him from falling out.

If anything, the people they passed looked even thinner and hungrier than on Faller's world. The streets weren't as straight and evenly spaced; they wound and meandered, intersecting other streets haphazardly. Otherwise he could have been on his world. The familiar scent of urine and shit came and went depending on the breeze. The four- and five-story buildings were tightly packed. Even the junk was the same—cars, trucks, and buses, rusting along the roads. There were red fire hydrants, brown telephone poles—all the things everyone could name but no one had any use for.

They veered to the right as they approached a long, high wall that stretched on and on. It was constructed of junk—cars, desks, cinder blocks—fit together like a huge puzzle. As Faller took it in, wondering what its purpose was, it started to drizzle. The cool, wet drops tingled wonderfully on Faller's face and arms.

"Shit," Bo said, picking up his pace as Faller opened his mouth to catch the silver droplets. "I knew this was a bad idea."

Turning right again, they'd gone a few blocks when suddenly the landscape opened onto a stunning vista. To Faller's left a white tower rose from a weedy field. It was tall and thin, tapering to a triangular point. To their right, beyond a green rectangular pond, a magnificent domed building sat above a long flight of marble steps. It was embellished with hundreds of columns, the whole thing white like the tower. His wheelers barely looked up as they turned toward the tower, then veered right before reaching it. They bumped along a walkway that edged another weed-choked field, then took a road that led toward another huge white building, this one with columns around the entrance.

They tipped the wheelbarrow at the foot of a long half-moon staircase leading up to the front doors, then dragged Faller up, his heels thumping painfully on each step. A man in a suit waited on the landing at the top, arms folded, watching their progress. The man had dark hair, and acne scars on his cheeks above his beard that made him look angry. He wasn't nearly as thin as the others.

The men set Faller down and a brief, muffled conversation ensued. Finally the acne-scarred man gestured toward the door with his head, his arms still folded.

Bo and the bald man picked Faller up and carried him inside, through a stunning vestibule. Faller marveled at an immaculately clean chandelier, ornately carved molding skirting a high ceiling, as they continued through to a long hallway.

Faller looked at Bo's face and was surprised at the wide-eyed fear so apparent there. Sensing Faller's attention Bo looked down at Faller, scowled, and tried unsuccessfully to appear less terrified.

They carried Faller into a big, wood-paneled room where a man was working at a desk, and set him on the floor beside a burgundy and black sofa with curled wood legs.

The man behind the desk rolled his chair out from behind it in one deft motion. Moonlark had a well-fed build, a big lion's head, dark hair, and heavy-lidded eyes. He was wearing a black suit that looked like it had been pulled off a rack on Day One and never worn.

From his chair Moonlark looked Faller over, his eyes narrowing. He leaned in for a closer look, pushing his face close to Faller's, going as far as running his finger over Faller's cracked, arid lips.

"How did you get like this?" Moonlark asked.

"Falling," Faller croaked. He tried to lick his lips, but his dried tongue only stuck to them.

"Falling? What do you mean, falling?" Moonlark tugged his flight suit. "What's this?"

"To fall," Faller said, knowing he was making no sense, but too weak to elaborate. "Please, some water?" His tone sounded pitiful and cloying even to him.

Moonlark turned to the acne-scarred man, who was standing in the doorway. "Get him some water." The man all but ran.

Turning to the men who'd brought Faller, Moonlark asked, "Why did you bring him to me?"

"He's a spy," Bo said immediately. "We found him on the roof of our apartment building, hiding under a big sheet."

"A sheet?" Moonlark sounded like he was losing his patience.

"A parachute," Faller said. "I fell."

"From what?" Moonlark pressed. "You keep saying you fell. You fell from what?"

"From the sky."

Moonlark squinted at Faller, his lips curled in confusion, or disgust. He looked up at the other men. "Put him on the couch." The two men who'd recently dragged Faller across a yard lifted him like he was an egg and set him on the couch, repeatedly glancing at Moonlark to gauge whether their lifting met with his approval.

"You've never seen him before?" Moonlark asked them.

Bo shook his head. "Never. But he can't be telling the truth . . ." His words trailed off, part statement, part question.

Moonlark glanced at Faller. "I appreciate you men bringing him to me. Your thoughtfulness won't be forgotten."

Picking up on the dismissal, the two men backed out of the room. The acne-scarred man squeezed past them carrying a glass pitcher. Faller reached for it when it was still halfway across the room. Pain shot down his arms and back, and he nearly fell off the couch straining to get to it. The man set the pitcher in Faller's hands; they shook so violently he sloshed water down the front of his shirt and he got more air than water. He sputtered, frustrated.

"Here," Moonlark said, lifting the pitcher and holding it for Faller. The first five or six gulps seemed to dissolve right into his mouth and throat, then the water started flowing, a cool stream he felt right down to his fingertips.

"Take a break," Moonlark said, drawing the pitcher away. "You'll puke if you chug like that."

Faller nodded, gasping, as Moonlark set the pitcher on a granite coffee table.

"So where are you really from?" Moonlark pointed at himself, then at Faller. "Just between you and me."

Faller struggled to sit up, feeling like he'd seem more credible if he was vertical. How to put this? "I fell off the edge of my world." He pointed at the ceiling. "There's another world above yours. Way, way up."

Moonlark crossed his legs. He was smiling. The smile seemed to say, *I'm amused by your bullshit, but I may kill you if it persists.* "That's an interesting story. An imaginative story." He rolled back toward his desk, reached into a wood chest next to it and pulled out a can of nuts. An honest-to-goodness sealed can of nuts. He pulled the vacuum seal like it was no big deal, helped himself to a few, then held the can out to Faller. "Nuts?"

Faller leaned forward and scooped as large a handful as he thought he could get away with without Moonlark cutting his throat.

When Moonlark didn't even look to see how many he took, Faller cursed himself for not taking more.

"So tell me . . ." Moonlark paused. "What's your name?"

"Faller."

Moonlark snorted. "Faller?" He canted his head to one side and nodded, as if allowing Faller to have his name. "Okay. So tell me, *Faller:* If you fell from the sky, how the fuck did you manage to *land* without breaking every bone in your body?"

"I had a parachute." He inhaled, intending to elaborate, then shut his mouth. Even to him it sounded absurd. He pointed at the door. "The men who brought me in took it."

"Ah, a parachute. I see. And what exactly does a parachute do?"

Moonlark probably had a vague image just from the word, but Faller thought it best to assume he didn't. "It's a half-circle of fabric with lines attached." He paused, took a moment to catch his breath before continuing. "A pocket of air forms under the fabric, letting you float slowly instead of falling."

Moonlark pressed his hands together, letting only his fingertips touch, and considered this. "Like I said, it's an imaginative story." He raised his eyebrows, smirked in a wholly unsettling manner. "Is there anyone who can corroborate it?"

"Two kids. Bo's kids—the taller man. I don't know if anyone else saw."

Moonlark grinned. "No one else saw you fall from the sky?"

"Not that I saw."

Moonlark watched him, still sporting that amused-yet-threatening smile. Faller wondered who this guy was. Someone with power, certainly. Someone who could have him killed if Faller couldn't convince him he was worth keeping around.

Faller pointed at a painting hung on the wall over Moonlark's desk, a landscape of cows grazing in a green field, a solitary farmhouse in the distance. "Is there any place on your world like that?"

Moonlark made no effort to look at the painting.

"No. It's some other place."

"Is that where you came from?" Moonlark gestured over his shoulder at the painting. "Have you seen those cows in that field?"

"What I'm saying is, why is it so hard to believe there's another place besides this one?"

Moonlark pushed out his lower lip and shrugged. "It isn't. I think there's a decent chance there are other places out there." His voice took on an icy tone. "What's difficult for me to believe is you *fell* from one of them." Moonlark stood. He held the can of nuts out to Faller. "Why don't you stay here for the time being, until we sort this out?"

Faller accepted the can. "Thank you." Clearly Moonlark thought he was lying, that he was a spy from Uptown, whatever Uptown was, and had decided to be patient with him for now. Chances were his patience wouldn't last. At least he had a place to stay and a can of peanuts. The rest he could figure out when he was stronger.

"Hammer?" Moonlark called. The acne-scarred man poked his head in. "Faller here is going to be our guest for the time being. Set him up in the Green Room, get him some clothes, get Powder to heat a bath down the hall."

A bath? *Heat* a bath? Faller couldn't imagine anyone hauling enough water to fill one of the tubs that sat useless in every house just so someone could sit in it, let alone heating the water first.

"Thank you," was all Faller could think to say as Hammer helped him stand. He was in a dangerous spot and would have to be careful, but compared to where he'd been a few hours ago, this was heaven.

V

Most of the restaurants along Richmond Road were closed, unable to get reliable deliveries. Peter watched out the window as he passed their dark interiors, Izabella's birthday present in his lap.

What do you get someone who's dying for her birthday? It certainly couldn't be a keepsake, or clothes, unless you happened upon a particularly lovely hospital gown. They'd considered making a professionally edited DVD from years of home videos, but that would only make her cry. In the end they'd concluded the best gifts were things she could use immediately, like the gift Ugo had given her the week before.

"I can't imagine what it cost Ugo to hire that string quartet." Peter shook his head in wonder, still staring out the window. "Whatever else you can say about the man, he loves Izabella."

"Mm-hm," Melissa said, her tone less than enthusiastic.

Peter looked at her. "What?"

Melissa seemed to consider as she stopped at a light. "I'm supposed to keep what's said on our girls' nights out to myself, but she's told me stories. Ugo's not all that easy to live with."

Somehow that didn't surprise Peter. He'd wondered how Ugo was able to so fully suppress his dickishness when he was around Izabella.

"What did he do?"

Melissa pursed her lips and made a popping sound. "The story that stands out is the time they were arguing about whether this woman on the news should have gone to jail for poisoning her neighbor's dogs. It was just a dumb argument, but Ugo wouldn't let it go. He kept lecturing her, and when Bella left the room he followed her, told her not to walk away when he was talking to her. She'd had about enough, so she went into their bedroom and locked the door."

All Peter could think was, *Surely this story does not involve assault. Surely Ugo didn't hit her.* Peter felt sure Izabella would take a tire iron to Ugo's skull if he hit her. She and Melissa weren't women who took shit, and growing up in their wacko family, they'd learned how to fight.

"Ugo pounded on the door. He kept saying, 'Don't you dare disrespect me.' When she didn't answer, he kicked the door in."

"Holy shit," Peter said.

"I know. Once he got inside he just went on lecturing her about why it was absurd to put someone in jail for killing an animal, when so many people had been murdered and raped in Bosnia."

Peter nodded. He'd heard some of Ugo's stories. His mother had been raped in front of him and his father by Serbian soldiers, then both parents had been killed, and he'd been placed in that postapocalyptic detention camp/orphanage. After the war he'd been adopted by the Serbian general, Valentin Stojic, and his wife. The breakneck shift to a life of privilege provided by his parents' killers must have been confusing as hell to a kid.

As they pulled into the hospital parking lot, Ugo was waiting, so they had to end the conversation there.

· · · ·

WHEN IZABELLA realized where they were going, she laughed with delight. Dunes blocked their view of the ocean as Melissa pulled into the sandy parking lot, which was completely empty, save for Kathleen's red Mini Cooper. There had been almost no cars on the road to Virginia Beach. Gas was too precious.

Heads bowed against a chilly breeze, they followed Ugo as he carried Izabella down to the water, with Harry, who'd hitched a ride with Kathleen, right behind him clutching her portable IV stand. Melissa pulled off her shoes and socks, and Ugo set her in a lawn chair and wrapped her in a blanket. It was agonizing to see Izabella like this. She trembled as if she were having a seizure, her face twisted by muscle contractions.

Ugo opened her gifts for her. When he unwrapped Peter and Melissa's gift, perhaps the last pound of macadamia nuts on the continent, Izabella acted as if they'd given her a new car.

What do you give to someone who's dying? Things she can use right now: food, and a trip to the ocean, so she can smell the salt air one last time.

Kathleen gave her a beautiful silk robe, sunset-orange, clearly hand-made. Harry's gift was a huge book of *Calvin and Hobbes* comic strips.

Ugo saved his gift for last: an exquisite emerald bracelet. Izabella acted as if he'd given her the Taj Mahal. Peter couldn't help picturing him kicking down their bedroom door.

When the gifts had been opened, Peter motioned to Kathleen to take a walk with him. She'd been a wreck throughout the gift opening, repeating words under her breath, eyebrows twitching, her right index finger air-writing madly. In grad school her symptoms had always grown worse around final-exam time, but they'd never been this bad.

"What's the latest?" On the ride down they'd studiously avoided talking about the war. Peter wasn't sure if Izabella was even aware that North Korea had entered it, adding the fifth-largest army in the world to the enemy's forces.

"Aspen and her advisors are scared shitless. We're taking too many losses." She whispered, "Losses, losses," under her breath. "They're instituting a draft. Immediately. Today."

"Jesus."

"With North Korea, it's going to get worse. By the end of the year we might see a billion casualties worldwide."

"It's hard to believe anybody wants this, even the crazies in North Korea. It's almost as if the war has taken on a life of its own, and even the warring countries can't stop it."

There were dark rings under Kathleen's eyes. Peter put an arm on her shoulder. "How are *you* holding up?"

"You know me." Kathleen laughed. "It takes me an hour to shower, with all the new rituals that have cropped up, but I'm okay."

Peter nodded. There was nothing to say that hadn't been said. Meds didn't help Kathleen; it was as if her obsessive-compulsiveness were part of who she was. "We're here for you. Any time you need a safe place, come stay with Melissa and me."

"Thanks. You know I love you guys. I don't know what I'd do without you."

Back where their towels and chairs were spread, the conversation was lighter. Melissa and Izabella were reminiscing about a summer trip to the Jersey Shore. They laughed about a time their drunk father almost burned down the boardwalk with illegal fireworks.

A storm front was on the horizon, with a roll cloud in the lead—slate grey with a flat blue-black bottom. It was still a ways off.

"What about you, Peter?" Izabella asked. "You have a favorite summer vacation story?"

Peter tried to think of some memory from his boyhood summers. He didn't like to think about his childhood. Besides his father's accident, his most vivid memory was being beaten by three of his classmates on the railroad tracks that crossed East Miller Street. One of them had been David Davison, who'd been his best friend once upon a time, before Peter had been placed in the gifted classes with the rich kids from Clarkston, thus somehow betraying the kids in his neighborhood.

His last year of high school, living with his chemistry teacher, Mr. Caruso, had been a revelation. Just seeing how a normal family functioned had opened his eyes.

"I wonder if that's what drew us all together," Izabella said. "Bad childhoods."

Ugo grunted. "I'd give a million dollars to trade childhoods with Peter."

14

It was still light when Faller woke. He had no idea how long he'd slept. When he got out of bed his legs felt rubbery and much too long; the room felt like it was listing to one side. His neck was stiff, and turning it in any direction sent waves of pain shooting down his upper back and shoulders.

After draining two glasses of water from a pitcher left on the nightstand, he looked around for something to piss in. He spotted a milk bottle set on the nightstand. It hurt to piss, but he filled the bottle a good three inches, which led him to believe he'd been asleep a long time.

Pulling back the curtain, Faller peered through the window past overgrown shrubs, at a field of tall grass shaded by thick-trunked trees. Beyond was a tall steel fence.

It was hard to gather his thoughts, standing there looking out on another world. Everything he thought he knew was wrong, leaving him almost as confused as on Day One. Something Moonlark had said nagged him: *I think there's a decent chance there are other worlds.*

Worlds, not world. He'd been too exhausted to process it when Moonlark said it, but now it seemed like the most powerful thing he'd ever heard. If there were two worlds, why not ten, or a hundred? There were so many paintings depicting so many different places, and it was a very big sky.

Faller let the curtain drop. He was eager to look around, see if there were clues here to explain things, clues that an outsider who'd seen another world might put together. He'd spent so much time digging through drawers in empty apartments on his world, poring over detritus from before the beginning of time. Maybe that effort would pay off.

Brand-new clothes were set out on the dresser—black pants and a pull-over sweatshirt. Faller put them on, then, bottle in hand, went into the hall and looked for a way to get outside to dispose of his urine. He passed door after door—all closed—turned a corner and heard raucous voices drifting from a big, brightly lit room down the hall.

Peeking into the high-ceilinged room, he saw a dozen or so people, mostly women and children, watching two others who were putting on some sort of performance. The audience was bright-eyed and well fed, sitting on chairs and couches that were old yet immaculate. The performers—a man and a woman—were pretending to be in a footrace. They jogged in place, sometimes the man in the lead, sometimes the woman. They were performing behind a big rectangle made from white plastic piping. Neither strayed outside the frame of the piping, giving the effect that this rectangle was a window into the actors' own imaginary world. It should have seemed odd, but it felt right to Faller. On his world performances could range anywhere, as if the watchers and the performers shared the same world, when clearly they didn't.

Before anyone in the room had time to notice him, Faller moved on. The place was immense. He passed an open door and paused to admire the longest dining table he'd ever seen.

"There you are." Moonlark emerged from a doorway, natty in a navy blue suit, a bright white handkerchief in the jacket pocket. Glancing at the milk bottle Faller was holding, he pointed to a room across the hall. "Just leave that, someone will take care of it."

As Faller returned, Moonlark put a hand on his shoulder and steered him down the hall, toward towering front doors, out into bright sunlight. "Let's take a walk." All signs of anger and impatience had vanished; Moonlark seemed friendly and relaxed as they strolled along a brick walk.

Two men in suits, pistols prominently tucked into their belts, fell into step a few paces behind them as Moonlark led Faller out the front gate, nodding at a guard leaning against a tree holding an assault rifle. Faller wondered if they still had bullets for the rifle, or if it was just for show.

They headed toward the wall he'd seen yesterday, walking the first few blocks in silence.

"You've never seen any of this before?" Moonlark asked, indicating the shop-lined street.

"I've seen streets that look like this, but never this one, no."

They turned left and headed through an empty park, then into an area choked with apartment buildings. Laundry hung from lines running above the street. Flies buzzed around layers of trash. Faller was growing tired, but he pushed on, trying not to let it show.

People noticed them as they walked. A few followed at a respectable distance, watching curiously, whispering among themselves. Moonlark ignored them, as if it happened all the time.

"I'd like you to do me a favor," Moonlark said, his tone conversational. "When we get where we're going, I'll show you various pieces of machinery. What I'd like you to do is look each over like you're familiar with it. Nod a lot. Touch the controls like you know just what they do. When I ask if you can work it, you say, 'Sure, no problem.' Loud, but not too loud. Can you do that for me?"

Faller nodded. "Sure, no problem." He kept his expression flat, wondering what Moonlark was up to. How could pretending Faller knew how to work machines benefit Moonlark, if he couldn't really work them?

"People from the Uptown side of the fence will be watching." Moonlark looked at him, raised one eyebrow. "Is anyone going to recognize you? Tell me the truth. Are you from Uptown? From one of the other boroughs?"

"I told you, no one on this world is going to recognize me, except the people who found me."

Moonlark chuckled. "Because you're from another world. Keep it up, my friend."

The walk reminded Faller of his march to the Tower. It was like a parade, with Moonlark and Faller leading a swelling crowd. Only the people following now were thinner, their steps less steady.

They passed through another business area, the empty shops long ago plundered.

"Here we go." Moonlark motioned ahead, at the wall Faller had seen the day he arrived. The wall must separate this place from Uptown.

When they reached the wall Faller thought he understood Moonlark's plan. The street that ran along it was lined with big, scary machines. The one closest to him looked like a giant dragonfly. The part of Faller's mind that always knew the right word for things whispered *Harrier*. Farther down was a five-legged steel bug with two turrets set on a swiveling head—a *drone tank*. Like everyone else, Faller could come up with a word for just about anything, even if he had only the vaguest idea—or no idea—what it was.

Moonlark led him to the Harrier first and said, "Can you operate a Harrier?"

Leaving the door open, Faller stepped inside the tight control cabin, touched the parts he assumed were controls in a manner he hoped denoted familiarity. He nodded. "No problem." On Faller's world, attracting too much attention to yourself had been a good way to end up dead. Better to keep your head down and look like someone who didn't eat much. Now it seemed Moonlark wanted to present him as someone who was extremely dangerous. Since he didn't have much choice, Faller would play along, but doing so made him extremely uneasy.

"I assume we'll need to come up with certain materials to activate it. You can tell me what you need?"

"Absolutely," Faller said. "That's right. No problem."

They paraded from machine to machine as the hushed crowd grew. More than a few faces peered over the wall from the other side. Faller could see someone watching through binoculars from the third story of a building behind the wall.

When the tour was complete, Moonlark led Faller toward the crowd. He had a way of steering Faller by the elbow that could pass for a warm, protective gesture. Moonlark positioned them in front of the crowd and raised his arms, gesturing for quiet.

"People, I'd like to introduce Faller. He has come from the heavens above to help us. More than fifty people witnessed his fall from the sky. A few of them are here with us." Moonlark gestured toward a group of twenty or so standing in the front of the crowd. He recognized the children who'd found him, and the people who'd wheeled him to Moonlark. The children were chattering excitedly to others near them; the girl pointed at the sky. "With Faller as our protector, those who would wish us harm will wish they had not."

Faller smiled, then realized that wasn't the right look for this role and tried for a distant gaze, to denote mystery.

"Where did you come from?" a man in the crowd asked, his arms folded tight.

"There's another world just like this one." Faller pointed at the sky. "Way, way up."

Moonlark squeezed his neck hard enough that it would have hurt even if it wasn't already injured. As it was, the pain was close to unbearable. "For now all that matters is, he's come."

"Is he one of the gods?" someone else called.

Ignoring the question, Moonlark drew Faller along the length of the crowd, probably wanting to give everyone an opportunity to see him.

· · · ·

"You DID great," Moonlark said as they headed back to his compound. "The people who found you are repeating your story all over the borough, and some of my trusted people are also claiming they saw you fall from the sky. Now we let the word spread, and more people will claim they saw you fall. You can count on people stepping up and laying claim to a piece of whatever's going on. It's human nature."

If Faller understood Moonlark's plan correctly, whoever was in charge on the other side of that wall was supposed to give him whatever it was he wanted based on accounts of Faller's legitimacy told by people on *this* side of the wall. That sure didn't sound like human nature to him.

When they arrived at the house Moonlark disappeared into a room with a long conference table after telling Faller to go to the kitchen and tell the cook to feed him. Tell the cook to feed him, and food would simply appear. That sounded almost too good to be true. He hurried toward the kitchen.

A woman wearing a lemon-yellow day dress and white heeled boots click-clacked past him with purpose. His thoughts firmly on the kitchen, Faller gave her a quick glance and a nod by way of greeting.

When he saw her face, he almost choked.

He skidded to a halt. "Wait!"

She turned, studied him. Faller studied her in turn, astonished, his jaw bobbing.

"Oh, you're the one who . . ." She trailed off.

There was no need to compare her to the photo. Her hair was longer, her teeth not as white, but the squared jawline, the freckles across the bridge of her nose, her strange green eyes that almost seemed to be slightly crossed . . .

Faller looked for some sign that she recognized him. "Yes, I'm the one who," he said, holding out his hand.

Her touch sent a shiver through him. Maybe the Believers were right, that the gods had set them on the world newly born on Day One with all they needed. In his case all he needed was a photograph of the woman he was meant to love, and a toy that showed him how to reach her. "They call me Faller."

"Storm." She examined him, frowning, as if he had something stuck between his teeth. "I keep thinking Moonlark must have misunderstood you. Did you tell him you fell from the sky?" She stifled a laugh, but not completely. Direct and to the point, no bullshit, no small talk. She had an easy confidence, she got things done. He could see all of this immediately. The air seemed to flicker as he looked into her eyes.

"I did fall from the sky."

"O-kay." Storm's eyes rolled toward the ceiling as she half turned, gestured down the hall. "Well, it was nice meeting you. I'm sure I'll see you again. Right now I have to be somewhere."

"*Wait.*" He reached out and nearly grabbed her wrist. She stopped, leaving a bit more distance between them. There was no mistaking her manner: she'd decided Faller was insane. He reached into his pocket, realized he'd left the photo in his jumpsuit, back in his room. He held up a finger. "Will you wait here?"

Storm's gaze shifted, settling over Faller's shoulder.

"Faller!"

There was no mistaking who had barked his name. Moonlark strode toward them, Faller's parachute under his arm.

"Is this the parachute you were talking about?" He let it unfurl across the floor.

"That's it, all right."

Moonlark studied him, his nostrils flaring, all hint of bemusement vanished. "Someone else swears he saw you drop right out of the sky. An adult this time." In one swift motion he reached into his pocket, yanked out a pistol, and pressed the muzzle under Faller's chin. It sank deep into the soft tissue there.

"Moonlark, don't," Storm said.

Faller tried to lift his head away from the pressure of the gun, but the gun followed. "I want you to tell me the truth, right here, right now. Where did you come from, and how did you get here?"

Faller spread his hands. "I told you. I fell here." It hurt to speak with the pistol jammed up in there. "I can show you. Give me the chute. I'll jump off a roof."

Moonlark retracted the pistol. Faller clutched the spot under his chin, turned his head from side to side, trying to relieve the throbbing.

Moonlark turned to Storm. "People swear on their lives they saw him float out of the sky. On their lives."

He handed Faller the parachute, straightened Faller's shirt, gestured toward the big front doors. "Show me."

Faller turned, then paused, looking at Moonlark, weighing the extent of his agitation.

"What?" Moonlark asked.

"I'm so hungry." Delicious as the nuts had been, it was all he'd eaten since a few sticks of dog jerky the first day of his fall.

Moonlark looked around. Not seeing anyone, he turned to Storm, put a hand on her shoulder. "Get him some food, will you?" Then he leaned in and kissed her.

Faller's insides withered as he looked away from the kiss.

VI

Fingers quavering violently, Izabella set down the TV remote when she saw Peter enter. MSNBC was replaying the video from yesterday, of Russian drones bombing the caverns that comprised the Bryan Mound strategic petroleum reserves in Freeport, Texas.

The world was fighting over a dwindling energy supply by reducing it further. It made no sense. Everyone was terrified that Russia and their allies—which now included most of Southeast Asia, Argentina, North Korea, the Middle East, and most of the former Soviet-bloc nations—were going to invade the United States rather than China, because invading a land mass and population the size of China's was suicide.

Peter picked up the remote and clicked off the TV. Willing himself to set aside his swirling war worries and give Izabella his full attention, he sat, took Izabella's hand. Her fingers were twitching as though an electric current were running through them. Her face was twitching as well, her mouth pulled to one side.

"This isn't funny anymore," she said, her words garbled.

"I'm not laughing."

He looked past her, at the fluid dripping out of the IV bag, into the syringe.

"Did you know I didn't like you when we first met?" Izabella asked.

Peter laughed. "And here I thought first impressions were my strong suit. It's funny, I liked you immediately." It had always baffled him why he sometimes rubbed people the wrong way. He'd gone through a lot of theories over the years. "What was it about me you didn't like?"

Izabella leaned forward to reach a long straw situated so she could get water without help. After two swallows, she fell back against her propped pillow, coughing violently.

"Are you okay?" Peter asked, leaning in, ready to pat her back.

Izabella nodded. "Happens every time." After one more big cough, she said, "You were hard to get to know." It took a moment for Peter to realize she was answering his question. "You have this affable, regular-guy veneer. Trying to get past it is like hitting a wall—but you *know* there's more underneath."

Peter digested this, surprised, staring at Izabella's water bottle, her barely touched lunch. He'd never thought of himself as closed. Izabella knew him better than anybody, except for Melissa and Harry, so he didn't feel like he could discount what she was telling him.

"In these past two weeks, I feel like I've gotten to know you better than in the whole previous twenty years." When he didn't say anything, she added, "Don't wait until people are dying to let them in."

He nodded. "I hear what you're saying. I'll try."

Izabella studied him intently for a moment, their eyes locked like lovers. Then hers brimmed with tears.

"What?"

"You know what."

He tilted his head, not sure he did know what.

Then it hit him. "Not the duplication thing."

She nodded.

"Bella, there's just no way. Even if I thought it was a good idea, I couldn't go behind Ugo's and Melissa's backs."

"It's not for them to decide. *I* want to do it. My opinion is the only one that matters here." Izabella tried to brush hair out of her eyes, but her hand wouldn't comply. Peter reached out and did it for her. "If you were in this bed instead of me, would *you* do it?" she asked.

"*No.*"

He let go of Izabella's hand, went to the window to escape the pleading in her eyes.

"Don't just say no—think about it first. Put yourself in my place. You're going fast. In two weeks you won't exist. Everything you were, all of your memories, the love you feel, all of it will just . . . stop."

Peter turned to face Izabella and closed his eyes, so she could see he was doing what she asked. He tried to imagine the rest of his life consisting of a few agonizing weeks.

He'd done this before. He knew if he thought about his own death deeply enough, there would come a moment when it stopped being an intellectual exercise and the hard reality of it would hit him in the gut, and real dread would set in. Reluctantly, he took himself to that place.

He had to admit, it was comforting to imagine another him carrying on with all the same thoughts, all the same memories. It wouldn't relieve all of the terror of dying, but it would blunt it.

"I think I understand why you'd want to do it," he admitted. "I'd probably want to do it, too." Before she could speak, he added, "But Bella, I can't. There's too much risk. It would be reckless to try it." He imagined dropping her through the iris, just like the mouse. The notion was horrifying. "Do you think Ugo and Melissa would just accept this duplicate you? They'd be so confused. It would turn into a huge mess."

"It would be *me*. I'd be standing right there, talking to them, acting just like I've always acted." She folded her arms, shook her head. "They wouldn't reject me."

Peter threw his hands in the air. "I don't even know if it's safe. That it works with mice is a long leap from knowing it works with humans."

"And if I died, look at the wonderful life I'd be leaving behind. Peter, look at me."

He hadn't realized he'd turned away. He looked down into her face, so different from Melissa's, so much rounder. Her eyes were blazing, holding his with their intensity.

"If it killed me, it would be a gift. You know that. I have absolutely nothing to lose."

A spectacularly selfish thought came to him: if he did as she asked, he wouldn't really lose her. He would, but he wouldn't.

"It wouldn't mean we're giving up," she said. "Ugo could still work on a cure." Her tone had taken on a hopeful note, perhaps because she could see he was wavering. She struggled to lift her head from the pillow. "We could look at it as insurance. I've always wanted a twin sister, so if I did survive, she wouldn't be a problem. Plus, I'd be famous."

Peter nodded, meaning to indicate that he understood what she was saying, not that he was agreeing to do what she asked.

15

MOONLARK CHOSE an abandoned six-story building a few blocks from his compound. It was shaped like a horseshoe, with an inner courtyard littered with vehicles. There seemed to be more abandoned buildings on this world than on Faller's, although there were plenty on Faller's.

"Look around, clear out anyone you find," Moonlark said to one of his men as Faller began climbing the steps of an external fire escape. "No witnesses until we know what we're dealing with."

On the roof, Faller connected the clasps to the suspension lines, then tugged on each half a dozen times. Setting the lines down, he watched the clasps for a moment, as if they might leap open on their own.

While he did this, he thought about the picture in his pocket, of him with a woman who lived on another world. The only way that seemed possible was if they had once known how to operate machines, and traveled between the two worlds.

Satisfied the chute was sound, he packed it up and stepped to the edge of the roof to assess the jump. After leaping from the Tower and falling off the edge of the world, six stories seemed like a distance he could jump without a chute. Across the courtyard, Storm was just joining Moonlark and his men, carrying a brown paper bag that Faller prayed had food in it.

Intent on making an impression, Faller waved to his audience, then backed up three steps and raised his hands in the air for dramatic effect. He dropped his head and closed his eyes, feigning deep concentration, even though it hurt his neck to do so.

He raised his head, got a running start and leaped. After dropping for a count of three, he deployed the chute. It popped open crisply; the jolt sent a stabbing pain through his tender neck, then he had a few blissful seconds to drift.

Faller landed a dozen yards from his audience and trotted to one side so the chute wouldn't deflate on top of him. A bow seemed in order to close out the performance, so Faller took one. As he raised his head he caught Storm's eye; from the layers of expression crossing her face, Faller suspected she almost believed him now, and everything she thought she'd known about the world was collapsing. Faller knew the feeling well.

Moonlark sauntered over while Faller was unhooking the harness. He reached into his vest pocket and shocked Faller by pulling out a pack of cigarettes. Shaking a cigarette partway out, he offered it to Faller.

"If you aren't who you say you are, I don't mean any disrespect by this, but if this is a hoax and you're just a fucking spy, I'll find out, and I'll cut you open and kick your guts across the sidewalk."

Smiling, Faller accepted the cigarette. "If this was a hoax I would have skipped the part where I went four days without food or water and just told you I fell after a big breakfast." He was painfully aware of Storm, hanging back with Moonlark's men.

Moonlark blew out a long trail of smoke. "I can't wrap my head around it." He grasped Faller's shoulder as something seemed to occur to him. "Then you really do know how to work the machines?"

"No—hang on—I have no idea how to work the machines."

Moonlark studied his face. "You know how to work the parachute. You knew we were here, or you wouldn't have jumped. You're telling me you're not one of the people who built all this?"

"I didn't jump—I fell. I was trying to jump off a skyscraper and I fell off the edge of my world."

Moonlark struck a match like it was something he did all the time, lit Faller's cigarette. "And what is your world like?"

Sweet smoke filled Faller's lungs, wafted in the air around his face. It was pure bliss. He blew a jet of smoke into the air. "It's a lot like here."

Moonlark looked toward the rooftop where Faller had recently been standing. "A lot like here. You mean buildings, roads, signs with writing, but no one knows what they say?"

"Yes. Exactly."

A yellowed candy-bar wrapper caught on Moonlark's shin as he considered this. Moonlark kicked it off mindlessly. "Maybe you were sent to teach us how to operate these machines and you just don't know it yet."

Faller laughed at the joke, then saw Moonlark wasn't laughing and reeled it back to a smile. "You're not serious. I told you, I don't know anything about machines. I don't know anything about *anything*—"

"You may not *know* you were sent. In fact, it makes a certain sense that you'd be ignorant of your purpose."

Faller threw his free hand in the air in frustration. "But I wasn't *sent*—I fell."

"Just humor me." Moonlark jerked his chin toward a pile of rust just recognizable as a truck, tucked into the corner of the courtyard. "Come on."

Faller followed, huffing in consternation but not daring to refuse.

Moonlark pulled open the truck's door, waved Faller inside. It smelled like wet rodent fur inside, and the seat cover was coming apart in strips. Storm and the men had sidled over close to the truck and were watching with interest.

"Just let your hands go," Moonlark said, waving toward the controls. "Play around."

Feeling like a complete ass, Faller set his cigarette on the edge of the passenger seat and put his hands on the wheel. He turned it left and right. He remembered from the early days, when a few of the vehicles worked for a while, that you needed a key to be in there, and you turned the key. He looked around; there was no key in the truck.

He jiggled the knob down by his thigh. *The shift* the voice in the back of his head offered. Fine, the shift. The words were there, but words like *shift* were just empty sounds that told you nothing.

He thumped the front (*dash*) with his fist, poked at buttons on the radio. Voices were supposed to come from the radio. It came to him in a flash of insight that startled him. He felt sure that was right, although he couldn't say why, or whose voices they would be. He fiddled with a few more knobs, then looked out at Moonlark and raised his shoulders. "Satisfied?"

Moonlark smiled, acknowledging his own folly. "Yeah. Let's go home and have a nice supper."

. . . .

"A NICE supper" was an understatement. They ate pigeon and potatoes. There was salt. Fucking *salt*. Then for dessert Hammer brought out three beautiful shiny red orbs. He set one in front of Faller. Faller gaped at it. It was one of those mythical things whose name he knew, that he'd seen in paintings in the museum and in books with pictures, but didn't exist. Only on this world, it did. An *apple*. His heart raced as he picked it up, sniffed it, watched Moonlark and Storm grip theirs in their fists and take a bite right out of the side of it. Tentatively, Faller sank his teeth into his, and as a chunk tore away he giggled with delight. It tasted like nothing he'd ever eaten; it was entirely new, and it blew the top of his head right off.

Moonlark seemed pleased by Faller's reaction to the apple. "So what were the early days like on your world, Faller?" he asked between bites.

"They were bad. Too many people. Not enough food. Everyone seemed well fed on Day One, with no idea how they'd become well fed or how to stay that way. About thirty days in, things came to a head and there was chaos—a war with a million sides. Shooting. Stabbing. Gangs going door to door killing everyone and taking their food."

He paused, took a bite of his apple to mask the sadness welling up. He didn't like talking about the early days. He didn't even like thinking about them, although memories often came whether he wanted them to or not.

"A lot of people died of disease. Eventually there were fewer people, and things settled down. People mostly get along now. At least, the people who are left." Neither Moonlark nor Storm seemed surprised by this account. "We have tribes—a hundred of them, maybe. No one can keep track of the alliances, the partial alliances, the feuds. What about here?"

"About the same," Moonlark said. "The chaos was more organized. Groups formed early—we called them clans back then. There were maybe fifteen in the early days. Some were wiped out in the early fighting, others merged, now we're left with seven. Seven boroughs." He counted them off on his fingers. "Uptown, Riverdale, Bordertown, Carterville, Far Corner, Greentown. And then there's us—Gateway. We control the center. All trade and movement from one side of the world to the other has to come through us." He pointed at his chest with both index fingers.

Faller thought it was interesting that Moonlark used *us* when clearly this was more a *me* operation than an *us* operation.

"Things haven't settled down here," Storm said. "There are always boroughs at war with each other, constant raids. Six months ago Uptown invaded and killed eighty of our people before we were able to drive them back."

"Yeah, but we killed a hundred and fifty of *their* people," Moonlark added, waving what was left of his apple.

Moonlark and Storm were sitting close together, making frequent eye contact. Faller tried to glean how permanent their relationship might be, how long it had been going on. He didn't dare ask.

"How many people are on your world?" Faller asked.

"Gateway has about twenty-eight hundred," Moonlark said. "We don't have exact counts for the other boroughs, but in total there are probably in the neighborhood of fifteen thousand."

Faller's world had less than that, although he had only a vague idea of how the worlds compared in size.

"A month before the war with Uptown our estimates were closer to thirty thousand. Who knows how many were here at the beginning. That's why you're so important—someone needs to unite the boroughs before they wipe each other out."

A flash of impatience crossed Storm's face. "There are other possibilities that aren't so all-or-nothing."

"Well." Moonlark pushed himself up from the table, ignoring Storm's comment. "I need to speak to some people." He nodded toward Faller.

"Many thanks for the meal. I've never had a better one," Faller said.

Moonlark waved it away. "Nah, don't worry about it."

Storm got up as well. Faller hung back, watching from the doorway as Storm turned toward a door while Moonlark continued down the long hallway. When Moonlark was out of sight, Faller followed Storm. The door led outside.

He found her standing, arms folded, on a patio beside a rectangular pool of black water. Crickets were trilling in the thicket of bushes surrounding the patio.

"Is this your quiet place?"

Storm turned. She didn't seem surprised to see him. "There are plenty of quiet places." She gestured toward a thirty-story tower a few blocks away. "That's empty, if you're looking for a quiet place. Every week there are more quiet places."

"Thanks, but I had plenty of quiet time while I was falling. I'm in more of a talking mood."

Storm smiled, shook her head in a "what am I going to do with you?" way. "You'd better get some rest. Moonlark has a big day planned for you tomorrow." She looked at him, smirked. "You're going to move the tank."

"Right." He didn't want to talk about Moonlark's plans, or the shrinking population. He wanted to show her the picture. He was also terrified to show it to her, afraid she would snatch it away and show it to Moonlark. Then Faller would have some real explaining to do, beginning with why he possessed a picture of himself with Moonlark's girlfriend, or whatever she was, and ending with why he hadn't shown the picture to Moonlark earlier. He didn't have good answers for those questions.

"So how did you and Moonlark meet?" Faller asked.

He watched Storm's profile as she watched the water. "Early on, two men got hold of my handgun while I was asleep. They attacked me. Moonlark came up behind them with a two-by-four and beat them both to death. When it was over, he picked up my pistol and handed it back to me."

Faller nodded. He could see how that would lead you to trust someone. "Where did you get the handgun?"

"It was in my belt on that first day." Storm turned to face him. "So tell me, Faller, have you considered how this all ends?"

"How what ends?"

Storm rolled her eyes at the sky. "Let's say Moonlark convinces the leaders of the other boroughs that you can work machines, and they give him what he wants. Then what happens?"

Faller waited, eyebrows raised.

Storm took on the tone Faller used when telling Daisy something she should already have figured out, like not to eat the mushrooms that grew on car tires. "At some point one of three things has to happen." She pried her first finger open. "One, you drive a tank down the street, or get water to come out of a faucet. We both know that's not going to happen. Two, Moonlark admits he lied about you to gain more territory, and God knows"— she laughed—"*that's* not going to happen. That leaves number three." She dropped her hands, looked at him, waiting.

Faller squatted, picked up a corner of stone that had chipped off the patio and tossed it into the water. "This is the part where you let me figure it out for myself, isn't it?"

"Yes, it is." She turned the full force of her gaze on him. "So tell me,

Faller. If you were smart enough to figure out how to jump from one world to another, this should be easy. What's number three?"

Faller had figured out number three in the middle of number one. He wasn't sure it was in his best interest that Moonlark's girlfriend knew he knew number three. Of course, it wasn't in her best interest to flat-out tell him that her husband was planning to kill him, so maybe he could trust her.

"Number three is that I have an unfortunate accident."

Storm pointed at him. "Bingo. You're not as clueless as you look."

"Why are you telling me this?"

Storm leaned in so close that for a moment Faller thought she was going to kiss him. "Because you're not the only one Moonlark's ridiculous plan is going to get killed." Her breath on his face made him giddy, despite the situation.

She drew her face away, folded her arms. "If you can disappear back to wherever you came from, now would be a good time."

"Well, that's a problem. I can't fall up."

"Then hide. Climb a wall into another borough where no one knows what you look like."

That made sense, but then Faller would be starving again, and there would be a wall separating him and Storm. The truth was, he didn't mind being in this kind of danger. Well, maybe "didn't mind" was an overstatement, but he'd rather be an apple-eating somebody with a target on his back than a rat-eating nobody trying to scrounge enough food to stay alive. If things got too dangerous, he could always run and hide then. For now, he'd see how things played out.

16

THE TANK was centered in the street, both of its muzzles pointed at the wall separating Midtown and Uptown. Thousands of Gateway residents lined the street. They churned and pushed, trying to see, but anyone who was pushed off the curb and into the street immediately stepped back onto the curb. Moonlark's men had told them no one in the street, and Faller was learning that the residents always listened to Moonlark and his men.

"How big a hole would it make?" Moonlark asked, loud enough for even the spectators on the Uptown side of the wall to hear. "Maybe that big?" He made a big circle with his arms.

Faller shook his head. "It wouldn't be a hole." He swept his hand across a big swath of the wall. "It'd knock out an entire section."

Moonlark beamed, apparently pleased with Faller's answer.

Because the turret looked like a giant gun, Moonlark assumed it would make a hole like a gun. Faller wasn't sure it made sense to assume a tank was like a gun. Sure, the turret *looked* like a giant gun, but guns worked. No one understood why guns worked when none of the other machines did. Maybe guns weren't machines at all; maybe it was better to think of them as tools, like hammers and saws. If his dream of the planes dropping bombs was anything more than his own twisted imagination, the things that came out of the drone tank would be nothing like bullets.

Faller and Moonlark climbed up to look at the tank's controls, just as they'd rehearsed.

"Can you make it move, without firing it?" Moonlark asked.

"Oh, sure." Faller stepped up to the controls tucked behind the turret.

Trying to appear deliberate, he gripped a handle with one hand, clutched a notched black knob with the other. The crowd hushed as he closed his eyes, as if concentrating deeply. He turned the crank and rotated the knob simultaneously, then, opening his eyes, he released the crank and flipped a series of switches set in a box.

The tank inched backward. The crowd gasped. It was a pretty sound: a thousand sets of lungs drawing in air all at once. Faller watched the mark they'd made on the street, and when the front wheel touched it he flipped the switches back where they'd been, then turned the crank in the opposite direction. The tank stopped.

As he hopped from the tank he could hear the men hiding in the manhole beneath the tank reeling in the chain they'd used to drag it those few feet. The manhole cover thunked quietly closed as Faller joined Moonlark and shook his outstretched hand. They posed for the crowd, their hands locked as if sealing a blood oath, their faces turned toward the throngs.

A face on the edge of the crowd caught Faller off guard. He took in her teardrop eyes and the tight, controlled line of her mouth, and let out a sharp yawp of surprise, dropping Moonlark's hand.

"Orchid?" Faller stepped toward her.

Moonlark caught his elbow, drew him back.

"Orchid, is that you?" Faller called. It *was* her, thinner, wearing heavily soiled jeans and a T-shirt, clutching a small boy's hand. Faller tried to break Moonlark's grip, but Moonlark only squeezed harder. Faller turned to him. "That woman is from my world! I know her. How did she get here?" He waved frantically to her. "Orchid, it's me!" Orchid looked over her shoulder, as if she thought he must be talking to someone else.

Moonlark yanked Faller in the other direction. "Let's go," he hissed. Orchid was watching Faller, no hint of recognition on her face.

"Orchid!" Faller pulled against Moonlark. Others in the crowd were now looking at Orchid.

Appearing confused and uncomfortable, Orchid pushed into the crowd. The little boy's hand, clutching a weathered toy race car, was the last glimpse Faller got as one of Moonlark's men grabbed his free arm and they half carried him away, his feet dancing just above the pavement.

"Fuck. You told me you didn't know anyone," Moonlark shouted when they were out of earshot of the crowd. He looked Faller up and down like he was assessing a turd on his shoe. "You lying sack of shit. You really had me going."

"I *don't* know anyone from this damned world. But *that* woman isn't from this world—she's from mine."

Moonlark stopped. He gawked at Faller. "You're not a con man, you're a fucking loony."

"No," Faller said quickly. He could guess what would happen to him if Moonlark decided he was insane. "I promise you, I'm not crazy. You can count on me." He made an emphatic show of not struggling any more, of standing with them, nice and calm. "I'm sorry about that, it won't happen again. She must just look like someone I knew. The resemblance is uncanny, really."

Moonlark studied Faller. Faller tried to look remarkably reasonable and lucid. Cursing under his breath, Moonlark resumed walking. "I guess I'm in too deep to cut my losses now."

Faller nodded as they rounded a corner, stepping into the street to avoid a collapsed wall.

"Okay, we'll go with it." He patted Faller's back. The pats were a bit hard. "No more surprises, you hear me?"

VII

PETER WHEELED Izabella into the lab as the door slammed closed behind them, echoing in the open space. Doing this in the middle of the night made it feel like a crime, and it was possible that, technically, it was.

"Is this starting to feel like a bad idea to you? Maybe I should take you back."

"Let's not go through this again," Bella pleaded. "I'm scared to death as it is." Her speech was a jerking, guttural mess.

The wheelchair left wet trails across the spotless floor from the rain outside. It was pattering on the big floor-to-ceiling windows, the water leaving trails down the glass.

Peter leaned Izabella forward, slipped his hands under her arms and lifted her from the wheelchair. Izabella could only watch as he struggled to carry her up the three aluminum steps of the scaffolding. Peter was too small and out of shape. Ugo the weight lifter could have hoisted her effortlessly, but Ugo couldn't know what they were doing until they were done.

Huffing, Peter set Izabella at the edge of the scaffolding closest to the iris—the portal to duplication.

Izabella pried off her wedding ring, handed it to Peter. "I don't want to lose this."

"I hadn't thought of that," Peter said.

"Shit, what about my clothes? I didn't think about bringing any, for me or for her."

The mention of *her* sent a fresh chill through Peter. He hadn't considered clothes, either. He was not a detail guy. "Maybe we should go back and get some."

"*No.* I don't want to risk losing my nerve. I can take off the hospital gown so I don't lose it. My double can hide in one of the offices until you bring her back some clothes. Shit. My *double.* Is this real?"

"That's what I'm saying. It is real. Too real." He looked away, untied the bow at the top of Izabella's hospital gown.

"Come on, Peter," Izabella said. "How are you going to drop me through without *looking* at me?"

She had a point. He turned his head about halfway back, fixed his gaze on a stain on the scaffold's steel floor as he slid Izabella's gown down her hips and pulled it off. Izabella was a blur of pale white skin and dark hair.

"I need you to look at me, Peter. Look at my eyes."

Peter did.

"I'm scared," she said. "I need you here with me."

He took her quavering hand, squeezed it. "I'm sorry. I'm here. Don't be scared. Nothing bad is going to happen." If only he was sure of that. The closer they came to actually going through with this, the more uncertain he felt.

He got behind Izabella and grasped her under her arms. His right hand bumped against her breast.

"Sorry."

She let out a panicky laugh. "Yeah, I'm pretty sure you're not hitting on me." She was trembling uncontrollably; whether it was all prion, or prion on top of fear, Peter couldn't say. His own heart was hammering wildly. In a few moments there would be two Izabellas.

"We're about to make history," he said. "Do you realize that? You're like the first person in space. Bigger."

"Just lift me, Boy Wonder. We can reflect on the significance of the moment when it's over."

He lifted her, her feet dragging until they cleared the edge and hung over the iris.

"If anything happens, tell Ugo I'm sorry I went behind his back. Tell Melissa I love her." She craned her neck, tried to kiss his cheek, but with her muscle contractions only managed to bump her nose against his ear. "Thank you."

"I'll see you in a minute; you can thank me then. In stereo." He stared into the aperture, waiting for her to change her mind. They could laugh over it as Peter helped her get dressed. It would be their little secret. For a few more weeks, at least.

Izabella was peering down into the darkness. "Let me go, Peter."

"Are you sure?"

She closed her eyes. "For God's sake, Peter, get it over with."

Struggling not to fall in with her, Peter let her go.

She disappeared into the aperture.

Heart racing, Peter scurried down the ladder, ran for the delivery ducts. He turned to the left, where the original Izabella would drop onto the cushioned gurney he'd set up.

Neither Izabella appeared.

The mice had come immediately. So had all the test organs and tissues. Peter stared at the duct. He resisted the temptation to plunge his hands up into it to see if she was somehow stuck, knowing his hands would simply poke out through the aperture above the duct.

He stood motionless, his heart hammering. Nothing had ever gone into the duplicator and failed to come out, in duplicate.

"Where is she?" he said aloud. He'd known there were risks. There were always risks when you knew so little about a process, but how could she be *gone?*

"Izabella?" he shouted. He waited, listening, then again, "Izabella?" His breath was coming in gasps.

He lunged toward the scaffolding, scurried up the ladder, nearly tumbled into the iris.

"Izabella?"

There was nothing there but the perfect blackness of the iris.

A soft thud startled him. He lifted his head, but couldn't see the delivery ducts. Scrambling, he leaped to the floor and stumbled to his knees before recovering. Peter could see the pale, white, naked forms of both Izabellas, each lying facedown. He reached the real Izabella and bent over her.

"Izabella?"

He rolled her over, stared into her glassy, sightless brown eyes.

17

As FALLER walked in the shadow of abandoned stores and houses, he had moments when he was sure the woman he'd seen was simply a stranger who looked a hell of a lot like Orchid. Then he'd picture that woman in the crowd—the pretty, long-lashed, teardrop-shaped eyes; the tight, clenched way she'd carried herself—and he was certain it was Orchid. It was a face he knew as well as his own.

Was she watching out for Daisy, as she'd promised? Of course she was; she loved Daisy almost as much as Faller did. They'd been like a family, except not, because of Storm. Although Storm had not been waiting chastely for him.

Faller paused on a street corner, stared off at storefronts smothered in dark green leaves. Some sort of climbing vine had taken over the block. This was pointless; he wasn't going to find Orchid, or whoever it was, by walking up and down streets. He wasn't even sure where the populated areas of the borough were—this part of town was deserted. Faller looked around for the white tower, headed back the way he'd come. There was no risk of getting lost with the white tower serving as a landmark.

Maybe the woman he'd seen in the crowd was Orchid's twin sister. She could have gotten there the same way Storm had, however that was. That would explain why the woman hadn't recognized him.

When Faller returned to Moonlark's house, Hammer told him Moonlark was looking for him, and sent him to Moonlark's office.

Moonlark was grinning so widely his ears were drawn back on his head.

He was missing an incisor. Faller felt a petty spark of joy—he still had all of his teeth. "Super wants to discuss terms for a merger."

"Who's Super? And what's a merger?" Moonlark hadn't invited him to sit, so Faller stood in the center of the big room.

"Super runs Uptown. A merger is tearing down the wall between the two boroughs and turning them into one. Under my control, of course. She wants to negotiate now, while she can still get favorable terms. She's probably hoping to become my second in command." Moonlark pushed back from his desk, strutted between two couches set facing each other, his hands behind his back. "With an army that size, and control of world trade, it'll only be a matter of time before we tear down all the walls and unite the world. None of the boroughs would stand for long, even after they figure out we can't really run the machines." He threw back his head and laughed. "Shit, am I brilliant, or what?" He looked at Faller, raised his eyebrows. "Am I brilliant?"

"You're brilliant."

Moonlark wrapped an elbow around Faller's neck, kissed him on the side of the head. "I have an excellent memory as well." He tapped his temple. "I don't forget the people who help me."

It was intended as a promise of rewards to come, but Faller couldn't help hearing it as a threat.

18

FALLER WOKE screaming. It seemed like the nightmare was trying to pull him back under, drag him to sleep despite his pounding heart and gasping breath. He got out of bed, stood clutching his pillow to his chest, waiting for the terrible images to abate.

Faller had been carrying a corpse through dark tunnels. The corpse was too heavy for him. She kept slipping, but he didn't want to drag her, because he'd known her. If he had to hear the sound of her feet dragging along the floor, he was sure he would lose his mind. He kept trying to get a better grip, but she kept sliding out of his sweaty hands. His fingers would grip her cold breast, her hair, a thigh. Then her hand had reached up and gripped his shoulder.

Pulling open the drapes, Faller opened his eyes wide to the early morning sunlight, willing the light to wash the images out of his head.

· · · · ·

STILL SHAKEN, Faller met Moonlark, Storm, and six of Moonlark's men in the long, open walkway that connected Moonlark's house and his center of operations. All of the men had guns tucked in their waistbands.

"Ready?" Moonlark asked.

Birds chirped in the trees and foliage as they set out.

"When we get there, you two hang back across the street," Moonlark said to Faller and Storm. "I'll call you over after a few words with Super.

Storm will say hello, then I'll introduce Faller. For God's sake don't say anything more than hello."

"No problem," Faller said.

"We're making history here. This is a day people will remember for the rest of their lives."

"I'm proud to be a part of it." That was definitely an overstatement of his enthusiasm. Once the deal was struck, Faller would have to be on his guard.

They reached the wall. He and Storm hung back. One of Moonlark's men ducked into a building behind them to serve as lookout on the roof.

"Did I detect a hint of sarcasm in your tone just now?" Storm asked, glancing at Faller.

"Sarcasm?" Faller pretended to consider. "I doubt it. My throat constricts a little when I'm kissing someone's ass. Maybe that's what you heard."

"Maybe."

"So why are you so dead set against this?" Faller asked as Moonlark and his men paused on the far curb.

Storm rolled her eyes up to meet his. "I don't think you're the ideal person for me to confide in."

"Wait, *I'm* not the ideal person for *you* to confide in?" When she looked at him, it was like biting into that apple. Everything else fell away.

"You and Moonlark seem to be getting pretty close. What would keep you from repeating what I say back to him, to win favor?"

"Hey, if I was going to squeal to Moonlark, I could have started with the little heads-up you gave me last night. I'm just trying to stay alive." He gestured toward the sky. "I fell for days, I landed here half-dead, and suddenly I'm in the middle of *this*." He waved toward Moonlark, as the gate in the wall began to swing open in a series of jerks.

The gate between the boroughs squealed as it swung open.

"Here we go," Faller said.

Six large men (admittedly less nattily dressed than Moonlark's) stepped through, followed by Super.

Super was grey-haired and fat. There'd been quite a few fat people on Day One, but none of them had managed to stay fat on Faller's world. The underside of Super's arms jiggled as she raised a hand and waved to Moonlark before putting her head down and pushing on.

Faller wondered what would happen once the agreement was reached. Did everyone start dismantling the wall right away, or what?

Super stopped abruptly, slowly raised her head.

"What the fuck's she doing?" Moonlark asked.

Super gave Moonlark a peculiar smile, one Faller didn't like.

She turned and lumbered back toward the gate.

"What the *fuck* is she doing?" Moonlark repeated.

As she approached the gate she raised her arms high. From the roof behind Faller a gunshot sounded—a *crack* that reminded him of the early days. He twisted to look at Moonlark's man on the roof. He was waving frantically.

"Run!" he screamed. His voice was partially drowned by shouts as people surged through the gate carrying weapons—axes, bats, kitchen knives. They sprinted toward Moonlark's group, looking eager to be the first to reach them and split a skull. Others came over the wall, too impatient to wait to get through the gate.

Moonlark's men drew their pistols. Faller turned toward Storm, but she was already gone. Behind him the shouts of the attacking mob built to a solid roar.

He took off after Storm. She was half a block ahead, running in bare feet, her shoes abandoned. She turned left into an alley, which would take her parallel to the mob rather than away from it. Faller took one glance back, saw Moonlark, gun raised, shooting a woman blocking his path point-blank in the face, then he turned and followed Storm.

They were the only two people on the narrow street—it was an opportune moment to disappear.

"*Storm.*" Storm glanced back, but kept running. "*This way.*" He rushed through an open door, into darkness. As his eyes adjusted he saw it was a restaurant kitchen, filthy, half an inch of water on the floor. He splashed deeper into the shadows.

A moment later Storm burst through the doorway.

"Over here," he hissed.

Gasping, Storm followed his voice and squatted beside him, behind a big steel cooking island, as voices rose and fell outside. A bell was ringing, deep and resonant, likely a call to arms for Moonlark's borough.

Faller was reasonably sure they were safe for the moment; in the heat of the first wave no one was going to poke around in an abandoned building.

"Did you see him? Did he get away?" Storm asked.

"He was alive the last I saw him."

She stifled a sob. "This is all because of his *brilliant* plan. Super must have figured she had to throw everything she had at us before you got the *tanks* working. He's such an *idiot*."

Given the results, Faller was inclined to agree. "Do you think this is a full-on invasion, or just an assassination attempt?"

"I have no idea." She swiped at a lock of hair hanging in front of her eye, glared at him. "I should get as far away from you as possible. I'm sure Super would prefer to capture you alive so you can run the machines for her, but dead and no longer a threat is probably a close second. Of course, you can't actually *run* the machines, so that will be a problem if they catch you."

"I suppose if they catch Moonlark's girlfriend they'll escort her home and tuck her into bed?"

There were shouts outside—not the sound of people running past, but desperate, angry sounds. Faller rose until he could see.

A man with an ax had cornered a white-haired man with a shovel. Back pressed to a brick wall, the older man was swinging the shovel frantically, trying to keep the other man back.

"Wait," he repeated after each desperate swing as the man with the ax waited for an opening, occasionally feinting. Faller had no idea which man was from Uptown, which from Gateway, or how they even knew they were from different boroughs.

The man with the shovel was tiring. "Wait," he cried out, sobbing, as the man with the ax took a swing that clanged against the shovel, knocking it down. He swung again and hit the man just below the elbow.

The man no longer holding a shovel screamed with a sharp, piercing clarity. His arm nearly severed, he grabbed for the ax with his other hand as it came down a second time. It split his hand in two and sank into his collar.

Faller squatted back down, resisting the urge to stick his fingers in his ears to blot out the man's death screams.

"We have to get back to the compound," Storm said. "It's heavily defended. They have boxes and boxes of bullets."

"How? The first Uptowners who catch us will cut us to pieces, and we have nothing to defend ourselves with." Faller gestured toward the street. "There's a shovel lying in the alley outside, but it didn't do the last owner much good."

Storm turned and peered into the darkness of the restaurant. "If we can get to a subway station, we can take the tunnels."

That hadn't occurred to Faller. Since things had settled down, the only reason anyone went into the tunnels on his world was to hunt rats.

"Where's the nearest station?" Faller asked.

"Come on." She ducked through the door leading toward the front of the restaurant. Faller followed.

There were broken dishes and silverware strewn around the main dining area. Nothing but butter knives, but Faller pocketed a shard of broken china. If it came to fighting for their lives it would be slightly better than fists—especially his fists.

Hidden by the gloom, they surveyed the street through a broken picture window. It was pandemonium. Just outside two men were beating each other senseless with bats. Faller spotted his friend with the ax. He had wounded a young woman (almost a girl, really) in the hip and was chasing her, bent on finishing her off. There were people everywhere; most appeared to be invaders from Uptown, but it was difficult to know for sure.

"There," Storm whispered, pointing down the street at steps descending underground, surrounded on three sides by a high green gate.

A big man gripping a length of pipe with a knife lashed to the end flew by the window. He rammed his makeshift spear into another man's spine, withdrew the knife before the man had time to fall, and was off to stab someone else.

"There's no way we can make it," Faller said. It was so apparent it barely needed saying.

They watched the stomach-churning display outside.

"Why don't we stay put, find a hiding place in the building?" Faller considered adding that he was remarkably adept at finding hiding places, having spent much of the first thirty days in one hiding place or another, but decided that might make him seem less desirable as a potential soul mate.

"And what do we do if Uptown takes control of this section? Stay hidden forever?"

"Do you have a better idea?" Faller gestured out the window. "As soon as we step through that door, someone is going to skewer us."

Storm studied the station, then looked at Faller. "How fast can you run, Faller?"

"Faster than you. I've spent my life running."

Storm smiled at his lame joke. "I say we run for it."

Faller gauged the distance to the station. No one would be expecting two unarmed fools to burst from an abandoned building. Maybe it was possible. And she had a valid point about the downside of his plan. "All right. You first."

She looked him up and down. "That's very valiant of you."

They ducked from the window as an unarmed man ran by holding his throat with a blood-soaked hand.

"Whoever goes first gets an extra couple of steps before the people out there with the sharp tools catch on," Faller hissed in Storm's ear. "If you want me to go first, I'd be happy to."

Ceding the point, Storm led them to the doorway (there was no door) and waited for an opportune moment to make her break.

A few minutes of watching made it clear that one moment was about as good as another. Storm turned, said, "Here we go. When you reach the tunnel, go left." She gripped either side of the doorway, took a breath, and launched herself out.

Already breathing hard from fear, Faller took off after her. He hurdled a blood-soaked body on the sidewalk, then turned it on, weaving to put distance between himself and anyone with a weapon, which was everyone still standing. A man with sunken cheeks and what appeared to be a scythe stared at Faller as he flew past.

"There he is!"

Storm was almost to the steps. A woman with a knife intercepted Faller, forcing him to skid to a stop. She slashed with the butcher knife as Faller feinted, trying to get around her. For an instant it was like they were dancing, then he got her to commit to her left by taking two quick steps in that direction before spinning to her right.

The woman had delayed him long enough that a tall, skinny man brandishing a crowbar now blocked the entrance to the underground. Others were closing in from all sides. There was no way around the guy.

Faller ran right at him, full tilt. The guy tried to time his swing with the crowbar, but flinched at the last instant, surprised when Faller just kept charging. The two men hurtled back into the darkness of the stairwell. The man broke Faller's initial impact, then Faller tumbled headfirst over him and bounced painfully down the concrete steps.

When Faller finally came to a stop the man plowed into him, knocking him farther down. Tangled together, they struggled to get up. A bare foot passed Faller's face on the step, and he heard clattering as Storm retrieved the crowbar. There was a hollow *thunk*, then another. The man went limp.

"Come on," Storm said.

Dragging himself from under the motionless man, Faller took the last flight of steps four at a time, landing in near darkness as pursuers piled down from above. Storm grabbed his hand and pulled him along. A dozen steps in, it was pitch-black. They edged along the wall, moving as quickly as possible. The smell of shit was overwhelming. The darkness and relative privacy made the stations perfect toilets. Faller didn't envy Storm her bare feet as shit squelched under his shoes.

"Spread out," someone behind them called.

Something clattered just ahead; silently, Storm placed Faller's hand on a turnstile, then he both heard and felt her clamber over it. He followed as their pursuers shouted to each other and rushed toward the sounds.

Clear of the turnstile, Faller waved his hand around until it bumped Storm's and she gripped his again. They moved quickly along the wall, their pursuers not twenty feet behind. It sounded like there were a dozen or more.

"Steps," Storm whispered as she drew him down. Clutching a handrail, they scrambled lower, the darkness growing thicker and damper. At the bottom they again moved along the wall until Storm whispered, "Jump," and Faller felt the edge of the platform and sprang blindly, landing on gravel in a three-point stance.

Storm pulled him to the right, although he was sure she'd told him to go left. They ran, holding hands. Faller held his free hand out in front of his face, praying they didn't run headlong into a train sitting on the track. The crunching of their feet on the gravel was mostly drowned by the shouts passing among their pursuers.

After only a few dozen yards Storm squeezed his hand, hard, and drew him to the wall. When she pushed him down, Faller grasped her plan. He crouched against the wall, trying to make himself as small as possible, then heard Storm moving in the gravel and realized she was doing him one better, lying on her side right along the bottom of the wall. He did the same, her feet pressing against his head.

Their pursuers were smart. They had spread out to cover the entire tunnel, and as they approached, Faller exhaled, willing himself to melt into the wall.

A foot brushed his cheek. He tensed, anticipating a shout, rough hands reaching for him. But the phalanx forged on down the tunnel, their voices growing dimmer.

Faller rose to his haunches, felt Storm do the same. Closing her hand over his, Storm silently led him back the way they had come.

VIII

HER LIPS were still warm. If Ugo had walked into the lab at that moment, found Peter's mouth on Izabella's as she lay naked on the gurney, what would he think?

"Oh, God, Izabella." He squeezed her hand. "Please. Please. Come back."

Peter had told her he wouldn't let anything happen to her.

Then he remembered her duplicate. He hadn't checked her duplicate. He rushed over, turned her faceup, searched for a pulse in her still warm neck.

Nothing. She was dead.

Peter lifted his face toward the ceiling and screamed.

What had he been thinking? He should have said no. No matter how hard she persisted, he should have said no. He pulled his phone from his pocket to call an ambulance, opened his contact list, searching for the number for emergencies.

The number wasn't under *E* for *emergency*. He scrolled down to the end of the list, passed *Woolcoff, Ugo,* and froze.

He should call Ugo first. He owed it to Ugo to tell him himself.

He punched Ugo's number.

"What do you want?" Ugo said, by way of greeting.

"It's Izabella. She's gone, Ugo. She's dead."

Ugo stammered. "My Bella? How can that be? I would have been contacted."

"No—she's not at the hospital. She checked herself out."

"What? Why?"

Peter swallowed, trying to wet his dry mouth. "She asked me to duplicate her. She—it didn't work."

Ugo howled into the phone. Peter squeezed his eyes shut, resisted the urge to pull the phone away from his ear. He tried to say he was sorry, but Ugo cut him off.

"Don't touch her, you son of a bitch." He disconnected.

· · · ·

IT DIDN'T seem possible for Ugo to arrive as quickly as he did. He burst through the door.

"Izabella."

He dropped to her side, across from Peter, lifted her hand and squeezed it in both of his. His entire body was shaking.

Izabella's mouth was partially open from Peter's useless attempt at CPR, her lips curled back in a grimace, or a smile, displaying her even white teeth.

She should be breathing. Why wasn't she breathing?

"I'm so sorry, Ugo. You have no idea. Bella kept asking—"

"Shut up." Ugo screamed. *"Don't you dare try to blame my Bella. Don't you dare. You did this."*

"I did, because she wanted me to. It was a chance, at least."

Peter didn't see the punch coming. It felt like a mallet smashing into his nose. He fell back, cracked his head on the hard floor.

"I *was her chance*." Ugo stood over him, his breath coming in huge, ragged gasps. *"My* research *was her chance*." He poked his chest. "*I* was going to save her. Not *you*."

Peter felt blood dribbling between his fingers as he clutched his nose. "If you want to bring me up on charges, I understand."

"Charges?" Ugo shook his head in disbelief. "I'll fucking kill you." He turned back to Izabella, knelt and pressed his fingers to her cheek.

She hadn't had many good days left. The rest of her life would have been torture. Surely Ugo could see that.

Ugo slid his arms beneath Izabella's legs and shoulders and lifted her.

"What are you doing?" Peter asked, sitting up. "You shouldn't move her."

"Shut up. My wife is not going to be remembered as the victim of some sick experiment. She died peacefully, in her own bed."

Ugo shifted Izabella's body, trying to get a better grip.

He studied her face. "You're sure I have my wife, not the abortion you made?"

"Yes."

Ugo headed for the door.

"What should I do with this one?" Peter called.

"I couldn't care less." Ugo pushed the door open with his shoulder and headed for the parking lot.

Grasping the edge of a lab table, Peter struggled to his feet. A few drops of blood dribbled to the floor; he pinched his nose to stop the flow.

The duplicate Izabella lay pale and silent under the fluorescent lights. If Ugo wanted people to believe Izabella died of the disease, this Izabella had to disappear. Peter squeezed his eyes shut, trying to think of what to do.

Nothing came. Izabella was gone; he'd killed her. That was all he could think of. He needed help.

Harry. Peter pulled out his phone. Harry would help him figure out what to do.

19

"Why don't invaders use these tunnels to cross under the walls?" Faller asked as they crept along.

"They're blocked off at the borders," Storm said.

Things had developed so differently on this world. Walls and boroughs, wars and dictators. Things had been a hell of a lot simpler on Faller's world. The people had seemed simpler as well.

The chatter of rats grew louder, along with a rancid stench, then it fell away as they moved past what must have been a side tunnel.

"Don't take this the wrong way, but I'm wondering how you ended up with a man like Moonlark."

"He wasn't always like this." Storm caught herself, paused. "No, that's not true. There used to be more to him, is what I should say. He stood out in the early days, when everyone was acting like animals. He helped me without asking for anything in return. He showed me respect when he didn't have to."

Maybe it was the sense of anonymity the darkness created, or fatigue bringing her guard down, but Faller felt like he knew Storm much better than he had a few minutes earlier. Did he trust her enough to show her the photo? It was in his back pocket.

The darkness shifted from black to dark grey, and Storm slowed. "I think this is our stop."

They climbed onto the platform and skulked along the wall until dim light and a staircase became visible.

They surfaced on a calm side street, but sounds of fighting were close. They were half a block from a weed-choked field that bordered one end of Moon-lark's compound, and decided their safest bet was to push straight through the field. Faller led the way, weaving through head-high weeds and brush until they emerged across the street from the gate.

Dozens of men patrolled inside the compound's fence. As soon as some-one spotted Storm and Faller they rushed them inside.

"Is Moonlark back?" Storm asked as Hammer met them at the door.

"No." From his tone and expression, it was clear he didn't expect to see Moonlark again. He grasped Storm's elbow. "Listen to me. It's not just Up-town. Riverdale and Bordertown are coming from the other side. There's a breach in the wall between us and Bordertown. It's only a matter of time before Gateway falls."

Storm's reaction confirmed what Faller already suspected: the news was a death sentence. They would kill Storm immediately, and string Faller up as soon as it was clear he couldn't operate the weapons. There was nowhere they would be safe.

At least, there was nowhere on this world they would be safe.

Faller reached for Storm's hand. "Come on."

Storm pulled her hand away. "What do you mean, come on? Don't you get it? There's nowhere to run."

"Yes there is." Faller held up a finger. "Wait there. Don't move." He raced down the hall, slid the last five feet on the slick floor and darted into his room. The parachute and his pack were bunched on the dresser with his jumpsuit.

"We need food and water," he said to Storm as he raced past her toward the kitchen.

"Wait a minute," she called after him.

In the kitchen he filled two empty glass jugs with screw-on caps from a trough of water under the window, grabbed a loaf of bread from the counter, slabs of cured meat from the pantry, half a dozen apples.

Storm appeared in the kitchen doorway. "Where are you suggesting we go?" She said it a word at a time.

"The only direction left." Faller pointed at the floor. "Down. If there are two worlds, why not three? Or a hundred?"

He shrugged on his pack while Storm laughed dryly. "You've got to be kidding. I'd rather take my chances with the invaders."

Faller stopped, looked intently at Storm. "Would you really?"

"I'm not jumping off the edge." She made a slashing motion with her hand. "Forget it. Even with your little parachute stunt, I'm not sure I believe your insane story. Even if I did, there's no way."

Faller pulled the photo from his pocket and handed it to Storm.

She studied it, her expression melting from bemused, to serious, and finally, to shock.

"Where did you get this?"

"I found it in my pocket, on Day One."

"Day One?"

"Day One. When time began."

Her usually pale skin was alabaster. She studied the picture, shaking her head in astonishment. "We look like lovers." She looked up from the photo, studied Faller's face carefully. "What is this?"

"I was hoping you'd know."

Storm brought the photo close to her face.

"Let me ask you something," Faller said. "In those early days, people discovered a lot of photos of themselves, with people they didn't know, in places that didn't exist. Did you find any pictures of yourself?"

She looked at him as if he'd performed a magic trick. "No. How would you know that?"

He tapped the photo. "This is the only picture of me. It's as if I'd just arrived there on Day One, while everyone else had been there a while."

Storm turned the photo over and examined the back, as if she suspected it might be two photos cleverly joined together.

"I really did fall from another world."

When Storm didn't respond, Faller reached out and clutched her hand, squeezed it. "Storm, I'm not joking. I'm not insane. I'm not full of shit. I. Fell. Here."

Her eyes flicked across his face, then back to the photo. "Why are you showing me this now?"

"I didn't show it to you before because I didn't want Moonlark to cut my throat."

Storm laughed. "Wise move. But why are you showing it to me now?"

Did he need to spell it out for her? The photo said they should be together.

"So you'll trust me," Faller said.

She handed back the photo. "Why should I trust you? You just admitted it yourself: you have no idea if there are more worlds below this one. You're just guessing. I'm not jumping off the edge of the world on a guess."

"It's an educated guess." He returned the photo to his pocket, tucking it beside the blood sketch. "It makes sense that there should be—"

The blood sketch appeared in his mind's eye: ovals, set one above the other. Only in Faller's mind, his world—as it had looked after he fell off it—was superimposed over the top oval.

"Faller?"

Faller pulled the sketch from his pocket, flattened it on the kitchen counter. His heart racing, he examined the sketch with fresh eyes—the eyes of someone who has seen worlds from a distance.

"What is that?"

"It's a map," he whispered. His fingers brushed the top oval, the one with a bloody thumbprint over it. Faller had assumed the thumbprint was a care-less smudge, but now he saw it for what it was: a marker.

You are here.

And the *X* on the lowest oval.

X *marks the spot,* the part of his mind that supplied the words offered up. He had to reach that bottom world. Whatever it took, he had to get there. That was where the answers were.

He looked at Storm. "I'm not guessing. There are more worlds below this one, and I have to reach the bottom one." He tapped the map. "On Day One I found this in my pocket, along with your picture. Look at it—it's a map."

"It's not a map," Storm said, frowning. "It's a bunch of ovals—"

"*It's a map.* I know how my mind works." He held up his left thumb, the one he'd cut to draw the map. "I drew it with my own blood so I'd know how important it was that I take it seriously, that I figure it out and reach that bottom world. I left it in my pocket, beside a picture of you—of us—because I was supposed to find you on the way." Faller lifted her hand, laced his fingers into hers.

"Tell me that doesn't feel right to you," he whispered. "Tell me it doesn't feel as if our hands are grooved to fit together, because they've spent so much time like this."

Storm disengaged their hands, drew hers away.

"*Trust me.*" Outside, the shouting had grown noticeably louder.

"*I don't even know you,*" she shot back. "And even if I did, you only have one parachute."

"We can share it. Look, Storm, at the risk of being blunt, you don't have many options. If you stay here, they're going to kill you. With me, at least you have a *chance*."

She reached into his vest, drew out the photo. She seemed to be studying her own face, perhaps marveling over how happy she looked. Faller guessed that since Day One she'd never once smiled like that.

She offered him the photo; but when he grasped it, she held on. "You're sure we can both land with just one parachute?"

Faller nodded emphatically. "Yes." At least, he thought they could. He'd figure out the details later.

"And you're sure there's another world below us?"

"Yes."

She let go of the photo. "We'll need a torch."

IX

THE CHURCH came into view at the top of the hill. Peter looked away, wishing it were still a hundred miles away, or ten thousand. Izabella and Melissa's Uncle Walt and Aunt Rose were on the sidewalk out front, heading for the big front doors wearing a black suit, a black dress.

There was no way he could do this. He would feign illness, drop Melissa off and go home and get into bed. He wouldn't have to feign illness—he was nauseous, sweating, his bowels roiling at the thought of going in there and facing Ugo, and Izabella's family and friends.

Beside him, Melissa was hollow-eyed from lack of sleep, the ridges of her nostrils pink from blowing.

He should tell her. If Melissa knew, and was still willing to stand at his side through this funeral, Peter thought he could make it through. But each time he tried, the words choked him. When he'd wheeled Bella into the lab he'd felt like he was doing a noble thing. Now it felt unspeakable.

Melissa parked behind the church. The van's engine went silent; they sat staring through the windshield at the back of the church, the mourners silently filing around to the front, their heads bowed, many of the younger ones recent draftees in dress uniforms.

Finally, Melissa opened her door, and Peter had no choice but to open his and follow her toward the church. Melissa reached out, took his hand, and he started to cry. She squeezed, thinking he was crying simply because Izabella was gone. He *was* crying because she was gone, but it was so much more than that.

Ugo was standing just inside the doorway, for once hatless, accepting condolences. Melissa fell into his arms; they hugged fiercely for a long mo-ment, Ugo's eyes squeezed shut, the veins in his temples bulging. When they finally broke off, Peter stepped up to Ugo, his legs shaking so badly he was sure he'd crumple.

He held out his hand. "I'm sorry," he managed.

Ugo turned to the next mourner in line, as if he hadn't seen Peter. Peter closed his hand, turned away.

Melissa was gaping. "My God, he just ignored you. Why would Ugo do that?"

"Maybe he didn't see me. He looks like he's in a daze."

"He saw you. Could this still be about the Nobel? *Surely* he wouldn't turn his back on family over something like that. Not at a time like this."

"I don't know what it's about." As he uttered the lie, he was back beneath the lab, carrying Izabella's duplicate through the chilly darkness of the old factory with Harry. He'd hidden the body like a criminal.

He flinched as a hand touched his back. It was Harry.

"How are you holding up?"

· · · · ·

HE LINGERED in Ugo's downstairs bathroom as long as he thought he could. As he stepped out, Bill and Audrey DeNiro surrounded him.

"We're so sorry for your loss." Audrey pressed her cheek to Peter's, the odor of Noxzema wafting from her.

"Thank you."

Ugo appeared around the corner. He waited there as Bill clutched Peter's hand.

When they were gone, Peter and Ugo had the hall to themselves.

"I understand that you had no choice in coming here—"

"Nothing could have kept me from coming. I loved Izabella like a blood sister—"

Ugo raised a finger, cutting him short. He stepped in very close to Peter. "Don't ever speak her name to me again. If I had my preference, you'd never speak to me again, period. Just stay away. If we have to be in the same room together, stay on the other side. Do you understand me?"

Peter nodded. He didn't want to be around Ugo any more than Ugo wanted to be around him. If not for being tied to him through family and work, Peter would do everything in his power to never see Ugo again. Now that Izabella's funeral was behind him, all he wanted to do was work, to forget that night, to devote himself to helping people suffering from these bloody bioengineered diseases and hope in time he would feel as if he'd done enough to balance the scales.

20

As THEY drew closer to the edge, no sounds drifted down from the streets. Evidently the fighting was concentrated inland.

"So who was the woman you thought you saw in the crowd?" Storm asked as they picked their way through the subway tunnel, the torch providing a circle of black-orange light around them.

"A friend on my world. Part of my tribe. Her name was Orchid."

"Just a friend? Did you have someone special on your world?"

"I did. Someone I loved with all my heart." Faller grinned as Storm tried to mask her surprise. "Her name was Daisy. She was about four feet tall—"

"About *your* height, then?"

Faller laughed. "That's right. I adopted her as a daughter, during the purge."

"The purge?"

"When it became clear there wasn't enough food for everyone, and a band of men began throwing the weak over the edge. They killed thousands—everyone who couldn't fight back. I wanted to stop them, but how could I? Then it occurred to me: I could save one, at least. I ran up to a child at random, waving the photo of the two of us, shouting that it was a picture of me and that child."

Some of the suspicion had melted from Storm's eyes. "You're just full of surprises."

Faller hadn't meant to tell the story to win points with Storm. Daisy deserved better than to be used as a ploy for sympathy. "I did it for myself, more than anything. If I hadn't saved at least one, I knew I'd feel sick with guilt for the rest of my life."

"Those men throwing children off the edge were also doing it for themselves. They were worried about their stomachs. You were worried about your conscience."

"The thing about it was, most of those men? They were crying. Sobbing. But they just kept on—" Faller choked up. He didn't want to return to that day.

Up ahead, a sliver of light announced the next station.

"That's the one we want." Storm picked up her pace. "It must be hard, knowing Daisy is still up there, thinking you're dead."

"I just hope the tribe is taking care of her. I'm sure they are; they're good people. Especially Orchid, odd as she is."

Storm tossed the torch down the stairwell behind them as they emerged squinting into the sunlight at the edge of the world. The streets were deserted.

The sky grew immense as they approached the edge; Faller's heart thrummed at the thought of intentionally leaping off the edge of this world.

Storm stopped well short of the edge, on chewed-up blacktop. "I don't think I can do this."

Faller kept going. He peered over the edge, checking for obstructions. There were none. "I faced this choice once before. Fall into the sky, or die. It's not much of a choice, if you think about it like that." He turned to face Storm. "I don't want to die. Beyond that, I need to see what's at the bottom. I drew that map for a reason."

Storm eyed the edge like it was a poisonous snake.

"Ever since Day One, we've lived with nothing but questions," Faller said. "Wouldn't you like some answers for a change?" He held out his hand.

She studied him for a long moment, then reached out and took his hand. "Storm!"

Over Storm's shoulder, Faller saw four men pushing a hollowed-out car, a fifth man steering. The fifth man was Moonlark. The car bumped and rattled toward them over ruptured pavement.

"Storm!"

This time Storm heard Moonlark. She turned, gasped at the sight of him, alive but clearly injured.

Faller squeezed her hand. "If you go to him, you'll die with him. You said it yourself, there's nowhere to hide."

Faller's heart hammered as Moonlark grew closer and Storm wavered, uncertain.

"Wait." Moonlark was close enough now that he didn't have to shout. It was the same word the doomed man with the shovel had used.

Storm tried to unclasp her hand from Faller's. If he let go, he knew he'd lose her.

He grabbed Storm's wrist with his free hand and pulled.

Startled, Storm pulled in the opposite direction. *"No."*

Faller pulled. Storm dropped to her knees, then stretched full-out, raking at his fingers with her free hand, screaming.

"You'll *die.*" Faller's back foot found nothing but empty space. He let himself fall backward, a death grip on Storm's wrist. Storm scrabbled to grab something with her free hand, digging at chunks of pavement, clutching at weeds that pulled free.

Faller's momentum dragged them over the edge.

As they plummeted past outcroppings of stone, Moonlark appeared above them, limping, one leg bloody. He shouted something Faller couldn't hear over Storm's terrified shrieks, then raised his arm. Gunshots rang out—three, four, five, six—each dimmer, less pressing than the last until Moonlark was nothing but a blur of bloody charcoal suit on a backdrop of powder-blue sky.

Faller felt a lash across his face. His first crazy thought was that one of the bullets had hit its mark far later than seemed possible. Then he realized Storm had hit him. She seemed less angry than panicked, a drowning woman reaching wildly for a branch.

"We're okay." He tried to secure her flailing free hand, but it swung wildly, matching the panic in her eyes. She seemed lost in her terror, completely unaware of him, every muscle tensed, as if she were bracing for impact. Still clutching her hand, Faller gripped her shoulder. "Storm. Look at me. Look at me." Her gaze flicked across his face for an instant before returning to the sky underfoot. "We're okay. There's nothing to be afraid of."

X

As THE front door to the lab swung open, a jolt of adrenaline shot through Peter.

It was Andrew Stone, one of the graduate students from UVA, looking bleary-eyed, probably here to gain access to a piece of equipment that wasn't available during the day.

Peter gave him a salute. Andrew returned it.

Ugo hadn't been to work in a week—not since before Izabella's funeral—yet a jolt of terror went through Peter every time the door opened, day or night. Ugo had to return eventually; one time the door would open and it would be Ugo storming in.

"Are we really going to do this?" He hadn't noticed Harry standing in his doorway.

Peter set his bottle of Zing on the desk, pushed his wheeled chair away from the bank of computers that surrounded him on three sides. "Why not? How often do you get to see how the fabric of reality reacts when you stick a whoopee cushion under it?"

"I hadn't realized that's what we were doing."

Although they weren't talking about her, the body of Izabella's duplicate might as well be hanging in the air between them. Peter felt it whenever they were together, and he was certain Harry did too, but Harry was too good a friend to bring it up, and Peter felt too ashamed. And what was there to say, really?

The lab was deserted except for Andrew. They headed for the iris, Harry holding the tray containing the anesthetized mouse.

With Ugo gone and the organ replication program stalled until the transplant team perfected their procedure, Peter was left with nothing to do but basic research. Most of the experiments they were conducting were aimed at understanding why Izabella had died, although only he and Harry understood that that was what they were doing. They now knew one crucial fact: no complex organism could survive the procedure if it was conscious when it went into the duplicator. Peter wanted to know more. He wanted to understand the duplicator inside and out. Right now he wanted to see how it reacted if he gave reality a good, hard shove. It was a wild experiment, best conducted in the middle of the night.

"So, what's your guess?" Peter asked Harry.

"Shit, I have no idea. If I had to guess, I'd say the mouse comes out duplicated, as if the loop never happened."

Peter grinned. "Fair enough." Peter was dying to see what would happen; it was like having an intimate conversation with the universe about how it worked.

Polchinski had first devised the physics version of the classic grandfather paradox: what happens if an object is sent through a wormhole and returns a millisecond earlier, but is sent *back* through the duplicator *less* than a millisecond later, and blocks itself so it can't enter in the first place? It creates a paradox. Polchinski had used billiard balls in his thought experiment, but the paradox was no different when the objects were sleeping mice. To create the effect, they'd fashioned an additional delivery duct that fed directly back into the iris.

Peter went to the delivery duct on the left—where the original mouse would be delivered, if it came back at all. "Whenever you're ready," he called to Harry. "This is exciting."

"Here we go," Harry called back.

A shadow dropped out of the duct.

Peter lurched backward; Harry shouted in surprise. It was not a shadow cast by an object—certainly not the shadow of a mouse. It was darkness. The size of a tire, it blocked out the grey tile floor beneath without replacing it with anything but darkness so deep it created the illusion of a hole.

The sight of it sent a wash of terror through Peter that bordered on superstitious dread, as if a demon, or a god, had dropped into his lab.

"Get Andrew out of here," he said to Harry. Peter had no idea what it was, no idea if it was dangerous. It had just fallen out of a wormhole, and it absolutely should not have, so it was by definition dangerous. He turned, found Harry still staring at the thing, transfixed. *"Now. Get him out."*

As Harry jogged off, Peter circled the object.

Nothing should be able to come out of the duplicator except objects they put in. It made absolutely no sense.

The lab door opened and shut; Peter heard the lock click into place. Five seconds later, Harry was back. "What the hell is that?"

"I'm not sure."

"What if it's bathing us in radiation right now?" Harry was standing a dozen feet farther back than Peter, as if that much extra distance would matter if the thing was doing them harm.

"If it is, it's probably too late."

It was three-dimensional. When he looked directly at it, it was difficult to see, as if his visual field were resisting it, trying to close up the blank space it created. Peter could see it better when he looked a few feet to one side; then it solidified into a spherical object resting on the laboratory floor.

No, not resting. The bottom of it was no longer perfectly spherical—it was flattened. The object was slowly sinking. There was a bluish glow where it was eating into the floor. It was ionizing the matter it was in contact with.

Peter giggled. He clapped his hand over his mouth, tried to get hold of himself. He thought he might be in shock. Taking a deep breath, he tried to think.

First, they had to neutralize this thing before it ate right through the floor.

Peter turned to Harry. "We need to introduce something charged. Come on." Peter sprinted toward the Van de Graaff generator.

"Something *charged*?" Harry said. He stood as if glued to the floor. "Holy shit. You think it's a singularity."

"Yeah. I do." He grabbed Harry by the arm and tugged him. "If we charge it, we can control it. Help me."

They set the Van de Graaff generator near the black sphere.

"Find two metal plates somewhere," Peter said as the generator began to spark as it charged up. If the object wasn't a singularity, it was sure doing a fine job of reacting exactly as a singularity should. He ran to get a battery.

Peter returned with two metal covers he'd torn off air-conditioning ducts. They set the metal plates on either side of the object, attached the positive pole of the battery to one plate, the negative to the other.

The object rose into the air until it was centered between the two plates.

It was neutralized and suspended; now they needed to get it out of the lab, to somewhere secure, and figure out what they were dealing with.

In his underground explorations with Ugo, they'd often passed a huge factory room with a thick steel door. That room would do nicely.

"Grab an end," Peter said, grasping one of the plates.

"Jesus," Harry breathed as he lifted the other plate.

The object rose as if by magic.

"If this is a singularity, why isn't it heavy?" Harry asked.

Peter nodded. A singularity with the circumference of a tire should weigh more than the Earth. "Hell, don't ask me. The paradox must cause some unusual quantum effect. There's so much debate about what happens when quantum mechanics and singularities come together, the only thing that would be surprising is if the result *didn't* surprise us."

They stood gawking at the object hovering between them.

"What the hell did we do?" Peter asked.

"Hey, don't look at me. I just work here," Harry said.

Peter smiled at him. "You practicing for when the feds find out?"

They located a wheeled cart to carry the battery and Van de Graaff generator, then slowly moved it all toward the hall. The stairs were going to be a bitch.

"Once we've designed a more professional electrostatic trap, let's start with a Geiger-Müller tube, alpha spectrometer, gamma and neutron detectors, to see if we need to set up a quarantine and call in the feds. I don't want to call the feds if we don't have to; they're liable to shut us down and then sort it out."

21

Storm's panic eventually subsided. What choice did she have? Your heart can only race for so long, as Faller and everyone else had discovered in the weeks after Day One.

As she grew less panicked, she grew angrier.

"I couldn't let you die." Faller had to shout to be heard over the wind.

"You have no idea if I was going to die. Maybe Moonlark was coming to tell me they'd pushed back the invasion." The constant pressure of the wind against her face made her look strange—her cheeks stretched, skin rippling, eyes wide in a look of perpetual surprise.

"The other boroughs were pouring in from all sides. They were going to kill you. You'd be dead right now if you'd stayed."

"It doesn't matter. It wasn't your decision to make."

"But will you admit there was no conceivable way you could have survived if I'd left you there?"

"Who the hell do you think you are? You think you can make decisions for me, just because you have a picture of me? If I wanted to stay and die with Moonlark, you had no right to stop me."

"He *shot* at us."

"He shot at *you*!"

Faller took a deep breath, tried to speak as calmly as possible, although the need to shout made it difficult to sound calm. "I'm sure he was primarily shooting at me, but you were right there, so he wasn't showing much concern for you. That's all I'm saying. If you care about someone, you don't shoot at something close to them."

"You dragged me over a *cliff*. Don't lecture me about right and wrong."

Faller fell silent. She had a point. He'd acted instinctively, because he'd had no time to do otherwise. It had seemed like the right thing to do in the moment. Even now, with time to think, he thought he'd done the right thing. But he had to admit an argument could be made that what he'd done was wrong.

"I'm sorry," he said, and again, it was hard to sound sincere while shouting. Storm didn't answer.

Not sure what else to say to make things right, Faller watched the sky. He followed the progress of a dozen dark, oblong clouds in an otherwise clear sky. They looked like fish swimming in an endless blue lake. Some on his world were convinced clouds were alive, that they ate sunlight and rain was their piss, or their tears. Faller was the only person in the worlds who knew clouds were nothing but misty air, though Storm would soon be in on the secret.

"Isn't it beautiful?" he finally asked.

"What?"

"The sky. Isn't it beautiful?"

She looked at him, apparently gauging whether he was serious. Then she shook her head in disbelief. "You've got to be kidding me."

Soon after, they fell through a cloud and came out misty-damp.

22

It occurred to Faller that he'd done nothing to address the issue of one chute and two falling bodies. He needed to be prepared when a world appeared. He reached for his pack. The simplest solution was to expand the harness so they could both squeeze into it, though when the chute opened they'd be yanked together.

"Can you hold this tight?" Faller held out the folded-up chute and lines. Storm glared at him, then, careful not to let them blow out of her hands, she took them.

After he'd been working for a while, Storm said, "It wasn't the same person."

Faller looked at Storm, questioning.

"Moonlark spoke to the woman you thought you knew. She's never seen you before."

Faller grunted a laugh. Moonlark was thorough, that was for sure. Or he had been thorough. "Well, that answers that question."

"What question is that? Whether you're delusional?"

"Very funny." Faller wondered if she would ever forgive him, whether she would leave him at the first opportunity. Maybe when they found another world and landed safely she'd realize he'd saved her life.

XI

PETER'S HEART leaped when Melissa was led into the lab by three members of his security team. She looked scared. Wait until she got a look at the thing in the basement.

She ran ahead of the security people, into Peter's arms.

"I missed you," Peter said into Melissa's hair. It had been three days since he'd seen her, and four days since he'd slept.

"I was afraid you'd done something stupid and injured yourself."

Peter leaned back so he could see her eyes. "But I wrote in my e-mail, 'Everyone is safe, no one's hurt. No one's in danger.'"

"What else are you going to say?" She laughed. "'I'm wounded, and in terrible danger. More in a few days'?"

Peter put his hands on his hips. "Have I ever come across as one of those 'I didn't want to worry you' guys? If I'm wounded, even if it's just a bad cut I get slicing tomatoes in the kitchen, I want credit for my suffering. I want sympathy."

"That I can't argue with. Remember when we had to prick our fingers in bio class to do that blood typing lab? I had to do it for you, and you carried on like I'd shot you."

"I did *not*." Peter laughed. "I didn't even flinch. I wanted to impress you with my bravery."

She grimaced. "Hate to break this to you, but that ship sailed when you couldn't prick your own finger." Melissa looked around the almost empty lab. "So what *did* happen?"

Peter took her hand. "It's downstairs."

"Your hand is all shaky and sweaty." Melissa lifted their clasped hands.

"Too much Zing. Not enough food." Peter headed down the long hallway.

"What have you been eating?"

Peter shrugged. "Mostly pizza and Chinese. I don't ever want to smell sweet-and-sour pork again."

At the end of the hall he flicked on the hastily installed lights in the stairwell, led Melissa down into a long-abandoned locker room. Filthy orange rubber raincoats hung in a row along the wall like skins. Rustling came from one of the bathroom stalls lining the wall. A rat, probably.

"Where are we going?"

"I wouldn't want to spoil the surprise. But I'll say this much: it's unbelievable. The world is never going to be the same."

"This from a man who created a duplicator. Now my palms are sweating."

Down another concrete staircase, where the air was danker, cooler. Through a largish room piled neck-high with World War II–era howitzer tires, with a narrow trail through the center.

"God, this is creepy."

"We had to store it somewhere no one would ever look."

Down another stairwell. At the bottom, Peter squatted to plug in two strings of Christmas lights. The long hallway glowed a ghostly blue and red.

They reached the doorway, its heavy steel door swung open, leading onto the cavernous factory floor.

"Hey, Melissa." Harry whisked toward them. "Wish I could stay and watch your reaction, but your husband is running me like a nine-year-old in a sweatshop." Peter tried to kick Harry's behind as he passed, but missed.

The factory floor was concrete, half the size of a football field. The foot-thick door suggested that back when this was a munitions factory, the room had been utilized for sensitive projects. Deep shadows hid the corners and ceiling. In the center was the isolation tank: eight cubic feet of space surrounded by a thick layer of military-grade blastproof glass. Peter's hand-picked team—four physicists he both respected and trusted—were working around instruments set on tables they'd lugged down from the lab on the first day.

Melissa went straight to the glass, peered in, then jerked away like she'd been stung. "What is that?"

No matter how many times Peter looked at the thing, it never failed to fill him with awe, dread, excitement.

Despite having come out of the duplicator, it wasn't alive. It didn't breathe, or have bodily fluids. It wasn't composed of living cells. It wasn't composed of *anything*, in the sense of being constructed of smaller particles; it was one unit, indivisible, like some enormous quantum particle.

"I was experimenting with the duplicator." As he looked in at the thing, his voice was soft, respectful, like he was in a church. "This came out."

"Oh my God," Melissa whispered. She covered her mouth, unable to take her eyes off the pitch-black sphere. "What is it?"

"Now you see the reason for all the secrecy. If the feds get word of this they'll seize the lab."

"What is it?"

That was the question, wasn't it? "We're pretty sure it's a singularity."

Melissa gawked at him. "You mean, like a black hole?"

"Not exactly. Black holes are one form of singularity."

"You were conducting an experiment and a *black hole* dropped out of your duplicator? From where?"

"I'm not sure yet."

"Did it come from outer space? Through time?"

Peter put a hand on her shoulder. "You need to reread your Einstein. Space *is* time, more or less, even though you can only move forward in time."

Melissa folded her skinny arms, bent one knee. "I didn't read my Einstein in the first place, as you well know." She stared at the singularity. "What sort of experiment were you conducting?"

Peter shook his head. "It's better if you don't know. Safer for you. We haven't recorded a thing, in case someone hacks our computers."

"Give me some sense of what you think happened. Is it dangerous?"

"Up to now, I thought of that portal as a simple loop—a wormhole that comes right back here a fraction of an instant earlier than our subjective time."

Melissa pinched the bridge of her nose. "Right, I got that."

"But I was wrong, because if that were the case, this couldn't come out"—he pointed at the singularity—"because there couldn't be anything in the wormhole beyond what we send in."

"So what do you think now?"

"I think the duplicator is a portal backstage. To the beginning of things, and the end. To the source." Peter closed his eyes. Images, impressions swirled. "But in the end, I don't really know."

Staring in at the dark sphere, Melissa pressed a trembling hand over her mouth. "It's too much, Peter. It's like you've summoned a god."

Two of the physicists—Jill Sanders and Natalia Komolov—passed, looking both exhausted and excited. Peter nodded. Despite being fairly good friends with Jill, Melissa didn't seem to recognize her.

Peter put his arm around Melissa, coaxed her to turn away from the glass. "Here's the important part: it contains a staggering amount of energy." Peter raised his hands, fingers spread. "I mean, a breathtaking, miraculous amount of energy. We've been experimenting on it with lasers: it turns out the center is rotating. You wouldn't believe what we've been able to do." He pulled a black felt-tip pen and a notepad out of his shirt pocket, leaned the notepad against the glass and sketched a circle. "This is the singularity." He added an ellipse around the circle. "This is the transition region surrounding it." He drew a series of dots entering the transition region. "We sent a stream of nanobots into the transition region, designed to break into two parts." He drew a line of smaller dots dropping into the circle, another line continuing out of the transition region. "One part falls into the singularity, the other comes back out." He looked at Melissa, aware that he was speaking way too quickly, but unable to slow down. "The part that comes out contains more energy than the entire nanobot that went in."

Melissa nodded. "You're saying you can use it as an energy source."

Peter nodded. "It contains enough energy to power the entire world for a decade. Just this one. And we don't have to settle for just one."

Melissa looked at him. "What do you mean?"

"If we want another, we can repeat the experiment. Create another paradox."

Melissa stared in at the thing, biting her lower lip. "No more oil, or coal, or nuclear to fight over," she whispered. "They could run everything."

"We could end the war in a day."

He was in possession of an inexhaustible, carbon-neutral supply of energy. His duplicator was, as Kathleen had pointed out, an inexhaustible supply of food. Between the two, so much would change.

"Send it back," Melissa whispered.

"What?"

"I've never seen anything that scared me so badly."

"You know I can't. If I put it back in the duplicator it'll come right back out, and it might bring a friend."

"I know." Melissa couldn't take her eyes off it. "How would you use it to supply the world with energy? Are you going to run power lines from the lab door out to India? Maybe hand out free singularities to Russia and North Korea?"

Peter smiled. "Far-field wireless power transfer. It's been around for a decade. We aim beams of electromagnetic radiation at fuel cells set on platforms. Anyone, from any nation, will be free to tap the fuel cells and help themselves to as much power as they want." He raised a finger. "As long as they agree to an immediate cease-fire and come to the table to negotiate an end to the war. If any country balks, no free power. They're cut off for some predetermined amount of time."

Tentatively, as if expecting a shock, Melissa touched her finger to the glass.

"The war would become moot in any case," Peter said. "It would be like fighting over seawater, or oxygen."

"You think you can do it?"

"I know I can. But I'm going to need billions. *Quiet* billions. I'll hire engineers to design the fuel cells and platforms without telling them what they're for." He took a swig of Zing. He felt exhausted, shaky, slightly headachy, like he might be coming down with something. "Kathleen is going to help me raise money through her connections."

Melissa stepped away from the isolation chamber. "Maybe I can help her. I'm barely able to work as it is now anyway."

Peter gave her a big hug. "Thank you. Thank you for believing in me. I don't know what I'd do without you."

23

FALLER DREAMED a thousand people were charging at him with axes and shovels. He was holding a gun. He lifted it, but instead of aiming at the mob storming at him—which was now led by Moonlark, clutching a machete—he pointed the gun at his own temple, and fired . . .

He woke with a jolt, which startled Storm and woke her as well, because their wrists were lashed together.

"Sorry. I had a nightmare."

The grogginess in Storm's eyes vanished, as if she'd been slapped. Faller didn't understand her reaction, then realized she wasn't looking at him, she was looking past him.

He turned.

In the distance, a world the size of his fist hung partially obscured by clouds in an evening sky.

"Hah!" Grinning, he looked back at Storm. "I told you. Didn't I?" They were lucky she'd spotted it.

"It's too far away." She stared at the world, seemed unable to take her eyes off it. "We're going to fall past it."

Faller twisted to appraise the distance. It was indeed far away, but it was also far below. Worth a try. They'd been falling for over two days; he'd rather not have to fall that long, or longer, before chancing upon another.

"Hold on to my feet." He shifted onto his stomach to get the full force of the wind. Once Storm had a grip on his ankles, he spread his arms and legs and began to glide. Maybe it was an illusion, but it felt like their horizontal movement was remarkably swift. Maybe two bodies created more pressure on the wind.

···.

IT WAS dark by the time they made it over, and the world below was nothing but an ever-growing starless patch of black in the sky.

"This is perfect," Faller said. "No one will see us land. We can parachute into a quiet part of the city and blend in." He could barely contain his excitement at the thought of seeing another world. The darkness blanketing it added a sense of mystery, of diving headfirst into the unknown.

Soon there were no stars at all visible in the blackness underfoot. Faller fumbled with the harness, cinching the buckles so their bodies were squeezed together, face-to-face, her body pressed tight against his.

It was unsettling, to fall toward a world in darkness. It was impossible to know how close they were to the ground, but if Faller deployed the parachute too soon they might drift right past the world.

Finally, he spotted a pinprick of orange light, then another. Fires. The reflected moon and starlight began to reveal more detail: vast fields and forests separated by strips that he guessed were roads. They were more than close enough to deploy the chute.

"Get ready for a jolt. Wrap your arms around your head. Try to keep your neck from snapping too violently, and your head from colliding with mine."

Storm did as he instructed. Her elbow pressed against his ear.

"Okay, on three. One, two . . ." He glanced down one last time, saw the ground fast approaching. *"Three."*

Storm let out a clipped shriek as the parachute snaked out and opened in one fluid motion.

As he and Storm were crushed together, it was like being squeezed by a giant hand. His vision went spotty.

Then they were drifting serenely under the stars, a new world below. Faller could make out smallish buildings spread here and there, with a concentrated cluster along one edge. The dark corner of his mind that housed the words grudgingly offered up *town.*

"It's like a picture in a book." Storm's tone was somewhere between fear and wonder.

A cool breeze blew them in the general direction of the town. A cylindrical building—a *silo*—passed below. The word sent a chill of pleasure through Faller.

"I think all the pictures in books are real places," he said.

Storm looked at him like he was nuts. "Have you seen a picture of an ocean? It would take up the whole sky."

That was true. There were also pictures of mountain ranges that went on and on until they disappeared in the distance. The world wasn't made to hold things that big; only an artist's imagination could hold them.

They were dropping toward a forest, which wouldn't do at all, so Faller spread his arms and coaxed them toward a weedy field. A hard breeze pulled them on a swift horizontal.

"Don't try to land on your feet," Faller said. "Just topple over as soon as we touch ground."

Weeds snapped against their shoes, then whipped their legs. Storm squealed as they hit solid ground and fell, tumbling in a heap.

Faller undid the clasps lashing them together, then stood, brushed himself off. The night was wonderfully silent, save for the chirp of crickets. Nearby, the parachute deflated.

There was a house on the edge of the field, partially enveloped in vines with big, teardrop-shaped green leaves. He pointed to it. "Why don't we rest in there until morning?"

"We've had plenty of time to sleep. Let's look around."

Faller had assumed that, as the person with the most experience falling onto unknown worlds, he'd be calling the shots. "I'm not sure it makes much sense to stumble around in the dark."

"Well, I don't care. I'm going to look around. If you want to hide out until morning, go ahead."

Faller was tempted to take out the photograph, to remind himself that the two of them could look happy together, but it was too dark for him to see it in any case, so instead he trailed Storm along a dirt path skirting the edge of the field, past a truck rusting beneath a blanket of vines, then some big piece of machinery rusting next to the truck.

They found a wider dirt road that led through the woods, away from the house.

Every so often they passed houses, most of them small and seemingly constructed as a single piece, like they came out of a mold. None appeared occupied.

The woods opened up, giving way to fields. They passed the silo and barn Faller had spotted from above, next to a big house with a long porch wrapped around it. The scene was beautiful. Together the trio of structures created a balance, a harmony he couldn't put into words.

"Are you crying?" Storm asked.

Faller wiped the back of his hand across one cheek. It came away damp.

"Why are you crying?"

Faller shrugged. "I don't know. It's just, seeing that farm. It gives me this warm feeling, and I feel like I should know why, but I don't."

Storm studied the scene. "But you've seen pictures of farms before, haven't you?"

"It's not the same."

Storm studied the farm for a moment longer, then pushed on.

The horizon was turning pink with the dawn when the dirt road intersected a paved road. They took the paved road toward the town.

24

THE TOWN lay at the bottom of a long, sloping hill. The buildings on one side of the main street hung right over the edge, some reinforced by steel beams sunk into the side of the world. Houses were sprinkled haphazardly around the rest of the small valley.

"Maybe we should stroll down the main street of the town, as casual as can be," Faller said. "See what we can see. Avoid talking to anyone until we learn how to blend in."

Storm gave him a bemused look. "No one saw us land. Who's going to suspect we dropped here from another world?"

For Faller, the memory of a man standing over him clutching a half-brick was still fresh.

"Just humor me, okay?"

Storm shrugged, then set off down the hill.

They passed a woman sitting on a porch, doing absolutely nothing. Faller waved; she squinted, partially raised her hand and gave a tentative flip of her fingers.

A few doors down a small pug-nosed dog rushed out from between two pickup trucks. It pulled up short at the curb and began barking, its butt popping into the air with each bark. All of the dogs on Faller's world had been eaten within a hundred days; Faller guessed this world must have more food. Faller knelt on one knee and held out two fingers, but the dog was not to be won over, so they moved on.

The main drag was just ahead; it was barely two blocks long, the curbs spotted with vehicles. A half-dozen people were visible. There was a man sitting in a wooden chair set out on the sidewalk while another cut his hair. Another man was hammering something, half in, half out of a doorway. A couple were crossing the street, and two young girls were drawing something on the sidewalk with a stone.

Stores lined the street, the snugness making Faller feel comforted. He hadn't realized how peculiar open spaces made him feel. Not a bad feeling—just untethered, as if he might fall up into the sky at any moment. The stores to their left and right were empty, their display windows mostly broken and displaying nothing but dust and dead moths.

"We should be talking," Storm said. "People usually talk when they're walking together."

"Good point."

They passed a store that wasn't empty. There looked to be food inside, along with some Day One things—shoes and such. Faller was tempted to stop and take a closer look, but stuck to his plan. There would be plenty of time later.

"Did I seem at all familiar when you first saw me?" Faller asked. "Like maybe we'd met before, but you couldn't remember where?"

"No. I heard someone had brought in a lunatic who claimed he fell out of the sky. I didn't want you to get too close, in case you were dangerous."

Faller laughed. "You may get a chance to see how it feels to tell someone you fell out of the sky."

Ahead, two men stepped out of a doorway, onto the street. Faller's heart thumped slow and hard as the men turned in their direction. This was it, their first test. They were older men, one wearing a leather billed cap, both in heavy boots held together with masking tape.

The men slowed as they approached, then stopped completely. They were gawking at Faller.

"Who are you?" A walrus mustache hid the movement of the man's lips, but he didn't have a beard. His face looked strange, sporting so much bare skin.

"Excuse me?" Faller said, trying to sound light and unconcerned.

"I've never seen you before." He said it like it was a shocking thing, looked at his companion, who shook his head slowly, as if in a trance.

Faller held out a hand. "The name's Faller. I'm from—" He jerked his thumb over his shoulder. "Off in the . . . far reaches—"

The men stared at Faller like he had the head of a goat. Faller wondered why they weren't staring at Storm. Certainly she was more stareworthy than he.

The man with the big mustache finally looked at Storm. "Emily, who is this?" He squinted at Storm. "Or is it Susanna?"

"Stuart?" the other man called, looking past Faller. Faller glanced over his shoulder. A tall man with a bland face partially obscured by a scraggly blond beard was heading toward them. This wasn't going according to plan.

Both men pointed at Faller. "Look at him," the mustached man said. "I've never seen him before in my life."

Stuart stepped onto the sidewalk, his head tilted as if trying to make sense of Faller's face.

"We keep to ourselves," Faller stammered. "We're hermits."

"It's like he appeared out of thin air," the mustached man said to Stuart.

Two women were crossing the street, their curiosity evidently piqued by the growing crowd. Faller lifted his head to greet them, trying to keep up his air of "oh, isn't this a silly misunderstanding?"

When he saw the women's faces, his polite smile crumpled.

They were staring wide-eyed at Storm, approaching her as one might approach a wild dog on a lead of indeterminate length. They were wearing blue summer dresses, worn but clean, and each had a yellow bow in her hair.

They both looked exactly like Storm.

One by one the men who'd been staring at Faller noticed these two Storms, and their eyes widened further as they looked from Storm to these women and back again.

"What the *hell* is going on?" Stuart finally asked. He looked at the two women. "Emily? Susanna?" The two women nodded, their eyes not leaving Storm. Storm looked like she might collapse.

Stuart turned to Storm. "Then who are *you*? What's going on?" He sounded on the verge of panic. Two others joined the crowd; yet more hurried toward them. So much for blending in.

"Look," Faller said, then fell silent. He wasn't sure how to continue. There was no remotely feasible lie he could tell. It hadn't occurred to him that a world could be small enough that everyone knew everyone else by name. His only recourse seemed to be to tell the truth.

"I can tell you who we are and how we got here, but you're not going to believe me. *I* wouldn't believe me if I were you." Faller heard a shout in the distance. There were at least a dozen people crowded around now. Some looked as if they weren't breathing for fear they might miss a word. Faller pointed at the sky. "There are other worlds, far above here—so far above you can't even see them." He took a deep breath and pressed on. "Storm and I fell from one of them."

The silence stretched on so long that Faller felt himself turning red with embarrassment, as if he'd just been caught telling an absurd lie.

Finally, Stuart asked, "Are you trying to tell us you fell out of the sky?"

"I'm not trying to tell you anything," Faller said. "We fell out of the sky. Well—" He shrugged the pack off his back, opened the pouch and pulled out the parachute. "Not exactly *fell*. We parachuted out of the sky. Obviously if we fell we'd have been killed. We parachuted." He partly unfolded the parachute, showed it to them. "It captures air so you float down slowly."

He looked at Storm, hoping for some support, but she was gaping at her duplicates, her mouth working soundlessly.

"Mister, you're so full of shit I can smell it from here," Stuart said.

Faller could feel his face growing redder, now out of anger. He took a step toward Stuart. "If I'm lying, you explain it to me." He dropped the parachute on the sidewalk. "How else could we have gotten here? Why have you never seen us before?"

"If I knew, I wouldn't be asking you, would I?"

Faller opened his mouth to say that he'd prove it, he'd parachute off a building and show them. But none of the buildings were more than two stories tall, not enough for the parachute to open. He turned his face to the sky and sighed in frustration. "How is us falling from another world any harder to believe than what happened to *all* of us a few hundred days ago?"

"*Hey*," Stuart said, "that's enough."

"What? I'm just saying." Faller pressed his hands to the sides of his head. "If none of us knows anything about what happened before that day, assuming we even *existed*—"

"I said, that's enough out of you," Stuart snapped. People were looking at each other as if Faller had pulled out his pecker. Stuart gestured toward two young, rather large men at the back of the crowd. "Jim, Billy, help me lock these two up. We'll sort this out after we can gather the City Council."

Stuart grabbed Faller by the shoulder. Faller tried to shake his hand off. "Why would you lock us up? We haven't done anything wrong."

"You're spreading bad feelings," James said, as if that explained everything.

XII

At the far end of the driving range a figure squatted to tee up a ball. From this distance Peter couldn't make out his face, but the Panama hat told him it was Ugo. He took a deep breath and, box of chocolates under his arm, headed across the parking lot toward the driving range.

The yardage markers set on the range were still standing, but the grass was knee-high and choked with weeds. Too much energy was needed to maintain the range and adjoining miniature golf course. Plus, who but Ugo went to a driving range in the middle of a world war?

Ugo wound, whacked a ball on a low, rising trajectory, out past the two-hundred-fifty-yard marker. As he turned to pluck another ball from a bucket he noticed Peter and froze for a moment, staring, before setting another ball on the tee.

Peter had tried playing golf with Ugo once, back when they were friends, and had quickly realized it wasn't for him. Too frustrating.

He squinted against the glare coming off the blacktop, feeling yet another headache coming on, and shifted the box of chocolates to his other arm. It was a good thing it was a cool day, or they'd be melting.

Ugo was wearing a white polo shirt, his hat, and wraparound sunglasses. Peter raised a hand in greeting. Ugo only stared. He didn't look surprised to see Peter.

"I still don't get what you see in this game," Peter said.

"No, you wouldn't."

Peter stopped a dozen steps from Ugo. "I thought maybe we could talk."

Gripping the club, Ugo looked down at the ball. "Is that right?"

"Ugo, I'm sorry. I want to make things right between us, but I don't know how."

Ugo glanced at him in what seemed a warning, then he looked away, as if he found it hard to look at Peter for long.

Peter pushed on. "I loved Izabella. I never would have done anything I thought would harm her. I only wanted to help her."

Ugo stared off at the field. "What do you have there?"

Peter offered the box to Ugo.

To his surprise, Ugo took them. He examined the box. "Knipschildt truffles. These must have been hard to find."

"I just want you to know how sincerely sorry I am."

"Nothing says sincerity like Knipschildt truffles." Ugo pushed the club he was holding into his bag, pulled out his driver. Peter took an involuntary half-step backward as Ugo turned, the club clutched in his fist. He strode to the tee, the chocolates in one hand, driver in the other.

"You're so transparent. Like a little boy. You want to repair things with me because you can't explain our falling-out to Melissa, and goodness knows, you can't tell her the truth." Ugo set the box in the grass, plucked out one of the truffles and set it on a tee. "I'm not particularly interested in helping you out of that little jam."

The truffle exploded when Ugo hit it, spraying chocolate a dozen feet in front of the tee. Ugo squatted, retrieved another and teed it up.

"I'm here because you're my friend. Or were. Because we're family." He wondered if Ugo had surmised that Melissa was the one who'd told Peter where to find Ugo. "Come back to the lab. Let's get back to work. The war is too important to let a personal conflict get in the way."

"A personal conflict." Ugo swung the club viciously, as if trying to bludgeon the truffle out of existence. Chocolate filling spattered his golf shoes. He paused, turned toward Peter. "What a nice, sanitary way to phrase it."

Ugo stuck out his bottom lip, surveyed the range. "When I was a twelve-year-old boy, a prisoner in the Omarska camp during the war, I was forced to bite off a fellow inmate's pinky finger while the guards cheered. If I'd refused, the other boy would have bitten off my pinky."

Peter put his hand over his mouth. "Jesus, Ugo. I had no idea—"

Without warning Ugo swung the driver at the box, sent it spinning toward Peter, one side torn open, truffles bouncing in the grass. "I don't want your sympathy. I want you to understand. You think I'm of no conse-quence. A lightweight."

Peter opened his mouth to disagree, but could see from Ugo's eyes that he'd probably swing the driver at Peter's head if he interrupted again.

Ugo gave a quick shrug. "Ugo doesn't agree with this, but I'm going to do it anyway. I'm going to send his wife through my duplicator. Who cares what Ugo thinks?" Ugo rubbed his long nose. "'Don't be a dick,' you once said to me, in front of the janitor." He shoved the driver into the bag. "I'm not who you evidently think I am. I'm not weak. When people cross me, I take their heads off." He spat in the grass.

Peter surveyed the chocolate massacre stretching from the tee box down the gentle slope into the weeds. "This didn't go down at all like you're thinking. Izabella pleaded with me—"

Ugo stabbed a finger at him. "If you speak her name again, I'll split your skull against that wall."

Peter was tempted to tell Ugo to go ahead and try. But win or lose, a fight would only make things worse.

"Now," Ugo said, "as to the *war*. It *is* too important. Too important to waste time helping you play with your toys. And too important to be left to a frail little dove of a president who doesn't have the stomach to do what has to be done."

"What do you mean?"

Ugo turned away. "You'll find out. Now get out of my sight."

Peter stood his ground as Ugo moved to a new, cleaner tee and went back to hitting golf balls. After a minute or two he headed back across the park-ing lot.

The war was too important to be left in the hands of President Aspen? Peter had no idea what that meant. The next election wasn't for another two years. What, was Ugo planning a coup?

Peter chuckled at the thought.

25

THEY WERE led to a cell occupied by the most fearsome-looking man Faller had ever seen. He was sprawled on the floor along the bars, one knee drawn up near his bare chest, which looked like two flat stones set beside each other. He had long, jet-black hair, reddish-brown skin, and ragged, almost gaudy scars on both his shoulder and stomach. He barely glanced at Faller and Storm as they took a seat on the long bench across from him. There was a puddle in the corner of the cell; from the dusky stink Faller guessed it was urine.

"That went well," Faller said. He looked at Storm, but his attention was on the stranger, whom he could see out of the corner of his eye. The stranger was staring at the floor between them. He didn't appear threatening, necessarily, but still, it was the sort of situation Faller liked to avoid.

"Why do those women look like me?" Storm asked. "They look *exactly* like me."

"It's just like the woman on your world who looked like my friend Orchid. Maybe we all have twins."

The stranger looked at them, then at his fingernails, one of which was missing.

"We must be sisters."

"Maybe."

Faller gestured toward the stranger. Storm shrugged. It was beginning to border on absurd to be in such a small space with someone and not speak to him.

Before he realized what was happening, Storm was standing over the stranger. She cleared her throat. The man looked up. He had remarkably sharp cheekbones and bright, angry eyes.

"I thought I should introduce myself, since it seems we're going to be roommates." Storm stuck out her hand. "My name is Storm."

The stranger studied her. "I don't understand. Why did you change your name?"

"No, I'm not . . ." Storm pointed vaguely. "I'm not one of the women you know. The twins."

"You just look exactly like them?" the man asked.

"That's right."

The stranger looked at Storm for a long moment. "Do you think I'm stupid?"

"No—" Storm began.

"No, honestly, she's telling the truth," Faller said. He tried to insert himself between the man and Storm, but Storm wouldn't give ground, so he ended up beside her. "I know it sounds absurd. But, honestly, if we were going to lie to you, wouldn't we choose something more believable?"

The man studied Faller, his face unreadable.

"I mean, look at our situation." Faller swept a hand to indicate the cell. "We're in a small, locked space with a stranger who can clearly snap both of our necks without bothering to stand. Why in the world would we agitate you?"

The big man considered this.

"I'm Faller, by the way." Faller offered his hand.

After a pause, the man reached up and shook. "Snakebite." The man's hand was so big Faller felt like a child shaking a grown-up's hand.

"Snakebite. That's an interesting name," Storm said. "How'd you get it?"

Snakebite rolled up his pant leg, exposing yet another scar—this one two puckered holes set about an inch apart. "I was bit by a snake." He looked up at Faller and Storm. A smile broke across his face.

Faller and Storm burst into laughter.

Snakebite rolled down his pant leg. "I heard you say everyone has twins on other worlds. What did you mean?"

Faller decided to take it more slowly this time. He retrieved his pack, pulled out the parachute and explained it to Snakebite, who examined the chute carefully, right down to the clasps and harness. Only then did he and

Storm explain exactly what they'd used the chute for, as shock and alarm grew increasingly apparent on Snakebite's face.

"Shit," Snakebite said when they'd finished.

"You believe us," Faller said, trying not to sound surprised.

"Why wouldn't I? You're here, aren't you?"

The outer door squealed open; the twins who looked like Storm were led in by Stuart.

"Now, I'm trusting you to watch your mouth, keep the conversation civil," Stuart said, wagging a finger at Faller. Faller nodded, confused as to why he was being singled out as a potential pottymouth.

"I'm Susanna," one of the twins said to Storm as the outer door closed. She pointed to her sister. "This is Emily."

"I'm Storm." A tear welled under her eye and broke down her cheek. "Are we sisters?"

Susanna stepped closer, grasped the bars. "We must be."

Storm swallowed, nodded agreement. She moved closer to the twins, clutched the bars.

Faller wasn't convinced it was that simple, given that Orchid also seemed to have a sister on a different world, but he kept his mouth shut, because he didn't have a better explanation.

"We're going to get you out of there right now. This is ridiculous," Emily said.

"I think Stuart is due for a good kick in the nuts," Susanna added.

Faller grinned. Maybe they *were* sisters.

They struggled for what to say to each other. Emily finally asked, "*Where are you from?*"

Storm stammered, seeking an answer, finally gave up. "I'll explain when we have more time."

Susanna and Emily promised to return, with a mob to string Stuart up if necessary.

Snakebite waited until the door had closed completely, then in a low voice, asked, "So what is this other world like?"

"Worlds. There are at least two others." They described their worlds while Snakebite listened intently. Storm and Faller began to pepper in questions of their own, though Snakebite was clearly more at ease listening than speaking.

"There were pigs, cows, crops in the ground when we woke," Snakebite said when Storm asked him about Day One. "People were hungry, and there was some killing, but most people were just scared and confused. It was when things settled down that it started getting strange here."

"Strange how?" Storm prompted when it seemed Snakebite wasn't going to elaborate.

"Everyone started pretending it never happened. If you brought up those early days, people acted like they couldn't hear you. They talk about 'making others feel bad,' which means talking about the early days. Now no one ever asks out loud what telephones are for, why some of us were born young and others old."

Storm looked at Faller. "Which explains what we're doing in here." Turning back to Snakebite, she asked, "Is that why you're in here, too? For talking about the early days?"

"Me? No," Snakebite said. "I know better than to disturb their little fantasy world. I'm in here because I won't apologize for cutting off Wayne's fingers."

Faller conjured a gruesome image of Snakebite pinning some poor guy's hand to a table and slicing off his fingers one by one, but the truth was less sinister. Wayne and three of his brothers had gone to Snakebite's place because Snakebite was using more water from a community trough than the brothers were happy with. Words were exchanged, and a fight broke out. Wayne went for a scythe leaned up against the wall in Snakebite's workshop, but grabbed it by the blade. When Snakebite kicked it out of his reach, Wayne's fingers went with it. The City Council thought Snakebite should apologize. Snakebite disagreed.

· · · ·

WHEN THE door opened a second time, Stuart was holding a key. Behind him, Susanna and Emily bore expressions of profound self-satisfaction.

"The City Council is assembling." Stuart unlocked the cell, and Storm and Faller filed out.

Snakebite put his hands on his thighs and climbed to his feet. "I guess I'm ready to come out as well."

"You're ready to apologize to Wayne?"

"I guess so." Snakebite struggled to look sincere.

"Come on, then." Stuart swung the cell door wide and led them outside.

26

FALLER WAS famished, but he kept his mouth shut, afraid to violate any other neurotic unspoken rules of this world he didn't know about.

The meeting hall was a big, high-ceilinged church with stained-glass windows depicting people herding sheep, looking down at babies, kneeling before people with circles of light around their heads. *Halos*. There was nothing Faller couldn't find a word for. On Faller's world churches were mostly abandoned, the windows knocked out. The space wasn't useful for anything and, although people had a vague idea that churches were for talking to gods, nobody knew exactly what you were supposed to say, and how to confirm they were listening.

Stuart escorted Storm and Faller to the front row and told them to wait. He hurried off to join one of the clusters of people forming in the back, speaking in hushed tones and glancing at Faller and Storm.

Faller was opening his mouth to tell Storm how uncomfortable the stares were making him when Orchid walked in.

"Oh, you've got to be kidding me," Faller said.

She was cradling a baby wrapped in a white blanket, her blue jeans free of mending or patches, rolled at the cuff to accommodate her small size. Her boots were in similar fresh-from-the-box condition. She was with a tall, white-haired, smarmy-looking man wearing wire-rimmed glasses. They were speaking to Stuart, and by the way Stuart was bending at the waist Faller could tell Orchid's companion was someone important.

"What? Who are you looking at?" Storm was scanning the back of the room when suddenly she inhaled sharply. "Wait a minute, that's—"

"Orchid. Again." Faller squeezed past Storm into the aisle. "I'll be right back."

Storm grabbed his arm. "Are you sure that's a good idea?"

Faller shrugged. "What's the harm? I'm sure she won't know me. I'm curious to see how similar she is to the Orchid I know."

As he approached he watched for Orchid's reaction and, while she stared at him with wide-eyed curiosity and perhaps a tinge of fear, it didn't look as if she recognized him. She whispered something to her companion, who was still talking to Stuart. The tall man turned to look at Faller.

His eyes, mouth, even his nostrils opened wide and he shouted a primordial, lung-emptying, *"Ha,"* as he stumbled backward. Orchid caught him, otherwise he might have fallen right through the open front doors.

The room went silent. All eyes turned to the white-haired man, who was breathing heavily, trying to compose himself but still gawking at Faller like he was a giant hairy spider or something.

The reaction left Faller stunned and confused. This man recognized him. Faller crossed the silent room and held out his hand.

"I get the sense you know me, but I can't seem to place you." He said it loud enough that everyone in the room could hear.

The man looked at Faller's hand. His nose wrinkled as if there were a bad smell in the room. "What? No." He took a half-step back, still not reaching to shake Faller's hand. "Of course I don't know you. Who are you?"

"My name is Faller." He grasped the man's wrist with his left hand, drew the hand into his own, maintaining eye contact. "And you are?" The man's palm was greased with sweat.

"My name is Bruce. Vice deputy of the City Council." The mention of credentials was a transparent attempt to regain the upper hand Bruce was clearly used to holding, but Faller wasn't intimidated. Maybe it was Bruce's reaction to him, or maybe having Storm at his side gave him confidence.

"A pleasure to meet you." Faller tried to read the man's birdlike eyes. Bruce disengaged his hand and, straightening a worn but clean corduroy jacket, headed toward the dais. Orchid's double (actually, it was triple now) followed after a final glance at Faller.

When Faller returned to his row, the twins were seated beside Storm. Snakebite was in the row behind them. Faller's head was spinning, trying to assimilate the perplexing details that had just been added to his understanding of the universe. There were at least three Orchids and three Storms. Had each world somehow started out comprised of the same people? If that were the case the Snakebite on his world had died early on, because if Faller had ever laid eyes on Snakebite before, he would remember. And of course he was quite certain there had been no Storm on his world.

As he scanned the faces in the room, none besides Orchid's was familiar, and Faller was certain he'd met every person on his world at least a handful of times. For that matter, no one on Storm's world had looked familiar to him, save for Storm and the other Orchid. So a few people had duplicates, others not.

People were settling into their seats, the meeting about to start. Faller had no idea how they should navigate this. He twisted in his seat to face Snakebite.

"Any advice on how to handle this?"

Snakebite leaned in so his mouth was close to Faller's ear. Storm leaned toward Faller so she could hear the exchange.

"Lie," Snakebite said.

"Lie?"

"Come up with an explanation that doesn't make anyone *feel bad*. Give them half a chance and they'll happily shove their heads back into their asses and pretend you've always been here."

Faller nodded slowly, wondering what possible explanation he could offer other than the truth.

On the dais a black-haired man with thick eyebrows called the meeting to order by banging two small sticks together over his head. Faller closed his eyes, trying to think. He needed something.

"My name is Carl. This here is Danny . . ." He went on to name the other seven men lined up in their folding chairs, then kept right on going, naming everyone in the room, maybe a hundred people, before asking Faller and Storm their names.

"I guess what we need to know is"—Carl turned his palms up—"where have you been? Why don't we know you?"

Faller looked at Storm. All Faller had thought of was, we've been hiding from you intentionally. It wasn't much of an explanation, and when Carl asked *why* they'd been hiding he wouldn't have an answer.

Still looking at Faller, Storm said, "We don't know."

"What do you mean, you don't know?" Carl asked.

The answer had caught Faller off guard. How was *we don't know* going to get them off the hook and out of this weird gathering?

Storm sobbed, buried her face in her hands. Faller patted her back and made soothing sounds, wondering what the hell she was up to.

"One moment we were just *there*, in that field. I don't know who I am, where I came from. I can't remember anything except my name."

A buzz went through the room. Faller glanced around, unsure whether Storm's admission constituted *spreading bad feelings*. From their expressions, no one else was, either. Storm wasn't talking about Day One, she was just alluding to it enough to make everyone uncomfortable, and hopefully sympathetic.

The members of the City Council were conversing, the men in the chairs on the ends stretching toward the center to hear and be heard.

Faller glanced back at Snakebite, who raised his eyebrows and shrugged. Apparently he had no idea how it would play.

Suddenly Emily and Susanna were on the dais as well, leaning into the conversation. Faller heard Carl tell them to go sit down, but the sisters went right on talking. He couldn't catch their words in the general din of conversation, but their tone was insistent.

Bruce was also doing a lot of talking, his eyebrows pinched, his voice just as pinched. He went back and forth with Carl, the sisters, and some of the others until Carl said something sharp and clipped, and the conversation came to an abrupt halt.

Carl clicked the sticks together until the buzz in the room died down. "There are things in the world that are unknowable." He looked at Faller and Storm. "We can't hold that against you. As long as you keep your speech civil"—he looked pointedly at Faller—"we don't see any need to discuss this further."

These were strange people. Faller rose from his seat along with everyone else, watching Bruce, who was watching him.

The crowd was pressed tightly together as they headed toward the exits, but a buffer of space, an invisible circle an arm's length in diameter, surrounded Faller and the three Storms. It was unsettling to see them so close together—like there was something wrong with his vision.

"Can I talk to you for a minute?" Storm asked as they climbed down the church's front steps. She grasped his wrist, led him a few paces down the street. "Susanna and Emily invited me to stay with them for now, and I told them I would."

Faller tried to mask the sting he felt. He'd assumed they'd stick together, because of the photo, the secret they shared. "I understand you're angry at me—"

"It has nothing to do with that."

"Okay," Faller said, realizing he'd been silent for too long. "But let's talk soon."

Storm nodded. "I think that's a good idea."

She rejoined her twins and headed off toward their home, wherever that was. Faller felt utterly lost and deflated without her.

He checked the sky: it was late afternoon. The thought of wandering around until he found an abandoned house to sleep in, alone, under dusty sheets, depressed the hell out of him.

He spotted Snakebite, halfway down the street. "Snakebite?"

The big man waited while Faller caught up.

"I don't have anywhere to stay." He paused, hoping Snakebite would jump in with an invitation, but Snakebite only waited. "Can I stay with you?"

Snakebite nodded. "Come on."

They didn't speak as they walked, and Faller was grateful for the silence. He needed time to think.

He wondered about Bruce. What would cause that sort of reaction from a grown man? Faller's presence had shocked Bruce, like he'd seen a ghost.

What if Faller had once had a double on this world, and Bruce had seen him die? That would explain a lot, actually. Bruce wouldn't be able to account for his reaction without referring to the early days, so he'd be forced to deny he recognized Faller.

What if Bruce had *killed* Faller's double in the early days? That would explain the bald shock on Bruce's face. Imagine coming face-to-face with a man you killed.

"Why are you smiling?" Snakebite asked.

Faller hadn't realized he was. "I'm trying to figure out why Bruce was so startled when he saw me."

"If something like that can make you smile, you must be a happy man."

Faller laughed, shook his head. "I'm just thinking crazy thoughts."

Turning onto the main street, they passed beneath storefront canopies, late afternoon sunshine alternating with blue shade. Despite the chipping paint, the stores were beautiful in their way, each a different color, each with a distinct face.

"Bruce is an important man," Snakebite said. "He got his position because he figured out things in the early days that kept people alive."

"Like what?"

Snakebite shrugged. "How to pump water from the ground. How to keep the crops growing. What some of the medicines did."

"How did he know those things?"

"I don't know. He figured it out."

"Do you like him?" Faller asked.

Snakebite looked at him, apparently annoyed by the question. "I don't like anyone. I'd just as soon live in the woods on the other end of the world."

"Then why don't you?"

"Because I like to eat."

· · · .

SNAKEBITE LIVED above one of the stores that hung over the edge, in an apartment with small rooms and narrow hallways. He invited Faller to choose either of the spare rooms with a bed (Faller chose the one with a window overlooking the edge), then, to Faller's surprise and delight, offered him a meal.

The kitchen was on the ground floor, behind the store, and it, like the store, was filled with broken things. Snakebite explained that he earned his food fixing things—shoes, chairs, brushes, bicycles, anything people brought him.

"How did you learn to fix so many things?" Faller asked as he watched Snakebite pull a rabbit off a hook in the pantry. His heart began to thud, his mouth water with anticipation.

Snakebite seemed confused by the question. "I didn't. I study each thing as it comes and I figure it out." He set the rabbit on a cutting board. "It's just common sense."

"I think you've bought into your world's discomfort with the past more than you realize."

Snakebite seemed startled by the observation. "How's that?"

"I can't tell you how many times I saw someone on my world pick up a flute, or darning needles, and their fingers knew just what to do, even if they didn't." Faller held up a hand. "Yet *my* fingers won't play a flute."

Clutching the rabbit in one hand, a knife in the other, Snakebite considered. "You're saying I learned how to fix things before the first days?"

"That's what I'm saying. Did you wake here in this house, on Day One? With all of these tools and things?"

Snakebite made a long slice across the rabbit's back, then set the knife down, grasped the rabbit in both hands, and peeled the skin back in both directions. "No. I was in a cemetery, behind the church where the meeting was held. I was sitting with my back against a headstone."

Faller nodded. Snakebite was like him, born homeless. Faller had envied the people on his world who woke on Day One in a house, with people around them, photos nearby that suggested they'd meant something to each other before Day One.

Snakebite glanced up at him. "What do you think happened?"

"I don't know, but I think I will, by the time I reach the bottom." Faller pulled out his map, smoothed it on the table so Snakebite could see it. "I drew this for myself, with my own blood, before Day One."

· · · ·

FALLER'S BEDROOM was littered with useless Day One things, as if Snakebite had never bothered to change anything. Colorful posters covered the walls: a human skull with three men's faces peering out the eye and nose holes; a winged woman rendered in a red so bright it seared Faller's vision. Small plastic replicas of cars, airplanes, ships were displayed on a shelf. There was a stack of comic books on a bedside table.

Faller grabbed the stack, sat on the edge of the bed and thumbed through them. They were mostly cartoon animals, not his favorites. On his world he'd looked at comic books now and then. Eventually he'd caught on that the pictures weren't random like in the art gallery; they told a story if you looked at them in the right order, which was always left to right and down the page.

Toward the bottom of the stack Faller came upon one that wasn't cartoon animals, and as he pulled it from the stack he laughed with delight, because he recognized it. Once, on his own world, he'd looked through the exact same comic. The man on the cover was wearing a tight blue and yellow costume that reminded Faller of his own jumpsuit. Maybe it had been the inspiration for Faller's costume, though he didn't recall thinking about the comic while choosing his outfit. Faller paged through the comic like it was an old friend. It wasn't surprising, really, to find the exact same comic on this world. Many of the cars were the same, even some of the people, so why not the same comic books?

When he'd finished reminiscing, Faller dragged the bed under the open window. Lying on his back with his hands propping his head, he gazed out at the bright swirl of stars as a cool breeze washed over him. He wondered how many worlds were out there, seeding that endless sky.

He withdrew the map from his pocket, counted the ovals. According to his map, there were seven. Maybe there were seven, but if there were a thousand, he wouldn't have had enough paper, or blood, to draw them all, so the map might not be representative. For all he knew there were a million worlds.

Were there more worlds to the sides as well as below? Maybe more importantly, was there anyone out there who could tell him why things seemed to have started in the middle, why the worlds were peppered with the same people? Someone, somewhere must have answers. Faller stared at the X over the bottom world. He was betting the answers were down there.

XIII

THEY STARED at the TV mounted on the factory wall in disbelief. On MSNBC, soldiers were swarming up Market Street in San Francisco. Foreign soldiers—Russian, Venezuelan, maybe North Korean farther down the coast. Foreign soldiers were invading. Russian T-90 tanks were on the beach in Santa Monica, firing on U.S. positions in the city.

Peter felt a hand on his shoulder, turned to find Harry beside him, stone-faced. "I think we have to bring more people into the fold. We need to move faster."

"The power stations are going to be the holdup." They had two hundred engineers working on the nanostructured fuel cells, three entire factories in the process of being converted to produce the cells. None of those employees knew *why* they were designing what they were designing, building what they were building.

"Then we need to put more people on that end of it."

It had never occurred to Peter that the Western Alliance might lose. Peter hadn't wanted *either* side to win; he wanted it to end in a draw, the war called on account of pointlessness.

"You're right." He squeezed his temples, trying to banish the relentless headache. It was always with him. No wonder, given how little sleep he was getting. His eyelids, his fingers were twitching with exhaustion.

"I've got to get back to work." Peter turned toward the station set up in the corner, stumbled, dropped to his knees. A loud buzzing hit his ears as his vision went dark.

"*Peter?*"

"Yeah. I'm all right." Peter struggled to his hands and knees. He'd fainted. He hadn't even realized he'd lost consciousness; it had come over him like a wave.

He felt a hand grasp him under the arm. "Take it easy. Sit. Just sit."

The feet and legs of his colleagues were all around him as he sat on the floor, still woozy.

"Call an ambulance," Harry said to someone.

"No. A trip to the emergency room will eat half a day. It's just fatigue."

"Peter, you just passed out. We've got to get you looked at."

Peter took a deep breath, trying to clear his head. It was pounding, and he had chills rushing through him that felt like an electric current. "What do we have, three M.D.s on the payroll? Get one of them down here."

· · · ·

TEN MINUTES earlier, he'd silently vowed to rest for five more minutes, then get back to work. There seemed to be extra gravity holding him down, pressing him into the cot. It was an effort to lift his arm to reach for the water Dr. Otero had left for him. He had a headache in two distinct places—behind his eyes, and in the back on the left side of his head. No one could do his work for him, though. Maybe he should give in, sleep for six or seven hours.

Dr. Otero came in carrying a printout, likely the results of the blood test. She was wearing a mask. She hadn't worn a mask during the examination.

"Dr. Sandoval." She paused. She looked deadly serious.

Potential diseases ran through Peter's head: cancer, ALS—

"You've contracted the Peterson-Jantz prion." She dropped her gaze. "I'm so sorry."

It felt as if the cot had been pulled out from beneath him, and he was falling. He was sure he was about to lose consciousness again. Maybe he had lost consciousness and was imagining this whole scenario?

He'd taken every precaution, should have had a zero percent chance of contracting the disease. It could only be passed through fluid—blood, semen, saliva. There was always room for error, wasn't there?

He had a month, at most. Most of it would not be quality time. A memory of Izabella, twitching, raced through his head like a spider scrabbling down his spine.

The terror—the black, sinking terror really kicked in, doubling him over, making his vision swim and his head spin. He was going to die.

"Do you want me to inform anyone for you?" Otero asked.

"No. Don't tell anyone." He needed to finish the project before he died. Did he have enough time?

No.

"You need to be hospitalized, under quarantine."

"I'll check myself in." He looked up at Otero, beseeching. "I've been carrying it unknowingly for days. If I were going to infect anyone, it wouldn't be now that I'm aware I have it. At least now I know not to share an ice-cream cone with anyone."

Dr. Otero nodded. "I'll leave you to rest and check on you in a few hours."

"Thanks."

As Otero's footsteps faded, Peter could hear work going on in the lab. He didn't see how they'd be able to finish the project without him. They'd have to turn it over to the federal government, who would undoubtedly try to turn the singularity into a weapon.

Maybe the diagnosis was a false positive; there must be cases where they misdiagnosed—

Peter laughed out loud. Here we go: denial—the first stage in Kübler-Ross's stages of dying. Next he'd start bargaining, although with whom, he had no idea. Maybe he could bargain with Ugo. *If you'll resume your work on Peterson-Jantz, find a way to isolate the prion-binding properties without the side effect of the complete obliteration of my memory, I'll*— He'd what? Bring Izabella back?

Ugo despised him. Maybe Ugo had a right to despise him.

His thoughts kept turning back to Izabella. She'd asked him to try to imagine what it felt like to be dying. He'd done his best; now he knew his imaginings were a pale shadow of what it actually felt like. You simply couldn't imagine what it felt like until someone was standing in front of you, holding your test results.

And now that he felt the full weight of dying, Izabella's desire to be duplicated made perfect sense.

He could do it, now that he knew he had to be unconscious when he went through. He could do it, if he wanted to.

He was so close to tapping the power of the singularity, to ending the war before it consumed the planet.

What about Melissa? If he did this, would the new Peter simply pick up where the old Peter left off, when the old Peter died? Did they start again from the beginning?

Was he really considering this?

Considering, yes.

Ugo would despise Peter even more, if Peter succeeded in duplicating himself after failing with Izabella.

Would *anyone* understand? Would his duplicate be allowed to carry on, to inherit Peter's lab, his grants? Or would he be whisked off to some CIA lab for study?

He'd have to do it secretly, in the middle of the night. Just like with Izabella.

27

As soon as the sun rose, Faller wanted to find Storm, but that would seem needy and pathetic. He might well be needy and pathetic, but he didn't want to seem that way to Storm.

Instead, he took out the photo. It was badly worn around the edges, the corners rounded, but Storm's smiling face was still crystal clear . . .

Then it dawned on him. Maybe Susanna and Emily's attire—the country dresses, their hair in identical yellow bows—had thrown him, because it was so different from the black blouse and jeans the Storm in his photo was wearing. Storm must have also realized by now that she might not be the woman in the photo. Maybe that was why she'd chosen to go with her twins, rather than stick with Faller.

He didn't want to believe either Susanna or Emily was the woman in the photo. They might look like Storm, but there was something about Storm, a feeling he got when he was around her, that told him she was the one he'd once loved.

The one he still loved. He felt sure his feelings for her had come through Day One intact, even if it had stripped away everything else. How else could he explain the love he felt for this woman? He'd felt it from the moment he'd met her.

She was beautiful, yes. But so was Orchid, so were a lot of women. They didn't make his stomach feel like he was falling when he was standing on solid ground. Only Storm did.

Despite the heaviness of her absence, Faller decided it was best to give her time, to let her come find him when she was ready.

In the meantime he helped Snakebite in any small way he could, holding two broken ends of an ax together while Snakebite set screws, finishing the stitching on a shoe once Snakebite had the pattern started. The first few times Faller tried to make conversation, Snakebite only grunted, or nodded. When Faller persisted, Snakebite stopped what he was doing and glared at Faller.

"Pay attention."

From then on the only time either of them spoke was to say something necessary, like, "Hand me that hammer."

Around midday they were working on a bicycle. The chain had snapped off, and Snakebite was replacing it with one he'd taken from a bike with no wheels propped in a corner of the store.

"One day there'll be no more spare parts, and then there'll be no more bicycles," Snakebite said as he threaded the chain through while Faller slowly rotated a pedal.

"It's safer to walk anyway," Faller said. "My friend Stripe hit an open manhole riding a bike and lost his front teeth."

Snakebite nodded. "Maybe you're right."

Faller watched carefully to see how Snakebite linked the two ends of the chain together to create a loop.

"What does it feel like, to fall?" Snakebite asked, keeping his eyes on his work.

The question took Faller by surprise. "At first it's bad. It feels like your heart is going to explode, like your stomach is falling faster than the rest of you. After a while it's almost peaceful, like you're not falling at all."

Snakebite wiped sweat from his forehead with the back of his wrist. "Do you twist and turn in the wind?"

"You can stabilize yourself by moving your arms and legs." He'd forgotten how difficult it was to imagine what it was like to fall.

Snakebite gave the pedal a trial spin; the bike's back wheel clicked smoothly along. Unlocking the bike from the vise, Snakebite flipped it effortlessly to the floor and, clutching the handlebars, pushed it toward Faller. "Would you deliver this to the owner? You can walk it; it's not far."

Faller smiled. "Sure. Where do I go?"

"It belongs to Bruce's wife." He pointed toward the street. "A few blocks past the Council Hall, big yellow house on the left. You'll see it."

Snakebite held the front door open for him. As Faller looked at him and nodded thanks, Snakebite kept his face even, betraying nothing, but Snakebite had to realize the opportunity he was giving Faller with this errand.

Wheeling the bike down the main street, Faller passed a man sitting on the bumper of a red car, eating an onion right out in the open, where anyone could run by and snatch it from him. Such an odd place.

There was a silver figure of a running horse set in the center of the car's grill. Faller wondered how these people could have cars lining the street, even sit on them, yet never talk about where they came from. Maybe they got it out of their systems late at night in bed, whispering their questions to their lovers.

The doors to the shop he'd passed on the way into town were still open. He slowed, peered in. There were three people in the shop—one behind the counter, the other two looking at things on the shelves and laid out on the floor. They weren't talking to each other. On his world people talked pretty much nonstop. Maybe it was a side effect of not being allowed to talk about Day One—they didn't look back, and if you didn't look back there wasn't much reason to talk except to ask someone to pass you a hammer, or to ask why you've never seen them before in your life.

Faller passed the Council Hall as the road sloped downhill. He spotted Bruce's house, a grand affair with mown grass and not one broken window.

As he turned the nose of the bike up the driveway the front door burst open and Bruce surged out. He stopped short a few paces off the porch, retreated back inside and reappeared clutching a tire iron.

"You're not welcome here. Not ever," Bruce said as he approached.

"You've never seen me before, you don't know anything about me, but you're out of your house with a tire iron when I show up with your bicycle?" He liked this world; it was softer than his, and way softer than Storm's. Old men thought they could threaten younger ones with a metal stick. "Come on, cut the shit. How do you know me?"

Bruce's Adam's apple bobbed. "I *don't* know you, but I know your type. You'll ruin this place if someone doesn't stop you."

Faller noticed movement, saw Orchid's doppelgänger watching from an upstairs window. He decided he liked the word *doppelgänger*. As far as he remembered, it was the first time he'd ever thought it.

"My type. You nearly jumped out of your shoes because you turned and saw me and recognized . . . *my type*." He let the words drip with sarcasm.

"I got a charley horse," Bruce said. "I turned wrong. It had nothing to do with you."

Faller could see he wasn't going to get anything useful from this man. He kicked open the kickstand on the bike and turned away without a word. On Faller's world it was a dire insult to turn your back on a man holding a weapon. Faller hoped it was on this world as well.

XIV

PETER SET the head of the hazard suit down and turned away.

He resisted the urge to double-check the doors to the lab. They were locked. He knew they were. Instead, he pulled off his sweatshirt, his hands trembling from exhaustion, and his illness, dropped his pants and underpants and stepped out of them, set them in a crumpled heap on his desk next to the handgun.

Steadying himself on the desk, he took a deep, whooshing breath, trying to muster the energy to do this.

The worst part was not getting to say good-bye to Melissa, but he couldn't imagine her going along with this plan, and it was the only plan that made sense. Too many lives were at stake.

The rungs of the short steel ladder were cold on the soles of his bare feet. He felt like a prisoner climbing a gallows.

Stepping into the steel cage with the trapdoor floor he'd rigged, he stared down at the iris, so like a giant eye staring up at him. Now that he was above that hole, he wondered if he really had the nerve to inject the methohexital and fall into it. His hands were clamped to the cold steel of the cage, as if nothing could possibly budge them.

This was the only way, though. Melissa wouldn't have to lose him. Millions of lives would be saved. All of this, in exchange for a few months of pain-ridden life.

He could have asked Harry to help him do this. He'd come close, but it wasn't fair to Harry. Peter could do it himself, and he'd already asked Harry to do more than any friend should ever have to do.

Peter took a deep breath, engaged the timer for the trapdoor floor. It would open in three minutes. He slid the syringe out of the plastic tube, into his palm, and thought about Izabella. Her pale, twitching body; the terror in her eyes.

I need you to look at me, Peter. Look at my eyes. I'm so scared.

Twice, he stabbed himself only to have the needle jerk free of his flesh because of his trembling. He stabbed more firmly the third time, pushed the plunger down with the heel of his hand.

Blackness enveloped him.

· · · ·

HE'D BEEN dreaming, but the dreams already felt old and faded, like they'd happened to him as a child. He couldn't remember the dreams, but just the thought of them made his skin prickle and his balls shrivel.

Peter opened his eyes. Rusty steel rafters crisscrossed far above. He turned his head; another Peter was sitting on an identical wheeled gurney across from him, gathering his wits. Peter suddenly remembered that the plan was for him—the real Peter—to die now. For one irrational instant, he considered running.

He laughed aloud.

The other Peter looked up. "What?"

Peter stood shakily. "For a minute I thought about running away from you, to escape my own carefully thought-out plan."

The other Peter smiled. "You know what's even funnier?"

"What?"

The other Peter waited, giving Peter time to figure it out for himself, but Peter had no idea.

"What's even funnier," the other Peter finally said, smiling wanly, "is that you don't even know which Peter you are."

Peter looked at the layout of the lab, realized he was facing the wrong way. He was sitting below the wrong delivery duct. And he felt fine—no headache, no tremors.

The other Peter—the real Peter—padded across the concrete floor and climbed into the chemical vat. It came to his neck. Peter remembered climbing into that vat a week ago, remembered the cold, awful, hopeless feeling it had given him to stand in it. Only it hadn't been him. He'd only existed for three minutes.

Happy birthday.

The pistol was lying on the corner of the desk where the other Peter had left it. For the thousandth time—and the first—he wondered if a gun was the best way. But he'd gone over it, and knew that, ugly and bloody as it was, a bullet to the brain was the least painful method, given the situation.

Peter hurried, aware that every moment of the real Peter's life was hell now. Time spent in a chemical vat waiting to die wasn't time worth having.

The other Peter was hunched inside the vat, his face twitching in terror, his mouth pulled back in a tight grimace. He was squatting in the cylindrical vat, his head below the top to minimize the chance of getting blood or tissue on the floor. The inside of the vat had been coated in elastic tiles to prevent ricochet. Peter had thought of everything.

Except that he wasn't a killer.

"I don't think I can do this." The gun felt like it weighed fifty pounds.

The other Peter looked up. "Jesus, just get it over with."

"I can't. We need to figure out another way." His mind raced, seeking a way out. "We're identical twins, separated at birth—"

"Don't make me do this myself," the Peter in the vat said, his voice near hysterical. "That would be so much worse. I'm giving you my life. Just do this one thing for me. *Please.*"

His hand shaking, Peter pointed the pistol at the base of the other Peter's skull and aimed downward, into the spinal column, as they'd planned. "Jesus Christ. *Jesus Christ,* Peter, I can't shoot you in cold blood."

"I'm fucking dying anyway. Just—"

He jerked the trigger. The back of the other Peter's head exploded and he collapsed into the vat.

Peter squeezed his eyes shut and turned away. "Oh, God. Oh, God." He was making a wheezy, keening sound and couldn't stop.

He needed to pull himself together, to get this finished. Then he could fall into the cot in the back office and have a complete breakdown. He could cry into a pillow, or scream into a pillow, and mourn himself.

Peter started the flow of perchloric acid into the tank. While it filled, hissing and steaming as it burned away the real Peter's body, he got dressed.

When the tank had drained, he staggered to the cot, took both Xanax tablets he'd left on the night table, washed them down with the paper cup of water.

He was Peter now, the one and only. No one else could ever know he wasn't the original. Not even Melissa.

28

THE DAYLIGHT had just begun to fade when Emily and Susanna came into Snakebite's shop, one of them carrying a three-legged chair, the other the fourth leg. While one consulted with Snakebite, the other set the broken leg on a table, then turned to Faller. "It's me. Storm."

Even after she said her name it took Faller a moment to understand. She and Emily (or was it Susanna?) were wearing identical paisley-patterned housedresses. Clearly she'd bonded with her sisters. Faller couldn't suppress a twinge of jealousy.

"I can take care of this right now, if you want to wait," Snakebite said to the other sister, glancing at Faller and Storm as he spoke.

"Can we step into the kitchen?" Faller gestured toward the door at the back of the store. He followed Storm through.

Hands on the Formica counter, Storm examined a display of blue and red floral-patterned plates hung on the wall. "I want to thank you for bringing me here. I still resent the way you did it, but I can see now that you saved my life." When Faller didn't reply Storm looked at him, and he nodded, not sure what she wanted him to say. "I stayed up half the night talking with Emily and Susanna. I explained where I came from, and they believed me and didn't pull any of that 'bad feelings' crap. I feel at home with them, at peace in a way I never felt on my own world."

It took Faller a moment to realize what she was saying. "You want to stay?"

"Yes."

"But we can't. I have to keep going." He pressed his hand over the pocket that held the map.

Storm nodded. "I know you do."

"But I thought—" Faller stammered. He'd thought they were destined to be together, that they were soul mates. Those words would sound foolish if he said them aloud. "Don't you want to know what's down there? Don't you feel like . . ." He searched for words. "Like there's a big piece of you that's missing, that slides just out of your grasp every time you reach for it?" He pulled the paratrooper out of his pocket, then the map, the photo, and slapped them all down on the kitchen table. "The answers are *down*. Before Day One I did everything I could to point myself in that direction. And then I added a picture of *you*. Could the message be any clearer? We're supposed to go down there. Together."

Storm went to the window, leaned against the frame. "Or you're supposed to go down there with Emily. Or Susanna."

"It's you in the photo. I know it's you."

Storm closed her eyes. "All I had in my pocket on Day One was a loaded gun. No maps. No parachutes."

No picture of Faller. She left that unsaid.

"Then forget the things in my pocket. The answers are still down. You feel it, don't you?"

"Oh, I feel it."

"Don't you want to know what it is?"

"No," Storm finally said.

"How can you not—"

Storm raised her voice, spoke over him. "Because it's something horrible."

The emotion behind her words took Faller by surprise, but he couldn't argue with her.

"If I could fall *up*, away from it, I would."

Her words sparked images from his nightmares, of giant intestines and bleeding skies, and suddenly the darkening sky framed in the kitchen window seemed ominous, unknowable.

Storm reached out, touched the side of his face. Her fingers felt cool and soft on his cheek. "The only thing that really matters in life are people. If you have people you care about, you have everything you need."

"I couldn't agree more." He reached out, took her hand. "That's why I want you to come with me."

Storm didn't pull her hand back, only smiled. "I can't leave Emily and Susanna. I have family. Can you understand how much that means to me?"

"Then I'll stay here with you."

Storm laughed. "You'd hate yourself if you stayed here. And me as well." Faller opened his mouth to disagree, to tell her he'd rather be with her and never know. She gave his hand a squeeze, then let it go. "I'm going to see how the chair is coming."

The door swung shut. Faller stared out the window, at black rain clouds in the distance.

When he finally pushed open the kitchen door and paused on the other side, Storm and Emily were talking in low tones by the door, their heads together.

When Storm saw him, she said, "Snakebite fixed the chair. We're heading back."

"I'll walk with you." He swallowed, trying to loosen a lump in his throat as he took the chair from Snakebite and followed them out.

As they walked, Faller lost track of which was Storm and which Emily, and no matter how carefully he watched them, there was nothing that gave it away. One of them lifted her finger, pressed it to her upper lip; the other canted her head to one side, her arms folded. All were Storm's mannerisms.

He wondered if he should say good-bye tonight, and leave first thing in the morning. Whatever waited at the bottom could probably wait a few extra days, but staying longer would only make leaving more painful.

A deafening *bang* made Faller jump.

Storm, or Emily, jolted violently to one side and dropped to the sidewalk, blood blooming just below her ear. The other Storm shrieked as three more quick *bangs* erupted, so loud they left Faller's ears ringing.

"Don't move. Stay right where you are." It was a man's voice.

Faller spun.

"I said, *don't move.*"

Two figures came at him, dressed in black, sheer black masks covering everything but their eyes. One, his gun raised, hit Faller in the face, just under his eye. Faller staggered, would have fallen if the other hadn't grabbed him. He yanked Faller's arms back.

Four or five other figures fanned out around them as Storm shrieked. Two of the figures were restraining her.

A big man dressed in military garb strode over to Storm, or Emily, pistol raised. "Be quiet, or I'll shoot you right here."

The man turned toward Faller. "Got you." He sounded jubilant, like a child who's found a can of chocolate pudding.

"You got who?" Faller asked. "Who do you think I am? Whoever it is, you're wrong, because I'm nobody. You just killed someone to grab nobody."

The man stepped closer. He had a beefy face, a long nose. "You're a terrible actor, Peter. If the blackout virus got you, how did you know you could jump from one island to another? Instinct? You're going to show me where you hid—"

There was a click, followed closely by an ungodly *boom*. The bottom of one of the figures' faces disappeared, replaced by bloody meat and bone. Another *boom*, and another figure dropped, twisting on the ground, clutching his ruined stomach.

The remaining figures fanned out, keeping low, guns raised, leaving Faller and Storm (God, he hoped it was Storm) alone in the open. Storm dropped to the pavement, crawled to her twin. Faller followed.

Faller saw the flash of a muzzle out of the corner of his eye, coming from the broken window of the store directly beside them. One of the figures in the street went down, hit in the thigh.

"*There.*" One of the masked men pointed. His comrades sprinted to either side of the store where the gunshot had come from.

Faller squinted at the window, spotted a large shape that had to be Snakebite, hanging back in the shadows. There was shouting in the distance, people alerted by the shotgun fire, heading their way. Faller hoped they had guns.

Pistol raised, one of the men in black made a run across the front of the store.

"*Look out,*" Faller shouted. He saw Snakebite drop and roll as the gunman fired, and kept firing until he was clear of the store.

Two others turned and barged into the store, firing into the darkness.

Two more shotgun blasts. Both men went down.

Faller looked around, realized their ringleader, the man who'd called him Peter, was gone. A handful of locals were in the streets, heading their way. The shooters still standing fled down the street.

Snakebite came flying through the door, sawed-off shotgun in hand, just in time to see the three figures duck between two buildings on the edge side of the street. Snakebite scanned the street for others, then lowered the gun as three locals pulled up short, surveying the carnage.

"My God, what happened?" It was Stuart.

Labored breathing was the only sound as Snakebite stood, his arms dangling at his sides as if he didn't know what to do with them now.

Storm was kneeling in a puddle of blood, cradling Emily's head, or maybe it was the other way around. The wound was a raw pit. Faller quashed a cry of despair at the blood leaking down the side of her face.

Glaring at one of the dead assassins lying nearby, Faller crawled to the lifeless figure, reached under his chin, found the end of the mask and yanked it up.

The air emptied from Faller's lungs. They stayed empty until black specks filled his vision, until he could no longer make out the face in front of him. Still, he couldn't inhale. He thought he was going to pass out, and craved that oblivion.

Snakebite yanked the mask off another corpse. That one, just like the first, looked like Faller.

"What's going on?" a woman cried. She was part of a gathering crowd keeping its distance from the carnage.

Stuart marched right up, surveyed the corpse, then glared at Faller. "You need to go back where you came from."

"Hey, they came after *me*."

"If I ever lay eyes on you again, I swear I'll hang you from that light pole." He pointed out the light pole, then looked at Storm or Emily. "Who are you? Who is that?"

Faller braced himself, afraid to hear.

The woman sobbed, took the lifeless hand of the other and held it to her face.

"Please," Faller said. "Tell me who you are."

Head down, her hair masking her face, she answered bitterly, angrily. "I'm Emily." She kissed the white knuckles, whispered, "I'm Emily."

Faller sank to the pavement.

A white-haired woman broke from the crowd, helped Emily up. "I'll take you back to Susanna."

Arms linked, the woman led Emily away, her bare calf slipping free of the back of her dress with each step.

Why couldn't it be Emily who was killed? It was an uncharitable thought, but Faller couldn't help it. It could just as easily have been Emily. He and Storm had been pulled apart by whatever had happened to fuck up this world, and somehow, *somehow*, he'd found her again.

All Emily seemed to have suffered was a scrape on her calf. As her calf appeared again he saw it was a bad scrape—three or four ragged lines running to her ankle, plus a few scuffed red patches.

Emily paused, as if she'd forgotten something. She said something to the old woman, turned and approached Faller. She held out her hand. "I'm sorry for your loss." Her eyes were red.

"Thank you." Faller took her hand. Her fingers were badly scraped. Especially her fingertips. The skin was flayed at her fingertips, leaving red ovals. The wounds were beginning to scab over. They weren't the sort you get cleaning a rabbit or picking blackberries, more what you'd get if you were clinging to something, scratching to hang on.

Faller searched her eyes. He let his lips form the name, *Storm.*

She swallowed, nodded, squeezed his hand hard, and he understood.

Don't give me away.

He nodded back. "Good-bye."

"Good-bye," she whispered.

XV

THE SINGULARITY hung suspended inside the containment chamber, in no particular hurry to give up its secrets. Peter wished he had all the time in the world to peel away the layers of this mystery, but he didn't. He was like an archaeologist forced to use a backhoe loader to excavate a fragile site.

Harry was hard at work on the most promising angle Peter had devised to convert the energy they harvested from the singularity into something usable.

Fifty spotlights were mounted on the factory wall, connected to fuel cells of varying design. It was like a contest, to see which of the brilliant minds in the room could figure out how to light one first.

Peter's small team buzzed around the factory floor, huddled in quiet conversations in corners, pecked at handheld computers, argued in front of dry-erase boards. He wondered if any of them had confided in a spouse, a lover, a relative about what was down here. At least the feds hadn't gotten wind of it yet.

It was so strange to Peter, so foreign, to have secrets. Before Izabella's death, what secrets did he have? None of any consequence. There were those Marvel superhero action figures he'd stolen from the local Walmart over the course of a couple of years. He'd never gotten caught. His parents never asked where a dirt-poor kid like him got all those action figures.

He was surprised how his memory went in a clear, unbroken line back to his childhood. He'd anticipated a clear division between the original Peter and him—duplicate Peter—but it was as if he were the exact same person, as if it were the duplicate Peter who'd died, not the original.

A buzz rose at the far end of the floor. Peter turned to find Melissa heading toward him. Peter met her halfway.

"What is going on with Ugo? I've left three messages in the past two days. I haven't heard from him since a few days after the funeral."

Peter nodded, not sure what to say.

"It's like instead of you two pulling together after Izabella died, it pushed you apart. Evidently I'm on the outside now as well."

"I'm not sure what to say. We had an argument—a couple of arguments, really—and the rift just kept growing until we're not speaking." He was blinking rapidly, felt horrible telling his wife such an utter lie. "I'm pretty sure he's still working for the Department of Defense, out at Camp Peary. They must have him working on biological weapons. It's possible he hasn't gotten back to you because he's busy."

"Can't you try to smooth things over with him?"

Peter spread his hands. "I brought him four-hundred-dollar chocolates and he used them as golf balls. What more can I do?"

Melissa sighed. "I know. It just kills me. We're family. Izabella would be heartbroken."

Peter wondered for the hundredth time if there was some way to confess everything to Melissa. The weight of it was suffocating him. He couldn't remember the last time he'd been able to take a deep, full, easy breath.

"Are you keeping up with the news?" Melissa asked.

"The TV is on in the lab, but not down here. Why?" He was afraid to ask.

"The E.U. has fallen."

Peter dropped his head. "Shit." It wasn't unexpected, but somehow he'd thought they could hold out for a few more months. The thought of Iranian, Pakistani, Russian troops controlling England, France, Germany was terrifying.

"You really think you can stop it with this?" Melissa gestured toward the containment chamber. "I wonder if it's gone too far."

Peter shook his head. "Kathleen thinks it may not be too late. There'd be some hard negotiations about territory already conquered; the maps aren't going to be the same as before. But she's convinced the major players would be open to a cease-fire in exchange for unlimited energy, especially under the threat of being cut out of the deal if they don't comply."

"Peter!" Harry screamed.

Peter spun in the direction of the cry, found Harry near the wall, pointing up at a spotlight that had snapped on, painting a portion of the floor in stark white light.

Another popped to bright life, then another.

Within a minute, looking at the wall was like staring into the sun. If he mounted a million spotlights to the wall, Peter had no doubt the grid could light them all.

29

SNAKEBITE OPENED his pantry, set a sack beneath it and swept the entire contents into the sack.

"No, that's too generous," Faller said, waving his hands. "I can't accept all that."

Snakebite turned his fierce eyes on Faller. Even now, knowing Snakebite wasn't a threat, they unnerved him. "I'm coming with you."

"What? Why?"

Snakebite disappeared for a moment, returned clutching a wallet. He dropped it on the table. "Here's what was in *my* pocket on Day One. Take a look."

There was a laminated card with Snakebite's photo on it, some cash, a folded-up piece of yellow paper, some plastic squares his mind insisted on calling *credit cards,* and, tucked in their own compartment, three photos of children. Two girls, one boy. All had Snakebite's black hair, his reddish complexion, his fierce eyes.

"You ever see any of them on your world?" Snakebite asked.

Faller shook his head. "I would remember if I had. Unless they, you know, were gone early." Faller handed the photos back to him.

"I never knew what to make of those pictures. Now I understand. You found your woman. I want to find my children." Snakebite shrugged. "I don't belong here anyway. I've always sensed that. Will you help me make a parachute?"

"Sure." Faller was overjoyed at the thought of a traveling companion, especially one with a shotgun and deadly aim. He touched Snakebite's shoulder. "Come on, we should probably be gone by dawn."

Behind what had once been a restaurant, they found a courtyard with steel tables and chairs, sheltered by a fabric canopy that was perfect parachute material. They cut it down and headed back to Snakebite's shop. Snakebite was carrying his shotgun; both kept an eye out for movement.

"I'm trying to understand how they got here, and why they came," Faller said as they walked.

Snakebite glanced at the sky. "They must have come the same way as you. They're chasing you, for some reason."

"The one man who didn't look like me thought I was some guy named Peter."

"Maybe they have your name wrong, but I bet you're the one they're after. You can move from one world to another, and so can they. I doubt that's a coincidence. Maybe they don't like that you're moving from place to place."

"The man who called me Peter told me I should have stayed hidden, like he'd been looking for me even before I started falling. Then he said something about a blackout. And just before you fired your first shot, he was starting to say he wanted me to show him where I'd hidden something. I think it's a case of mistaken identity."

"Or maybe your real name is Peter," Snakebite said.

The thought of that made Faller's bones shiver. "How would he know that?"

"Maybe he didn't forget."

The possibility struck Faller like a brick. If it were true, that man would have all the answers.

30

HALF A dozen shops from Snakebite's store, one shop had burned and been cleared away, leaving a gap like a missing tooth, nothing but a cracked foundation hanging over the edge. Each hefting a heavy backpack, they stood in a silent row along the edge and looked out at the sky. Bystanders hung back on the sidewalk. Storm wasn't one of them. Faller was relieved; they'd said good-bye, seeing her again would only make jumping that much harder.

After they'd finished Snakebite's parachute, Faller had lain awake, his stomach in knots, wishing he could stay on this repressed little splinter of a world with Storm.

Faller turned to Snakebite. "Ready?"

Snakebite nodded.

"On three, okay?"

"Faller."

He turned toward her voice. *"Storm?"*

She was dressed in her old outfit—jeans and a white shirt, a pack strapped across her back. Susanna was with her, their eyes still wet with tears.

"Is there room for one more in your parachute?" she asked.

Faller raced over, swept her into a fierce hug. "Really? You're really going with us?"

"I convinced her she should go," Susanna said. "The more we talked, the more obvious it was that—" She paused, searching for words. "Her place was with you."

Storm broke away from Faller's embrace. "We'd better get going. Susanna said Stuart is just dying to find you still here."

Snakebite laughed gruffly. "Yeah, I'm shaking in my boots. Are we ready?"

Susanna poked Faller in the chest. "You take good care of her." She looked at Snakebite. "You, too."

They took their places on the edge of the world. This time Snakebite counted to three.

They jumped in unison.

He gave Snakebite a few minutes to get accustomed to falling, then he drifted over.

"Landing lessons," he shouted.

Snakebite nodded.

Faller set out to teach both of them everything he knew about navigating and landing. On the next world, they could fashion a parachute for Storm, then they'd be set.

XVI

THE WILLIAM and Mary campus passed on Peter's left: darkened red-brick buildings spread across a smooth green lawn. The campus was deserted, in the middle of what should have been fall semester. So many of those kids were out West now, on the front lines, or fighting in Southeast Asia, or North Africa. Or dead. So many were dead. The press couldn't provide even a partially accurate estimate of how many Americans had been killed in the war. Millions was all anyone knew at this point. *Millions.*

Pulling up their long driveway, he could see through the fence that the pool area was lit, the fountain spraying a plume of water into the sky. As the sun went down their neighbors would see this decadent display of electricity from their dark houses, as they sat reading books, or playing board games, by flashlight. He felt guilty enough that they had a generator, and enough pull to be able to acquire fuel to run it. Flaunting it wasn't a great idea.

Most people thought Peter's income paid most of their mortgage, but the truth was Melissa brought in more than he did. Peter took a salary, but he felt funny earning too much doing scientific research. Melissa's work was always in demand, especially the miniature golf courses. Disney World had one, and so did the Metropolitan Museum of Art.

Melissa stepped onto the porch as he came up the walk.

"We having a party or something?" Peter joked. He gave her a kiss. As they drew apart he noticed something in her eyes—an uneasiness.

"What is it?" Peter asked.

"Come on in and have a drink, and I'll tell you."

"I definitely don't like the sound of that." He followed her inside, through the high-ceilinged, marble-floored vestibule, down the hall and out onto the verandah that overlooked the pool, where Dalia, their cook and housekeeper, had set three places for dinner.

"I thought it was just us tonight," Peter said.

"That's what I want to talk about. After you have a drink."

Peter stopped in his tracks. "Why? Who's coming?"

The expression on Melissa's face was answer enough. "He doesn't know you're going to be here; I told him you were staying at the lab—"

Peter's heart began to drum.

Melissa swept strands of hair out of her face. "I'm sorry I lied. It was the only way I could think to get the two of you in the same room." She put her hands on her narrow hips, looked through the wide arched doorway into the hall. "He's family. Whatever's come between you two, you need to sort it out."

The doorbell rang. Peter's first thought was to slip out the back while Melissa answered it, but he couldn't do that to her. He and Ugo would just have to tolerate each other's presence for one dinner. They could discuss neutral topics. Music. Fine chocolates.

The sound of his booming baritone, the clipped Slavic accent, made Peter cringe. The voice grew louder as Melissa led him down the hall. "I should have called you weeks ago, but I've been—"

When he saw Peter, he stopped in his tracks.

"Ugo," Peter said as amiably as he could manage.

Ugo tried to pull his jacket back on as Melissa took his elbow and all but dragged him toward the table. "Ugo, *sit*." Reluctantly, Ugo allowed Melissa to shove him into a seat. She looked at Peter. "Sit. Please."

Peter took a seat at the opposite end of the table, with Melissa between them.

"You two have been friends for ten years. You really want to give that up because of an argument?" She looked from one of them to the other.

Peter shrugged. "Sometimes people just drift apart."

Muttering under his breath, Ugo reached across the table and poured himself a generous martini from a silver shaker. Peter stared off at the brass and silver fountain set in the center circle of their trilevel pool.

"Remember the time you two city boys decided to go camping in the wilderness?" Melissa asked. "It was freezing out, and it started to rain, so you headed back toward the road in the dark, and you got lost. You spent the night shivering under a tree, and in the morning it turned out you were a hundred feet from a restroom." She looked at Ugo, then Peter. "Right?"

Peter tried to smile, but the corners of his mouth just wouldn't lift. Ugo was staring at his empty dish.

"The first night we all went out together, Peter traded *shirts* with you on the way to the bar because a bird pooped on yours." She waited for some sort of reaction. "You don't throw away that sort of friendship. You just don't."

Peter mustered a weak nod.

"You can't even *look* at each other." Melissa turned to Ugo. "Peter says you're angry with him because he didn't make a public statement about you deserving to share the Nobel."

Ugo plucked a shrimp from an iced dish, popped it in his mouth. "If that's what he says it's about, who am I to argue?"

No words would come to Peter. It was excruciating, to sit here pretending this was about the Nobel, to watch Melissa try to fix something that was not fixable.

"I should have put more effort into appearing on late-night talk shows, and wheedling invitations to be guest of honor at science fiction conventions," Ugo said.

Peter sighed heavily. "You got me, Ugo. I won a Nobel Prize because I cozied up to the science fiction community."

Ugo folded his arms. "You painted this image of yourself as a lone-wolf genius who did everything by himself. You've done a lot of things behind my back, but research isn't one of them."

Peter tried to mask how badly the insult shook him by trying to look annoyed. He reached for the shaker, poured himself a drink, and spilled half of it on the tablecloth.

"What do you mean, Peter's done a lot of things behind your back?" Melissa said.

"Nothing." Ugo waved a hand in disgust.

"Peter certainly did nothing to *intentionally* get you excluded from sharing the prize. You can't think he would do that, do you?"

Ugo looked right at Peter. "No. All of Peter's mistakes are *accidents*."

Peter took a long swig of his drink, trying to mask how badly his hand was shaking. "Why don't we talk about something pleasant?" Out beyond the pool, the setting sun bathed Melissa's miniature golf course in golden light. He pointed toward it. "Melissa just finished her thirteenth hole. Stonehenge."

Melissa sprang from her seat. "Let's play it." Without waiting, she headed down the winding staircase to the pool area. Peter followed, leaving Ugo sitting alone with his drink.

Melissa handed Peter a putter and ball, then leaned two spare putters against a bench by the newly completed hole.

Peter's ball hit one of the broad, flat stones and ricocheted off to the right. As he turned he saw Ugo standing with his hands in his pockets a dozen feet behind them.

Melissa's overshot the hole by about six feet.

Peter headed toward his ball.

"Hang on." Melissa lifted one of the spare putters. "Who's going to play for Izabella?"

Peter froze.

Melissa stood holding the club, waiting for one of them to claim it. "I miss her. I know both of you do, too. Maybe you don't realize it, but I think a lot of the problem between you two has to do with her. If she were here, I don't think this falling-out would have happened."

Ugo barked a laugh, the harshness of it clearly startling Melissa.

"What's funny about that, Ugo?"

Peter retrieved the extra putter, his knees shaking badly. "I'll play for Izabella. Let's just get this over with."

As he was setting the orange ball on the mat, the putter was ripped from his hand. He looked up to find Ugo looming over him, clutching the putter.

"Don't you dare. I told you to never speak her name in front of me, and I meant it."

Melissa pushed her way between them. "What the hell is going on? Someone tell me. Right now."

Peter should have insisted they call the police, that night in his lab. He'd taken the easy way out when Ugo offered it, but in a situation like this, there was no easy anything.

Ugo glared at Peter. "Go ahead. Tell her. I'm tired of our friends thinking I'm the villain in this."

He wanted to tell Ugo to shut the hell up. He wanted to run.

"Tell me what?" Melissa looked at Peter, frowning, confused. Possibilities must be flying through her head, the worst probably being that he and her sister had had an affair. If only it were that simple.

"Better yet, why doesn't *Peter* tell her?" Ugo looked up at Peter. "Why don't you see if the real Peter can join us? Or is he too ill?"

The words hit Peter like he'd been punched. Surely Ugo couldn't know. No one knew, except his doctor.

Melissa looked from Ugo to Peter, and back again. "If you're trying to make some sort of profound existential point, Ugo, it's lost on me."

Ugo shrugged. "I'm simply asking if Peter can join us."

"He's right there," Melissa nearly shouted.

Ugo shook his head. "That's not Peter." He looked at Peter, grunted. "I assumed your wife, at least, was in on that secret. You really haven't told her any of this?"

How could Ugo possibly know? Dr. Otero wouldn't violate Peter's confidence, would she? If she did, she would have told Melissa, not Ugo.

Ugo tsked, shook his head as if he were disappointed in Peter. "Do you really think I'd miss the early symptoms of a disease that my own wife suffered from?"

Peter tried to think of when Ugo would have even seen him. The driving range? *Peter* hadn't even known he had Peterson-Jantz that day at the driving range.

Melissa studied Peter, lingered on his quavering hands. "Sweetie, are you sick?"

"He's not sick; the real Peter is sick. Very sick, by now."

"Shut up," Melissa said. "I'm asking Peter." She turned to Peter, her eyes pleading. "Tell me what's going on."

Ugo took a seat on the bench beside the thirteenth hole, leaned back, folding his hands across his belly. "Where should we start?" He cocked his eyebrows.

"What is it you think you know?" Peter asked.

"All right. Two weeks ago, you were exhibiting the early symptoms of Peterson-Jantz. Now"—he gestured toward Peter's hands with a flourish—"they've absolutely vanished. Either you've developed a cure for Peterson-Jantz—in which case I'm sure the Nobel Committee will have a prize in medicine and physiology for you in no time—or you duplicated yourself."

Melissa gaped at Ugo. "What are you *talking* about? Are you out of your mind? It's *Peter.*"

Peter considered denying it all, insisting Ugo had gone off the deep end. Ugo had no proof. Izabella's duplicate body was at the bottom of a shaft, deep under the lab. Peter's body was gone.

Melissa grasped his arms, her face suddenly close to his. "Do you know what he's talking about? Because you don't look confused, you look terrified. And that's scaring me."

Peter looked at Ugo, who raised and lowered his eyebrows. The bastard was enjoying this.

"Can we go sit?" Peter whispered, his voice shaking.

He followed Melissa back to the verandah, with Ugo trailing a dozen paces behind.

Before he began, he drained his martini glass in three big gulps.

"Right before she died, Izabella asked me to duplicate her." He couldn't catch his breath; he felt like he'd just been sprinting. "At first I said no—"

"*We* said no," Ugo interrupted. "She asked us together, and we told her no."

"Do you want to tell her?" Peter hissed.

Ugo shrugged. "If you want. But you're doing fine. Why don't you go on?"

Peter wanted to hurl a plate at his bald head. "Later, when I was visiting her alone, Izabella begged me to help her. I kept telling her it was too dangerous. She didn't feel she had anything to lose at that point. So I agreed to help her." He looked at the slatted floor, his voice dropping to a near whisper. "And she died."

Peter knew she'd be shocked, but he wasn't prepared for the utter devastation on Melissa's face. When she'd recovered a little, she turned to Ugo. "You need to go home."

Ugo shrugged, rose from the table. "I understand. It was a shock to me, too, when Peter called me in the middle of the night to tell me my wife was lying dead in his lab."

"Please. Go," Melissa said, her voice barely controlled. She was crying, her face down, hidden by the veil of her hair.

As Ugo turned, Peter saw the hint of a smirk beneath his somber scowl. He was thrilled by Melissa's reaction; it was exactly what he'd hoped for.

"You're such a bastard."

"Why don't you buy her some chocolates? That ought to fix things." Ugo paused, as if considering. "Better yet, give her a bottle of Zing energy drink." Ugo stood very still, staring pointedly at Peter as if those words, *Zing energy drink,* were profoundly significant.

Peter watched him wind down the staircase.

Her breathing ragged, head still bowed, Melissa waited for Ugo to be gone.

Why had Ugo waited so long? If he was going to reveal the truth about Izabella, why wait?

The only thing that had changed was Peter had contracted Peterson-Jantz. Ugo hadn't been around to see him popping Motrin like mad, drinking Zing because the caffeine helped the headaches. How could he possibly know?

Why don't you give her a bottle of Zing energy drink?

In his mind's eye Peter saw Ugo jamming a syringe down through the neck of a plastic Zing bottle. So the bottle wouldn't leak, so Peter wouldn't notice the tiny hole when he pulled the bottle from his refrigerator . . .

He inhaled sharply, held his breath. Who had easier access to the Peterson-Jantz prion than Ugo? He leaned over the rail, shouted, "*You* did this to me."

Ugo stopped, halfway down the staircase, looked up at Peter, and smiled. "I have no idea what you're talking about."

Peter grabbed a steak knife from the table and launched himself down the staircase after Ugo.

"*Peter.*"

Peter could hear Melissa chasing him down the iron stairs. That's why Ugo hadn't called the police that night in the lab. If Peter was in prison, Ugo couldn't get to him.

"You murdered me," Peter shouted. "I was only trying to *help* her, and you murdered me for it."

"*Peter!*"

Ugo was only a few steps below, waiting, when he saw Peter had a knife. He took off down the remaining steps with Peter right behind, and Melissa screaming at Peter to stop.

When Ugo reached the patio the big man sprinted for the gate. Rage fueling his steps, Peter chased, but when he had his chance, when Ugo had to slow to open the gate, Peter couldn't bring himself to use the knife. Instead he slashed at the air a few inches from Ugo's shoulder.

Melissa grabbed him from behind and yanked him around. "What are you *doing*? What's the matter with you?"

"Didn't you hear what he said? He infected me with Peterson-Jantz."

Behind Melissa, the fountain pattered like a heavy downpour. She pressed her hands to her face, dragged them, tugging her skin, exposing the bloodred rings under her eyes.

"Why didn't you tell me?"

Ugo's Porsche roared to life, backed down the driveway.

Was she talking about Izabella, or Peter's duplication? Had she even caught on yet, that he was not the original Peter? She must have. Everything was spinning out of control.

Melissa was waiting for an answer.

"I was ashamed, and afraid. Ugo offered me an out, because he didn't want anyone to know how Izabella died. At least that's what he said."

"Did a duplicate of Izabella come out?"

"Yes. She was dead as well." He knew what question was coming next, and he dreaded it.

"What happened to her body?"

Peter put his hands on his head, turned away from Melissa. "I hid it. In the factory." He saw no point in bringing Harry into this.

"You dumped my sister's body in a factory?" Melissa sounded horrified. Disgusted. Just as Peter had imagined, every time he thought of telling her.

He turned to face her. "It wasn't her body. It had never been alive."

"So you hid it." Her eyes were brimming with tears; she reached up, brushed a strand of hair aside with badly trembling fingers.

"Yes."

Melissa waited. When Peter didn't say anything more, she said, "Go on."

"I started getting sick. Headaches, trembling. Susanna Otero diagnosed me with Peterson-Jantz. I thought I caught it from Izabella. Now I know the truth." He glanced toward the driveway, although Ugo was long gone. "I needed to finish the singularity project; too many lives are at stake for me not to. So I duplicated myself."

It seemed to take time for the words to register. When they did, Melissa broke down. She sank to the pavement, clutching her stomach. When Peter sank to one knee, tried to console her, she shoved him away.

"You're not Peter? Is that what you're telling me?"

"Of *course* I'm Peter. I remember the first time I set eyes on you, coming out of your trailer on the way to the bus stop in fifth grade. The first time we kissed, outside Regal Cinema, after we saw that Tom Cruise movie—"

"You're the duplicate, though—that's what you're saying."

Reluctantly, Peter nodded.

Melissa stood. "Where is Peter?"

"*I'm* Peter." He poked viciously at his chest as he stood to face her. "The only way I could save my life was to create a second me. It was the only way. I knew if I involved you, you'd try to stop me—"

"Where is *my* Peter?"

"It was the only way. I duplicated myself, and then I killed myself—my dying self—"

Melissa cried out, clapped her hand over her mouth.

"—so there'd be no question that I was me."

He reached out with both hands, held her shoulders. She shook him off as if she'd been touched by snakes. "Don't touch me. I'm not married to you. I'm a widow." Her eyes opened wide for an instant, then she laughed harshly. "You're not even the Peter who killed my sister and hid the body. You didn't even *exist* when that happened."

"Technically that's true. But you're wrong. I did do it. I still have night-mares about it."

She looked just as she had at Izabella's funeral—shell-shocked. Gut-punched. "I fell in love with Peter because he was so sweet, so honest." She wiped her nose with the back of her hand. "Now I'm standing in my back-yard, hearing about bodies stuffed in basements." She held her stomach. "God, my stomach hurts. Is this a nightmare? Please let this be a nightmare."

For a second time, Peter reached out, grasped her shoulder, trying to steady her. Again, Melissa pushed him away. "*Leave*. Leave or I'll call the police and tell them what you've done."

"Melissa, it's *me*. It's still me. I didn't mean to do anything wrong. Please, can we figure this out together?"

Melissa held up a hand in warning, fresh tears wetting her face. "Go."

He went through the gate, to his car, and sat in the driveway, shaking. He'd done everything wrong, made the wrong choice at every turn. The thought of spending even one night away from Melissa right now was intolerable. With everything that was happening, all the stress and fear, Melissa was what kept him sane.

The only place he could think to go was Harry's apartment.

31

FALLER WATCHED Storm, her white shirt flickering in the wind. He wanted to believe she was the woman in the picture, but as she'd said, it was silly to pretend there was no chance it was poor Emily or Susanna. And who knew? There could be more Storms.

As the hours passed his concern drifted outside of him, until it became something he could put on or take off at will, or turn over in his hands and examine.

None of them spoke much. It was like being back in Snakebite's repair shop, only instead of "Pass me that hammer," it was "Do you want some berries?" Faller was glad. Talking broke the spell, dragged him back from that blissful place where he was standing motionless, his thoughts slowing to a stop.

He enjoyed watching Storm fall, her hair in a ponytail, snapping in the ceaseless wind. He wondered if she was still angry at him for pulling her off her world.

It struck him that he'd never really said he was sorry for making that decision for her. He'd explained himself, defended himself, but never apologized, and in all fairness it should have been her decision to make, even if staying meant dying.

Faller drifted closer to Storm.

"I'm so sorry," he shouted. "I don't know why I tried to defend what I did. All I can say is—" The temptation to add that he'd only done it because he cared about her was strong, but that would just be more excuse-making. "All I can say is, I'm sorry."

Storm's expression told him he'd just gone a ways toward redeeming himself in her eyes.

"I'm sorry, too."

Faller frowned. "What did you do?"

She reached out with one hand. Faller took it, and they drew together until their faces were close enough that they didn't quite have to shout. "I let you think I was dead."

Faller shook his head. "Only for a moment."

"That was only because you figured it out. I was going to tell you it was me, as soon as I could get you alone."

Faller nodded. "And I swear to you, what I did wasn't calculated. I did it without thinking. I'm impulsive sometimes. It gets me into trouble."

"Like falling off your world? That kind of trouble?"

"Like that, yes."

They fell past an enormous cloud, taller than it was wide and drenched in pink and peach from the setting sun.

"Do you miss Moonlark?" Faller asked.

Storm smiled wanly. "I do. He wasn't my idea of the perfect man, but he'd been a part of my life almost from the beginning. It's strange, to think I'll never see him again."

Chances were, no one would ever see him again, but Faller kept that thought to himself.

32

THEY FELL side by side, but didn't speak much. He was happy just to fall with Storm, to let the wind air out his head, to sweep away the sight of Emily lying dead in Storm's arms, and all the corpses that looked like him.

Faller hadn't realized he'd fallen asleep until Storm's voice woke him.

He moved closer to her. "I didn't hear you."

"I keep wondering about the photo, about Emily and Susanna."

"Forget about the photo."

"I can't."

"You're the woman in the picture. I know it."

"But you *don't*."

And they never would. That doubt would always hang over them.

"I don't care what we meant to each other in the past. I care about now." He pulled himself closer, and kissed her. The kiss missed because of the turbulence, catching part of her lip and a nostril.

Storm's expression was unreadable. "Remember how that impulsiveness always gets you in trouble?" Storm grabbed his nose between her thumb and forefinger and twisted until he yelped in pain. Then she let go of his hand and drifted away.

XVII

THE BEEPING of the moving van backing into the driveway pulled Peter out of the imaginary conversation he was having with Melissa. He rose from the bench by the thirteenth hole, went around front.

Melissa was just stepping out of her van wearing sunglasses, her hair pulled back tightly. When she saw him, she looked away. "You promised you'd stay away until I was finished."

"I know. I'm sorry. I realized it might be the last time I ever see you." The rims of his eyes were burning, from crying earlier.

"I don't even know what to call you," Melissa said.

Peter looked toward the heavens. "I'm Peter. It's me, it's just me."

One of the movers joined them. "Miss Deveraux, if you'll walk through the house with me, show me what goes."

"Sure."

Peter watched her go. She was wearing black pants, a black silk scarf, as if she were in mourning.

He had a terrible thought: what if she held a funeral for him? Surely she wouldn't do that. He was just caught in a spiral of terrible thoughts.

He went back to the bench, watched for glimpses of Melissa as the moving men carried furniture out of their house. He tried to watch the clouds, a low ceiling of cumulus and stratocumulus, the tufts tinged in plum purple, but it didn't calm him. Every box, every piece of furniture the moving men carried out burned in the pit of his stomach, but he couldn't stop watching.

The French doors opened and Melissa came out. As she walked toward him he felt a fresh surge of irrational hope that she was coming to forgive him.

The look on her face dashed those hopes.

"Do you really believe we're not married, or are you planning to file for divorce? Last time I checked, I was still legally Peter Sandoval."

Melissa pulled her hair back with both hands, lifted her face to the sky. "I don't even want to think about that now. I want to go home to New York and spend time with friends, but I can't even do that."

No, that was for sure. Parts of New York were under enemy control. Parts of the city were rubble.

"Where are you going to go?"

"I'm staying with Kathleen in D.C." From the way she was standing, arms folded, shifting from foot to foot, Peter knew she wouldn't be here much longer. If he was going to give the little speech he'd been rehearsing night after night while he wasn't sleeping, now was the time. Not that it would do any good.

"Whatever you think of me, of the things I did, I want you to know: I meant well. I only meant to help Izabella. It was the only thing in my heart when I said yes to her." He took a breath, expecting her to argue, to tell him to shut up, but she only went on staring into the pool. "When Ugo tried to kill me, all I could think was: I can stop this damned war. If I had more time, I could keep millions of people from dying.

"You said you married me because I was kind. I still am. I'm a good person. I could have used the singularity to become the richest person on Earth; instead I'm risking my life to give it away. Don't you dare try to paint me as some sort of psychopath."

Still staring into the water, Melissa unfolded her arms. "Okay."

As she started back toward the house, two women wearing black suits and dark sunglasses passed through the gate, heading toward Peter. Melissa paused.

When they reached Peter, one of the women held up a badge: FBI. "Mr. Sandoval, my name is Special Agent Shannon Mitzner, and this is Special Agent Patricia Cortez. We'd like you to come with us."

"Why?" Peter said.

"We're investigating two suspected murders: Peter Sandoval and Izabella Deveraux-Woolcoff."

Ugo.

"*I'm* Peter Sandoval."

Agent Mitzner nodded. "It's a complicated matter. Please come with us and we can discuss it."

"Why would federal agents be investigating murders?" Peter asked.

"There are national security implications to the murder of Peter Sandoval."

"Do I have a choice? Am I under arrest?"

"Yes, I'm afraid you are," Agent Mitzner said.

Peter looked to Melissa, for help, for compassion—he didn't know what he wanted from her. She turned and headed for the driveway, sobbing.

33

AFTER TWO days of falling, Faller was just beginning to worry when he spotted another world. Their stores were just about depleted, partly because they'd only counted on there being two of them. He and Storm moved over to join Snakebite.

Snakebite stared right through him, at something a thousand miles away. Faller tapped his shoulder. Slowly, Snakebite's eyes regained focus.

Faller pointed at the world. Snakebite nodded.

Moving quickly, he and Storm strapped themselves into the harness together, and deployed their single chute.

It was small, a U-shaped sliver, nothing but wreckage and rubble. Melted vehicles, piles of bricks and concrete, twisted steel beams. It reminded Faller of the bombed-out part of his own world.

Faller and Storm came down hard in a pile of bricks; the falling chute drifted past them and crumpled. Faller watched as Snakebite kept drifting . . .

"Shit." Faller shrugged out of the harness and ran after Snakebite, who was heading toward the edge. *"Look out,"* he cried, as if he couldn't see he was in trouble.

Snakebite reached out and hooked his arm around a steel beam, part of the blackened skeleton of a high-rise, thirty feet above the ground. The velocity almost tore away his grip, but Snakebite clung tight, the muscles in his arm tensing as the parachute collapsed, fluttering and dropping limply.

Faller and Storm waited at the bottom as Snakebite shimmied down.

"Can you tell me what I did wrong, so I'll know not to do it again?" Snakebite asked as he examined abrasions on his arms.

Faller thought about it. "Aim for the middle."

Snakebite grunted.

They found a handful of bodies, all but one wrapped in blankets and set in a neat row in the lobby of a mostly intact hotel. The last body was propped against a concrete traffic divider, right by the edge. They were little more than skeletons in clothes. There were buckets, plastic tarps, bathtubs set out all around the hotel, and no obvious source of water, so not much mystery about how they died. They found a few empty cans, one a can of peaches that reminded Faller of Daisy.

"I guess it's safe to assume this isn't the world we're looking for," Storm said.

"Why don't we head toward the edge?" Faller was eager to find the X on his map; they could sleep in shifts while they fell.

Faller caught his ankle on the steel post of a bent-over sign still fixed in the broken concrete. As he pulled his foot free, he noticed the image on the sign: it was a tower, twice as tall as those around it, its surface formed so it looked as if it had been twisted. It was wider at the bottom, tapered at the top, crowned with a long metal pole resembling a spear. There was an arrow on the sign, pointing to the left. When the sign was standing upright it would be pointing right off the edge.

Faller bent, gripped the sign in both hands, then brushed dirt caked over the top of the tower. He knew that building like he knew his own face.

"How did I miss it before?" he said aloud.

Storm bent beside him, looked at the sign. "What is it?"

"It's the Tower—the skyscraper I jumped from. This sign is pointing to a building on my world."

"How could—" she began, then gasped as realization dawned.

He could picture exactly where this little sliver of world would fit up against his, over a divot that jutted out over the edge, in the bombed-out section of his world.

"Someone or something tore the world apart. It caused all this suffering. The hunger. The purges. I want to know who or what did this." Faller pulled out his map, unfolded it. "That's what the X is for—to show us where to find the answer."

XVIII

PETER WENT to his filing cabinet, rummaged around until he found the bottle of tequila they'd presented to him at the surprise birthday party the lab had thrown for him last year. He was tempted to drink straight from the bottle, but there were still dozens of people moving around the lab at two A.M., so he opted for a mug commemorating the Eighty-seventh International Conference on Theoretical Physics. That had been a good conference. He took a swig of the tequila, felt it burn as it trailed down his esophagus.

The bail hearing still haunted his exhausted brain. They'd declared Peter Sandoval dead. The prosecutor had referred to Peter in the past tense.

He took another swig of tequila. He hadn't eaten in three days, had barely been able to get water past the fist of anguish lodged in his throat.

He wondered what Melissa was doing. It still didn't seem real that he couldn't pick up the phone and call her, tell her what a crappy day he was having, tell her how much he loved her.

She was never coming back. The alcohol provided a distance and clarity that allowed him to see that. Melissa was never coming back. They weren't even legally married. She was a widow.

The door to the lab whooshed open. Peter half stood to see who it was as Kathleen breezed in. His first thought was she was here with a message from Melissa, but why would Melissa send Kathleen on a three-hour drive from D.C. rather than call Peter herself, or send a text? He raised his hand and waved to Kathleen.

She stopped in his doorway, took in the tequila, then, laughing, raised what was in her hand: a bottle of Jack Daniel's. "Great minds think alike."

Peter motioned toward an empty chair. "What are you doing in Williamsburg?"

"I came to see you." She half-filled a plastic cup with whiskey.

"How did you know I'd be in the lab at two A.M.?"

Kathleen chuckled. "A lucky guess? I would have tried your house next."

Peter laughed, though there was no amusement in the laugh, and it didn't feel good the way laughing used to feel.

Sipping his drink, Peter looked out at the duplicator, so full of promise to change the world for the better, yet the cause of all his problems.

"She's never coming back, is she?"

It was a complete non sequitur, but Kathleen didn't blink. "She doesn't talk about it, so I don't know what she's thinking, but no, I don't think she is."

Peter went to the window, stared out into the darkness. "She's why I'm still here at two A.M. On those nights when I'm too tired to work, I sleep here, because I don't want to go home. I should sell that house, but every time I think of doing it I convince myself she'll be back, and the house will go back to being a good place."

Booze dribbled into his mug; Peter turned to find Kathleen refilling it. "Thanks."

She lifted the bottle in *salud*, sat again. It took her a moment to find a satisfactory place to set the bottle down on the floor. Evidently some spots were better than others, or at least that was what Kathleen's OCD told her.

"She does the best Mick Jagger impersonation you've ever seen. She pulls over on highways to carry *toads* out of harm's way. She wears Green Lantern pajamas. I really fucked things up."

Kathleen sighed, crossed her legs. "If you want my opinion, you get sixty percent of the blame for the breakup, mostly because you're the dumbest genius on the planet for thinking Ugo would keep quiet. Melissa gets forty percent for holding you to an impossible standard. She wants to be married to Galahad, Gandhi, and Prince Charming all rolled into one." She shook her head. "You know what's ironic?"

Peter took a deep, huffing breath. "No."

"You're about as close as it gets, and she can't even see that."

"Yeah." He closed his eyes, because her words, despite their good intention, hurt. Once upon a time he'd thought that highly of himself; now it sounded like the sort of lie you tell a depressed friend to cheer him up. "You said you came all this way to see me?"

"Believe it or not, I'm here to deliver an offer from the president."

Peter raised his eyebrows. "Wow, you've come up in the world. Last I heard you were sharing an office, drafting PR releases."

Kathleen waved the compliment away. "She asked me to do it because I know you personally."

He leaned forward, laced his fingers over his knee. "So, do tell. What does President Aspen want?" Peter had little doubt about the nature of the offer. They had him over a barrel.

"Turn the duplicator over to the U.S. Government. Teach our people everything you know about it. In exchange, you get a full pardon."

"Just the duplicator. Not the singularity?"

Kathleen tsked. "Peter, she doesn't know about the singularity. I don't betray my friends."

"I was guessing one of the four physicists working with me would have cracked by now."

"If she knew about it, she'd have already taken this facility. By force, if necessary."

Peter frowned. "What does she want the duplicator for, if not to create a singularity?"

"I don't need to tell you that we're taking heavy, heavy losses out West and in Europe. She wants to make more soldiers."

Peter jolted. Some of the tequila in his glass splashed on his fingers. "She wants to—" Peter pictured the same soldier—obviously one with high intelligence and superior battlefield skills—being spit from a duplicator over and over, day and night. They'd feed duplicates of him back in like a conga line.

"This isn't only about the war for her," Kathleen said. "Aspen is seriously worried about a coup. I'm sure you've seen General Elba trashing Aspen in the media. She's testing the waters, seeing how people would react."

That frail dove doesn't have the stomach to do what needs to be done, Ugo had said at the driving range.

"Ugo's involved in this, isn't he?"

"Big-time," Kathleen said. "He seems to be getting more powerful in that camp by the day."

Peter wondered if he should take the deal, sick as the image of a million twin soldiers made him. Did he have a choice? They'd probably take the duplicator by force if he didn't agree. The president was playing relatively nice for now, because it wasn't just about the duplicator itself. His expertise was valuable as well.

Even if he did have a choice, it was probably unpatriotic, even treasonous, to withhold this advantage from his country, because they were going to lose without the singularity. China and India were mauling Russia, bombing Moscow and Saint Petersburg mercilessly—but if he had to bet his life on the outcome, he wouldn't bet the home team. If he were forced to hand the singularity over to one country it would be the U.S. and its allies, but he was convinced the best route was to release it to everyone at once.

"I'm guessing you think I should take the deal?"

Kathleen propped her foot on his chair. "Oh, no. Definitely not." She burst out laughing at Peter's dumbfounded reaction. "They're afraid of you, Peter." She raised her nonexistent eyebrows. "You do realize that, don't you? You've cracked reality open like an egg; no one knows what you're capable of. That's why they're leaning on you, trying to pressure you, instead of simply coming in and taking what they want. They don't know about the singularity, but I doubt it would surprise them."

It seemed impossible that they were having this conversation. Peter wouldn't kill innocent people, not for any reason. That his own government would murder him seemed almost as inconceivable.

Kathleen leaned forward, narrowed her eyes. "Do you think you could turn D.C. into a crater, if you wanted to?"

Peter shrugged. "Maybe. I never would. Plus I'm focused on tapping the singularity as an energy source, not developing it as a weapon."

"I know. That's why I'm telling you all this. If she knew about the singularity, Aspen would immediately develop it into a weapon. I like your plan better."

She whispered, "Better, better," under her breath.

"It's interesting." Peter took another swig. "You're ruthless, but your ruthlessness is driven by good intentions. It's an oxymoronic combination, but you pull it off admirably."

Kathleen gave him a wry smile. "I'll take that as a compliment."

He'd just called Kathleen ruthless. It was probably a sign he should stop drinking. He lifted his mug, took another swig.

"I'd seriously recommend you hire a private security force to protect this facility. I can hook you up with people you can trust."

Peter did not miss the warning in her tone. "I'm not sure I can afford it. I need cash; I'm burning through what Constantinides and his billionaire friends have given me. The war's making it hard for them to stay liquid."

"I'm working on finding you more. With Melissa's help."

"Melissa?"

Kathleen nodded.

"I wish you were working for me. I could use help navigating the political side of things."

Kathleen stood, spread her arms for a hug. "When the time is right, I'll come. For now I'm more valuable to you in Washington."

Feeling somewhat wobbly, Peter stood and wrapped his arms around her. "Thank you. So much."

She kissed him, full on the mouth but briefly, then stepped away and capped her bottle of Jack. "I'll be in touch. Be careful. Be paranoid."

34

IT WAS night when Faller spotted the next world, blotting out a patch of stars beneath their feet. He couldn't make out much of this world in the darkness, but as they dropped, the shadows of medium-tall buildings loomed to his left. Off to his right were bizarre things he wasn't sure he recognized, yet they tugged at him, called to him in a peculiar way. Naked loops snaked through the sky; skeletal steel towers, like big ladders, rose; a giant wheel—

Ferris wheel, his mind whispered. Yes, that was it. Faller could remember that a Ferris wheel turned, and that people sat in it, but not why. Looking at it gave him an all-too-familiar falling sensation in the pit of his stomach.

They dropped onto a wide, flat, chewed-up four-lane road, with no buildings in sight, the tandem landing with Storm once again jarring. Along with food and water, Faller needed to find materials to make Storm her own chute.

Once their chutes were stashed away in their packs, they came together in the middle of the highway.

"Which way?" Faller asked, looking around.

Storm pointed. "I want to see the amusement park."

Amusement park—that's what it was called. "Do you know what it does?"

Storm looked at him like he was the dimmest sop she'd ever seen. She set her palm on his forehead and gave a gentle shove before setting off toward the amusement park. "I'm guessing it amuses."

For a moment he just watched her go, then he caught up to Snakebite.

They were approaching an enormous overhead road sign, with nothing on it but words. Faller stared at the words, squinting. "They're as familiar as my own hand. I know they form words, but no matter how much I struggle, I can't make them speak."

Snakebite considered the sign.

"So many of the words I know don't mean anything," Faller said.

"Italy," Snakebite said.

"Exactly. Boot? It's a kind of boot, I think."

Snakebite shook his head. "It's a white building with marble poles in front."

That seemed right as well. Maybe it was one of those words that meant more than one thing. Like orange. "I used to think a lot of the words I knew were imaginary, like the talking animals in comic books. But the more I see, the more I believe they're all real."

Snakebite pointed at the behemoth structures rising above the trees ahead. "Ferris wheel. Roller coaster. I've never seen one before, but there they are."

A flash of insight came to Faller. "You ride them."

Snakebite thought about it, then nodded. "That's right. You ride them. For amusement."

They passed another sign, this one big and colorful, set among dead bamboo trees. Farther on was the biggest expanse of pavement Faller had ever seen, then a high fence and sheltered gates. The gates were open.

The sun was rising as they passed into the amusement park. There was no one in sight. Straight ahead, the roller coaster sat behind a low fence. It was an enormous beast, a mad set of twisting, looping train tracks. Seeing it up close, it was obvious to Faller that you rode it, although it clearly didn't go anywhere.

They passed a fenced-in field littered with bones and rotting pieces of brown and white fur. Snakebite pointed to a sign mounted on the fence that sported a picture. "Giraffes." Yet another thing Faller had suspected was nothing but a fantasy. Evidently this world was inhabited, because the giraffes looked like they'd been eaten. He wished he could see one alive.

There was a pirate ship, dozens of well-plundered stores, empty booths with pictures of delicious-looking nonexistent foods. People began to appear here and there; a few glanced their way, but no one paid them any special attention.

They passed a small train on a circular track, a merry-go-round, toy planes on the ends of steel poles, also set in a circle. Ahead, they heard the murmur of voices.

A market was in progress, tables of goods set out in an open cobblestoned area surrounded by squat brown and white buildings, with a clock tower in the center. Hands in their pockets, they strolled along, studying the goods and the transactions.

"Do you have anything for me today?"

Faller looked up. An old woman was standing behind a table of herbs and vegetables, looking at Storm expectantly. Her bright red hair was silver at the roots. When Storm didn't answer, the woman added, "Who are your friends?"

Storm kept her expression flat and matter-of-fact. "This is Faller, and Snakebite."

Faller nodded hello; the old woman smiled and nodded back.

Over the old woman's shoulder, Faller spotted a woman on a bicycle cruising toward them, her arms covered in colorful tattoos, her long black hair snapping in the breeze. She kept the bike remarkably steady as she weaved among people and merchandise.

"Why are you dressed like that?" the old woman asked. "And what's with the packs? Are you—"

The woman on the bicycle looked up, locked eyes with Faller, and shrieked.

She slammed into a tall steel rack of homemade shoes, knocking them everywhere. She tumbled across the cobblestones before coming to rest against the legs of a table.

Faller rushed to help her. She had a long, ugly scrape up her arm from elbow to shoulder; the knee of her pant leg was torn and streaked with blood.

"Are you all right?"

She looked at him, seemed baffled by the question. Storm, Snakebite, the brown-skinned man who evidently owned the shoes, and a few others hovered over them. "Can you stand?"

"I don't know," the woman said. She had a peculiar voice, high-pitched and warbly. Faller helped her as she got to her knee and stood. When her right foot touched the ground, she yelped in pain and buckled into Faller's arms.

Snakebite squatted, rolled up her pant leg, and examined her ankle. "There's no swelling."

"It hurts," the woman said. "I think it might be broken."

"Come on, let's find some cool water for it," Faller said.

Snakebite grasped the woman's other arm while Storm got her bicycle.

"Which way?" he asked the injured woman.

"I live in Wild West Town." She was looking up the paved trail leading out of the square, so Faller headed in that direction, not wanting to let on that they had no idea where, or what, Wild West Town was. The woman hopped along on one foot, leaning heavily on Faller and Snakebite. Her tattoos started at the wrist, disappeared up the short sleeves of a loose orange blouse. The ones on Faller's side were a tapestry of thorny roses, young and old faces, words and abstract designs. They were like someone's dream—chaotic, nightmarish, yet beautiful. There were lines in the corner of her eyes and on her forehead, setting her about square in the middle between young and old.

"It would be easier on your ankle if I carry you," Snakebite suggested.

"I'd rather you didn't, if you don't mind. I appreciate the offer, but the worse off I seem, the more likely someone notices, and takes advantage. You know?"

Snakebite nodded.

"I'm Penny, by the way."

Faller, Storm, and Snakebite introduced themselves.

"I've seen you around," she said to Storm, "but not Faller or Snakebite. Are you two from the other end?"

"We are." Faller could have sworn Penny had shrieked at the sight of him. It reminded Faller of the first time Bruce saw him. Maybe something had happened to her bike at that moment, and that's why she'd shrieked.

"Were you driven out, or are you just here to trade?"

"Just to trade," Faller said. Driven out? That didn't sound promising. He hoped they weren't in for a replay of Storm's world. At least this time no one saw them fall from the sky, and they weren't defenseless.

They reached a fork in the road; Faller allowed Penny's hopping to draw them to the right.

"What happened back there?" he asked.

"Oh"—she waved in the air—"I was going too fast; I hit something slick and the tire went out from under me." It had looked to Faller like she barreled straight into the shoe shelf, but he kept his opinion to himself.

They passed under a rickety wooden sign that, along with words, sported the silhouette of a cowboy. Beyond was a dirt road running between old unpainted buildings made of rough-cut planks. Here and there, bicycles were tied to wooden railings. The only vegetation in sight (if you could call it vegetation) was a big, dead tree poking up through the planked sidewalk on one side of the street. There weren't many people around.

"This is me, up there." Penny gestured at a staircase clinging precariously to the outside of one of the rustic buildings. They helped her up the steps, which creaked ominously. From the landing Faller could see they were fairly close to the edge, maybe a thousand steps away. A sweeping, raised semicircular track ended abruptly, jutting out into space.

Penny fished a key out of the back pocket of the baggy pants she was wearing and unlocked the door.

Her apartment was packed with useless things. Rows of dolls lined the shelves of one bookcase, some of them soiled and worn, one—a man dressed in a black tuxedo sitting beside the shelf—was life-sized. There were stuffed animals of every size, and shelf after shelf of books. The walls were covered with paintings of nothing more than blotches of color.

"Will you be all right here?" Faller was eager to look around, find some food and water, plus materials to fashion a parachute.

"No," Penny nearly shouted. More calmly, she added, "Please don't go. I'm sure I'll be fine in a day or two, but right now I can barely walk."

"Don't you have a friend who could help you?" Storm asked.

Penny looked slightly embarrassed as she answered. "That depends on what you mean by a friend."

Faller looked at the others, not sure what to do.

"I have food," Penny offered.

Faller wasn't sure he had the heart to leave Penny in any case, but the promise of a meal clinched it for them. While Snakebite went to the kitchen to get a meal started, Faller stepped onto the outside landing with Storm.

"What do you think?" he asked.

"I can stay with Penny while she recovers, so there's no chance of me bumping into my newest twin." It was clear the prospect of yet another look-alike didn't sit well with Storm. Faller could relate. "We're near the edge, so if we run into problems we can leave in a hurry. You and Snakebite could see about restocking our food supply."

"Plus, we need to make a parachute for you. Not more than a couple of days, though."

"No, two or three at most," Storm said.

· · · ·

THEY MADE two new parachutes—one for Storm, plus an emergency backup in case one got damaged. With the chutes safely stashed in their packs, they sat in Penny's living room as the light faded.

"You've got an interesting apartment. The decorations, I mean," Faller said, working to keep the conversation on innocuous things that would avoid exposing their ignorance of her world.

Rubbing her sore ankle, Penny looked around the room. "They're all carnival prizes. They were just lying around in bins inside the games. I went around and collected a bunch." She shrugged. "They're comforting to me. I don't know why."

"They're soft and innocent," Storm said, smiling. "I think we all craved friendly faces, especially in the early days."

"What about the books?" Faller asked. One of the first things he'd done when he claimed his room on Day One was dump all the books out the window.

"Oh, they were already here." Penny waved dismissively.

They kept the conversation light and vague—their greatest food discoveries in the early days, speculations about the origins of Day One. Penny told them about her Day One experience: she woke in the park, huddled on a bench by the elephants. She told them what elephants had been like, and giraffes, and zebra. She didn't ask them any hard questions that might expose their ignorance of the world, probably eager to please so they'd stick around until her ankle healed. She was nervous, constantly twirling her hair, or biting her nails, but quick to laugh.

"So, are you and Snakebite planning to go back to the other end when you leave here?" she asked Faller when the light had almost completely drained from the room. "It's safer here in the park."

Faller looked at Snakebite. "We're not sure what our plans are. We tend to move around a lot."

"The reason I ask," Penny said, "is because I could really use some friends, and I like you. All of you." She looked at each of them in turn. "I feel like I can trust you."

Faller gave Penny a warm smile, feeling like shit, as Storm muttered something vague about seeing how things unfolded.

When it was so dark they couldn't see each other's faces, Penny announced that she was spending the night right where she was, on the couch, and they were welcome to the bed in her bedroom. Snakebite grabbed his pack and unrolled his blanket on the floor in the kitchen. Storm headed toward the bedroom. At the door she turned to Faller. "Are you coming?"

35

"Stop grinning. It makes people suspicious," Snakebite said.

He couldn't help it. Whenever he wasn't thinking about his mouth, it immediately formed a wide smile. He'd never felt so light and warm. It was as if he'd now emptied two thirds of the objects he'd found in his pocket on Day One. He'd gotten off his world, and had reunited with the woman he'd lost. Only the map was left to weigh him down.

Snakebite whacked his chest, not hard, but hard enough. "Stop grinning."

Snakebite was always looking around, scanning in every direction. Faller thought he must be watching for threats, but then another explanation occurred to him.

"You're watching for your children."

Snakebite went on scanning. "Only way I'm going to find them."

"I'll keep an eye out, too." When they had some privacy, he'd have to take a closer look at their photos, although he thought he'd recognize them from their complexions and angular faces.

The market was, if anything, busier than the previous day. The old woman with the herbs and vegetables was there. So was the man selling shoes, his merchandise looking no worse for wear.

The thing was, all Faller and Snakebite had to offer in trade were guns and ammunition. Even if they kept two guns for each of them, they had two to spare. If this world was anything like his, or Storm's, a gun was worth a great deal of food, but it wasn't something you simply pulled out in a marketplace. It would draw unwanted attention.

As it was, people kept eyeing Snakebite. He was the sort of man you didn't forget, and suddenly everyone on this world was seeing him for the first time.

"I think our best bet is to find a rough neighborhood, assuming this world has one." Faller looked at Snakebite. "You didn't have a rough part of town on your world, did you?"

"My house was the rough part of town."

Faller laughed.

"Hold on a minute. I've got an idea." Faller paused as they reached the old woman's table, gave her his brightest smile. "I'm wondering if you've seen my friend today—the woman I was with yesterday?"

"Melissa? Nope. Have you checked if she's working?"

Faller set his hands on the table, leaned in, lowered his voice. "To be honest, I don't know her that well. I just met her yesterday, and she took off after helping Snakebite and me take Penny home."

The woman smiled slyly. "And you're hoping to bump into her again."

Faller covered his eyes, feigning embarrassment. "You caught me. Can you blame me, though?"

The woman put a hand on Faller's shoulder. "If you don't know where Melissa works, you need to get out more." She gave him directions to a theater on the edge of the amusement park.

"You going to go up and introduce yourself?" Snakebite asked as they walked.

Faller laughed. "Just a little reconnaissance. If there's another Storm on this world, I want to see her with my own eyes. The look-alikes are the only clue we seem to have about what's going on."

They passed a group of seven men, three carrying rifles. The men slowed and eyed them as they passed. Faller smiled and nodded; Snakebite acted as if he didn't notice them, even as they had to leave the path to let the men by.

Faller heard a voice in the distance, clear and strident, almost singing, but not quite. They were on the paved walk; the open-air pavilion the merchant woman had directed them to was just ahead.

"Where are you, Robert? Turn your back on your people, or if you won't, tell me you love me and I'll turn my back on mine." Her voice was unmistakable as she all but shouted the words with such eloquence, such passion. It set his heart racing to hear it.

Faller picked up his pace as a male voice called out, "Tell me more. Or should I answer now?"

"What is a clan, really?" Melissa replied. "It's not a hand or a foot. It's just a word. What's a word, really? If you called a rose by any other name, it would smell just as sweet."

The pavilion—nothing but a wide roof supported by posts—was packed. The perimeter was roped off. Faller lifted the rope, and he and Snakebite ducked under. A tall man with a machete intercepted them.

"You have to pay first." The man gestured toward a little white booth just outside the pavilion.

"You would be just as perfect—" Melissa stopped speaking, mid-sentence.

Faller looked toward Melissa. She was staring right at him, her lovely face filled with such shock, such horror. Her mouth was moving, but no words came.

The man on the stage with her stammered some line, trying to cover for her, but Melissa went on staring as the audience began to rumble.

She leaped from the low stage and ran, as if she were running for her life.

XIX

THERE WERE so many bombers, so perfectly spaced, that it looked as if there were a steel mesh curtain gliding over Boston. Peter could barely breathe as skyscrapers crumpled in on themselves.

"I can't take this," Harry said, pressing the heels of his hands against his eyeballs. "I can't take this anymore. Holy Christ."

Peter put a hand on Harry's neck, gave it a gentle squeeze. "I know. Hang on, buddy."

The North Korean bombers just kept coming. The same image was echoed on each of the big screens mounted along the factory wall. While the rest of the East Coast was dealing with rolling blackouts every three hours, they could watch as many TVs as they cared to, could light the factory floor like it was Christmastime, because their generators were fueled by the singularity. If they would just give him time, he could do it for everyone on Earth.

Jill Sanders was sobbing. She'd grown up in Boston.

"We're not going to be done in time," Harry said.

"Then we have to get it done faster." Maybe he should turn it over to the feds. Their resources were almost endless; his were anything but.

"Dr. Sandoval?" Peter turned to find Denny De Rosa, one of his other physicists, running toward him. "The prototype arrived."

Peter turned his face to the ceiling and shouted with joy and relief. Finally.

"They're loading it onto the winch at the south end of the building," De Rosa said. "It should be down here in half an hour."

Peter's phone rang: it was Kathleen.

"How's your progress?" she asked with no preamble.

Someone on the floor called Peter's name. He gestured to Harry to go see what whoever it was wanted, then headed upstairs, to make sure the prototype made it down safely. "Better, now. I don't want to jinx us, but I think we're a month away. Work on eighty of the platforms is under way, with the other fifty-six scheduled to begin this week. Our engineers in Germany just delivered the fuel cell prototype, and if our test charge is successful they're ready to start manufacturing them immediately."

"There's something you need to be aware of."

Kathleen's tone made Peter's stomach clench. "What's that?"

"Secretary of Defense Elba and her Joint Chiefs—Perez, Holland . . . and Ugo Woolcoff—tried to issue a press release stating Aspen was unfit to serve as commander in chief. Aspen blocked the release."

Ugo. How had that bastard suddenly become a Joint Chief? "Are they strong enough to push her out?" Peter asked as he climbed a dank, dimly lit staircase.

"At this point it's hard to say who holds more power—Aspen or the military. You're going to get a call from the president in a little while. She's going to ask you to provide her with the means to manufacture her own duplicator."

"*What?* No. There's no time." He lowered his voice as he pushed open the heavy door, stepped out into the hallway leading to the main lab. "What if she finds out about the singularity? No."

"Just wanted to give you a heads-up."

"I appreciate it. I won't ever forget this."

Hands on hips, Peter surveyed the lab. It looked like a marine barracks. "Security" people—his own private army, really—were communicating with others outside the campus perimeter with headsets. A few techs weaved among them, going about their own business, oblivious to what was going on belowground. There were so many pieces of this to keep track of, so many details. Peter hated details, but he needed to get them all right. So much depended on it.

36

FALLER RACED around the edge of the pavilion with Snakebite on his heels. He spotted Melissa running down the walkway, the way they'd come. She cut onto a narrower path behind a toy elephant ride, glanced over her shoulder.

"Wait," Faller shouted. "I want to talk to you." Why was she running? She must recognize him, or someone who looked like him. There must be someone on this world who looked like him, someone Penny didn't know. They were closing on her. She hadn't gotten much of a lead, and her long, flowing white dress and matching shoes weren't conducive to speed. Seeing them close behind, Melissa raced up a half-dozen steps and disappeared through a wide doorway.

Barreling through the doorway, Faller slammed into a pane of glass and fell on his ass as a dozen Melissas fanned out in different directions.

"Are you all right?" Snakebite gripped his armpits and helped him to his feet.

He'd struck the window with the side of his face, which throbbed. His cheek stung when he touched it; his fingertips came away somewhat bloody.

"I guess so. Come on." Faller headed into the maze more carefully, his arms outstretched. It was a baffling mix of windows and mirrors, all coated in a relatively uniform layer of dust and grime. Melissa was in fifty places at once. He had no idea how to reach her.

"Melissa?" All of the Melissas' heads turned when she heard her name. "Melissa, I'm not sure I understand what's going on, but I promise you, I'm not out to hurt you." He glanced at Snakebite. "And my friend Snakebite looks scary, but he's harmless, too."

"I know who you are," Melissa said.

"Who am I? I'm dying to know."

"Melissa?" a voice near the entrance shouted. "Are you all right?" Reflections of five or six men filled a dozen mirrors. One was the man who'd been onstage with Melissa.

"Planter?" Melissa called. "Help me."

"*Help you?* I just told you, we just want to talk. You don't need help." Faller's words were partially drowned by shouts as the men bulled their way into the maze. Two came around a corner, spotted Faller and Snakebite.

Suddenly Snakebite was pointing a handgun at the oncoming men. *"Everyone calm down."*

The men froze.

"Melissa, stand still." Snakebite eyed Melissa through the maze, his threat unspoken.

Melissa froze.

Faller didn't think Snakebite was the sort of man who'd shoot people who weren't pointing guns at him, but he sure looked like the sort who would. "Now, Faller is going to come to you. He'd like to ask you a few questions. Then he and I are going to leave. No one is going to get hurt. All right?"

After a pause, Melissa said, "Yes."

"Thanks," Faller muttered to Snakebite.

"So much for keeping a low profile."

Faller slid his hands along the glass, worked his way through the maze until the flesh-and-blood Melissa was standing in front of him, her back against a mirror.

"Please. Just explain who you think I am."

Melissa was quivering, as if she were sure Faller was about to kill her.

He'd forgotten about the photograph. He took it from his pocket and held it out. "Can you make any sense of this?"

Melissa came off the glass, took a half-step toward Faller, looked into his eyes. "You've got to be kidding me." She took the photo from him, turned it over, then back again.

"You *recognize* it?"

"How the hell did you get here?" she whispered.

Faller took the toy paratrooper out of his pocket.

Melissa pressed her palms over her eyes and started to laugh. It wasn't happy, joyful laughter; more the sort of laughter Faller associated with lunatics. "I can't get rid of you. You're like a disease that keeps coming back." She dropped her hands. "I thought you were one of Ugo's assassins, coming to get me. Jill and I decided to hide on the same island. They caught her. They almost caught me." She kept her voice low, evidently so the others couldn't hear.

Melissa studied him. "Jill Sanders? Your colleague?"

Faller shook his head.

All of the hostile bravado drained from Melissa's face. "Oh, no." She covered her mouth with one hand. "The virus got you."

"The virus? It was a disease?"

She was crying. "Yes and no. A disease and a weapon." She shook her head. "Shit, Peter."

"My name is Faller," he insisted, although he was getting a terrible sinking feeling. He almost didn't want to ask, but he had to know. "Is that you in the picture?"

"Yeah. Mm-hm. That was taken on our honeymoon. Costa Rica. We asked a local to take it."

"We're married?"

Melissa's laughter was bitter. "No, sweetie. We're divorced."

Faller felt his heart break. He thought of Storm, waiting back at Penny's apartment. "That can't be. You're lying."

"I'm *lying*?" She held up her left hand, wiggled her finger. "Where's your ring?" She held up the photo, tapped the image of Faller's hand around her waist. "You have it on in the photo."

Faller had no idea what a ring had to do with any of this. "Why do you remember, and I don't?"

"It's a long story."

He motioned toward the front. "Come on, you can tell me over a meal."

She didn't move. "You're going to get us both killed. Ugo's looking for us—for you, especially—and you're moving from place to place like an idiot."

He couldn't believe this was the woman in the photo. She was so jaded.

"That's why I have to know what's happened. I don't want to get myself killed, or anyone else for that matter. If I'm doing something ignorant, convince me to stop."

She folded her arms, looked away, then dropped her arms and stormed off, navigating the mirrored maze effortlessly.

As they returned to Penny's apartment, Melissa walking between Faller and Snakebite, Snakebite handed Melissa the photos of his children.

"Have you seen any of them?"

Melissa studied each photo carefully. "I'm sorry, no. If they weren't on your island, they could be on any one of ten thousand. More."

Snakebite remained stone-faced as he digested this nugget.

Faller was dreading the moment Storm learned she wasn't the woman in the photo. For his part, Faller was trying to sort out how this new information affected his feelings for Storm. It did, and it didn't. It didn't change who Storm was, but knowing their coming together was all predicated on a case of mistaken identity was disturbing.

He and Melissa were divorced. All of that time he'd spent mooning over that photo, yearning to find her. Early on, it had been the only thing that kept him going.

"What should we do about Penny?" Snakebite asked as they approached the apartment.

That was a good point. They could ask Storm to come outside and leave Penny out of it, but then anyone passing would see Storm and Melissa together, and that might raise eyebrows.

"I say we risk telling her the truth," Snakebite said.

"Who's Penny?" Melissa asked.

"A woman we met from your world," Faller said.

Melissa only nodded.

At Penny's door, Faller took a deep breath before pushing it open. Storm, who was sitting on the couch across from Penny, gave him a bright smile as he stepped through. When Melissa followed, she sprang from the couch.

Penny looked from Melissa to Storm and back again. "I don't understand. What is this?"

For her part, after looking Storm up and down, Melissa only shook her head, as if Storm's presence were only mildly surprising.

"This is Melissa," Faller began. "Apparently she knows some things and has been kind enough to enlighten us."

"Can someone please tell me what's going on?" Penny's voice was shaking.

Faller held up both hands. "Please. Penny, just bear with us." He turned to Storm. "Melissa claims she's the woman in the photo."

Storm blinked rapidly, trying to keep her reaction from showing. But it did show, at least to Faller.

"You're sure?" Storm asked Melissa. "You remember?"

Melissa looked at the ceiling. "All too well."

Faller went to Storm, put a hand across her shoulders, and as gently as possible said, "Melissa and I are divorced."

Storm covered her mouth and ran into the bathroom.

Melissa was gaping at Faller in disbelief. "You're in *love* with her?" She looked as if her legs might give out, like she might cry, laugh, scream, or do all three at once.

Faller didn't respond.

"Would you mind telling us who you are, and why you remember what Faller doesn't?" Snakebite said, folding his arms across his broad chest.

Her hand trembling badly, Melissa swept her hair back, clearly trying to compose herself. "As I told Faller, it's a long story."

"Why don't you get started?" Snakebite said.

"Wait a minute." Faller went to the bathroom door, rapped on it gently. "Storm, you're going to want to hear this."

The door opened. Storm looked composed, her expression unreadable. "Thank you."

Melissa took a seat in a white stuffed chair. Snakebite set a cup of water on the table beside her and took a seat on the floor against the wall. Faller led Storm to the couch, his heart thumping, sensing that some of the confusion he'd lived with since Day One was about to be lifted.

Melissa stared at him and Storm. "This is just . . . I can't believe what I'm seeing."

"Please," Snakebite prodded.

Melissa pressed her fingers against the sides of her nose and closed her eyes. "There was a war. Peter and I—" She cleared her throat. "Excuse me—*Faller* and I were active in the war on the losing side, so according to the winning side, we're war criminals."

She opened her eyes, looked at Faller and Storm. "I guess it makes sense. If you've been lobotomized, lobotomies seem sexy."

Pinching his lower lip, Faller waited for her to continue. He had no intention of interrupting this.

"The war went on until a scientist on the enemy side, Ugo Woolcoff, developed a weapon. It was called the blackout virus. It spread like a disease, but instead of making you sick, it erased your memory."

And just like that, the mystery of Day One came clear. It wasn't gods or guilt that had done it, but war.

"The thing was, our side had a weapon of a sort, too." Melissa took a sip of water. "A scientist on our side developed it, not as a weapon, but as a way to end the war peacefully. The scientist was rushing to finish his device when Ugo Woolcoff released the blackout virus." Melissa shrugged. "He finished it just as Woolcoff released the virus. Only it didn't do what he expected."

"What did it do?" Faller asked.

"It tore the world apart."

Penny looked about to say something, then rose and limped into the kitchen area and poured herself a glass of water.

"How big was the world, before it was torn to pieces?" Snakebite asked.

"You'd have to walk . . ." Melissa looked at the ceiling, "for about five hundred days to go around it."

It had taken Faller half an hour to cross his world. And that was lengthwise.

"Why do you and I look alike?" Storm asked.

Melissa folded her hands in her lap and stared at them for a long moment. "The machine responsible for tearing the world apart could create duplicates of people."

It felt as if someone had poured ice water down Faller's back.

"There wasn't much time, and there was a lot to do if we were going to end the war, so some of us duplicated ourselves. When the world was torn apart, the duplicates ended up scattered—"

"Wait a minute," Storm interrupted. "Are you saying I'm a *copy* of you?"

A copy. That's why Melissa had reacted so harshly when she realized Faller and Storm were in love. Suddenly Faller wasn't sure he wanted to hear the truth, if that was what this was.

"Yes," Melissa said, speaking gently. "That doesn't mean you're not just as real as I am."

"Oh, I'm real. Well, that's reassuring." Storm got up, turned toward the front door. "You're out of your fucking mind."

"Storm," Faller called as the door slammed behind her. He half stood, intending to go after her, then, reluctantly, sat. He needed to hear this.

Snakebite was now standing beside Penny in the kitchen. He was show-ing her the photos of his children, speaking quietly. Evidently Penny's an-kle was feeling much better.

Peter pulled out his map, handed it to Melissa. "This was in my pocket on Day One. It looks like a map to me. Do you know what it leads to?"

Melissa studied it. "It's telling you to go down. The land mass with the X over it is probably where you lived. Williamsburg."

The front door flew open. Storm rushed in and slammed the door closed behind her. She looked at Faller. "I just saw you outside."

Everyone sprang from their seats.

"I told you you'd get us killed," Melissa said.

Snakebite pulled the shotgun and a pistol out of his pack, then slung the pack over his shoulders. He went to the door, cracked it open and peered out. "I don't see anyone, but they're not going to stand in the middle of the road after spotting Storm."

"Who isn't?" Penny asked.

"Do you have more guns?" Melissa asked, ignoring Penny.

Snakebite turned. "Can you shoot?"

"Not really. Enough that I won't accidentally shoot you, or myself."

Faller squatted by his pack and fished for the pistol Snakebite had given him.

Snakebite raced around the apartment, peering out the corners of win-dows. "Grab the parachutes. I want everyone to climb out the bedroom window. There's only two feet between this building and the next, so you can shimmy down. When I shout, run for that long blue trough."

"The log flume ride," Penny offered.

"Fine. We're going to take that right over the edge. When I start shoot-ing, get out that window."

Snakebite grabbed Penny's life-sized doll and set it beside the kitchen window, which faced the log flume ride. He disappeared into the bedroom, returned carrying a mattress. Partially folding it, his biceps bulging from the strain, he shoved it through the window. He snared Penny's doll by the throat, took two deep breaths, then tossed it out the window as well.

Gunshots rang out as ambushers mistook the doll for a person. Snakebite stepped onto the windowsill, gripped the frame and swung himself outside, fired a quick burst toward the roof. A body dropped past the window.

"*Go.*" Snakebite let go and dropped toward the mattress.

They ran for the bedroom. Melissa went through the window first, bracing her feet against the opposite wall, her back against the wall of Penny's building. As she attempted to shimmy down, she immediately dropped five feet, managed to wedge herself again, then half slid, half plunged the last dozen feet. Gun drawn, she motioned for the others to follow as more shots rang out behind the house.

Faller sent Storm down next.

When Penny lifted her leg to step through the window, Faller said, "Stay! You're not part of this."

"I doubt they'll see it that way when they burst in shooting." Not waiting for Faller's reply, she plunged to the ground, clawing the walls trying to slow herself. She didn't limp at all as she moved off.

As he was climbing out, Faller heard a sharp whistle—Snakebite's signal. He landed hard, staying on his feet only because the space was so narrow. Maybe Snakebite could shimmy down between two walls, the rest of them might as well have simply leaped.

"Go." Melissa was at the back edge of the tiny alley, waving them on.

Snakebite was at the far back corner of Penny's building, exchanging shots with however many assailants were in front, pinning them down. Faller ran like hell to the log flume, then rolled into the big semicircular raised canal where Storm was waiting for him. They climbed a steep incline on hands and knees. It would slow them down, but Faller recognized the brilliance of Snakebite's plan: the log flume provided excellent cover, and gave them a clear view of anyone moving below.

The problem was, Penny and Melissa were with them. No: the problem was, Penny was with them. If Faller had his way, Melissa would leave with them. Ex-wife or not, she knew what was going on. He hadn't gotten a chance to ask what the flag at the bottom of his map meant.

It occurred to him that he didn't have his map; Melissa had been holding it. Hopefully she'd stashed it in a pocket.

Faller heard footfalls below. He raised his head to look, and suddenly Snakebite was half on top of him, pushing his face into the grit and rotting leaves lining the flume ride.

Snakebite let go, gestured to Faller that they should rise together on either side, guns raised, and shoot. Faller nodded, suddenly realizing the flume probably wasn't bulletproof. Once the shooters below pinpointed their location, they could shoot right up through it.

Snakebite held up three fingers, then two, then one . . .

Gripping the side of the flume, Faller rose to his knees, immediately spotted one of his duplicates, sans mask, squatting in a copse of trees. The gun seemed to go off on its own, spraying bullets left to right, then right to left, all shy of the figure in the trees.

The figure jerked three or four times as bullets ripped into his chest, shoulder, thigh. Snakebite's shots. Faller spotted another duplicate directly below, just as Snakebite got him, his shots incredibly accurate.

Melissa and Storm were at the top of the rise and on their feet, shooting off either side. They would have looked like mirror images if Melissa hadn't been wearing that long white dress.

"Let's go," Snakebite barked.

Scrambling on all fours, Faller climbed as fast as he could.

"Keep moving," Snakebite said behind him. A second later, Snakebite was firing again. Faller kept his head down, his breath coming in ragged gasps, his arms and legs absolutely burning with fatigue as he clambered the last ten yards and reached the peak.

They had to be seventy feet in the air. Ahead was a steep drop that tapered off at the bottom before it simply ended, sticking out over the void.

He turned to Penny. "Just hide until we're gone. When they see us go, they'll have no reason to climb up here."

"Come on." Storm waved him on. "Snakebite will catch up."

"I'm staying," Melissa said. "They haven't had time to count heads."

"But we need you," Storm said.

Melissa gave her a look. "That doesn't mean I'm parachuting into the sky with you."

"I'm sorry." Storm shoved Melissa in the chest with both hands, hard. Shrieking, Melissa tumbled backward, hit the steep incline and plunged headfirst, building remarkable speed. Storm leaped after her as shots rang out, peppering the steel framework directly below them. Faller jumped onto the slide and plummeted, the wind growing louder in his ears as he gained speed. Just as he leveled out, the slide ended. Sharp pain lanced his bicep as he caught a jagged edge on the way off.

Then he was falling, headfirst, the whistle of the wind growing louder.

Faller righted himself. He clutched his arm, pulled it against his side. It stung. Blood oozed between his fingers. They were alive, though. That was the important thing. And they had Melissa, so they weren't fumbling in the dark anymore.

A panicked shriek drew his attention. It was Penny, thrashing and screaming. Her shrieks reached him on and off through the whistling air.

"What did you do?" Faller shouted, knowing no one would hear.

Snakebite was diving toward Melissa, who looked to be in shock. Snakebite pointed at Faller, then at Penny. Faller gave him the "okay" sign, spread his arms and legs and waited for Penny to catch up.

37

"Breathe," Penny said, evidently to herself. "You're okay." She was cling-ing to Faller with both arms and legs. She had remarkable stamina.

"I have to check on Storm," Faller shouted. "Will you be all right?"

"*No.*" She squeezed tighter.

"I still don't understand why you jumped."

"You think those men were just going to walk away? I was dead if I stayed."

Faller wasn't sure those men would have gunned down a woman they hadn't been after, but he had to admit he didn't know what they were capable of.

"I'm so scared," Penny said. "I'm having severe heart arrhythmia; I think I may be having a heart attack."

Faller wasn't completely sure what a heart attack was. "It'll get easier. I promise. But right now I need to speak to Storm." He peeled one of her hands off his back. "You'll be fine."

Penny moaned uneasily, gripped him harder. He felt bad about tossing her into the deep end of the pool like this, but he had to check on Storm.

"Deep breaths," Penny said. "Promise you'll come right back? I don't have a parachute."

Faller couldn't help laughing. "I had noticed. Yet you still jumped off your world."

"Well, you pushed Melissa off without one. I assumed you had a plan."

"We'll fix you up when the time comes." Faller pulled free. Whispering urgently, Penny hugged herself and squeezed her eyes shut.

Faller dropped toward Storm.

He offered Storm a hand, and was relieved when she took it. Her eyes were red.

"How are you feeling?"

"Confused," Storm said.

Faller wanted to tell her it didn't matter, but he doubted that would be comforting. Storm had just learned she'd been manufactured.

"How can I help?"

Storm smiled. The buffeting wind made it look as if her face were twitching. "I don't think you can."

"What does this mean for us?"

She squeezed her eyes shut for a moment. "You're drawn to me because you were drawn to *her*. I'm attracted to you because I'm a *copy* of her. I'm guessing you've noticed that she doesn't like you much, and I'm guessing before your memory was wiped, you didn't like her much. So we know how this story ends."

"I don't believe that. You're not her."

"Evidently I am, more or less."

Faller tried to respond, but Storm cut him off. "Can we talk about this later?"

"I'm sorry. I shouldn't have brought it up. I'm going to talk to Melissa, see what else I can find out." He squeezed her hand.

As he let go, she asked, "What sort of world was this, where they made people like it was nothing?"

Faller had no answer for that.

Melissa was overhead, clutching Snakebite's arm for dear life, probably because he was the only person with a parachute who was neither her duplicate nor her ex-husband. Faller spread his arms and legs, allowed the pair to drop toward him as he decided what to ask first.

"Why are my duplicates trying to kill me?" It seemed a sound place to begin.

Melissa shrugged. "You left four behind. Ugo caught one and made more."

Faller didn't have much to go on when it came to finding holes in Melissa's logic. "How do I know how to fire a gun if I can't remember ever firing one?"

"Completely different part of the brain. The virus works on autobiographical memory, and the reading centers. Firing a gun is procedural memory. Totally different thing."

It was as if she'd switched to a foreign language. "The brain has different parts?"

"God," Melissa said, shaking her head, "the virus burned so deep."

In other words, "God, how incredibly ignorant you are."

"There's a woman. Pointy eyes, hard and pretty at the same time. She was on my world, and two of the others."

Melissa laughed. Her laugh was like Storm's, but with a bitter edge. "Kathleen Choi. Her original insisted on being dropped on the same world as you after the blackout virus had run its course, when we all ran and hid. I think she was in love with you."

He pictured Orchid's distraught face as she carried his pack up flight after flight of stairs. "She still remembered everything?"

"Yes." Melissa licked her lips. "Do you have water?"

Faller reached back, deftly unzipped a side pouch on his pack, produced a canteen. "Put your entire mouth around it." Drinking in free fall was a challenge.

After managing a drink, she handed the canteen back with a nod. "That whole time, she never let on?"

"No."

"Either she was scared you'd do something rash if you knew about Ugo, or she didn't want you to leave her and come looking for me."

That sounded about right to Faller. Maybe a little of both. "Why is Ugo after *us*?"

"He may think we know where to find something he wants. An energy source. Also a weapon. Plus he hates you and wants you dead."

"Do you know where this weapon is?"

Melissa smiled. "I do now."

"What's that supposed to mean?"

"You wrote it on your map. You know the flag, with the number thirteen?"

His map. Faller patted his pockets. "Where did that map go? You had it in Penny's apartment."

Melissa thought about it. "I think I left it there. I'm sorry."

Despite knowing every line of it by heart, Faller felt an acute sense of loss.

Melissa looked up. Faller followed her gaze, but there was nothing up there.

"It may take them a while to rendezvous with their transportation, but eventually they're going to come after us." She looked down. "It's not going to be difficult to figure out where we went."

She had a point. The ninja Fallers were persistent. He thought for a moment. "Let's move laterally. They won't know which direction we went in." Waving to get Snakebite's attention, he said, "Hang on to my feet. Snakebite can get Penny." He shifted from a feetfirst position to mimic a bird in flight. Melissa grabbed his ankles, forming a train. He motioned for Storm to follow, as Snakebite got Penny to do the same with his ankles.

It didn't feel as if they were making much horizontal progress, but Faller knew from the times they'd tried to intercept worlds on their periphery that that was deceiving. They'd be out of sight of pursuit in a matter of hours.

Faller's head ached, trying to assimilate everything Melissa had told him. Each answer she gave further shifted the shaky ground he stood on.

He looked back at Storm. Even from a distance her figure looked forlorn, as if she might dissolve into smoke and become part of a passing cloud, or melt into raindrops.

XX

As THE newscasters debated President Aspen's fitness to continue leading the country on the iPad Harry had propped in the grass, Peter closed his eyes, turned his face toward the sun. The heat on his skin felt remarkably, unbelievably good. He was so tired of those walls and the dusty, dank smell. He was sick of feeling exhausted.

He unwrapped the white wax paper, lifted half a tuna sandwich, pried out the tomato and set it on the paper beside the other half of the sandwich.

"You should eat that," Harry said.

"I hate tomatoes."

"You need the vitamin C."

"I'm taking multivitamin tablets every day."

Harry shook his head. "Not the same."

On a day when he was less exhausted, Peter would have taken pleasure in having one of their pointless debates while leaving the pathetic slice of tomato to bake in the sun, but today he picked it up without comment and shoved it back into his sandwich.

Harry patted him on the back. "That tomato was all that stood between you and scurvy."

Grinning, Peter took a bite. With his mouth full he said, "I owe you my life."

Peter watched a gorgeous, classic incus drift overhead. It was powder blue, a flat-topped mushroom.

"Oh, what now?" Harry asked.

The talking heads on the news had given way to a familiar sight: MSNBC's Special Alert graphic.

"There is word this hour of an outbreak in Malaysia of a never before seen virus. The victims show severe disorientation and memory loss. For more we go to Angie Lo in Kuala Lumpur."

Harry stopped chewing. "Memory loss," he breathed.

They watched images of brightly dressed people clutching their heads, crying, shrieking, begging for help.

"Now we know what Ugo's been working on for the past three months." Peter should have guessed. The terrible side effect of the Peterson-Jantz suppressor virus made it a perfect bioterror agent. It was remarkably hearty, and could be contracted through the air. In fact, it was almost too hearty. "But Sumatra's right across the Strait of Malacca. They're our allies." Peter leaned in closer to the screen. "That whole area is a patchwork of enemies and allies. How are they planning to control the spread?"

The whine of an aircraft engine rose in the distance, growing louder. A Harrier broke over the trees, flying low.

A dozen of their security personnel carrying assault rifles raced to set up sheltered positions as orders were shouted back and forth. Two security people escorted Peter and Harry inside.

"Hang on," Peter said. "If they wanted to attack, they wouldn't be landing in the middle of the lawn."

They watched the Harrier set down a hundred yards away. The engine died. Kathleen jumped out.

Grinning, Peter jogged toward the Harrier.

He stumbled, then slowed to a walk as Melissa stepped out behind her.

Kathleen gave him a big hug; Peter looked over her shoulder at Melissa, who hung back.

"What are you doing here?" he asked as Harry joined them.

"The coup is under way in Washington. Elba and her Joint Chiefs."

Peter pressed his hand to his cheek. "Is she going to be successful?"

"I think so. We got out before they started lining up Aspen's people for the firing squad."

Although Kathleen was speaking, Peter's gaze kept drifting to Melissa. Her expression was tight, serious. She opened her mouth and spoke for the first time.

"We're here to help you in any way we can."

A man in blue air force fatigues stepped out of the Harrier. His otherwise handsome, square-jawed face was marred by close-set, beady eyes.

Kathleen looked over her shoulder. "Brandon Dawson. Good people. We can trust him."

Peter and Dawson exchanged nods.

"Let's get inside," Peter said. "We're so close. A week away."

"That's not soon enough," Kathleen said as they headed for the door. "Elba might start nuking North Korea at any time. And Peter"—she turned, gave him a hard look—"Elba's people released Ugo's virus without the president's authorization. I think that virus is a big part of their battle plan. That's why Ugo gained so much power so quickly."

· · · ·

PETER WAITED outside the door to their impromptu strategy room, which had once been a factory office. The far wall was dominated by a checker-patterned chalkboard, with a hook in the corner of each square to hold a key. Beneath it was a desk, a concrete-encrusted rubber boot sitting on top.

When Melissa and Kathleen arrived, Kathleen went past him, into the room.

"Melissa?" It came out sounding tentative; Peter cleared his throat. "Do you have a minute?"

"I'm not sure any of us have a minute," she said, but she stopped.

"I just wanted to thank you for coming, after all that's happened." A lump rose in his throat; he swallowed, trying unsuccessfully to banish it.

Melissa toed a loose piece of concrete. "If anyone can get the world out of this mess, it's you." She looked up. "We need to focus our attention on that."

Peter nodded. Her unspoken message was clear enough.

38

In his nightmare, he'd been crawling in a tunnel, only it wasn't so much a tunnel as a huge, greasy intestine. It went on and on, each twist opening to another short length of stinking, twitching meat. He could still smell the place—an acrid, pungent odor like vomit on coal.

He woke with Snakebite's hand on his shoulder. It was dark; the moon and most of the stars were hidden by clouds.

"There's a world below," Snakebite said in his ear. "The others are ready."

They landed on the outskirts of a large town. It seemed deserted, but it was nighttime, so it was hard to say. Choosing a street at random they walked between windowless half buildings, empty foundations, buildings with one wall peeled away that were otherwise intact. There was something strange about the place that Faller couldn't quite put his finger on.

"It's clean," Snakebite said, his voice low.

That was it. On other worlds there was trash everywhere. Where a building had been knocked down or damaged, there was rubble. Bricks, wood, broken glass. Faller saw blackened, twisted steel girders, and plenty of vehicles, but no rubble. Not even food wrappers.

They turned left at the next cross street.

"It's like a giant vacuum sucked up everything that wasn't bolted down," Melissa said.

Faller had half expected Melissa to have some explanation based on her vast store of memories, and was almost pleased that some of this, at least, was still confusing to her. What must it be like, to have memories traveling all the way back, in an unbroken chain? How different life would be.

"Look at that. Holy shit, look at that." Penny was pointing half a block ahead.

It was like an invisible line. On one side, the landscape was picked clean; on the other, rubble and trash lay scattered and heaped just as on any other world.

A lone figure stood at the divide between cluttered and clean, piling bricks into a wheelbarrow. It was a woman, slender to the point of skeletal, her back to them.

They paused a respectful distance away. Who wouldn't be frightened by a group of strangers coming up behind you at night, especially when one of those strangers was Snakebite?

"Hello?" Storm called softly.

The woman turned. "I couldn't sleep—" When she saw them, she screamed.

It was Orchid. A few worlds back Faller might have been startled or surprised, but now he pretty much expected to encounter an Orchid or two everywhere he went.

Orchid took a step back, screamed again, then bolted.

They watched her go.

"God. This is going to take some getting used to," Penny said.

"I'm *still* not used to it," Faller said.

"What do we do now?" Storm asked.

"Let's keep walking," Snakebite said. "If there are people living here, there's food and water."

Faller looked at Penny's legs. She was walking fine, no hint of a limp. "Your ankle seems a lot better."

She looked down at her feet. "Yeah. It's like something just popped back into place."

"There may not be many people in this town," Melissa said. "It looks like it was heavily bombed during the war. Most of the residents who survived would have moved to refugee camps. Kathleen made a lot more duplicates than the rest of us. She couldn't stop. When all the duplicates took off a few hours before the apocalypse, hers looked like an army. It doesn't surprise me that some of them would end up in peculiar places like this."

"If there aren't many people here, how did they clean out so much of the world?" Faller asked.

"I don't know. Kathleen had serious OCD issues, so it makes sense that she'd clean up."

"What's OCD?" Faller asked.

Three women came flying out the front of a mostly intact apartment building. They headed straight toward Faller's cadre. All three were Orchids.

"Guns." Snakebite squatted, drew his shotgun. Faller pulled his handgun, cursing under his breath.

"I told you." The voice came from behind. Faller turned. Five more Orchids were behind them, handguns raised. Half a dozen more raced toward the scene.

"You've got to be kidding me," Faller said.

"Drop your weapons," a voice called from above.

Armed Orchids were on the roofs on either side of the street.

Snakebite's shotgun clattered to the blacktop. Faller and the others dropped their handguns.

Orchids approached warily from either side, chattering to each other. They were all Orchids. Every one of them.

One raised her voice. "Where did you come from?"

"From up above." Faller pointed. "There are more worlds up there. We're completely friendly."

The Orchids looked baffled. They exchanged wide-eyed glances as even more joined them.

"He's telling the truth," Penny said. "I didn't believe it, either—"

"Their *faces*," one of the Orchids said.

They'd never seen a person who didn't look like them, Faller realized.

"Do you have food?" asked one of the Orchids who looked better fed.

"Not much," Snakebite replied. "We were hoping to trade with you for food and water. And if you have anyone who's good with wounds, my friend has a bad gash on his shoulder."

Faller wasn't sure he'd call his wound bad. The throbbing had mostly subsided over the past day.

"Take off your packs," the Orchid said.

Never taking her eyes off Snakebite, she grabbed each of the packs in turn and handed them off to her sisters.

. . . .

AT LEAST it wasn't a prison. They were moving up in the world, Faller thought, eyeing the crown molding and the ornate wooden door locked from the outside.

"I'm trying to understand how this happened," Penny said to Melissa, flipping her remarkably straight bangs out of her eyes. "You just stepped into a machine and spit out copies of yourselves? *Why* did you do this?"

"Just drop it, okay? I don't want to talk about it."

Penny cupped her hand to her ear. "I'm sorry, can you repeat that?" She gave Melissa a pointed look. "Maybe with a little less hostility this time?"

"Sorry," Melissa muttered. "I'm a little agitated."

"Join the club," Penny shot back. She retreated to a corner, sat cross-legged facing the wall, back straight. She pulled her ankles up over her thighs.

"What are you doing?" Faller asked.

"Meditating." She inhaled deeply, let it out. "It calms me."

Faller shook his head, turned away. The more he got to know Penny, the odder she seemed.

The lock on the door rattled; the door swung open.

"Come on," said one of the four Orchids standing outside.

They headed away from the center of town, down a road lined with one-story buildings festooned with colorful signs. As they walked, Snakebite studied the Orchids leading them, his eyes narrowed.

"Why do all of them carry pistols if there's no one here but them?"

That hadn't occurred to Faller. If there were no threats, you'd think they'd let their guard down a bit. "Maybe they only started when we arrived?"

"They had us surrounded two minutes after we were spotted. They were on the roof with rifles. They had to be carrying them to get there so quickly."

Faller nodded. The Orchids had odd patches on their shoulders. One wore a yellow one with the image of a tree stitched into it. Another had a purple one, with what looked to be a brick on it.

"Excuse me." Faller caught the eye of an Orchid walking to his left. "What are the patches for?"

She looked away.

One of the others looked over her shoulder. "It's how we tell each other apart."

They turned into a big parking lot, headed toward a huge blue and white building. As they reached the doors, one of the Orchids told four others to stand guard outside.

"Let someone else," one of them protested. "I want to hear."

As Faller was whisked inside, they were still arguing about who would stay outside.

The roof was collapsed in several places where bombs must have hit, but the vast floor was spotless. He'd never seen such a clean floor. Words in tall letters were affixed high on the walls.

Faller and his companions were led to five folding chairs set in the middle of the store, where dozens of Orchids were congregated.

"I'll bet you anything those chairs are in the exact center of the floor," Melissa muttered. "They paced it off, walking heel to toe from the walls."

They *did* look to be perfectly centered. Faller's Orchid had been peculiar, with her step-counting and twitches and such, but her behavior hadn't been this extreme. Maybe when there was no one around but people just like you, your peculiarities seemed normal, so you did nothing to suppress them and they went wild.

When Faller and the rest were seated, the Orchids—forty or so—gathered in a circle around them.

"One thing's for sure," Snakebite said under his breath. "I'm not going to find my kids on this world."

Melissa fielded most of the questions. No one seemed to be strictly in charge. The ones who stood toward the front asked most of the questions. Faller guessed they held higher status than the others. The ones hanging toward the back were thinner, more desperate-looking.

When someone asked how they had landed safely if they'd fallen there, Faller asked for his pack. He showed them his parachute, explained how it worked. Here and there in the crowd, multiple Orchid hands dug into the other packs and pulled out parachutes, chattering excitedly as they examined them.

"We'd be happy to teach you to make your own," Snakebite offered. He'd been silent to that point, no doubt watching for opportunities to extract them from an uncertain situation. Faller didn't have a clear sense of whether these women meant them harm. The Orchids hadn't threatened them, but it was also clear they were not free to leave.

Five or six of the Orchids closest to the front huddled together out of earshot. When they broke, one clapped her hands. "That's enough for now.

If your duties don't involve these strangers, it's time to get to work, if you want to eat."

That most definitely sounded like the words of someone of higher status. Evidently even in a group of people who were all exactly the same, some ended up in charge.

39

A CHURCH bell sounded in the distance. All of the Orchids in sight—save for the four who were in charge of "escorting" the five newcomers around—burst into frantic motion.

They disappeared into various intact structures and returned carrying pails, tubs, bowls, plastic tarps, which they set out in neat rows.

"What's going on?" Penny asked one of their Orchid guards. Based on her patch, Faller was fairly sure her name was Purple Brick. Ever efficient, the Orchids had evidently picked out a dozen objects in sight at the time—brick, cloud, tree, bird, et cetera—and a dozen colors, and everyone's name was just a combination of the two.

Purple Brick motioned toward the horizon, where a cluster of dark clouds had gathered. "There's rain coming." It would have made more sense to simply leave the containers out. Evidently that was more clutter than the Orchids could tolerate.

A second guard, Orange Boot, encouraged them to move along, toward, Faller assumed, yet another interrogation. The Orchids kept thinking of new questions, yet felt no compunction to answer any themselves. Most pointedly, Snakebite had repeatedly asked whether they would eventually be allowed to leave, or should consider themselves prisoners, and, of more immediate concern, when they would be fed. It had been two days since they'd last eaten, though they had been given water.

They passed through a new, slightly more bombed-out part of town that had already been cleared and scrubbed clean. The buildings left standing were taller than in other areas, and more elaborate. They didn't look like stores, exactly, but definitely weren't homes.

As they passed a tall, broken first-floor window, Faller spotted figures in beds. "Hang on." He stepped closer. "What *is* that?"

"The dying center," Purple Brick said matter-of-factly.

"The *dying* center?" Penny asked, eyes wide. "What the heck is a dying center?"

"Can we see?" Storm asked.

Purple Brick shrugged. "If you want."

"No they *can't*," Orange Boot countered. Or maybe it was one of the other guards. Faller couldn't see her patch.

"Why not?" Purple Brick asked.

"Because it's none of their business."

Purple Brick rolled her eyes and motioned them inside as Orange Boot went on arguing, asking Purple Brick who exactly put her in charge.

The beds inside were evenly spaced, set in a perfect rectangle, and filled with emaciated Orchids.

"Jesus." Penny went to the closest bed, bent over the gaunt woman lying there, her breath coming in a harsh rattle.

"What's wrong with them?" Melissa asked the Orchid watching over the dying women.

The woman shrugged. "Nothing's wrong with them. They're too weak to work, so they're starving."

"Well, why don't you *feed* them?" Storm asked.

The caregiver frowned, looked at Storm like she was slightly deranged. "They didn't earn it, and they didn't win it, so they don't get it. If we handed out food to everyone whenever they wanted it, we'd *all* starve."

Faller had to admit, there was a logic working there. Of course where he came from, food went to whichever tribes could get it, whether through murder, intimidation, theft, or alliance. There had to be better ways to decide who lived and died. Seeing them lying there with their meatless arms and sunken cheeks, these old, old young women sent a knife through his heart.

"How do *we* earn food?" Storm asked.

"I don't know," the caregiver said.

Storm turned to Purple Brick, eyebrows raised in a silent question. Purple Brick shrugged. "Ask the women in charge, when you see them."

From what Faller could tell, there were about a dozen women in charge, with a dozen others trying to push their way into the mix. It reminded him of chasing Melissa through the hall of mirrors, only this wasn't an illusion.

They needed to get away from this place. Seeing how they treated each other, Faller had little doubt they'd shoot him and his friends, or let them waste away until they were in one of these beds. But even if they could get hold of their parachutes and get to the edge, they needed to replenish their food and water supply first.

"We've got a long walk," Purple Brick said. She led them outside into a light drizzle.

Storm fell into step beside Faller. "I'm starting to get a bad feeling about this."

This would be their third meeting with the Orchid intelligentsia since they'd arrived.

"Me, too," Faller said.

The lead guard headed up a steep flight of stairs set into a hill.

"Based on what I know of Orchid—the woman who—" He caught himself. He was about to say he thought he understood how their minds worked, because he knew the woman whom they'd been made from. That was like saying he could understand Storm by watching Melissa, and he didn't think Storm would appreciate that assertion.

"It's okay." Evidently Storm had seen where he'd been going.

They reached the top of the stairs, followed a brown brick path between two wide, identical three-story buildings with evenly spaced windows. The one on the right was heavily damaged, the one on the left, untouched. Beyond them a dozen similar brown brick buildings were scattered in the open, weedy space.

"How are you doing?" he asked Storm. "Any better, now that you're back on solid ground, and had some time?"

"To be honest, I'm too hungry and scared to think much about it."

They were led to the base of a tall building that was mostly intact. Actually it was more like a tower than a building, narrow and windowless, with a pointed crown and a clock set below three slatted openings near the top. The Council of Orchids was waiting at the base.

"We want you to show us," one of them said.

"More than happy to." Faller accepted the pack from one of the council members. The tower must have been the tallest structure on their world.

The interior was nothing but a winding staircase that left him rubber-kneed as he reached the top. There, he knelt and prepared the chute, checking and double-checking the clasps before refolding it and strapping the pack to his back.

Everyone was looking up as he took two quick steps and leaped out of the tower. The chute deployed perfectly; he floated toward the ground, treated to a view of the city spread out below the hill, and clear sky beyond the edge.

Faller flinched as a familiar *bang* lit the air. Shouts erupted and people ran, most heading into the tower, a few Orchids running in the opposite direction. Suddenly Faller's progress felt glacially slow. He was a perfect target, dangling below the chute.

One of the Orchids fell as Faller scanned the landscape for the attackers. He spotted two, in a second-story window of the building they'd passed. He couldn't be certain from this distance, but they looked like Orchids.

Faller jolted after each shot, expecting to be hit at any second. Three of the Orchids lay injured or dead in the courtyard. He looked for his people, saw Snakebite inside the base of the tower as he finally touched ground. Immediately, he dropped flat on the pavement, allowing the chute to cover him as the gunfire continued. He slithered across the bricks in the direction of the tower, hoping the chute would make him a harder target. No one was shooting at him, though; the assailants seemed to be targeting his captors.

Suddenly the parachute was gliding over him, being pulled away.

"Hurry." It was Storm. She led him inside the tower, where twenty people huddled away from the doorway.

"We don't want to be shot, either," Snakebite shouted at the Orchids by the stairs, his jaw rippling with anger. "We're pinned down. They can burn us out, or pick us off one by one if we try to leave. Give me my shotgun. I can help." He held out his hand, left it there, fixing the women with a glare that could melt stone.

One of them shoved Snakebite's pack at him. He dropped to one knee, pulled out his shotgun and a handgun, went to the door.

"Cover me," he said to a handful of Orchids standing near the door with pistols drawn. Then he was gone.

Renewed gunfire rang out.

"Cover him, damn it," Penny said.

Two Orchids were already poking out the corners of the doorway, firing at the buildings on either side.

As Snakebite disappeared behind the building on the left, it grew quiet.

"We should have people at the top of the tower," Faller said. "We can't see behind us from this doorway."

"They're on their way up," Purple Brick answered.

Muffled shots coughed somewhere outside. It sounded like Snakebite's shotgun. Faller scanned the rise up to the building, watched for movement through the windows, but it was impossible to see inside from their angle.

"*There,*" Purple Brick shouted. Snakebite appeared from around the front of the building, his shotgun trained on two unarmed Orchids walking ahead of him.

Armed Orchids poured out of the tower, raced toward the trio.

"Get his gun," someone behind Faller shouted.

Some of the guards took control of the captives, while others trained their pistols on Snakebite.

"Drop the shotgun."

Snakebite's mouth dropped open. "You're kidding me, right?"

They raised their guns higher. "Put it down."

Snakebite flung the shotgun at the nearest woman in disgust; she lifted her foot to avoid being hit. "You're welcome. There are two bodies in the building as well. I'm sure you'll want to clear them out and scrub the blood from the floor."

"I don't understand," Faller said, "why were they shooting at you?"

It seemed as if no one was going to answer.

"They're insurgents," Purple Brick finally said. One of the other Orchids gave her a look. Purple Brick stared her down, gestured at Snakebite. "He just risked his life while we stood with our tails between our legs. I think they deserve to know." She turned back to Faller. "A group that wasn't happy with the status quo attempted a coup. When it failed, they ran."

Which explained why everyone carried a gun.

"Let's go," Orange Boot said. "In the morning we'll put a noose around their necks."

For an instant, Faller thought she meant his and his friends' necks, then realized she was talking about the insurgents. But he suspected their turn would be coming soon.

XXI

HARRY PUSHED the box of Dunkin' Donuts down the table to Peter. He took a chocolate one, slid them across to Kathleen. "Kathleen, hold up a cue card, let me see how they look," Peter said, squinting under the bright camera lights.

"How long is this message?" Roberto Sanchez asked. Peter still hadn't gotten over his surprise that Roberto Sanchez had flown down personally for this interview. Likely thanks to Kathleen's powers of persuasion.

Kathleen swallowed a doughnut. "Don't worry. Under five minutes, then you're free to ask any follow-ups you like."

Peter looked at Melissa, sitting off to the side, hands in her lap. Having her and Kathleen here felt a lot like sunshine on his face. He hadn't realized it, but part of the strain of working in the lab nonstop had been seeing the same five faces, day after day. Having someone new join them had given him a boost; that one of those people was Melissa felt like a miracle.

Sanchez got into position; the cameraman counted down with his fingers, pointed at Sanchez. After a brief introduction, Sanchez turned it over to Peter. He began reading the statement off the cue cards.

This was a risk. They weren't giving away the precise nature of this "new, revolutionary, limitless energy source" that would be free to all, but each side's brightest minds would be able to make some decent guesses. If they could get all sides to agree to a cease-fire, even a slowdown in the ever-escalating aggression, it would be worth it.

As he neared the end of the statement, he looked at Melissa, who gave him a tight, encouraging smile.

"We're on the brink of a new era that will render this terrible war pointless," Peter read. "We're not asking any party on either side of the conflict to make concessions. All we ask for is ten days. Just ten days to prove that these are not hollow promises."

Sanchez followed up with thirty minutes of questions. He all but accused Peter of treason, pressed him repeatedly to reveal the nature of the power source, and reminded viewers that he faced charges of murdering the "real" Peter Sandoval. It took all of Peter's willpower to suppress an urge to tell Sanchez to go fuck himself.

40

SNAKEBITE AND Storm were in a corner of the room, speaking in low tones. From the snippets he caught, they were exchanging Day One stories, just as Faller and his tribe had done every so often, sitting around a fire. He remembered Daisy, legs pulled up to her chin, her face so serious as she described coming awake in a classroom, huddled together with twenty other children and one adult man.

God, he missed her.

Penny was in her corner, meditating, her two hands forming a cup at her abdomen, eyes closed.

Melissa was sitting on one of the beds, her legs crossed inside her filthy white dress, head back.

"What was that story you were acting out on your world?" Faller asked. "Just from the snippet I saw, it was much better than anything I ever saw on my world."

The question amused Melissa. "It was a bastardization of a play by a man named Shakespeare. Once upon a time, I wanted to be an actress, and I figured now was my chance, since no one else remembered any plays and I did. You could only get away with ripping off Shakespeare on a world where everyone's memory had been wiped."

Despite the splendid mattresses the Orchids had provided, they'd all waked before sunrise, likely because they were hungry.

"Melissa?" Snakebite said. "Do you recognize me from before the fall?"

Melissa gave him a sympathetic look. "I'm sorry. It was a big world back then."

Snakebite shrugged. "Just curious. I'm not sure it makes a difference who we were in that world."

"Given your scars, your fighting ability, there's no doubt about *what* you were. You were a soldier. Probably in one of the elite forces."

"Clearly you were also a master chef," Faller added. "I'll never forget that oatmeal and ham stew you made for us in Penny's apartment."

Snakebite smiled. "I bet you wish you had some now."

"Hang on," Melissa said. "Snakebite, did you find a wallet in your pocket, after your memory was wiped? That might tell us something."

Snakebite dug into his pack, pulled out the worn black wallet and tossed it to Melissa. She pulled out a laminated card, studied it.

"You lived in Bethesda, Maryland. That was a big military town. That's probably where your children are." She dug into the center compartment, pulled out more cards, and a folded piece of yellow paper. "Ah, here we go." She smoothed the paper on the bed. "Your name is Robert Harjo. You were on leave, to visit your dying mother." Melissa looked up from the paper. "I'll bet you anything that's why you were in that town. Your mother lived there."

Snakebite's eyes were unblinking, wide with interest. "Bethesda, Maryland. It's a start. Thank you." He turned toward Penny. "Penny? What about you? Did you have anything in your pockets on the first day that Melissa could read?"

Penny shook her head without shifting position. "I was wearing a dress. No pockets."

The locks on the door clicked open. A contingent of Orchids motioned them out. They were led to what had once been an ornate building, with a dry fountain outside, moldy burgundy carpeting on the floor of what had been the inside. Remnants of two walls remained, but that was it—nothing of the roof remained but a single naked support beam. A few badly beaten wheels and tables stood in the otherwise clean and empty space, plus some colorful, boxy machines.

Casino, Faller's little voice said.

Twin ropes dangled from the support beam, nooses already tied. One of the prisoners cried out and began to struggle when she saw the nooses. The other just stared.

The prisoners were led to one of the tables, where a wheel lay inside a bowl. A hundred other Orchids closed the space around them, trying to see.

"Roulette," Snakebite said to no one in particular. That struck a chord with Faller's little voice.

An Orchid whose name must have been Black Bird, based on her patch, pointed at the prisoner on her left, the calm one. "What number?"

"Twenty-eight," she answered, her voice a shaky mess.

Black Bird pointed at the other prisoner, who only shook her head.

"It's a chance, at least," Black Bird said. "You'd rather have no chance at all?"

"I can't choose." The woman was so breathless with fear she could barely speak. "I can't."

"Okay," Black Bird said. "I'll choose for you. Your number is zero."

She gripped the wheel and sent it spinning, then flipped the steel ball along the wall of the bowl, heading in the opposite direction.

Everyone watched, silent, mesmerized, as the ball slowed, dropped onto the wheel, and clattered for a moment before sticking in the hole above the number 3. Two spaces away from zero.

Everyone began chattering at once.

"Oh, well." Black Bird struggled to be heard over the din. "Bad luck." She gestured at the makeshift gallows. "String them up."

Three Orchids had to drag the skittish prisoner to her noose, while the other walked under her own power.

The nooses were tightened around their slender throats. Without word or ceremony, a line of Orchids picked up the slack end of each rope and walked it away from the gallows.

The prisoners jerked into the air, legs kicking frantically, their faces turning purple, until they were a dozen feet above the casino floor. The ropes were tied off on the brass pipe that ran along the foot of a bar.

The woman on the left stopped kicking first, followed shortly by the woman on the right. They hung limp, their eyes bulging, swaying gently at the end of their ropes, canted for some reason at a slight angle from the floor.

All of Faller's companions were looking away from the scene, even Snakebite. Suddenly Faller felt ashamed for watching, although he'd taken no pleasure in it. He looked away.

This was insanity, these exact copies of a woman living on the other side of the sky fighting each other to the death, over nothing.

Faller looked up at the dead women. It was strange, how they were hanging at an angle to the ground, as if pulled by some invisible force. Others in the crowd seemed to notice as well. Murmurs rose from the crowd.

Faller reset his feet. He felt unsteady; he definitely wasn't feeling well.

"What's going on?" Storm asked. "Do you see that? It's like they're being *pulled*."

To Faller's right, Penny grasped Snakebite's forearm, as if to steady herself. Were the hanged women canted at a slightly more extreme angle than before? It could have been his imagination, but it looked as if they were.

Faller looked to his left, and had the most peculiar sensation: the *ground* seemed off. It was as if it weren't the hanging women that were angled, but the ground.

"Faller, Snakebite," Black Bird said. "Choose a number."

Faller sputtered; fear cut through him like a blade. "We haven't done anything."

Black Bird shrugged. "You're a risk. You can't be trusted. Pick a number."

An Orchid was at his side, pressing a pistol to his temple as his friends screamed protests.

"Pick a number, Faller." Black Bird glanced around, as if noticing the slight tilt of the ground for the first time.

The barrel of the gun pressed harder into Faller's temple. He looked at the table, at the dead women beyond it, hanging at that disturbingly crooked angle. "Twenty-eight."

"Snakebite?" Black Bird said.

"Fuck you all," Snakebite replied, his tone no more hostile than usual.

"Fine," Black Bird snapped. "Faller's number is twenty-eight, Snakebite's is fuck you all."

She spun the wheel, sent the ball flitting around the lip.

It bounced, landed on 3. Three slots from 28.

"Bad luck," Black Bird said over rising murmurs of confusion.

On the roulette table, the steel ball popped from its slot, bounced over the numbers 35 and 12, and settled into 28.

One of the Orchids in the crowd shouted, "What's going on?"

There was no doubt now: the casino floor was tilting. The crowd wasn't perpendicular to the floor; everyone was leaning toward the gallows.

"Does anyone understand what's happening?" Snakebite asked, his voice low. "Melissa?"

"No."

Everything looked off. Was it worse than it had been a moment earlier? Orchids were leaving, staggering away, steadying themselves on whatever they could grasp. Three Orchids hurried past, holding each others' hands, speaking in urgent whispers.

In the street, a wagon piled with bricks rolled past. No one was pulling it. It collided with the curb and tipped, spilling bricks.

There was an unnerving groaning/squealing coming from across the street. The hanged women looked like they were levitating.

"We have to get off of here," Snakebite said. "Find our packs while everyone is preoccupied."

Across the street, a building collapsed with a roar, sending an avalanche of bricks spilling into the street. A cloud of dust and debris rose into the air. Farther in the distance, Faller heard another crash. If the tilting didn't stop soon, all the buildings would come down.

The Orchids were moving in a dozen directions. Snakebite grabbed the arm of an Orchid rushing past, shouting directions and looking important. "Where are our packs?"

She tried to yank her arm free, but failed. When she instead tried to draw her pistol, Storm beat her to it and pointed it at her head.

The Orchid shouted for help. In a heartbeat, a dozen guns were trained on Storm and Snakebite. Storm lowered the pistol; Snakebite released the Orchid's arm.

"Take them back to the lockup." Faller checked the speaker's patch: Yellow Tree.

A few blocks away, another building crumpled.

One of the Orchids holding a gun on Snakebite stepped away, lowered her pistol and hurried off. Seeing this, others followed. Soon there were no pistols trained on them; the casino was emptying, the Orchids fleeing.

"Oh, my God," Melissa said. "They found the map, and now Ugo has the singularity. He's doing this."

"Doing what?" Faller asked. "Making a whole world tilt?"

"Yes."

Faller folded his arms. "A whole world is tilting because of *us*?"

"Because of you. If he found the map, and the singularity, he doesn't need you alive any more. He wants you dead, especially if he doesn't know your memory was wiped. I just don't understand how he knows where we are."

"Why don't we split up and look for the packs?" Storm suggested.

The only places they could think to look were the buildings on the street where most of the Orchids seemed to live, and the big store where they'd held the first meeting.

"We'll check the store." Melissa tugged at Storm's arm, drawing her away. "The three of you check residences."

Storm gave Faller an unreadable look, then took off with Melissa.

Faller's group headed off to find the street with the residences. "Anyone know which way?" Having been led around for the past few days, Faller hadn't paid much attention to directions.

"This way," Penny said. "They were on Lexington."

Faller didn't remember anyone referring to the street as "Lexington," but he followed Penny, since she seemed sure.

It was, mercifully, downhill. Faller ached all over, but ignored the pain, pushing to keep up with Penny and Snakebite. It was a strange sensation, running on streets that were so uniform in their downward tilt. Twice, Penny took a detour to avoid fallen buildings. Soon Faller recognized the façade of a movie theater they'd passed when they first landed.

Orchids were rushing to and fro, wide-eyed and confused, shouting directions at each other. The landscape was badly tilted now; looking up the street was like looking up a steep hill, except the buildings left standing were all leaning toward him, threatening to pull loose from their foundations and tumble down on him.

"Let's each take a building," Snakebite said. "I don't know if they'd be in a closet, or sitting in the open." He wiped sweat from his forehead.

"This seems hopeless," Faller said. "How are we going to find them when we don't even know what building to look in?"

Snakebite looked around, spotted an Orchid coming out of an apartment building. "Hey. Excuse me." He ran over to her, fell into step beside her as she hurried up the sidewalk. If she was armed, her pistol was hidden. Maybe she'd forgotten it in her rush to get out of the building.

Faller eyed the row of seven or eight intact buildings. He did not relish the thought of going inside them.

"This is just fucked up," Penny said. "What if it just keeps tilting? Everything will come sliding down on us."

Movement drew Faller's attention. Down the street, the theater was tipping. It fell silently until it hit the building beside it. When the second building was hit, it tumbled over like a domino, spewing wood and concrete as it landed on the roof of the squat row of bomb-damaged stores beside it.

Snakebite ran back toward them, his gait awkward and uneven as he moved perpendicular to the slant. "These two, if they're anywhere." He pointed to the two apartment buildings on the end of the row.

The end apartment building peeled off from the one beside it.

"*Look out,*" Snakebite shouted to an Orchid hurrying along the walk beside the building. It was too late; she had time to look up, raised her hands as the building crashed down on her. Faller couldn't help but imagine Storm's face, not Orchid's, on the woman. He wished Melissa hadn't separated them.

"Shit. Oh, shit. We have to get off of this thing," Penny said.

A *crack* caught their attention. A tree growing alongside the road had fallen, crushing a van, its upper branches burying a truck parked across the street.

"We have to find cover." Snakebite looked around. "Something solid that protects us from falling objects."

Faller looked around as well. Nowhere looked safe. From near and far, the crack and boom of falling buildings filled the air, mixed with screams. Down and across the street, there was a block where most of the buildings were gone, leaving nothing but a row of foundations cleaned out by the Orchids. From his vantage point he could see that one foundation was sunken, where there had once been a basement.

"Down there." He pointed. "That basement."

"I see it," Penny said. "Let's go."

It was no longer possible to run full-out—the drop was too steep. Instead they half ran, half skipped to a concrete basement about a dozen feet deep, completely empty thanks to the fastidiousness of the Orchids. There were concrete steps leading down. Faller felt better—safer—as soon as he was standing on that sunken floor.

A crash got their attention. A semi, trailer and all, was tumbling down the hill at them.

"Look out," Faller shouted, his words drowned by the deafening rattle of steel as it slammed over them.

Faller ducked.

The steel trailer banged to an abrupt halt, three feet above his head.

"Is everyone all right?" Snakebite called from nearby.

Penny shouted that she was all right. Faller crawled toward the high wall of the basement, the wall of steel rising, giving his head more clearance, as he went. One end of the trailer had wedged in the basement against the far wall; the other was still aboveground, creating a lean-to.

Penny ducked into the space, looked up. "Perfect."

They hunkered down with their backs against the wall, waiting, with no plan beyond avoiding being crushed. The foundation was so severely tilted that when Faller propped his feet flat on the concrete, his knees were parallel to his hips.

Something crashed into the semitrailer. Faller jumped as blocks of concrete rained down on either side of their makeshift lean-to. He hoped Storm was safe, maybe waiting at an edge, ready to jump. He had to admit, it was an unlikely scenario. If the world didn't stop tipping, he couldn't imagine a way out of this for any of them without their parachutes.

A shriek snapped him back to the present. Ducking low, Faller crawled out from under the trailer, with Snakebite and Penny at his heels. The stairs were blocked by rubble, but he managed to climb up the side of the partially crushed semitrailer and jump to the wildly tilted ground beside the cab of the semi.

There were three Orchids lying in the street. Two were motionless, the third was trying to push herself up, but her legs looked like they'd been broken, or crushed. A fourth was still on her feet, clinging to a light post. The angle was so severe now that if she stumbled and fell, she'd tumble down the street until she slammed into something.

Up the street, a tree fell, releasing a yellow school bus that had been wedged against it. It toppled down the street, ricocheting off the remnants of a store, bearing down on the Orchid. Seeing it was coming right at her, she dropped down on all fours and scrabbled sideways, trying to get out of the way.

"This way," Faller called. The Orchid ran for them. She looked like she was running on a wall; her momentum would have plunged her straight into the rubble-filled basement if Penny and Snakebite hadn't grabbed her from either side as she flew by.

As they led her into their shelter, Faller took one last look around, hoping to spot some other survivor, willing Storm and Melissa to appear from behind a building. Debris crashed down from above, an avalanche building steam. It was an awesome and terrifying sight.

Faller jumped onto the semitrailer, then vaulted to the basement floor and ducked beneath the trailer. It wasn't going to stop, he realized. And if this was the work of Ugo Woolcoff, then he'd underestimated how much hatred he could create in the heart of another human being. Could this really be about him? It was hard to believe. He *couldn't* believe it, actually. For some reason Melissa wanted him to go to his grave believing he was responsible for all the death in the world, but he wouldn't. No one would tip a world just to kill him.

"I'll be right back." Snakebite disappeared from under the trailer.

A moment later he was back carrying seat belts, cut from the truck cab. Snakebite cut the buckle off a seat belt with a knife he must have had strapped on him, slid it behind a pipe running along the base of the wall, then lashed it around the Orchid. He repeated this on each of them until they were all attached to the wall.

There was nothing to do but wait, and hope the world stopped tilting. Faller looked at his companions. Penny was clinging to Snakebite.

"I'm sorry, Penny," Faller said. "I'm sorry you got tangled in this mess."

"No, I got myself tangled." Tears welled in her eyes. "I should have stayed out of it."

"Stayed out of what?"

Penny shook her head. "It doesn't matter now." She looked up at their low steel roof. "He knows I'm here. He doesn't care."

Faller frowned, trying to follow. "Who doesn't care?"

Penny buried her face in Snakebite's shoulder. Snakebite put his arm around her.

A wave of affection for Snakebite washed over Faller. He raised his hand to Snakebite, who saw the gesture, and raised his in return.

The wall was now as much ceiling as wall, the floor as much wall as floor. Outside, some tipping point was reached, and the sound of things falling escalated until it sounded like it was raining bricks, trees, cars, and people.

The seat belt around Faller's waist tightened as he slid down the floor as far as his tether would allow. The trailer groaned.

It lifted free, and toppled out of their basement. Suddenly steel and shadows were replaced by bright blue sky.

Tentatively, the Orchid turned to Faller and wrapped her arms around him. Maybe it was seeing Penny and Snakebite, maybe just an instinctive need to seek comfort at the end of the world. Faller put an arm around her shoulder.

They drew their legs in toward the wall as steel, wood, and stone dropped from overhead, some of it landing just beyond their sheltered space and rolling to the far end. Much of it hit the mountain of junk piled against the far wall and bounced back out.

If not for the belts they would have toppled down the wall of this world with the rest of the things that had been on it.

"What's happening?" the Orchid asked. "Do any of you understand this?"

"Not really," Faller said. "Our friend thought an evil scientist tipped your world to try to kill us, but I think that's unlikely." He thought of Melissa, silently cursed her for pulling Storm away. He wanted to say good-bye to her, to tell her he loved her, that he didn't care if she was a copy of someone else.

Soon they were hanging from their straps with the sky below their feet.

Nearby, an Orchid fell from whatever she'd been clinging to. She plunged, screaming. There were other people falling as well, scattered among the trucks and trees and detritus. It occurred to Faller that Storm was probably down there somewhere. If he went headfirst the whole way, arms pressed to his sides, he might catch her, and they could at least die together.

"I'm going to cut loose." Now that he'd thought it through, he could feel Storm getting farther away with each passing moment.

Penny looked at Snakebite, who nodded.

"You're not serious," the Orchid said, eyeing the endless sky below.

"You're welcome to come with us," Faller said.

"I don't understand. Why would you do that? The world might still right itself. If you fall, there's no hope."

"Even if it does," Faller said gently, "there'll be nothing left. We'd all starve."

The Orchid clutched his shoulder. "Please don't leave me here alone."

Faller reached out, brushed the back of his fingers against her cheek. "I'm sorry. Come with us."

He nodded to Snakebite, who pressed the knife against the seat belt above Faller's head and, with one quick motion, sent him plummeting.

Below, the sky was filled with chunks of buildings, vehicles, rocks, and thrashing, screaming Orchids. Some were still clinging to broken pieces of their world.

Faller rotated until he was diving headfirst, pressed his arms to his sides and willed himself to fall faster. Storm was down there somewhere.

41

WHEN IT became clear the two specks he'd been tracking weren't just float-ers in his eye, Faller's heart soared. There were two of them, two tiny *X*s in a cloudless blue sky. They could have been Orchids, but Faller was sure they weren't. They were Melissas, arms and legs stretched to slow their descent, hoping Faller and the others would catch up. Faller spun to find Snakebite and Penny, who were falling side by side, and pointed emphatically.

Snakebite gave him a thumbs-up.

Faller repositioned himself in a headfirst dive, and closed the gap.

As he drew closer, his heart started beating slow and hard. Each of them was clutching something. He tried not to get his hopes up; it might be food or water, although that wouldn't make much sense if they were going to die anyway. They looked like packs. Faller squinted, straining to see, battling the wind that blurred his vision.

They were black, they had straps. He inched closer, willing himself to see what was actually there, not what he wanted to see.

Storm was looking up at him. She was wearing a pack on her back, and was clutching two more, one in each hand.

· · · · ·

FALLER HELD Storm, her long hair snapping against his face.

"If this doesn't prove we're meant to be together," he shouted, "I don't know what would."

Below them, and off just beyond the edge of the debris field, Faller noticed a silver-grey object that was growing larger as they dropped. Faller squinted, trying to see what it was.

He pointed. "Look at that." It was clearer now. It was shaped like a cross, or a bird, but larger.

"An airplane," Storm shouted. "My God, it's *flying.*"

They waved their arms over their heads to get the others' attention, then pointed at the object. It was closer now, holding its position as they dropped toward it. Could these be the people who had tipped the Orchids' world, coming to finish them off? If they could fly a plane, they must be powerful. Maybe Melissa had been right. Maybe Ugo Woolcoff really was behind it.

Snakebite was moving toward Faller, waving his arms, screaming something. Faller strained to hear him.

"*Spread out.* As far apart as you can."

Of course. Clumped together, they were an easy target. Faller spread his arms and legs, and glided away from Storm.

The aircraft was closing, heading right at him. The massive machine cruising under its own power was awesome, and horrible. It reminded him of his dream of aircraft shitting bombs.

Overhead, a green car was falling side first. Faller would make a more difficult target if he was hiding behind something. He strained against the buffeting wind, allowed the car to drop to him.

Faller angled alongside it, then lowered his arms to try to match its speed. Reaching out, he grabbed the bumper with one hand. The aircraft was close enough that he could hear the *wheem* of its engines over the howling wind. Faller pulled himself along the car's greasy undercarriage, putting it between him and the aircraft. The *harrier,* his mind offered. Not an airplane, a *harrier.*

It occurred to him that it would be better if he could get *in* the car. Then the Harrier wouldn't have a clear shot at him. Faller hooked his foot under a steel rod connected to one of the wheels and reached until he grabbed the handle of the rear door that was facing downward. Clutching the handle with both hands, he dislodged his foot. His body whipped free, his toes pointing up. Gasping from exertion, he worked his legs into position to brace his feet against the side of the car. He strained, pulling the door open against the force of the wind. Then, feetfirst, he squeezed inside. The buffeting wind slammed the door against his shins, then his knees, then hips as he dragged himself into the backseat.

Panting, he grabbed a seat belt and pulled himself to the center of the seat. The Harrier's engine was deafening. Faller glanced through the side window, then the back, as he fished the handgun out of his pack.

The Harrier rose, filling the car's sideways windshield. It rotated, exposing an open side hatch, where two of his duplicates squatted, huge black rifles raised.

Faller dropped to the floor as rifle fire erupted. The windshield and driver's side window shattered as bullets *thunked* into the body of the car.

The firing stopped. Faller leaped up, aimed out the shattered windshield. The two gunmen had retreated out of sight.

Faller waited, gun trained on the open hatch, finger on the trigger. Both the car Faller was in and the Harrier were rocking and shuddering, making it difficult to keep the gun aimed anywhere close to his target.

Snakebite appeared below the Harrier, spread-eagled, allowing the Harrier to drop toward him. Relief washed over Faller as Snakebite clutched the bottom of the aircraft's front end and hung on.

Faller kept his gun trained on the open doors as Snakebite looped something—the seat belt from the truck, Faller realized—through a catch beneath the front of the Harrier, then lashed it around his ankle. Snakebite pulled it tight, then let go.

The wind whipped him upright, so he was staring straight in through the front windshield of the Harrier. Snakebite raised his handgun, fired point-blank, calmly squeezing off shot after shot. The windshield cracked.

Movement in the doorway caught Faller's attention. One of the gunmen leaned out, clinging to something inside the Harrier, and trained his rifle on Snakebite.

"Look out," Faller shouted. He fired at his look-alike, his shots flying wild as his look-alike's assault rifle roared to life.

Snakebite was jolted backward by the force of the bullets.

The shooter ducked back into the Harrier as Faller, screaming, clambered over the seat, pushed himself out through the car's windshield.

As blood whipped off his body, forming a spiral of red mist above, Snakebite lifted his gun and fired. The canopy shattered. Snakebite fired three more shots.

The Harrier spun out of control.

Faller glided toward it, arms outstretched, as Snakebite whipped around, still strapped to the Harrier's nose.

His look-alikes appeared in the doorway. One pushed off, leaping from the Harrier. The wind kicked him into a spin; he pinwheeled his arms, trying to right himself, unaccustomed to falling. Faller clutched his handgun with both hands, fired three shots, but the wind made it impossible to aim.

The second look-alike jumped out. As he flew outward from the careening Harrier, the tail swung around and hit him squarely in the face. Faller didn't need to watch further to know he was dead.

Faller had drawn to within fifty feet of the other duplicate, who'd finally stabilized and was falling feetfirst. Drifting headfirst toward him, Faller raised his handgun, tried to take aim as his duplicate pointed the assault rifle at him.

The muzzle of the rifle jerked upward as the rifle's kick threw his duplicate into a backspin. Moving ever closer, Faller missed four more times as his duplicate repositioned himself and again raised the rifle.

Something splashed into Faller's eyes, blinding him. Burning agony in his shoulder came a heartbeat later, and Faller realized it was blood in his eyes. Gasping in pain, he wiped his eyes with his good arm.

His duplicate was struggling to get into position to fire again, his eyes trained on Faller so intently he didn't notice Storm below him, closing fast. She was falling faceup, her arms and legs spread. When she'd closed to within just a few dozen feet, she raised her gun and fired.

Storm didn't stop firing until she plowed right into him. By that time he was dead, his blood spraying upward in sheets.

Careful to avoid the swinging tail of the pilotless harrier, they headed toward Snakebite, who was limp, his arms flapping in the wind.

Faller wrapped his arms around Snakebite from behind. When he saw Snakebite's eyes—open, sightless—Faller pressed his face into Snakebite's back and screamed. He cried on his friend's big shoulder.

Fingers touched the back of Faller's neck. He lifted his head and, ignoring the pain in his shoulder, reached out to wrap one arm around Storm, who was clinging to the seat belt holding Snakebite to the Harrier.

"He's gone," Faller said.

Storm pressed her face close to Faller's as they clung to Snakebite.

"I just want to keep falling," Faller said. "I don't want to land anymore."

Storm nodded. She lifted her head, stared at Faller's shoulder, her red-rimmed eyes widening. "Is that your blood? Are you shot?" She looked around; Melissa and Penny were nowhere in sight. "We have to get you help; we have to stop the bleeding." She reached up to where the seat belt was tied to the Harrier, tried to pry it loose.

"His left leg," Faller said. "There's a knife."

Storm strained, pulled up Snakebite's pant leg, unsheathed the hunting knife and cut the seat belt. With Snakebite between them they pushed off the nose of the Harrier and got clear of it.

"*Faller?*" Storm's cry seemed to come from far off. He opened his eyes, realized he'd blacked out. He grasped the webbing of Snakebite's suit with his good arm, pulled himself closer.

"We have to let him go," Storm said.

"Unzip his pack," Faller said. He had his bad arm tucked close to his body.

Storm unzipped Snakebite's pack a few inches. Wrapping his legs around Snakebite, Faller felt around inside the pack until his fingers brushed the photos, tucked in an inner pocket. Faller slid them into his own pocket, against the photo of him and Melissa.

"I'll find them." He choked up, felt his tears whipped from his eyes before they could reach his cheeks. "I promise I will. And when I do I'll keep them safe. Like they were my own."

"We both will," Storm said.

They unstrapped Snakebite's backpack, then let him go.

XXII

"Dr. Sandoval?" Paula Tankersly, his head of security, stood under the archway between the factory floor and the main passageway. "You have a visitor. We've detained him outside."

"Who is it?" Peter asked.

"He wouldn't say. Big guy, early forties. Accent."

Peter found Ugo standing just outside the door to the lab, facing away, hands in his pockets, straddled by two security people. His Panama hat was gone, replaced by a snappy maroon U.S. Army beret to go along with a black and army-green dress uniform. Ugo turned when the outer door opened.

"There's a face I never expected to see again," Peter said.

"This isn't a social call. With so many lives at stake, we can't always choose who we speak to."

"I can't argue with that." Peter's thoughts were spinning, trying to anticipate what Ugo could want. Certainly it had to do with their plea for a cease-fire. They were responding quickly; the interview had aired on MSNBC two hours earlier.

"Shall we walk?"

Peter shrugged. "I could use some air." He turned to Paula. "We're fine."

"Impressive setup," Ugo said, nodding slowly, hands behind his back as they walked. "You've got your own little army."

"And you've got a big one."

Ugo laughed. "I'm *part* of a big one. The people in charge sent me. They caught your TV appearance."

"And?"

Ugo held out his hands, looked toward the sky. *"Unlimited energy forever?* Come on, Peter. Or should I call you Peter the Second? That's quite a claim."

They wanted to know what it was. They were dying to know. Of course they were. "We can back up our claim in ten days, if the rest of you can keep from destroying the planet for that long."

"No one's going to destroy the planet."

Peter slowed, studied Ugo's crooked profile. He knew that smug tone well. "Why is that?"

Ugo tilted his head, lifted one shoulder toward his ear. "You have your secrets, I have mine."

To their right, a huge smokestack rose out of the yellow weeds; beyond it three rusting tanker cars sat on a dead-end strip of railroad track.

"Only your secret's not so secret," Peter said. "Right now it's ravaging Singapore and Indonesia."

"Ravaging." Ugo waved a dismissive hand. "No one's dying. They're not even getting sniffles or sore throats."

"It's wiping their memories."

Ugo glanced at Peter. "Tough to fight when you can't remember who you're fighting, or why."

Peter stopped walking. After taking a few more paces, Ugo stopped as well. "Singapore is an ally. You can't use the virus because it's too difficult to control. If you released it on Russia, South America, and North Korea, eighty percent of our own people would end up contracting it."

Ugo smiled. "That would end the war, though."

Peter laughed dryly.

Ugo wasn't laughing; he was looking at Peter, eyebrows raised.

"Wait. You're not seriously considering releasing that virus on a large scale?"

He gaped at Peter as if Peter were being incredibly dense. "Why wouldn't we be? If the war goes on much longer, someone is going to start launching nuclear weapons. Maybe North Korea, maybe India. China would be my dark horse–pick. As soon as someone goes down that path, there's going to be retaliation. How many will die then?" His eyes were wide, the vein on his forehead bulging. "How many more will die when the radiation drifts to neighboring countries? The blackout virus stops it *now.*" Ugo chopped his palm for emphasis.

"What if the virus is too efficient? What if it wipes *everyone's* memory?"

Ugo shook his head. "Central command will wait out the infection in an airtight underground facility."

"I take it you're part of central command."

Ugo didn't respond. They were planning to wipe everyone's memory, ally and enemy alike. Intentionally.

Out of nowhere, Peter had a flash of memory: he and Ugo, sprawled on couches in Ugo's living room watching *The Usual Suspects*, drunk on Ugo's cognac, stuffed with pizza delivered from Chanello's. How had they possibly gotten from that moment to this?

"Give me ten days, then all parties can sit down and negotiate a permanent armistice." He wished Melissa and Kathleen were here to help reason with Ugo.

"Where is this boundless energy?" He made a show of squinting and peering toward the lab. "In there? What are we going to do, put a chorus line of salmon through your duplicator and run the world on fish oil?"

It was possible Ugo was bluffing, trying to force Peter to show his hand. The thing was, Ugo didn't sound like he was bluffing. He sounded like he was convinced his plan was better than the alternative.

Removing the singularity from the equation, he might even be right.

"Come on," Peter said.

· · · ·

THE LOOK on Ugo's face as Peter led him to the window on the containment chamber was gratifying. His smugness, his air of importance, melted away, and left a little boy staring openmouthed at a miracle.

"What is that?" he said, once he'd regained some of his composure.

"It's exactly what it looks like. A singularity." Peter spread his hands, mocking the gesture Ugo had made outside. "*Boundless, unlimited energy,* right here in my lab." Peter couldn't remember the last time he'd enjoyed a moment this much. Ugo had been so proud of his little virus. "I'm on the verge of transporting energy to nanostructured carbon fuel cells all over the world. The energy will just keep flowing; the fuel cells will be inexhaustible."

Ugo went on staring into the chamber. "Where did the singularity come from?"

Peter laughed. "Trade secret."

His nose almost pressed to the glass, Ugo grunted.

"Can you get Elba to agree to the cease-fire?" Peter asked.

"Now, why would I do that?" Ugo stepped away from the glass and folded his arms across his chest. "So you can close your eyes and poke at some buttons and hope this *singularity* responds the way you're hoping it will?"

Harry was crossing the floor to join them. Peter waved for him to stay away.

"This is the equivalent of how many nuclear warheads?" Ugo asked. "A thousand? A *million*? And you're screwing around with it, lighting light bulbs." He gestured at the wall of spotlights. "You don't need ten days. You need ten years, of careful, controlled experimentation." Ugo spun, headed for the exit. "And you don't have ten years, so if I can help it, you're not going to get ten minutes."

"Oh, I see. That's how you're going to rationalize it to yourself. I have a solution that doesn't involve you becoming a god. One of the supreme rulers of the lobotomized masses." Peter took a few steps toward Ugo's swiftly retreating form. "You're a sociopath. What you're planning is no different from genocide."

Ugo stopped, spun, pointed at Peter. "What you're planning *is* genocide. You're a loose cannon. You always have been." He disappeared through the doorway.

Peter called Kathleen, asked her to return to the lab, immediately. They were out of time.

42

SOMEONE WAS slapping his cheek. "Faller. Wake up. You have to drink."

Faller peeled one eye open as the canteen was pressed to his lips. He took a few swallows, pushed the canteen away.

"How long have we been falling?" He'd been drifting in and out of consciousness for what felt like a long time.

"Three days."

His shoulder was bandaged with white strips—from Melissa's dress, he assumed. The strips were mottled with dried blood, none of it fresh as far as he could tell. His shoulder was aching worse than the day before, and he felt so exhausted his eyes kept closing on their own.

Melissa and Penny were nearby. When they saw he was conscious, they came over.

Melissa unwrapped the bandage.

"I don't feel well," Faller said.

"The wound is infected. The bullet is still in there," Melissa said.

Faller spotted a lone figure, falling through the clear blue sky a few hundred yards away. Snakebite.

"Am I going to die?" he asked.

The wind tore the softly spoken word away before it reached Faller, but he could read Melissa's lips.

"*There*," Storm said, pointing straight down.

Faller closed his eyes. He didn't have the strength to look, but he knew what she'd found. He didn't care.

Cries of disappointment cut through the howl of the wind. He pried one eye open, gently rolled on the wind until he could see what was below.

The world was nothing but sand and rock.

"We must have drifted over what's left of the Atlantic Ocean," Melissa said.

"We have to land," Storm said. "Faller can't keep going."

Storm deployed Faller's parachute for him.

Snakebite plummeted past, down into the endless sky.

. . . .

FALLER KEPT his gaze on Storm, tried to muster the strength to tell her he loved her. Storm pressed the back of her hand to his forehead.

"He's burning up."

Penny tapped Storm on the shoulder. "Get out of the way."

Startled, Storm looked up at her. "What?"

"I said, get out of the way." Penny tugged her baggy pants down to her knees, exposing white panties, and what looked to be a rough brown bandage wrapped around one thigh, only the bandage was bulky, bulging in places.

"What *is* that?" Storm asked.

"It's a fucking medical kit," Penny said. *"And you don't deserve it, goddamnit."* She shouted this at Faller. Faller couldn't understand why Penny was angry at him. She peeled a strip of Velcro from around the kit and unrolled it beside Faller.

Melissa knelt, slid a vial out of a pouch and examined the label.

"Give me that." Penny plucked the vial out of Melissa's hand.

"Morphine? Jesus, do you have antibiotics?" Melissa asked. "Why didn't you tell us you had this?"

Faller watched as Penny straightened his bent arm and injected something into the crook of his elbow with a remarkably bright, tiny syringe. Then she pulled something thin and silver from the pouch.

"A *scalpel*?" Melissa said.

Penny paused to give Melissa a look. "Would you prefer I leave the bullet in?" She turned her attention back to Faller. "I gave him a dose of morphine, but I don't have anything to knock him out completely, so you two will have to hold him still. This will hurt even with the morphine." She gave Faller a cold look. "I'm tempted to make it hurt more than it needs to."

"How the hell do you know how to get a bullet out of someone?" Storm asked.

Penny drew another vial from her pouch, shook red liquid into her palm and rubbed it all over her hands. "I'm a doctor. A psychiatrist. I don't have much surgical training, but extracting a bullet isn't exactly brain surgery."

"You *did* recognize me." Faller's tongue felt slow and thick. The medicine she'd injected into his elbow was sending a warm flush through his body, right down to his toes. "That's why you fell off your bike."

"Oh, I recognized you all right." She tossed the bandages aside, picked up the scalpel, looked at Storm and Melissa. "Hold him down."

Faller's eyes flew wide as fresh pain cut through the warm haze of the drug. The urge to pull away was almost irresistible. He squeezed his eyes shut, ground his teeth, and tried to hold still.

It took only a few minutes, but it seemed like an eternity. While Penny was packing the wound, Faller fell asleep.

43

SHOUTS WOKE him. It was pouring. Storm, Melissa, and Penny were shouting, encouraging the rain to keep falling.

Faller was afraid to move. He felt as if he'd been beaten by a mob with pipes, dragged up and down a flight of steps, then stomped with combat boots.

It occurred to him that he should open his mouth, catch some of the rain.

Penny interrupted the celebration. "He's awake."

Storm appeared with a canteen. She bent, poured water into his mouth, which absorbed right into his lips and cheeks, none of it reaching his throat. The next dollop allowed him to swallow.

Penny watched, hovering in the background. She had a medical kit. Even more astonishing, she'd known how to use it. She'd also been furious at Faller for no apparent reason.

"What happened?" Everyone was blurry, because the rain was in his eyes. He felt too weak to raise his arm to clear them.

"Penny is a spy." Melissa pushed her soaking-wet hair away from her face.

"I'm not a *spy*," Penny said. "I'm a *psychiatrist*. I was doing research. Monitoring the effects of the blackout virus."

"The *effects*?" Melissa took a step toward Penny as if she were going to take a swing at her. "The *effects* are a billion people dead."

"I didn't release the fucking virus," Penny shot back, "so get out of my face. And the blackout virus wasn't responsible for most of those deaths. Peter's little black hole had something to do with it as well."

That diffused some of Melissa's anger. "We wouldn't have had to rush to deploy the singularity if that asshole Ugo hadn't been about to lobotomize the world's population. How did *you* avoid infection, by the way?"

"Peter's *what*?" Faller gasped. "I thought you said I was Peter?" He was so confused. Penny was a spy?

Penny pointed at him. "Yes. You're Peter." There was no mistaking the heat in her eyes. "How am I supposed to hate you when you don't even remember what you did?"

"What *I* did?"

The rain eased, shifting from a torrent to a steady drizzle.

"You want to find the person who did this?" Penny squatted, rifled through her pack. She held a small round mirror to Faller's face. "There. There he is. Tell him what a son of a bitch he is."

"You're out of your mind," Faller croaked. He pushed the mirror away and looked at Melissa, who stared at the ground.

"Melissa's been lying since you met her," Penny said. "*You* did this. You're the greatest mass murderer in history, and you don't even know it."

"You are so full of shit," Melissa said. "I was there, right in the middle of it—"

"Oh, I know you were," Penny said.

"Elba and her people are the murderers. *Ugo* is a murderer. Not Peter."

"I'm not a murderer." He wanted to say more in his defense, but he was still so weak.

"You're right. You're not," Penny said. "Ugo Woolcoff turned you into an innocent." She turned away. "That's why I couldn't sit back and watch you die."

Peter looked at Storm, who was squatting beside him, knowing she didn't have any answers. At least she was someone like him, someone from the world he knew, the world that had begun on Day One. Storm reached out, stroked his good shoulder. The tenderness of the gesture brought a lump to his throat.

"We were born on Day One," Storm said, speaking softly. "You, me. Snakebite. This has nothing to do with us."

Faller wished he could believe that. He'd done this? He'd torn the entire world into pieces? *Him?*

"Oh, and don't worry too much about Storm being a duplicate of Melissa,"

Penny said. "You're a duplicate, too. You murdered the original Peter San-doval and took his place."

He looked to Melissa.

"Peter was dying. Ugo intentionally infected him with a disease," Melissa said. "It was Peter's idea, not yours."

There was no way Faller would ever understand this world he had lived in. He felt like he'd been hit with a brick. He, personally, had created a machine that ruined the entire world?

"Is anything you told me true?"

Melissa sat on the ground beside Storm. Her dress, which had been so clean and white when he'd first set eyes on her, was filthy, and ragged at the knee where she'd torn strips to make bandages for him. "I didn't want to burden you with this. In your case the blackout virus was a mercy."

"That's for sure," Penny said.

Melissa shot her a warning glance. "The broad strokes of what I told you were true. I left out the part you played."

"The broad strokes," Faller repeated. He thought of the early days, after Day One. He'd been a nobody, not even worth killing. If they'd known, he would have been the first one tossed over the edge.

"Penny's the reason the assassins were able to locate us on her world, and on the one we just left," Storm said. "She's been communicating with them using a machine. A walkie-talkie."

"They don't know where we are now, though," Penny said. "They probably think we're dead."

"Why didn't you tell them where we are, now that we have nowhere to hide?" Faller asked.

Penny looked at him like he was the dimmest of insects. "When I told Ugo they'd taken your parachute and you had no way to escape, I thought he was going to send more assassins. Instead he tried out his shiny new toy—your singularity—and killed hundreds of innocent people. He thought it would kill *me* as well." She looked from one of them to the next. "*You're* supposed to be the ruthless ones."

"Evidently he also killed the original me, so you shouldn't be *too* surprised," Faller said.

Penny shook her head. "I've never heard that before. I'm not sure I believe it."

Melissa laughed bitterly. "Fine. Go on living in your hermetically sealed fantasy world." She folded her arms. "You never explained how you avoided the blackout virus. How *did* you get chosen to be one of the lucky few?"

"My father worked in the Department of Defense, under General Holland."

Melissa sighed heavily, rolled her eyes.

"Don't look at me like that. The rest of my family had their memories wiped. Three brothers, my grandparents, aunts, uncles, cousins. I got in because I had skills they needed." She looked at Faller. "Two of my brothers died before we could get to them. Plus my grandparents, and an uncle." She looked around, spotted her medical kit, pulled out a small bottle and fished a blue oval pill from it. She set it on her tongue. "Xanax. I've been sneaking them since this started. I was scheduled for pickup in two weeks."

"Then why did you come with us?" Faller asked.

"Because Peter Sandoval showed up, and they told me to stick close to him. Believe me, going down that slide was the bravest thing I've ever done. You have no idea."

"You said a few thousand people weren't exposed to the virus. Where are they?" Melissa asked.

"Some are on the base world with Elba—a piece of Andrews Air Force Base, near D.C. Others are with Woolcoff, at Peter's lab in Williamsburg. The rest are spread all over, trying to establish order on strategically important islands, or they're intelligence-gathering." She shook her head. "For the most part, it's chaos. There's no power, no food."

"Except now they have the singularity," Melissa said, "and all the notes and recordings in Peter's lab to understand how to use it. They'll establish themselves as the leaders of the world, make it over in their swinging dick image."

His notes. His lab. It was still hard for Faller to grasp.

"You came from Ugo's world?" Storm asked Penny.

Penny nodded. "After the apocalypse Ugo quietly shuttled people to some of the nearby islands for reconnaissance, and to keep an eye out for Peter, you, Harry Wong, the others who might know where the singularity was, or how to make another."

"With the other power sources gone the singularity is more valuable than ever." Melissa looked for a relatively clean spot on her sleeve, used it to wipe rain off her face. "Now he has it, thanks to me."

XXIII

PETER AND Harry were waiting outside when Kathleen and Melissa barreled onto the lawn in Kathleen's Lexus, skidding to a stop half a dozen feet away.

Talking with rapid-fire speed, Peter filled them in on Ugo's visit. When he got to the part about wiping the memories of everyone on Earth, save for a small cadre that would become the de facto rulers of the planet, Melissa cut him off.

"No way. There is no way Ugo would be complicit in this. He was bluffing to get you to show him the singularity."

"Melissa, he tried to kill me," Peter said. "Or *did* kill me, depending on your—"

"This is different."

"Not from where I sit, it isn't," Peter shot back. He pointed at his temple. "The man is a nut. A psychopath."

Harry held up his hands. "Come on, let's not argue. We have to decide what to do."

"If they really are planning to release this blackout virus, knowing the singularity exists is going to accelerate their timetable," Kathleen said. "But they're military. They're going to have a strategy meeting before they act. We have a day, maybe two."

"I'd need *five* of me to get everything done in a day," Peter said. "Most of it only I or Harry can do."

Kathleen tapped her lip, thinking. "Then we'll make five of you."

It took Peter a second to understand what she meant. He held up both hands. "No way, Kathleen. I'm not going down that road."

"Not just you. All of us," Kathleen said. Down at her side the index finger of her right hand looped and swirled, writing out the crucial words as she spoke them.

"Come on, Kathleen," Harry said, but Kathleen ignored him. She touched Melissa's shoulder.

"Melissa and I will sound the alarm on Elba's plan, try to stop it before it's implemented. Actually, we could use a hundred of us for that." She laughed delightedly at the thought. Peter thought she sounded slightly deranged, and wondered if the pressure was getting to her.

"Kathleen, no. That's an insane idea. We're not duplicating ourselves."

Kathleen shoved Peter in the chest, hard, with both hands. "*Wake up.* The world as we know it is about to end. We have to do *everything* we can to stop it. If that means jumping through the fucking duplicator, we jump through the fucking duplicator."

Peter looked to Melissa for help.

Melissa took a deep breath. "If you really think Ugo is going to do this, then I agree with Kathleen. But I hope to God he's not playing you."

"He's not."

"Then let's go." Melissa pointed toward the lab.

. . . .

"WAKE UP, Peter." Someone was slapping his face.

Peter groaned, lifted his hand to ward off the light but exceedingly annoying blows.

"Peter? Time to wake up." It was Kathleen.

Not far away, Harry was saying, "Peter, wake up."

Peter pried one eye open. Kathleen was leaning over him, her face very close. "There you are."

Everything came flying back to him. He opened his eyes wide, tried to shake off the grogginess of the anesthetic. Kathleen helped him sit up on the gurney. Peter looked around, noting that he was on the left, on the side where the original comes out. So he was the original, or, at least, the original duplicate, rather than a duplicate of the duplicate. It didn't matter, really, but somehow it felt important to know this.

The other Peter stood, limped over woozily. He stuck out his hand. Peter shook it.

"This is just too bizarre," the other Peter said. "You want to head to the lab while I go through again? Seems only fair, since evidently I'm the copy."

"That's okay," Peter said. "You go ahead to the lab." He wanted to be there when his friends went through, although again, it made no real difference that it was him and not his duplicate.

· · · ·

"WAKE UP, Peter," Peter said as he slapped his fifth duplicate's face, while Kathleen tried to wake his fourth duplicate, who had gone through to produce the sixth. His fifth duplicate opened his eyes, groaned, closed them again. "Come on, Peter, we don't have time."

· · · ·

KATHLEEN ADMINISTERED the injection of methohexital to another Kathleen as a third Kathleen waited to help lift her into the iris. The Kathleen giving the injection looked up at Peter. "You might as well get busy. I'm going to make of lot of me, send them off on various missions as they come out."

The Harrys and Melissas were already gone; Kathleen was right, there was no need for him to linger, save for a feeling that the duplicator was his baby, and he should watch over it while it was being used.

"Remember when I asked if you could turn D.C. into a crater, if you wanted?" the other Kathleen asked him.

"Sure."

"It might come to that. We have to power up the fuel cells first, but if it looks as if Elba and Ugo are going ahead with their memory-wipe plan, we may be forced to take them out."

Peter looked out through the big window, at the lawn, the crumbling brick remains of the building across the way. Two security people—one of them Paula—were standing on the lawn with their arms folded, talking. "We've done some trials. I'm fairly sure I can use the singularity as a weapon, if necessary."

She lifted the now unconscious Kathleen's legs while the Kathleen who'd spoken first took her arms.

"The problem is verifiability," Peter said. "The blackout virus has something like a twenty-four-hour incubation period. They could release it and we wouldn't know for a full day." He dragged his hand through his hair. "For all we know they've already released it."

Outside, Paula sank to one knee. Her companion grasped her arm, said something. He lunged for his rifle just as the side of his face exploded.

"*Soldiers,*" Peter screamed. "Everyone downstairs." More of his security forces appeared. The tatter of automatic rifle fire erupted, muffled through the glass. *"Downstairs."*

Through the glass door Peter spotted Melissa—one of the Melissas, anyway—in the lab's business office, on the phone. He threw open the door. "Soldiers attacking. Downstairs."

Melissa dropped the phone and ran.

They raced through the long hall, down the dimly lit stairs, through the locker room. Peter had no doubt these were Elba's troops, sent to seize the singularity, probably with orders to take Peter alive. In all likelihood they were elite troops—Special Forces. His security people had no chance against them.

As they rounded a corner three of his security people passed, running in the other direction.

"Hang on," Peter called.

They paused. One of them, a small, stocky man, said, "We need to get up there—"

"No," Peter said. "They're Special Forces. Get on the radio and tell your people to get downstairs, *below* the level of the off-limits factory floor. It's very important they're below." He continued toward the factory floor. Releasing a burst of energy into the air from the singularity was simpler than directing it into fuel cells. It should take him no longer than sixty seconds to set it up.

"Peter? What's going on?" Harry was heading toward them, from the direction of the factory floor.

"We're under attack," Peter shouted. "Get everyone down in the subbasement below the factory floor."

With Kathleen at his heels, Peter raced through the doorway, onto the factory floor. He screamed, "Everyone downstairs." The Peters and Harrys sprang into action, helping to corral the few who weren't duplicates down the stairwell, which was half blocked by rotting plaster and concrete from the partially collapsed roof.

Peter turned to Kathleen. "Go on. I can do this myself."

She ignored him. Peter didn't have time to argue. He grabbed the laptop that was interfaced to the singularity and set to work creating the algorithm that would release several hundred joules of energy—enough to kill, but hopefully not bring the building down on top of them.

"Shouldn't we seal that big door?" Kathleen asked.

"No. I can't send energy through it, and they'll just blast it open," Peter said. "Come on, press right up against the containment chamber."

The faintest patter came from the hall. Peter typed frantically, stabbing the keys.

Louder footfalls, someone running, breathless. A series of soft pops, like champagne corks loosed from bottles.

Harry burst into the room, stumbled toward them. *"Peter."* He landed facedown, ten feet from Peter. There were three bullet wounds in his back.

"Harry," Peter screamed.

He and Kathleen dragged Harry close to the containment chamber as soldiers stormed in, automatic rifles raised, pressing close to the walls.

"Hands on your head," the soldier closest to the door shouted, his face shaded by the brim of his helmet.

Tensing, expecting to hear more muffled gunshots any second, Peter reached out to the laptop sitting on the floor beside him, and sent the algorithm to the singularity.

The soldiers exploded.

There was no blinding flash, no indication of the energy coursing through the air, only soldiers bursting like water balloons, becoming nothing.

Peter felt droplets of liquefied warrior strike his face and arms as he turned to Harry. Each of Harry's breaths brought a sharp squeal. He was bleeding from his mouth, his eyes unfocused.

"Oh, Jesus, Harry. What did they do?" Peter lifted Harry's head and slid it into his lap, wondering if he was the real Harry, or one of the duplicates. He hated himself for thinking that it mattered.

"I'm okay," Harry said. "Just need one of the doctors to take a look." He was lying in a pool of blood. Peter could feel it seeping through his jeans.

Kathleen was on the phone. "No one's answering. No one's answering nine-one-one." It wasn't surprising, really. The U.S. Government had just been overthrown.

The sharp squeal of Harry's breathing went silent as they were carrying him up the steps to the lab, and daylight.

44

WHEN FALLER woke, he was falling. Storm was beside him, her hair tied in a tight bun to keep it from snapping in the wind. When she saw he was awake, she handed him a canteen. His hand trembling, he drained what little was in it, then turned away, chose a direction that was relatively private, and relieved himself. His urine, which was a dark yellow, whisked off into the air. Through practice he'd grown adept at avoiding the spray.

Storm angled in close when he finished. "We've passed three worlds so far. All of them are barren. We're trying to glide back to where we were, but we don't know which direction that is."

Faller nodded. He didn't have any suggestions. If Melissa, who remembered everything, didn't know which way to go, he certainly didn't.

Now that he'd had a chance to rest, he felt as if he had a better grasp of the situation. This man, Ugo Woolcoff, had murdered him, taken his and everyone else's past away, forced his hand in causing this apocalypse (as Penny called it), and stolen this thing he had created. The first way he made use of it was to tip a world, killing everyone on it. Then he'd killed Snakebite.

That was why Peter had used his last lucid moments to draw that map: he was crying out to Faller to get this singularity before Ugo and this General Elba did. Ugo was a lunatic. He'd turned the world into an awful place, and seemed intent on making it even worse.

If Faller had been able to create this singularity, this thing that could upend worlds, surely he could figure out a way to get it back. Then he would learn how to use it to fix the damage he'd done.

He took Storm's hand. "Let's go talk to Penny."

"Hang on." Storm got her attention, waved her over.

"How can I get to him?" he asked Penny.

"Hang on," Penny said. "I may have saved your life, but if you think I'm going to help you, you're wrong."

"Ugo killed those people. He tried to kill you. Do you think he should be allowed to rule the worlds? And this thing he took—this singularity. Couldn't we use it to help all of these people who don't know what's going on?" It was difficult to speak loud enough to be heard, with the howling wind, and so little strength.

"You killed people, too. You killed my brothers, my grandparents, so many people I can't even begin to list them. What makes *you* qualified to rule the world?"

"Wait a minute," Storm said. "Maybe Faller was a bad guy back then, I don't know. But he isn't the same person now. You said that yourself. You can trust him. You know you can."

Penny considered Storm's words. "It's a moot point anyway. Ugo has an army. His world has unlimited power now. Faller would be doing Ugo a favor if he went there."

If only he'd understood who Ugo Woolcoff was, back on Snakebite's world. One way or another, this would have ended there.

"Can you get Woolcoff to come to us?" Faller asked. "He came once before."

Penny shook her head. "He thought you were defenseless, and he was eager to find the singularity. Now he has it, and he knows you're armed and have allies. If I told him you were still alive, and where you are, he *might* send another Harrier full of assassins after you, but that's all."

That was the last thing they needed.

He allowed himself to drift away from Penny and Storm. He needed time alone in the sky to think. There didn't seem to be many good options. Run and hide seemed their best bet.

If they knew the assassins were coming they could set up an ambush. They had Snakebite's shotgun, plus three handguns. But what good would that do? Woolcoff could make more assassins—as many as he wanted.

It was remarkable, how little difference there was between Faller and these assassins. Penny said they were made from a Peter whose memory had been wiped by the virus as well. If not for what he had seen and done in the past few hundred days, and what they had seen and done, they would all be exactly alike, inside and out.

"Wait a minute," Faller said aloud.

45

WHEN MELISSA called it a coral reef, his inner word supplier agreed. It was a jagged and twisty wall that formed an L-shape on two sides of them. Lying in the crook of that *L* gave Faller an uneasy, claustrophobic feel. It was the ideal place for an ambush, though.

Penny swept her dark hair out of her face with a trembling hand. She was more anxious than he, if that was possible.

"Remember back on your world, when those assassins had us pinned down in your apartment?"

"Yeah?" Penny said.

"Why didn't you just shoot me and run to them?"

Penny shook her head vigorously. "I couldn't shoot a dog, let alone a person. No matter how much I thought they deserved to die. Plus, I didn't have a gun."

"What about the people we're about to kill?"

Her eyes clouded. "Don't make me have second thoughts about this. I'm still not sure which side I should be on. Neither, probably. I should just walk away. But I want to see it end, and you and Storm have me convinced this is our best chance of reaching that point."

Penny's walkie-talkie—a paper-thin steel rectangle, started flashing.

"They're coming." Penny raised her hand, signaling to the others. Faller lay flat on his stomach and feigned unconsciousness. As far as the bad guys knew, he was in the late stages of something called sepsis, and Snakebite and Melissa were dead.

What seemed a hellishly long time later, Penny called, *"Here."* Faller heard the thump of boots. He hoped the coral formations between Faller and his attackers would shield him from their gunfire long enough for this to work.

Storm and Melissa opened fire. Faller rose, pistol ready.

Three Fallers were charging, pistols flashing. Two others had stopped and were firing at Storm and Melissa. Three were already down. Faller kept his head low, not allowing them a clear shot. He squeezed off shots at his duplicates, trying to remember what Snakebite had taught him during the rare peaceful moments they'd had, but all of his shots went wide, or high, or something. Part of the problem was he couldn't raise his left arm, so he had to shoot one-handed after using two in practice.

"Jesus. I don't like this," Penny cried out as she fired from a few feet away. "I don't like this."

Faller tried aiming lower, fired again. A bloody hole materialized in the chest of one of the look-alikes, and he went down. Faller let out an involuntary grunt of surprise, felt a stinging pain in his own chest. He'd killed someone. He wondered if it would have felt more or less terrible if the person didn't look like him.

The final two duplicates were almost on top of them when Penny shot one in the face. His jaw exploded, leaving nothing below his upper teeth.

Storm and Melissa appeared from behind cover on the far side of the coral canyon.

"Drop your fucking weapon," Melissa shouted.

The survivor's pistol dropped to the sand. Some of his comrades were writhing in pain on the moonscape; the rest were dead.

Storm covered the sole survivor as Melissa approached one of the wounded, who raised his hand. "Wait. Please."

Melissa shot him, point-blank. Her expression a tight mask, she strode to another wounded Faller. Another shot rang out. Faller wondered how she felt, shooting duplicates of her ex-husband.

"I still think this is a terrible idea," Melissa said to Faller as she joined them. "You have *no idea* what you're doing. Everyone in Ugo's stronghold is going to be armed. They have video surveillance, a fleet of Harriers, tanks. You can't just waltz in there and take the singularity."

Faller spread his arms wide, looked out at the darkening sky. "I made it this far. Evidently I'm a resourceful guy, and I have resourceful allies."

"I don't think you understand the extent of the damage you've suffered," Melissa said. "You're not capable of making an informed decision about this."

"We're disabled, you mean," Storm said. "Handicapped. Those are the right words, aren't they?"

Melissa stared at the sand. "By definition, both of you have suffered severe brain damage."

"Based on that map I drew, I believed I could do this even before I suffered the brain damage," Faller said.

Melissa closed her eyes, as if trying to be patient. "*Listen to me*. I remember what happened, I *know* what's possible and what's not. Let's take the Harrier and run."

"Run where?" Faller asked. "You said yourself, this guy has an army and unlimited power. Eventually his soldiers will take control of every world."

The prisoner was looking from one of them to the other, trying to figure out what was going on.

"Penny," Melissa said, "tell them I'm right."

"She's probably right," Penny said. "We've got transportation now. We could run and hide."

"I don't *want* to run and hide. I'm sick of running and hiding."

Melissa walked off.

Trying to quell his heart, which was still pounding from the ambush, Faller struggled to his feet. He was still weak, still in pain despite Penny's painkillers. He hoped he'd feel better in a few days.

He turned to Penny. "Ready to make the call?"

Penny took a deep breath, nodded. "Here goes." She pulled out her walkie-talkie, moved a few paces away.

"He's dead. Sandoval is dead." She listened for a moment, then laughed. "I know. It's incredible." A pause as she listened again. "A wonderful day for humanity—that's a great way to put it, Dr. Woolcoff."

Faller looked at the sky. He hated this man with an intensity he hadn't realized he was capable of.

"Here's the thing," Penny said into the walkie-talkie. "All of the Peters you sent are dead except the one who got Sandoval. He suffered a gunshot wound to the shoulder. I treated him, but it's going to be a few days before he can fly the Harrier." Pause. "I know. They put up a hell of a fight. They're all dead. Yes." After some additional discussion about how great it was that Faller was dead, Penny signed off.

"That should buy you three or four days," Penny said. "Or it buys us a three- or four-day head start, if we run."

"I'm not running." He was done running from this bastard.

XXIV

PETER SWEPT equipment off a long lab table, and they laid Harry's body on it. Three members of their surviving security forces were outside, rifles leveled, sweeping the area.

"Harry. Oh God, Harry," Melissa cried out when she saw his body.

A moment later, another Melissa rushed into the lab and shouted pretty much the same words.

Harry followed right after her. Looking stunned, dread-soaked, he approached his dead doppelgänger, stopping well shy of the table. "This is too much. I don't think I can take this."

Peter wrapped an arm across his friend's shoulder, gently turned him away. "Just a little more work to do, then we can rest. We'll have a movie marathon, eat popcorn till we're nauseous."

"I'm nauseous now."

"I know. Me, too." He patted Harry's back.

Peter clutched a table as two more Harrys spilled into the lab, along with three Peters, a Melissa, several Kathleens, all led by Paula wielding a rifle. The sight of them made him reel, made him feel as if he might drop through the floor, or float away, at any minute. He squeezed his eyes shut, took a deep breath. He needed to hold it together.

One of the other Peters raised his hands to get people's attention. "We have to get back to work. Keep pushing; we're almost there."

That was all it took. People hurried away in different directions, others huddled to confer.

Peter went to join two other Peters.

"How close are we?" he asked.

"Three hours."

"I hate to toss another complication into this, but I think we should move the singularity out of the lab. Hide it somewhere." Peter was going to go on, explain that even after they powered the cells, Elba and Ugo might come after the singularity again, maybe using the blackout virus, but there was no need. He was effectively talking to himself.

"I'll give you a hand," one of the other Peters said. They hurried off to rig something to transport the singularity. They'd need a vacuum-sealed chamber, and an electromagnetic field. Then they'd need to think of a hiding place.

Out of the corner of his eye, Peter spotted three Kathleens at the duplicator, two of them prepping the third for duplication.

"Kathleen," Peter called. The two who were still conscious looked over. "How many have you made? It's enough."

"Just a few more," one of them called back, her finger twirling in the air, air-writing the words she'd just spoken.

46

THE LOCALS—SIXTEEN of them by Faller's count—watched from the edge of the forest. They were getting bolder in their curiosity, maybe realizing that if the people who'd shown up in a functional Harrier meant them harm, they'd already be dead. Still, they kept their distance.

"Into the wind. Into the wind," his look-alike (who insisted his name was One-Thirty-one—the number on his shirt) said. "Watch your thrust vector."

Faller had allowed his attention to drift, which wasn't a good idea, even if the Harrier did most of the work itself. One-Thirty-one insisted it was still possible to crash the thing.

The Harrier landed with a double thump.

One-Thirty-one nodded, satisfied. "It's still ugly, but it gets the job done. I think you're ready."

Faller hopped down the steps, feeling self-satisfied. Although One-Thirty-one had been stingy with praise (likely because he thought Faller was the devil), Faller thought he'd picked piloting up pretty quickly. Two days, maybe thirty or forty landings, and he was ready to solo, at least for the short, one-way trip he was planning.

He was still surprised how quickly One-Thirty-one had agreed to teach him to fly the Harrier in exchange for his life. One-Thirty-one had claimed it was because he disliked Ugo only slightly less than Faller, and hoped they'd find a way to kill each other. Given that he and One-Thirty-one were basically the same person, Faller hoped that was the reason, not simple cowardice.

"We're set. He says I'm ready," Faller announced to Storm and Melissa, who were waiting by the pond. Faller looked to One-Thirty-one, who nodded.

Melissa rose, pulled the pistol from her belt. "Then let's get this over with and get going." Head down, she approached One-Thirty-one.

One-Thirty-one took a step backward. "Hang on, what are you doing? I did everything you asked."

Storm sprang to her feet. "Wait a minute. What are you doing?"

Melissa kept walking. One-Thirty-one glanced at Faller, looked about to take off for the tree line.

"Hold on—" Faller said.

Storm grabbed Melissa's wrist from behind, yanked her. *"Stop."*

"What?" Melissa said.

"You're not planning on shooting that man, are you?"

"That is my plan, yes."

"No you're not," Storm said.

"Let go of my arm," Melissa said.

"We had an *agreement*," One-Thirty-one said.

Faller rested a hand on One-Thirty-one's shoulder. In a low voice he said, "It's okay."

Penny, who must have slipped off to go to the bathroom, appeared from out of the bushes. She paused, took in the confrontation.

"Put the gun down," Storm said to Melissa.

"We're exactly one world up from Ugo's. If Ugo's people found him, he could tell them everything." Melissa yanked her wrist free. "This is a *war*. Someone has to be the grown-up."

As Melissa turned away, Storm whipped her arm around Melissa's throat, put her in a headlock. "Drop the gun."

Melissa grabbed Storm's wrist, tried to break free. Storm tightened her grip until Melissa gagged. Faller considered intervening. If Storm had been the one in the headlock, he would have, but he thought maybe Melissa had this coming.

Melissa dropped the pistol. Storm stepped on it, then released Melissa, who stumbled, clutching her throat.

"We're not shooting people just because we can," Storm said. "I get it— we're fighting for our lives. Some lines you don't cross, even if you're fighting for your life."

"That sounds just like something I would have said before the war." Melissa was looking at Faller, pain in her eyes.

"Oh, I've seen plenty of people die," Storm said.

"Evidently not enough," Melissa shot back.

47

FALLER EYED the meager supply of food beside the Harrier. After that, they'd have to rely on foraging, or trading with the locals.

"I wish I could go with you," Storm said.

"So do I," Faller said. Actually, he didn't. This was likely to be a one-way trip. He didn't want anyone else to die, least of all Storm.

Penny was holding a sketch she'd made on the back of a piece of paper she'd found in the Harrier. It was a map of Ugo's world. "If you and Melissa do need to parachute in, there aren't many places you can drop without being noticed, even at night. There's a forested area over on this end that would be your best bet." She pointed it out on the map.

"Faller, you're not going to be able to move around unnoticed, after you take credit for killing Peter Sandoval," Penny went on. "Sandoval duplicates are scum in this place, but you're going to be king of scum."

"Sounds delightful. Maybe I won't want to leave."

Penny ignored the crack. "Don't speak to anyone who doesn't speak to you first. Not even me. Once you and I land, I'm going to treat you like a complete stranger. No offense."

"Fair enough."

XXV

WITH *IRON LIVES* howling from the CD player, Peter sped up. He was doing close to a hundred miles per hour, but there were no troopers lying in wait for speeders, so the only risk was an accident.

His mind needed to be focused on the situation at hand, but he kept thinking about Harry. He didn't know how to grieve. He hadn't grieved much for his original self, either, because he hadn't felt *gone*—only moved. The same with Harry, although from the original Harry's perspective, he had in no uncertain terms been shot, suffered, and died.

Lifting his hips, Peter pried his phone from his jeans pocket and dialed Harry's number.

"Hey, Doc."

"How are you holding up?" Peter asked, fighting the feeling that he was speaking to a stranger, an imposter. How ironic that he of all people should feel that way.

Harry's duplicate took a big, huffing breath. "I'm hanging on by my fingernails. This is all so messed up; there are two other mes walking around, and *I'm* not really me. The real me is dead."

"You can't think about it that way."

"How can I not think about it that way? It's true. I'm not me. Me is dead."

"You're you. It's just that there's more than one you now. Try to focus on what you need to do."

"That's what I'm doing. One of the Harrys is already gone, in the Harrier with the original Melissa and Kathleen, so we're shorthanded. Hey, you just walked by! You want to talk to yourself?" Even hanging by his finger-nails, he was still a comedian.

As he headed around a gentle curve, the George Washington Bridge came into view.

"I'll pass. I'm just getting into Manhattan. Tell me I said hi." He discon-nected, wondering if Melissa, Kathleen, and the Harry duplicate got out before the blackout virus hit, if Ugo had released it at all. Peter wondered if *he* got out in time. He'd know soon enough.

The lanes leading out of the city were clogged, while Peter nearly had the incoming lanes to himself. Many were afraid New York was going to get hit again soon, although it was of little importance militarily. Maybe word was getting out that deposed President Aspen was hiding in Manhattan, and they were afraid General Elba was going to bomb it to finish her off. Peter wished Aspen had chosen a hiding place closer to his home; he hated being so far from his friends at this crucial moment.

His phone buzzed, alerting him to an incoming text.

The message read: *I sent you a box of chocolates.* The sender was blocked.

"Oh, no. *Oh, no.*" Peter dialed Harry.

"I just got a text from Ugo. He claims he released the blackout virus."

"Shit. How widely? Did he say?"

"No. At the very least, he's releasing it right at you. The message was personal, meant to let me know I was about to get it. Are you ready to go?"

"Just about," Harry said. "Minutes away."

"As soon as you do it, get everyone out. Cut everyone loose, tell them to run and hide, far and wide. Hopefully some of you can avoid being cap-tured if this doesn't work." If the blackout virus ran its course and Ugo's group took complete control, Peter had no doubt Ugo would come after not just him, but Harry and maybe Kathleen and Melissa as well.

"I have to go. I love you. Tell the other Harrys and Kathleens and Melis-sas I love them, too." Peter disconnected. He was flying down the Henry Hudson Parkway, the river on his right, no one shooting hoops in the parks he passed, no one walking a dog or rollerblading. Everyone was inside, watching the news, or fighting in California, or China, or Saudi Arabia. Or they were dead.

He took the Thirty-ninth Street exit. President Aspen was at U.N. Head-quarters, on Forty-second Street along the East River. Hopefully she'd man-aged to get a television crew inside to air the announcement that the energy supply was in place. Whether that announcement would restore Aspen to power, Peter didn't know.

A wave of longing hit him unexpectedly, for Melissa to be here with him. One of the Melissas. Any of them.

A billion stars exploded outside. Peter hit the brakes.

· · · ·

PETER WAS alone, in black space that wasn't space. It felt as if it were pushing in on him, suffocating him. He was seeing in every direction at once, surrounded by vast, twisting ladders comprised of ink-black spots. The ladders twisted in on themselves, shot off in straight lines to pinpoints. They filled the black, starless void like endless strands of DNA.

· · · ·

HIS BMW thumped over the curb and onto the sidewalk. Peter braked to a stop just in time to avoid slamming into a building.

Back in the direction of the river, people were shouting. Screaming, really. Peter wanted to sit in his car on the sidewalk and try to make sense of what he'd just glimpsed, but it sounded like there were people who needed help. He got out and jogged in the direction of the screams.

Singularities. Those billions of spots he'd glimpsed in that instant had been singularities, strung together in an elaborate fabric.

Passing in and out of the long shadows of high-rises, he crossed Eleventh Avenue, spotted a crowd a block away, on Twelfth, staring out toward the river.

Only as he drew closer, the Hudson wasn't its usual dark grey-green—it was light blue, blending perfectly into the sky. It had to be an illusion; some strange reflection of the sky that camouflaged the water . . . and the shore of New Jersey beyond.

Peter slowed as he drew closer. The people seemed distraught beyond all reason, and the illusion of the powder-blue sky existing where the Hudson should have been only grew stronger. A big, billowy cloud drifted serenely where Hoboken should have been.

He reached the crowd, clumped together a dozen feet from the ragged edge of a seemingly endless drop that began halfway across what had been Twelfth Avenue. There was nothing beyond but sky.

Peter kept walking, through the crowd, over broken chunks of Twelfth Avenue until he'd gone as far as he could without falling.

He looked out at what he'd done.

Then he turned and headed to the right along the drop-off, threading his way past thousands of sobbing, screaming, terrified people. Twice, he stumbled and fell.

Peter picked up a fist-sized chunk of concrete and hurled it over the edge. He watched it plummet. Which was impossible, because he was standing on a chunk of Manhattan that was *not* plummeting. By all rights it should be plummeting.

48

DEAFENING MUSIC filled the cockpit, making it difficult to concentrate. Faller needed to concentrate. His head ached, trying to remember everything his doppelgänger had taught him about flying. It would be a miracle if he was able to land the thing without raising suspicion, or killing himself and Penny. When he was practicing he'd been more relaxed. And there hadn't been loud, shitty music playing.

"Can you turn that off? It's terrible."

Penny killed the music.

"Thank you."

"It's not terrible," Penny said.

"It's terrible."

She folded her brightly tattooed arms. "I happen to know Iron Lives was one of your favorite musical groups before your memory was wiped."

"Then I had terrible taste."

Something smelled bad. He wondered if it was the bodies. Did corpses start to smell after only three days? Probably if you were closed in with them, they did.

"What else do you know about me, apart from my being the biggest mass murderer in history?"

"You were brilliant. You took a razor, sliced open the air, and pulled a god out through the wound."

How lyrical. "But I didn't know the god would do this, when I set it loose?"

Penny shrugged. "Melissa says you didn't. Woolcoff tells everyone you couldn't stand losing, so you unleashed the furies of hell on everyone—your friends as well as your enemies."

If that was true, he was a monster. Of course, all of Penny's information had been filtered through Ugo Woolcoff, who most definitely was a monster.

He took out the walkie-talkie.

"What are you doing?" Penny asked.

"Calling Melissa. I want to understand why I unleashed the furies of hell. I need to practice using this anyway."

Melissa answered immediately.

"How did I end up wrecking the world? I want to understand."

Melissa's voice grew uncharacteristically gentle. "We were trying to stop a war, before Ugo unleashed his blackout virus. You ran out of time, and took your best shot. You're an arrogant asshole, but you're not a psychopath. Far from it. Ugo is the psychopath."

Peter laughed. "I never thought I'd feel grateful to someone for calling me an arrogant asshole."

"Well, you're welcome."

He envied and pitied Melissa for remembering all of this.

"What did I do to make you hate me?"

She tsked. "I don't hate you. I'm angry at you. You were so impulsive. You *are* so impulsive. I guess it's hard to learn from your mistakes if you can't remember them."

"We divorced before I made the big mistake. What did I do? Why did we split?"

When she finally answered, her voice was thick with emotion. "You lied to me."

Faller nodded, then remembered Melissa couldn't see him. "I'm sorry I lied to you, even if I don't know what I lied about."

"You didn't have much choice. It took me a long time to understand that."

They were getting close to their destination. "Can I speak to Storm?" Faller didn't want Storm to think he'd called solely to speak to Melissa.

He could hear Melissa choke up, across all those miles. Her voice got very low—so low he could barely hear her words. "Do you have any idea what it feels like for me, to see the two of you together?"

Her words startled him. "I don't, Melissa. I honestly don't."

"Hold on."

"Melissa, wait."

"Hey." It was Storm.

Faller struggled to compose himself. "I just wanted to hear your voice before I do this."

"It's so strange. I'm talking to you, but you're not here."

"I know. Meanwhile I'm flying in a machine that actually works. I'm not sure if this is better or worse than the world we met in."

"Me, neither."

"This whole plan is probably going to fail. As Melissa points out, I'm a simpleton compared to them."

"You'll figure it out. If you don't, run and hide, and we'll come and get you."

· · · ·

UGO'S WORLD hung a thousand yards below, a mix of smallish buildings, roads, a few wooded areas.

"Well, I'll say good-bye now, because once that hatch opens, I can't speak to you again," Penny said.

Faller reached out, squeezed Penny's hand. "Thank you."

Penny handed him the Harrier's microphone set. "They'll expect you to call in before you land."

He used the voice-responsive feature, as One-Thirty-one had taught him.

"Hello?" Faller said into the mic.

"Who is this?" an annoyed male voice snapped.

"This is One-Thirty-one." Faller tensed, hoping his look-alike hadn't fed him false information about their referring to themselves by number, despite Faller's promise that he'd come back and cut off his feet if he did.

"Well, hero or not, since when is *hello* proper hailing protocol, One-Thirty-one?"

"I'm sorry. I'm not myself since the injury. I hit my head when I went down. I'm experiencing some disorientation and memory loss." Step one of the plan was now implemented. Whenever he appeared ignorant, he would blame it on a head injury.

"Don't worry about it. Given the circumstances, you could probably say anything and get away with it. Holy shit, One-Thirty-one. You got him.

You left here a dupe nobody, but you're coming home a legend. Congratulations, man. Congratulations."

"Thanks." He would have liked to use the guy's name, or number as the case may be, but hadn't thought to ask the real One-Thirty-one what it was.

49

FALLER'S KNEES felt like they might buckle as he carried the corpse dressed in his jumpsuit down the Harrier's stairs, onto an airport runway. Dried blood from the corpse's bullet wounds stained his tan assassin-wear as hundreds of people applauded. About a third of them, packed close together and set apart from the others, looked just like him.

Two men in overalls took the body from Faller. A third confiscated Faller's handgun and patted him down.

Faller recognized Ugo as soon as he stepped forward, grinning, dressed in a shiny uniform. They set the body in Ugo's arms. Clutching the bloodied corpse in one arm, Woolcoff raised his fist in the air. The applause grew deafening. He let the body roll to the tarmac, set his foot on its head as photographers circled.

Faller smiled tightly, straining to keep his burning hatred for this man from showing.

Woolcoff motioned Penny closer. She faked a wide, jubilant smile as the photographers snapped pictures. Faller stood a few steps away, not sure what to do.

"Did he die immediately?" Woolcoff asked, raising his voice as the cameras flashed and the cheers rolled on. When Penny didn't reply, Faller realized Woolcoff must be deigning to speak to him.

"He was wounded. I ran up and shot him point-blank to finish him off."

Woolcoff nodded. "Nice work. I'm sure your comrades will want to honor you with a private ceremony." He raised his voice to the crowd. "The monster is dead."

As cheers rose again, Faller couldn't help noticing how much pleasure Woolcoff derived from them. His expression was somewhere between that of a little boy being praised by his daddy, and the smirk of a bully who's just pushed someone over the edge.

"What should we do with the body?" an old man with a droopy mouth asked Woolcoff.

Woolcoff nudged the body with the toe of his shiny black shoe, then knelt and examined Faller's jumpsuit before grunting and standing. "Put it on ice. We'll take it on tour, display it island by island as we reclaim them."

That was all Faller heard, as his look-alikes crowded around and led him away.

"You got him. I can't believe it," one of them said.

"I can't, either." Faller glanced at the number on the man's sleeve. One-Twenty-eight. He needed to remember who was who.

"It's not just Sandoval's face anymore, it's also the face of the dupe who killed Sandoval."

"That's right." Faller tried to sound enthusiastic.

They filed through a gate in the cyclone fence at one end of the runway, crossed a field and headed down a shady street. A truck rolled past. Faller willed himself to ignore it, as the rest of the Peters were doing. The town wasn't as clean as the clean parts of the Orchid world, but it was cleaner than any other place Faller had seen. More astonishing were the lights glowing inside buildings, the hum of machines coming from all around.

They crossed a remarkably green, perfectly flat lawn that left flecks of moisture on his boots, then headed into one of many redbrick buildings that formed a circle around the lawn. Down a flight of stairs, they filed into a huge gymnasium. Colored lines created geometric patterns on the polished wood floor.

"It's been great associating with you, One-Thirty-one," Peter One-Twenty-eight said.

Faller opened his mouth to ask where One-Twenty-eight was going, but thought better of it. A hand rested on his shoulder; Faller turned to find a bare-torsoed Peter holding out his shirt. Faller accepted the shirt. It had the numeral 1 on the sleeve.

"It's yours, now," the shirtless Peter said solemnly.

"Oh. Okay. Thank you."

The shirtless Peter waited. Faller pulled off the shirt he was wearing, and donned the number one.

Every other Peter in the room pulled off his shirt. It was not exactly an impressive display; each had the same three or four chest hairs, scrawny pecs, and bony shoulders. No one seemed to notice that they were all a bit thicker and better fed than Faller. They exchanged them with each other. The previous wearer of shirt number one pulled on shirt number two. Everyone was moving down a number to make room for him.

"Come on," Peter Two said now. "Let's get your things moved to your new room so you can get some sleep." He flagged down three Peters, all with numbers in the one-thirties and -forties, and told them to move Faller's possessions from his old room to his new one. They sprinted away.

The numbers weren't just to tell the Peters apart, like the patches the Orchids wore on their world. They indicated status. Faller was now Peter One. King of the Peters. King of scum. It would be difficult to slip away, disappear over the edge without anyone noticing, if it came to that. On the other hand, maybe he could use his newfound status to his advantage. Maybe the other hundred and fifty-odd Peters would do what he said. Or maybe he could use his status to get hold of another handgun.

By the time they crossed the quad to another redbrick building, this one divided into small, narrow dorm rooms, Faller's room was ready. He thanked Peter Two, pulled down the shade, and slept.

·· ·· ·

A SHARP knock woke him. His door swung open.

"We're going to be late." It was Peter Two, with others standing behind him.

Faller hopped out of bed, pulled on his shirt, and headed for the door.

Peter Two gave him a peculiar look. "Sorry. I didn't mean to suggest you didn't have time to brush your teeth."

"Oh. Right." Faller headed for the bathroom and closed the door. He'd never brushed his teeth before, but he knew what a toothbrush looked like, and had a vague idea what to do with it.

Waiting outside with Peter Two were Peters Four, Seven, and Eight. Faller did his best to make it look as if he knew which way they were headed while following their lead. Walking in the center of the road, they crossed a bridge with a stream running under it, headed uphill, followed a brick sidewalk to the side entrance of a big four-story building.

The Peters led him into a semicircular classroom filled with built-in desks and chairs, a big screen at the front. They took seats in the front row as a stooped old woman fiddled with the technology at the front of the classroom.

Before long, the woman began to speak, or, more specifically, teach. Everyone seemed to understand what she was saying. Faller couldn't follow a word of it.

"The velocity is L over T, plus or minus Delta over T. What you're doing here is measuring the velocity accurately, but you're measuring it after . . ."

Everyone was writing down the numbers. He tuned the woman out, tried to guess what was going on. Why were they teaching the Peters? Assuming these men had started out understanding as little of this as Faller, they had been learning it for some time if they were able to follow what the teacher was saying.

". . . but you can think of it simply as a vector space with an infinite number of axes . . ."

Faller closed his eyes and mentally repeated this one phrase until he'd committed it to memory. Melissa might know what it was, although the plan was for Faller to hold off contacting his comrades until he was ready to rendezvous, to minimize his risk of being exposed.

· · · ·

AFTER CLASS, Peter Two suggested they go for a hike and get acquainted. It surprised Faller that they wouldn't know each other pretty damned well by now, if they'd lived like this since Day One, but he was happy to do something that would help him get oriented, maybe help him locate the closest edge.

They almost collided as Peter Two abruptly veered to his right. Faller adjusted his step, spotted the opening of a narrow trail through the woods.

A dozen paces later, the road was out of sight. "The single digits are wondering if you'll be making changes to the strategy moving forward," Peter Two said.

The strategy? "No. No major changes," he mumbled.

Number Two clasped him on the shoulder. "I appreciate the vote of confidence." They crossed a shallow stream, single file, using three flat stones. "While you were on your mission, Seventeen and his people have been lobbying hard for more aggressive action." He looked at Faller. "They say we should negotiate from a position of strength, which in their minds means refusing to obey orders until we get concessions. That's beyond risky. It's suicide."

"Mm." Faller tried not to react. They weren't happy. Of course they weren't. How could a bunch of Peters be happy being treated like shit? This was wonderful news.

A plan took shape in Faller's mind. Peter Seventeen and his people were chomping at the bit for decisive action? Faller would have to get to know them better. As Peter One, maybe he could fan the anger burning in his brothers.

XXVI

No ONE bothered him, no one even looked at him as he walked along the hall of the twenty-first story of a luxury high-rise, kicking in doors.

He came to another door where no lights appeared to be on inside. He knocked, then waited.

When no one answered, he knocked harder.

It took a dozen good kicks to break this door in, but no one came to investigate the racket. If they had, Peter would have explained who he was, and how important it was that he get his hands on a telescope.

As it was, he went inside, called out to confirm no one was home, then spotted a telescope by the window. Sitting on a stool beside it, Peter peered into the eyepiece and scanned the endless sky until he found what he was looking for. It was up high, so all he could see was the bottom.

Scanning lower in the sky, he spotted another. This time he could see the top. It was a neighborhood—raised ranch houses, lawns, pools, suburban streets, ending in a ragged, broken edge, as if it had been dug out of the ground by a giant excavator, or yanked like a weed.

There was a six-pack of beer in the refrigerator, still cool if no longer cold. He pulled one, twisted off the cap and drained half of it.

What had he done? People would die. Billions of people, because of him. He drained the rest of the beer, opened a second. As he drank it he wondered if the windows of the apartment were shatterproof, or if he could throw a chair through one and jump out after it.

Given the laws of physics as Peter understood them, this was impossible. Chunks of the Earth's crust couldn't hover in the sky, and the people on those chunks couldn't possibly be alive. The only quasi-rational explanation was that the singularity had completely re-formed their world, given it new properties. In theory, singularities could create universes, so it wasn't impossible.

Peter went back to the window and looked out. It was almost evening, the sky fading from blue to grey.

Gravity was still acting on smaller objects, so it must be working on the large islands hanging in the air. If he assumed that, then some other force was holding the islands aloft. Some force pulling from space?

This piece of Manhattan reminded him of the singularity, hanging suspended between two forces. The other possibility was just that—repulsion. Steepling his hands and pressing them to his mouth, Peter pictured a million tiny islands, locked together because each repelled the others surrounding it. On the subatomic level this was commonplace, given the Pauli exclusion principle: any two electrons with identical properties repelled each other. If those quantum properties now applied to macroscopic objects, or if these chunks of land had some type of charge that made them repel each other, the world outside Peter's window would be possible.

He drained the last of his beer, tossed the bottle onto the spotless ivory carpet. Numb, wondering if his friends were all right, he went to the refrigerator and got a third beer.

What would tomorrow be like, with a million souls living on this island with no power and limited resources?

50

FALLER PRETENDED he was utterly engrossed in eating his lunch—and to some extent he was, because it was damned good, spaghetti and tomato sauce—while eavesdropping on a conversation at the next table.

"Nothing's going to change," Peter Eleven was saying. "We're going to stay filthy in their eyes."

"One? One?"

Faller suddenly remembered that was his name. Someone had called it at least a half-dozen times. Peter Twenty-six was standing at a distance, as if afraid to approach. "Sorry. Hard to get used to the new name. I keep expecting people to call me One-Thirty-one."

Peter Twenty-six smiled a little tightly and nodded. "Defense wants to see you."

"Oh. All right." Who was Defense? If he was going to play the head injury card, now was the time, but if he could avoid it he'd like to. It might raise suspicion, especially if his odd behaviors started piling up. "Seventeen?"

Peter Seventeen looked up, fork hovering above his plate.

"Take a walk with me to Defense?"

"Sure." Peter Seventeen stood eagerly.

Faller gave him an *after you* gesture, and followed him out.

"I asked you to join me because I wanted to talk to you about the strategy."

Peter Seventeen glanced at him. "You know I'm behind you, whatever you decide."

"I don't doubt that. But I know you have your own opinions, and I want to hear them. I'm wondering if maybe we need a bolder plan."

Peter Seventeen laid out his thoughts for open resistance to their low status on Ugo's world. He argued that Ugo was keeping them where they were out of hatred for Sandoval, and always would, that they were smarter and more capable than anyone on this island and shouldn't allow themselves to be treated like scum.

He kept talking as they walked along a brick sidewalk, speaking quickly and passionately, probably seeing it as his one chance to make his case directly to the big kahuna.

If only he knew who he was speaking to.

When a group of nattily dressed people appeared, heading toward them, Peter Seventeen led Faller into the street, giving them a wide berth. Faller waited until they were out of earshot, then asked Peter Seventeen if he thought it was possible to take Ugo out.

Seventeen's eyes got huge. "Don't joke like that."

"I've never been more serious."

"They'd tear us apart and throw us off the edge a piece at a time."

"What if we didn't stick around to be cut into pieces? What if we hijacked Harriers? Ugo's the one who hates us. If he were dead, would the rest of them waste their time chasing us?"

Peter Seventeen looked at the road. "I need some time to digest what you're suggesting. I don't mean to be disrespectful, but it makes me nervous to discuss it, even here." He looked more than nervous—he looked terrified.

"All right. We'll talk more another time."

Looking into the sky, Faller thought of the Orchid world, turning upside down. *He'd* invented the thing that did that, the thing that had the power to tear the whole world apart. If he could do that to stone and sky, he could figure out a way to kill Ugo. Once Ugo was dead, he could see Storm again. They'd figure out a way to help people. He'd like to return to Daisy and the rest of his tribe in a Harrier packed with food, medicine, and power. What an entrance that would be. He grinned, imagining Daisy's and Orchid's expressions when he stepped out of that Harrier.

Peter Seventeen led him down a road flanked by big, squat buildings surrounded by parking lots. It was a warm day, the sun beating on Faller's head. They walked in silence, Peter Seventeen probably mulling what Faller had suggested.

They passed a billboard: a giant picture of Ugo's face, sporting a humble, almost coquettish smile. Peter Seventeen led him through a gate. A guard dressed in fatigues nodded as they passed.

The dozens of buildings beyond the gate were a mix of old, crumbling factory-looking structures, renovated buildings that were shiny new material built on the bones of the old, and a few brand-new glass and steel structures. Peter wanted to ask Peter Seventeen who exactly Defense was, but that would be admitting too much ignorance.

Peter Seventeen led him into the most imposing of the renovated buildings, past a checkpoint guarded by two serious-looking military types, along a hall, down stairs, past a heavy door and into a large room. The room was packed with technology of all sorts, all of it lit and operational. At the far side, a small steel chamber with a thick window stood alone.

Dozens of people sat at stations, including two Peters, one with *B* on his sleeve, the other, *E*. They were sitting side by side wearing goggles, hard at work. Their gloved fingers tapped keys and waved at the air as if there were something there Faller couldn't see.

"Go on," Peter B said without looking up. "Go look at it. You know you want to."

Peter Seventeen headed toward the steel chamber. "I know *I* do." Faller followed, looked over Peter Seventeen's shoulder at a ball of utter blackness. The sight made his balls shrink. The sphere was blacker than he'd known black could be—blacker than the tunnels he and Storm had stumbled through on her world, fleeing people with knives and axes.

He knew what it was immediately.

Defense. It meant *protecting yourself*, but sometimes it meant *military*. The place where the weapons were held.

When they returned, Peter B glanced at the number on Peter Seventeen's sleeve and said, "Wait outside." Without a word, Peter Seventeen spun on his heel and left. Evidently letters trumped numbers in the Peter hierarchy.

Peter B eyed Faller. "Congratulations."

"Thank you."

"Now, since you're the new Number One, listen up."

"All right."

Peter B eyed him suspiciously, as if there might have been a hint of sarcasm in his reply. "You need to keep your people in line. We know they're unhappy with all the classwork. We hear the complaints. Keep them motivated. Just because we've recovered the singularity doesn't mean they can relax. We could always use more of them."

"I see." It made a certain sense: if you have exact copies of the man who created something, teach them what he knew, and they could create it as well.

"A couple of your people are getting way out of hand with the complaining, and *that* guy"—Peter B pointed at the door—"Seventeen, is at the top of the list. If he and the others like him don't settle down, I'm going to wipe them clean."

Faller nodded, trying to appear concerned about Peter Seventeen's bad behavior.

"I'm serious," Peter B went on. "We've got all the B-Virus in the world, and I'm not afraid to use it."

"I don't doubt you," Faller said earnestly. "I'll do everything I can to settle them down."

Peter B seemed satisfied. He moved on, briefing Faller on various mundane aspects of his new position. Being king of the scum wasn't going to be terribly glamorous.

51

A BOTTLE peeking up in the back of the little pantry in his room caught Faller's eye. Pushing boxes and jars aside, he drew out a tall, square bottle made of brown glass, with a black label and white lettering. Unmistakably a booze bottle. Faller had only seen a handful before, but had made a point of remembering what they looked like.

He unscrewed the cap and sniffed, savoring the sharp, acrid scent as he silently thanked the real One-Thirty-one for his foresight. He took a swig, but just a small one. This was something to be savored. The burn in his throat brought back memories of the last time he'd had booze. While hunting for food he and Fish had found a half-bottle of clear stuff in a fiftieth- or sixtieth-floor apartment, under the bed of what had obviously been some teenaged boy's room. Their excitement at the find had fueled enough adrenaline for them to race up the last ten stories to the roof, where they'd passed the bottle until it was empty, then whooped and howled and jumped around like idiots until they fell asleep.

Faller took another drink—a bigger one. That night with Fish the booze had taken away his doubts and fears like nothing ever had; Faller hoped it would do the same tonight.

The more he drank, though, the sadder and lonelier he felt. He kept seeing Snakebite's face, his eyes vacant and unseeing, his hair snapping in the wind. Faller withdrew the slender communicator from its hiding place in his boot, turned it over. He could reach out across all those miles right now, bring Storm here to him, although they'd agreed it was a bad idea for him to contact them until he was ready to leave.

Faller took another drink, then slipped the photo of him and Storm out of his boot as well. In his mind it would always be Storm in the photo. He thought about what Melissa had said, that it hurt her to see them together. He wondered if he would have fallen in love with Melissa if he'd met her first. This was such a complicated situation. All he could do was follow his heart, and his heart said he loved Storm.

Faller pressed the button in the center of the walkie-talkie then moved it to his ear.

"Hi," Melissa said. "What's happened?" Funny how he could tell it was Melissa from just a few words.

"Nothing, really. They're teaching us physics, and I'm now the leader of the Peters."

"Are you *drunk*?"

He lifted the bottle, studied the level of the liquid inside. "Not as drunk as I will be."

"Have you seen Ugo?"

"I saw him. He's a smarmy prick."

Melissa burst out laughing.

"Can I talk to Storm?"

Silence on the line. "That's why you called, isn't it? You're drunk and mooning for your girlfriend."

Another pause.

"Faller?" Storm said.

Faller laughed with delight. It just burst out of him. Yes, he was drunk, and it felt good. "I just had to call, to tell you I love you." He took another swig from the bottle; some of it sloshed out of the corner of his mouth, splashing on One-Thirty-one's standard-issue brown blanket.

He looked up to find Peter Two standing in the doorway, his hand on the doorknob. "Are you out of your mind?"

"I have to go." Faller lowered the walkie-talkie.

Peter Two yanked him off the bed, dragged him down the hall and into the darkness of the quad. "How bad was that head injury? Bad enough to forget the *cameras*?"

"What?" Faller's mouth felt thick and awkward, unable to form words properly.

Peter Two studied him, scowling. "What happened to you out there?" He pressed his hand over his forehead. "Look, if you have something going on with a woman, that's your business. But you just flaunted it in Woolcoff's face. Number One or not, they're going to come after you for it."

Peter Two thought Faller had been talking to a secret lover. But, surveillance cameras? Woolcoff's people had been watching? Faller tried to remember what he'd said to Melissa and Storm. Had there been anything that would give him away?

Nothing he could recall. He'd called Woolcoff a prick, told Storm he loved her, but he hadn't called Melissa by name . . .

A cold dread washed over him.

The photo. He'd taken out the photo of him and Melissa.

He was dead. They were probably on their way. His friends would never reach him in time.

Peter Two's eyes narrowed. "You did it on purpose, didn't you? Your memory can't be *that* far gone. You did it to force us to act."

Faller's racing pulse slowed. He gave Peter Two his best calm, level stare. "That's right."

Peter Two shook his head in wonder, whispered, "You crazy bastard."

"Someone had to wake us up. We can't spend the rest of our lives with our heads bowed, stepping into the gutter to let people pass. I'd rather be dead."

Peter Two considered him with something bordering on awe. "It wasn't luck that you were the one who got Sandoval. You're a leader. A true leader." He nodded. "All right, One, I'm willing to die for a chance to live. Tell me what you want to do."

That was the question. A hundred and fifty unarmed Peters couldn't take on an army. And as soon as the Peters learned who Faller really was, Faller would have no allies at all. All he could possibly hope to accomplish was to take Ugo with him, though even that seemed unlikely. Ugo wasn't going to show his face until Faller was dead.

Peter Two waited for orders.

"I'm going to Defense. Can you get me a gun?" Maybe he could force someone to use the singularity to kill Ugo.

"Come on." Peter Two led Faller away from the campus at a jog, toward a side street, and stopped in front of a small white house. "Wait here." Peter Two paused, added, "You're not the only one with a girlfriend."

It felt as if Peter Two were inside a long time, but that was probably because Faller was so painfully aware of each second ticking by, moving him closer to being found out. Finally, Peter Two came out, pressed close to him, lifted his T-shirt and slid a handgun into his belt.

"Try to convince the men to rise up," Faller said. "I'm going after Ugo." He turned to go, then had an idea. "Hold on."

Peter Two turned back.

"Would you give me your shirt?"

Peter Two pulled his shirt over his head, handed it to Faller, held out his hand to accept Faller's in return.

"We should probably toss this one in the bushes. It might as well have a target drawn on it."

Two shook his head, pulled it on. "It might buy you time."

Faller clapped Peter Two on the shoulder, feeling terrible. If Two survived, he would hate himself for being duped into helping the monster Peter Sandoval. He'd never understand that Faller didn't know Peter Sandoval any better than he did.

As Faller ran toward Defense, he called his friends. Storm answered.

"Everything's gone to shit." He jumped a low stone wall on the edge of the campus. Cutting across the sidewalk, he almost collided with a young couple. "Sorry," he called over his shoulder as he crossed a street, then, into the phone, "If you don't hear from me within two hours, go ahead and jump, see what you can find below this world. Don't waste any more time."

"No. We'll come and get you." She was fighting back sobs.

"It's too late." Faller worked to keep his emotions in check. He needed his air to run. His lungs were already burning, his thighs rubbery, his shoulder wound shrieking from the jostling. The booze made him feel as if he were running on slanted pavement. He cut down a tree-lined side street. "It was a long shot from the start. At least the rest of you will be safe." Surely Ugo wouldn't bother chasing the others once Faller was dead.

A helicopter thumped in the distance. Faller ducked under a tree, leaned on the rough bough to steady himself.

"I shouldn't have let you go. I should have talked you out of it."

"We all would have ended up dead," he said, panting. "You can't fight someone who can flip worlds." The *whupping* of the helicopter faded. Faller ran. A group of four men and women wearing natty suits coming the other way paused as he approached. Faller cut into the street to pass them.

"Slow down, *Peter*," one of the men shouted as Faller passed.

"I'd better go." It was difficult to run holding the phone to his ear. "I love you, Storm. I wish this had turned out differently."

"Don't give up, Faller," Storm shouted. "You sound like you're giving up."

Faller cut up a stairwell between two buildings, pushed past an old woman, mouthed "Sorry," before pushing on. "I'm just being realistic. You know, that wasn't exactly the reply I was hoping for."

"I love you, too," Storm shouted into the phone. "That's why you can't give up. Find a way out. You fell off a fucking world and found a way out of *that*."

"That's true." He'd been lucky, though. He didn't feel lucky now. "I have to go. I'm sorry, but I'm running for my life."

"Run fast, Faller." Storm disconnected.

With each step, his legs responded a little more sluggishly. He was nauseous, dizzy, clutching the handrail like the old woman he'd almost knocked over.

He turned at the sound of gunshots in the distance. Peter Two must have convinced the Peters to join him. Faller wondered if he was still wearing the Number One shirt.

When he reached the road that led to Defense, he ran headlong into a platoon of soldiers heading the other way, lined up single file. Shouts rose from the soldiers. Rifles turned his way.

He raised his hands. "Easy. I'm on your side. I'm on my way to Defense to—" He stammered, not sure what a Two would be going to Defense to do. "For support action. Communication. Those Peters with the guns, I don't know if they've lost their minds, or what."

The commander of the platoon waved his troops past as Faller rambled on.

"Good luck," Faller called. He walked off, keeping his pace brisk but dignified until foliage blocked his view of the soldiers, and vice versa. Then he broke into a run again.

He thought about the armed guard at the gate, the soldiers at the checkpoint inside. He wasn't going to talk his way past them. Someone was going to get on a radio and check his story, even if he came up with something convincing.

Movement in the road ahead caught his eye. More soldiers. Faller looked around for somewhere to hide. A tall cyclone fence ran along one side of the road. Across the street, a squat concrete building sat among mountains of gravel and sand. Big yellow machines—bulldozers, front loaders, steamrollers—lined the back of the lot. He ran through waist-high weeds to the concrete building.

Inside he found the remains of an office. There was a desk, an overturned swivel chair, a shattered computer screen, a bag of golf clubs leaned up in one corner, golf pictures on one wall. Faller pulled the gun from his pants, sat against the wall to one side of the doorway. The gunfire he'd been hearing in the distance had gone silent. Maybe all the Peters who'd risen up were dead. Melissa had said this plan would only lead to more death, and she'd been right. The Peters were people trapped in a bad situation, nothing more. They didn't deserve to die.

The footfalls of the soldiers in the road faded. Faller peered out through the doorway. A spotlight traced a path across the sky before dropping out of sight.

He needed to get moving. He pushed through weeds, wound behind old buildings and over low fences, staying parallel to the road, periodically eyeing the high fence topped with vicious curls of barbed wire on the other side. Either he needed to find a way over or through it, or he had to storm the gates of the compound. Alone, with one gun.

It occurred to him that he didn't even know how much ammunition he had. He paused, knelt in knee-high yellow grass, released the clip as Snake-bite had taught him. It was full. He had that going for him, at least.

From down the road, Faller heard voices. He dropped onto his stomach.

"Check those buildings." Faller recognized the voice immediately, because it was his own. "Fifty-six, did you hear what I said? I want someone stationed every two hundred yards."

"Sorry," Fifty-six said.

Faller heard footsteps to his left, swishing through the grass. He held his breath, stayed perfectly still as a voice called, "Clear," from a dozen feet away.

"All right, let's move."

As the Peters moved on, Faller raised his head ever so slightly. Thirty Peters were heading farther down the road, with Peter One—formerly Peter Two—leading. Peter Fifty-six was fifty yards to Peter's left, standing in the middle of the road, a pistol holstered at his hip.

Faller was royally screwed. Now he couldn't even get across the road, let alone into Defense.

Faller's gaze lingered on a drainage pipe close to the road, on his side. It disappeared under the road.

There we go. The voice in his head was Snakebite's. He could almost see Snakebite squatting beside it, asking, *How are you with closed-in spaces?*

Faller eyed the blackness inside the pipe. He honestly didn't know how he was with closed-in spaces. He belly-crawled through the grass until he reached the opening, then wriggled into the drain, his arms in front of him, his wounded shoulder screaming.

It smelled like a cross between a swamp and a shithouse. Thick goo from the bottom slid down the neckhole in Faller's shirt.

The shoulder made crawling excruciating. He used his feet as much as he could, pushing against the sides of the pipe with his toes, walking himself forward on his elbows.

It grew dark quickly. He couldn't help thinking about how much earth was between him and the road above, and what would happen if this pipe just kept sinking lower, into some underground drainage system. There was no way he could back out—it was too tight.

The pain in his shoulder was blinding. Blinking away a mix of tears and sweat, Faller squinted into the darkness ahead, and realized he could see a circle of dim grey light. Encouraged, he pushed on, his feet churning, scraping the drainpipe, his elbows raw.

The circle of light grew larger, but not much brighter. He looked up, saw the pipe led into a larger, vertical pipe with a ladder set into the side of it. He saw this through the vertical slits of a metal grate.

Reaching forward, he grasped the grate, tried to push it open. It rattled, but held firm.

"Shit."

Faller's heart was hammering wildly.

Hang on. Snakebite's voice again. He imagined Snakebite lifting his torso until it pressed the top of the pipe, fumbling at his belt and pulling out a gun.

Faller couldn't hold himself up on his bad arm, nor could he use it to draw his own gun, so he rolled onto his back in the muck to pull it from his belt.

Aware there was a decent chance the bullet would ricochet right back into his face, Faller pointed the muzzle at the bottom hinge, closed his eyes and fired.

He squeaked like a startled pup at the deafening report, even though he'd been ready for it. The hinge was shredded. He shot out the other one, reached out and pulled open the grate, hoping he was far enough underground that no one had heard the shot.

He surfaced behind an unlit concrete behemoth of a building.

Getting his bearings, Faller ducked around to where he could see the Defense building. It was brightly lit. Through the glass doors Faller could see the guarded checkpoint. They'd be watching for his Number Two shirt. He scraped off some of the filth that streaked his shirt, smeared it across the Two on one shoulder, then the other, obscuring both.

Faller took a few huffing breaths. "You can do this."

He jogged into the open, pushed through the front doors.

"We got him," he shouted, breathless, excited.

The three people in the room—two men and a woman, all dressed in fatigues, lowered their assault rifles, their faces relaxing.

"Where was he?" the woman asked. She looked Faller up and down. "Looks like he put up a fight."

Faller walked right up to the trio, smiling. He raised his gun and kept firing until all of them were dead.

As he retraced the route down to the control room, Faller struggled to keep himself together. They would have shot *him* if they'd had the chance, he told himself, then they would have gleefully paraded his body down the road at the end of a rope.

When he reached the heavy door, he paused again, trying to calm himself. There hadn't been anyone armed in the control center the last time he'd been there, but this time they knew Faller might be on the way.

It was harder to put a big smile on his face this time, but he did his best.

"We got him," he cried out as he hurried in.

Everyone in the room looked up, including two Peters: A and C.

There looked to be only one armed person in the room—a soldier watching a big screen over the shoulder of a woman, his assault rifle propped against the desk nearby. Faller walked over and plucked the rifle away from the desk.

The soldier jerked as if startled awake. He lunged for Faller; Faller took a step back, pointed the handgun at the soldier's chest.

He eyed the big steel door. It was six inches thick, clearly intended to keep unfriendlies out, unless the unfriendlies happened to have a bazooka. This would be simpler if only a few people were locked in with him.

Keeping his back to the door, Faller brandished his pistol at the Peters. "Who here knows how to work the weapons?"

Peter A curled his lip at Faller. "Go to hell, Sandoval."

Faller aimed the pistol at his thigh. "Either answer the question, or I shoot you. You know me. I won't hesitate."

The look Peter A gave him was filled with such contempt, such bald hatred, that Faller had to resist stepping back.

Faller raised the pistol, pointed it at Peter A's forehead. "On the count of three, you're dead."

Peter C rolled his eyes up to meet Faller's. "It's not theoretical physics, Sandoval. All you need is me."

Faller glanced at him. "Fair enough. You two stay. Everyone else, out."

"I said, everyone out," Faller barked, training the gun on the now unarmed soldier.

The room cleared. Never taking his eye off the Peters, Faller swung the heavy door closed and dropped a huge steel bar in place.

"I'm guessing you're no more a fan of Ugo Woolcoff than I am," Faller said to Peter C.

Peter C leaned back in his swivel chair. "Don't try to seek common ground with me, Sandoval. Just tell me what you want, and I'll decide if I'd rather do it or get shot in the head."

"I want you to kill Woolcoff."

Peter C shook his head. "This is a military facility. We deal in weapons of mass destruction. I can't kill one individual from a distance. I don't even know where Woolcoff is right now. For all I know he's standing outside that door."

Faller pounded the table. "I want him *dead*. How do I do it?" He was flying blind; he knew nothing about this place, and he couldn't expect any help from the Peters. He didn't even know what the singularity could do, and the only other weapon he knew about was—

"The last time I was here your colleague, Mr. B, threatened to use the blackout virus on Peter Seventeen."

Again, Peter C shook his head. "Unless you can bring Woolcoff to this room so I can inject him with it, the B-Virus is no help to you." He shrugged. "I could release it, but in a few hours we'd *all* be blanks." He gestured toward the door. "And I mean all. That's a heavy door, but the room isn't airtight. Wipe Woolcoff and you wipe yourself."

Faller leaned against the desk. Wipe himself? The thought of going through Day One all over again made Faller want to shriek. He would forget Snakebite, and falling. He would forget Storm. He didn't want to start again, an empty glass, a little boy lost and confused.

What other option did he have, though? Stay there until he died of thirst?

"What the hell. Let's hit the reset," Faller said.

"Wait," Peter C said. "You're joking, right? You don't really want to—"

"Do it."

Peter C studied him.

"It's the only way you and the rest of the Peters will ever be their equals. We can all be ignorant together."

Peter C laughed dryly. "I don't want to be equal that badly."

Faller suspected it wasn't quite that simple. "Is it because you hate me too much to give me what I want, even if it will make both me and Ugo suffer?"

Peter C leaned back, drew a sack from under the console. Faller snatched it from him.

"My lunch," Peter C said. "I'm hungry."

Faller looked inside, then handed it back. Peter C drew out an egg, cracked it on the desk, began peeling off the shell. "At this point I hate both of you about equally." He looked to Peter A. "Would you say that's accurate?"

Peter A waggled his hand. "Sandoval still a little more."

"Then send us both back to the Stone Age."

Peter C took a bite of his egg.

"Was your memory wiped?" Faller asked.

Peter C shook his head. "The copy of Peter that I'm a copy of had *his* memory wiped."

"Then you remember how terrible it is, to wake up after it happens." Faller shrugged. "I'm asking you to inflict that on Ugo and me both."

Peter C finished his egg. "And myself."

"If you waste much more of my time," Faller said, doing his best Snakebite imitation, "you can do it using the one finger I'm going to leave you." He slung the rifle over his shoulder. Still holding the handgun in his good hand, he propped his foot on a chair, withdrew Snakebite's knife, which was sheathed against his calf.

It looked as if Peter C had some difficulty swallowing the last bit of egg with Faller and his knife so close.

The console buzzed. Peter A checked it. "It's Woolcoff." He tapped a key and Woolcoff's image appeared on the screen mounted on the wall. "You think you're pretty damned clever, don't you?"

"Evidently I'm the smartest person alive." Faller glanced at the Peters. "Although now I guess it's a hundred-and-fifty-way tie."

Woolcoff leaned closer to the screen. "'Evidently.' So I really did get you with the virus. I didn't realize until I found the map you drew."

"It got me. But it didn't stop me."

Woolcoff folded his arms. "And what are you going to do now, Mr. Genius?"

"I'm working on it."

Woolcoff grunted. "I could bolt the door from the outside and leave you to rot. In fact, that's exactly what I'm going to do."

Faller gestured at A and C. "I have hostages. Innocent men." He waited for what he knew was coming.

"*Innocent* men." Woolcoff waved a dismissive hand. "They're *you*, down to the last cell. I'm looking forward to the day when I can line every one of you in front of a firing squad, but for now, I'll settle for three."

Faller couldn't suppress a half-smile. Let his companions chew on that little nugget for a moment.

"Would you mind refreshing my memory, since you took the liberty of erasing it? I understand you murdered the original me. What were we fighting about, exactly?"

Ugo uncrossed his arms, moved his face closer to the monitor. "Among other things, you killed my wife."

Faller was sick of people telling him he'd been a cold-blooded killer before Day One. He knew who he was, and people didn't change just because you wiped their memories. That was becoming clearer to Faller by the day. "You mean I took a gun, or a knife or something, and murdered her with it?"

"You might as well have." Ugo's anger was coming to the surface. "You're such an idiot. You have the worst judgment of anyone who's ever lived, and still you go barreling on, leaving ruined lives, a ruined *world*, in your wake. No more, though."

Ugo's face vanished.

Faller turned to Peter C. "Do you still hate me a little more—"

Peter C raised his hand. "Save it. I'll do it."

"You need help?" Peter A said.

"No, I've got it." Peter C looked up at Faller. "Peter Sandoval and I are going to finish what he started." He shrugged. "Who knows, maybe afterward we'll all meet nice girls, settle down in houses along Jamestown Road, raise kids. Whatever happens, it has to be better than this." He leaned over the console. Faller watched his hands sweep the air, his fingers tap.

A sheen of sweat formed on Peter C's brow as the smile faded, replaced by tension, maybe fear. Finally, he swiveled to face Faller.

"We're one function away from blackout. There's no taking it back once it's released. What's it going to be, Sandoval?"

"Do it. And my name is Faller. Don't call me Sandoval again. I'm no more or less Sandoval than you are."

Peter C spun back to his console, tapped the air once. He got up, went to the far end of the room and peered in at the singularity.

"You said it would take a few hours?" Faller asked.

"Sixteen to twenty," C said from across the room. "The air is so permeated that we're all going to be patient zero simultaneously."

Whatever that meant.

"Can I make a suggestion?" C asked. "If I were you two, I'd move away from that door."

Faller looked at the door, back at C. "Why is that?"

Mr. A, who was already moving toward the back of the room, answered. "Ugo's not going to be satisfied leaving you to starve. He's going to try to get that door open."

XXVII

PETER WOKE with a start. He'd been dreaming that a hole had opened under his bed, and he was falling right down through the core of the Earth. He woke to a reality no less bizarre.

He found a new toothbrush under the sink, brushed his teeth using pink lemonade instead of water.

Using the telescope, he checked out the street below. Most of the people who passed were carrying things, or pushing carts. Peter felt no impulse to race outside and join them, although he was aware that every moment he delayed gathering food, water, and weapons reduced his odds of survival. He wasn't afraid. Guilt currently crowded out the possibility of any other emotion.

There was no possible way he could build a new duplicator with the materials available on this island, so there was no chance of acquiring another singularity. Even if he had a singularity, the odds of ever understanding it well enough to repair the world seemed remote. What he should probably do is seek out President Aspen. Presenting himself to her wouldn't solve anything, but he could explain what happened, and, using what authority she retained, perhaps she could help the rest of the population understand. Of course, doing that would dramatically increase the odds he would be hung from a street lamp or burned alive.

It would be nice to have a handgun for protection. He went from room to room, looking in drawers and cabinets, hoping to get lucky.

The apartment's second bedroom was a child's room. From the abundance of action figures and military vehicles, Peter guessed its resident had been a boy of seven or eight.

A toy paratrooper hung from the lamp on the nightstand. Peter unhooked it from the light switch, looked it over. The figure was about an inch long, dressed in brown camo fatigues and a matching helmet. His parachute was light green, round, with slits in three of the panels.

He crumpled the parachute and figure together and tossed it toward the ceiling. The parachute deployed crisply. Peter swept the paratrooper off the floor and stuffed it in his front pocket as a plan began to form.

What were the odds that Williamsburg was below Manhattan in this new world order? Maybe using the telescope he could examine each of the islands within range, identify them, and form some working hypothesis about how the various land parcels had shaken out. Maybe.

Even if he had to jump blind, though, Peter would take the chance if he could locate a parachute, or make one. He had nothing to lose, and, besides his lab, Melissa was out there somewhere. Five Melissas were out there, actually. He knew she would never forgive him; odds were she'd lost all faith in him after what he'd done. But he still needed to find her. Even if she despised him, he would give anything to see her, to be near her.

He wanted to find his friends as well. For an instant, he couldn't remember Harry's and Kathleen's faces, then they came rushing back, and with them Peter felt such sharp longing to see them, mixed with a strange tangled grief from Harry's death. He still didn't know how to grieve for someone who was both gone and not gone.

They were all gone, now, unless he could find them.

The sky was mesmerizing. So enormous from his vantage point, dotted with cumulus humilis, like so many giant marshmallows.

. . . .

HE FELT like he was coming awake, but he hadn't been asleep, he'd been watching the clouds. Peter stood, dragged his hands down his face, tried to banish the fog from his mind. He had to get going, locate a parachute somewhere on this island in the sky so he could find . . .

A sick, crawling sensation slid through his gut. For a moment he hadn't been able to remember who he wanted to find. He'd forgotten Melissa.

He headed for the stairs.

People were hard at work foraging for supplies. A young guy in a purple shirt and sunglasses passed on the sidewalk pushing a cart loaded with bottled water, a pistol pinned between his hand and the cart handle.

An altercation on the corner half a block away caught his eye. Peter edged closer until he could hear a man and woman arguing. The woman was terribly distraught.

". . . get away from me, I said."

The man held out his hand. "Sabrina, please. I don't understand what's the matter with you. It's me. It's Joey."

"Don't touch me. Leave me alone."

"Sabrina, you're sick or something. We gotta get you somewhere safe. To a doctor or something."

Peter jogged back in the other direction, then stopped, looked around, not quite sure where to go. He'd done it—he'd really done it. Peter tried to think of the man's name, but came up blank. Big guy, always wore a hat. If the symptoms were manifesting now, he must have released the blackout virus sixteen to twenty hours before he sent Peter the warning.

They'd had an argument, he and the big guy, but Peter couldn't remember what it had been about. A woman.

A girl, thirteen or fourteen, passed Peter on the sidewalk, crying hysterically. She reached up, pressed her palms over her ears, screeched, "Where do I live?"

He had to think of a way to hang on to who he was.

Then he remembered the singularity. Its energy could be used to alleviate some of this. It could be transported in fuel cells to these islands. He and the other Peter who'd helped move it were the only people who knew where it was hidden. He had to write it down before he forgot.

Only, victims of the blackout virus couldn't read. He wouldn't remember how to read in a few hours. The thought was terrifying. He took a few deep breaths, tried to calm himself.

What if he drew pictures? Or a *map*?

He pulled out his wallet. There was nothing big enough to write on, only his ID card and a few photos. One of him and his wife, on their honeymoon. If she had known he still carried it around, she would have laughed that harsh, sarcastic laugh he'd only heard for the first time after everything went bad.

He dropped the wallet and its contents on the sidewalk, saving only the photo. When he tried to put the photo in his pocket, his fingers brushed something already in there.

He pulled out the paratrooper. He'd forgotten all about the parachute. Was there time to locate one?

Peter closed his eyes, tried to get a sense of how quickly the virus was doing its work. He had no idea where he'd grown up, had no memory of being a child, of having parents. He was a physicist—he still remembered that. His name was . . .

It wouldn't come.

He had to hurry. Patting his pockets, he realized he had nothing to write with. He could go to the closest apartment building, find an empty apartment and kick in the door. That would take time. He might forget what he wanted to write down by then.

He froze. What *did* he want to write down?

Straining to remember, he spotted the paratrooper in his hand. It came back to him.

There was a penknife on his key chain. He could cut his finger and use his blood. That was good—it would convey to his memory-wiped future self that the map was important, something he'd literally bled for. Glancing around, he spotted a discarded Milk Duds box in the gutter. He tore it open at the seam, flattened it on the sidewalk.

He opened the penknife, and without hesitation sliced into the pad of his thumb in one quick, violent pass.

Blood pattered onto the sidewalk in thick drops. Dipping the fingernail of his index finger into the blood, he started at the bottom, drawing a flag. He steadied his trembling hand by clutching it with the other, smearing both with blood in the process.

As he sketched out the ovals to represent the world as it was now, he kept forgetting what he was doing, and why. To fight against forgetting, he repeated aloud, "I'm drawing a map," over and over as he worked.

52

FALLER CALLED Storm.

"Are you all right?" Storm asked.

"I'm fine. I need you to ask Melissa how long it takes after the blackout virus is released before it's no longer contagious."

Faller heard muffled conversation as Storm spoke to Melissa. "About four days."

"It can't spread from one world to another, can it?" Although it was a little late to be thinking of that.

Storm consulted with Melissa. "Not unless someone who's infected carries it there. Why? What did you do?"

"I released it on Ugo's world."

Melissa whooped.

"The thing is, I'm still on Ugo's world."

"Hang on, you released the blackout virus on *yourself*?"

Faller had started pacing without realizing it. He stopped. "It was everyone or no one. At the time it seemed like the best of a lot of bad options."

"When I see you, you're not going to recognize me. It'll be Day One for you all over again."

Her words set off a crawling dread inside him. Day One all over again. He'd almost rather die. "I could stand the thought of Day One all over again if it didn't mean forgetting you."

"I'll remember for both of us," Storm said.

"Listen, I'm the guy in the shirt with the number two on it. I don't want you to ride off into the sunset with one of these other clowns."

"Very funny," C said.

53

Soon Faller wouldn't remember thinking the thoughts he was thinking now. It seemed impossible. He wondered if he could hang on to some of his memories, or even just one, through force of will. What if he held it firmly in his mind, repeated it while the virus did its work? If it were possible, which memory would he choose to keep above all others? Which memory of Storm was the quintessential moment in their time together?

Storm inviting him to join her in Penny's bedroom?

Their reconciliation, while they fell from Snakebite's world?

Faller thought of their midair reunion, after Woolcoff tipped the Orchid world. If not for what had followed, that would be his fondest memory.

A muffled explosion shook the room, knocking Faller off his chair.

"Here we go," C said from the spot on the floor where he'd landed.

The steel door was still in place, but there was a deep, jagged crease toward the bottom. Faller crawled a bit closer to inspect the damage. There was a six-inch breach where the door had pulled away from the wall. He could see into the hall, and heard voices, although he couldn't make out what they were saying.

Peter C coughed. "Here we go—a little tickle in my throat. That's how it starts. Another hour or so and we'll be vegetables."

Faller eyed the door. "I'm not sure we've got an hour."

. . . .

ANOTHER EXPLOSION rocked the room, sending electronic equipment tumbling from the tables, shooting chunks of debris toward the back of the room, where Faller, A, and C were sitting behind an overturned table.

"That almost got it," a voice said from behind the door. "We can batter it down from here."

"Can you see them?" a second voice asked.

"No."

From behind the table Faller flung the assault rifle toward the door, followed by the handgun. "We're not armed." He coughed again. The tickle in his throat was getting persistent.

There was a *bang* as something hit the door. The massive hinges holding the door squealed.

"Come on, let's try to look passive." Faller pushed the table aside, got down on his knees and put his hands behind his head. The others followed his lead, A to Faller's left, and C to his right. Hopefully if they gave themselves up without a fight, Ugo would pass up shooting them on the spot in order to plan a more public and festive execution.

"It's true what Ugo said, you know," Faller said as they knelt on the floor. "I don't know why you hate *me*. We're all the same guy, so you're just as responsible as I am. And really, from what Melissa told me, this is all Ugo's fault."

"Who's Melissa?" C asked.

At first Faller thought C was being facetious, but he was serious. "If no one here told you about Melissa, they've been telling you lies."

The door crashed to the floor. Faller held perfectly still as half a dozen soldiers rushed in pointing automatic weapons at him. At all three of him.

Two soldiers grabbed him under his armpits and dragged him out of the room. His knees and feet bumped the concrete steps as they dragged him to ground level and outside.

Ugo was waiting outside, hands on hips, with at least fifty other people. They dropped Faller at his feet.

"Are you sure you have the right one this time?" Ugo asked.

"I thought you said we were interchangeable." Faller pinched a piece of grass from his tongue.

Hands grabbed his ankles, pulled off his boots. A soldier walked around and handed Ugo the photo Faller had been carrying since Day One.

Ugo coughed as he tore it in half and dropped the pieces into the grass. "Get up."

Faller considered defying Ugo, but figured all he'd get for his trouble was a kick in the ribs from one of the soldiers. He stood.

Ugo punched him in the face. The blow landed between his mouth and nose like a sack of rocks, knocking him backward a step. Another punch, to his eye, landed before he could recover.

Faller retreated a few steps as people cheered Ugo on. The thing was, there was almost as much coughing as cheering. Faller had no idea whether he knew how to fight. He raised his fists close to his face, lunged and threw a punch that glanced off Ugo's cheek. Ugo buried a fist in Faller's stomach, doubling him over. It surprised Faller how much it hurt. Much worse than getting hit in the face. Ugo was much bigger than him, and looked in shape for a guy with greying hair. And evidently Faller didn't know how to fight.

Ugo kicked upward, at Faller's bent face, but missed badly. Faller straightened, even though it sent jets of pain through his stomach, and raised his fists again. He needed to drag this out until the blackout virus knocked Ugo out for him. Faller threw three or four punches in quick succession. Two landed with a satisfying smacking sound.

Howling and red-faced, Ugo stiff-armed Faller in the face, drove him backward until he tripped over someone's foot and tumbled to the ground. Ugo grabbed him by the hair, lifted his head and punched him, three, four, five times. The last punch caused a sickening cracking sensation in his mouth. Some of Faller's teeth had broken.

Ugo stepped back. His knuckle was gashed and bleeding, and he was panting heavily, but he was grinning.

The grin wavered. A look crossed Ugo's face, as if he were trying to remember something, then it vanished. He kicked Faller in the face.

Faller was gone for a moment, lost in pain, disoriented, not sure where he was, or what was happening.

"I'm going to beat you to death." Ugo stood over him, hands on his hips. "I want you to be aware of what's happening. You're going to die right here in this grass."

Faller touched his nose, which felt much too big and thick. It was numb on the outside, but pain raged deeper inside.

Ugo kicked him in the stomach, higher up this time. Faller felt a rib snap.

"There was a time when . . ." Ugo trailed off, his mouth forming an O, his eyebrows clenched.

"You're forgetting something, Ugo," Faller said. He waited for Ugo to catch on, but Ugo just stood there, his face pinched in concentration. "Fine. You'll . . ." Faller trailed off, the thought he'd formed vanished. There was a fizzing/popping sensation in his head, as if he were feeling each individual memory as it was extinguished.

"What am I forgetting?" Ugo asked, his tone almost pleading.

"I'm not going to tell you." The truth was, Faller couldn't remember what he was going to say, but he wasn't going to tell Ugo that. He hated Ugo. Although at the moment he couldn't remember why.

Ugo turned to one of the soldiers, held out his hand. The soldier put a crowbar in it.

"Hang on, I'll tell you," Faller said.

Ugo waited.

Faller strained to remember what he was about to tell Ugo. It was something he'd done, something Ugo wouldn't like. It was so hard to think, though. Something was wrong with him. Something—

"The blackout virus. You're forgetting the blackout virus."

Faller could see the wheels turning in Ugo's head. "You released it? Here?"

It felt as if the back of Faller's head had vanished, replaced by inky blackness. Faller reached up, pressed his fingers against the back of his head to make sure it was still there.

It was.

"I'm bringing a hundred fifty copies of you up to speed in astrophysics," Ugo said. "At the pace they're going, in two years they'll know as much about . . . something . . . as you knew. Then they'll put their heads together and—" Faller could see the thought get away from Ugo as he pressed a palm to his forehead, trying to concentrate. "God*damnit*, you little *fuck.*"

The big man swung the crowbar at Faller's face. Faller raised his hands to ward off the blow, caught the brunt of it on his fingers. The next blow landed on his kneecap. Then his thigh. His hip. His ribs again, the pain blinding.

He wrapped his arms around his head and steeled himself for the next blow. The pain was blinding, excruciating. When the next blow didn't come, he looked up.

The big man stood over him holding the crowbar with the most peculiar expression on his face.

"Where was I?" the big man asked. "I—" He licked his lips, looked at the crowbar. "Was I hitting you?"

"No." It seemed the safest answer. "Why would you hit me?"

"Him, yes," a woman in a uniform said, pointing. "He's—"

"Because you—" The big man dragged his hand through his thinning hair. "It was something. You did something to me. You took something."

The pain was terrible. Intolerable.

What was happening to him? Then he remembered: blackout virus. He was being erased. Soon there would be nothing left. Was there anything left now? He closed his eyes, tried to remember something. Anything.

"I was falling. I remember that." He was falling through the sky, the endless sky, toward a thin woman with black hair. He loved her.

The crowbar thunked to the ground. The big man clapped his hands over his ears.

Something was wrong. Had they been in an accident? Were they sick?

54

CHIRPING WOKE him. Stabbing, burning, throbbing pain radiated from so many places in his body he couldn't focus on any one. He'd been in some sort of accident. Maybe he'd fallen.

He peeled open one eye, expecting to find himself in a hospital bed. Instead he was lying in the grass, surrounded by other people.

He waited for memory to follow, for reminders of why he was badly hurt, who these people were, but nothing came.

The chirping was coming from a thin metal rectangle lying in the grass near him.

"Do you know me?" a voice asked.

Slowly, gently, he got to his hands and knees, tried to rise. Stabbing, agonizing pain shot through his knee and he dropped back into the grass.

"Do you know me?" the man repeated.

"No." The chirping stopped.

There was another man nearby who looked exactly the same as the first: sandy-brown hair, a roundish face. He had an *A* on the sleeve of his shirt. The other man had a *C*. "Do you know either of us?" Faller asked him.

"No," the man said.

The standing man, C, frowned. "How can you not know each other? You're brothers or something. You look exactly alike."

Slowly, gingerly, he pointed at himself. The pain in his ribs doubled. "*I* look like him? So do *you*." He looked around. There was a building nearby, all glass and steel. Other buildings nearby. Nothing was familiar. He craved something familiar to stave off the awful lost feeling he had.

Other people were walking around, speaking to each other in urgent tones. They all looked terribly confused and scared.

A click behind him made his shoulders clench. He turned. His twin with a *C* on his sleeve was holding up a rifle, examining it.

"It's loaded," C said.

"We must have been fighting someone. Maybe they did this to us," a big man said. He had a bruise on his cheek, a drooping, slightly swollen left eye.

Maybe there was something in his pockets that would give him a clue to who he was. He checked them, and found three photographs. They were of children of varying ages with bronze-colored skin and black hair.

The big guy was standing over him. "Maybe they're your family."

Seeing what he was doing, the other men went through their own pockets. A had a half-empty pack of gum, two keys on a ring. C had an identical key ring and a pen.

"Are those your children?" the big man asked him.

He shook his head. "I don't know."

"Amnesia. That's the word for this," A said.

The word sounded strange, like it was the first time he'd ever heard it, yet the man was right. That was the right word.

The thin rectangle started chirping again. He picked it up, held it in his palm. "Phone?" The word sizzled in his mind like he was giving birth to it.

All three men nodded. "You talk to people on it," C said.

"How?" He turned it over, looking for buttons, but it didn't have any. It stopped chirping.

"We should find food and water," the big man said.

55

He needed something to drink, but the distance between his cot and the sink was a thousand miles to his eye—the one that wasn't swollen shut.

Pain. It was his whole world.

A woman was shouting outside, her voice muffled. The sound drew closer. He wanted to go to the door to see what the commotion was, but that, like the glass of water, would mean more pain.

Of course he had to get the water sooner or later. Maybe he should get it over with, and see who was shouting, and what they were shouting about, while he was up.

He swung his leg over, pushed himself into a sitting position, wincing from the stabbing pain in his ribs and knee. Grasping the broom handle he leaned on when he walked, he pushed himself to his feet and staggered to the door.

"Faller?" a woman was calling. She was jogging beside a woman who looked exactly like her, both of them looking all around. They were skinny, green-eyed, freckled. He hadn't noticed them before, which was odd, because he thought he'd met just about everyone in the world over the past few days. One of his look-alikes was following a few paces behind them.

One of the women spotted him, and stopped short. "What number was on your shirt?"

"Excuse me?"

"On the first day. What number was on the sleeve of your shirt?"

He looked at the floor. The shirt was lying where he'd dropped it when he discovered clean ones in a drawer of the room he chose.

"Two."

The woman's face lit up. She raced toward him. "*Faller*. Oh, my God." She grasped his arm and leaned in to study his face, hand over her mouth. "Oh, my God. How did you get like this?"

"I don't know."

The woman wrapped her arms around him. Faller hissed through his teeth, grasped her arms. "I could really use a hug right now, I admit it, but it hurts too much."

The other woman, who was hovering a few feet away, said, "We need to get you out of here."

"Out of where?"

The woman who'd tried to hug him touched his arm gently. "We're your friends. We know what happened to you, and we'll tell you, but right now we have to get you and a few other people off this world. Bad people are coming."

He fought back tears of relief. The thought of having friends who wanted to help him was overwhelming. "Do you know my name?"

She let him go. "You're Faller. I'm Storm, that's Melissa, and that handsome devil over there is One-Thirty-one." She pointed at his look-alike.

"Faller." He liked the sound of it. He didn't think much of his face, but he liked his name.

"Can we save the introductions for the ride?" One-Thirty-one said.

Storm smiled. "He's our ride."

"Sure, that's all I am to you. A means of transportation," One-Thirty-one said. "Once we're safe you'll probably try to shoot me again."

Laughing, Storm put a hand on Faller's shoulder. "Can you walk?"

As she led him away, she explained what had happened. He wasn't surprised to learn he and Storm were in love, but his mind reeled when Storm went on to explain that he and Melissa were divorced. And that was just the beginning.

56

FALLER WATCHED the ground approach, the whine of the aircraft deafening.

"This is definitely it." Melissa studied the landscape through a window. "I knew it was five or six islands directly up from where I was dropped off. We were in a hurry to get hidden, so we ended up clustered together."

"Finally," Ugo said. "I'm so airsick I'm not sure I'll ever feel normal again."

Faller studied the big man's profile. It was hard to grasp that they'd been mortal enemies. He looked like a pleasant enough fellow.

It was a pretty world, with two lakes and a lot of trees in the center, the rest of the land cut up into parcels with houses on them.

When One-Thirty-one swung the stairs into place, Melissa went out first, glancing this way and that, rifle pointed at the ground, as a crowd gathered.

"We're looking for a man named Harry," Melissa called. "This tall." She held her hand out a bit higher than the top of her own head. "Asian."

"He's probably at home," a grey-haired woman said. "Who *are* you?"

"We're—" Melissa hesitated, cast about for the right words.

"We're the good guys," One-Thirty-one said. Under his breath, he added, "At least, I'm a good guy. The jury's still out on you."

"Shut up," Melissa said. "I may still shoot you."

A contingent of locals led Faller—who was still getting accustomed to his crutches—Storm, Penny, and Melissa to Harry's house, which backed onto one of the lakes. Some children had run ahead, and as Faller and his companions approached the house a man came barreling down the street, laughing and screaming like a lunatic. Melissa had told Faller they were friends, so he tucked one crutch under his arm and held out his hand to shake. Harry just kept coming, arms open.

He might have plowed right into Faller if Storm hadn't stepped between them. "Gentle, gentle. He's injured."

"Oh, my God. Oh, my God, I can't believe it!" Harry kissed Faller on the forehead. "You don't remember me, do you?"

"Don't take it personally. I don't remember anyone."

"Yeah, there's a lot of that going around." Harry nodded sympathetically. He went and hugged Storm, and Melissa.

"You'll never guess what we have on our aircraft," Melissa said.

Harry tilted his head. "Tons of food, I hope. Vodka would be nice. Maybe some Xanax? I'd kill for a Xanax."

Melissa waved her hands at him. "Think big. What one thing would you most want us to have with us?"

Harry frowned, thinking. Then his eyes got huge. "No. Seriously? You got it? *Seriously?*"

"Can we use it? We can't go back to Peter's lab—Elba is in control there. Are there other places we can go where you can find the equipment you need?"

"Absolutely. Just find me an R-1 university with a decent physics department. UNC Chapel Hill. UVA."

"We also have Peter's notes," Melissa said.

Harry clutched his chest. "Seriously?"

"Is there any chance we can fix this mess?"

Harry considered. "It'll take time—years—because God knows, we've learned our lesson about rushing things. I don't know. It's possible."

57

MELISSA WAS standing by the cargo door, staring out at empty blue sky, one hand on the wall. She went on staring as Faller joined her.

"You look sad. The worst parts are over, you know."

Still, she didn't look at him. "It was supposed to be you and me who ended up together, not you and one of my duplicates." She sighed. "It makes sense, though. She's me without the past. You're you without the past. It's like when we first met."

The words surprised Faller. Since they'd gotten divorced, he'd assumed Melissa didn't like him much. "I'll be the first to admit I'm still getting a grasp on all of this, but I'm not the original Peter—the one you met in high school, right?"

Melissa sighed. "You insisted you were. You told me I was getting hung up on bodies and being too literal-minded."

Peter pointed at One-Thirty-one. "So how am I different to you from that guy over there?"

Melissa glanced at One-Thirty-one. "We have a shared past. Mostly a bad one filled with pain, but we fought Ugo together."

"Aren't you getting hung up on bodies again? I mean, either you're willing to accept that I'm just a continuation of the original Peter, or you're not. And if you are . . ." Faller pointed at One-Thirty-one again. "So is he."

Noticing Faller pointing, One-Thirty-one raised his eyebrows, then jokingly looked over his shoulder before pointing at himself in a "Who, me?" gesture.

"Look at him," Faller said. "He's in love with you. When a Peter looks at a Melissa, he can't help but love her. We need to locate all the Melissas, and introduce them all to Peters."

Melissa burst out laughing. At the sound of her laughter One-Thirty-one glanced her way again.

"I'm serious. We're meant to be together. Look at him. He loves you. We're all in love with every one of you. Every damned one of us."

Melissa leaned over and kissed Faller's cheek. "And I love every damned one of you, too. Just—" She shook her fist in mock frustration. "*Think* before you jump."

"I'll try." It was hard to learn from your mistakes when you didn't remember making them. At least now he knew what most of them were. Maybe that was enough.

58

THEY HOVERED a thousand feet above the world, which was packed with towering buildings on one end, punctuated by one skyscraper that seemed much too tall to stay upright.

"This has to be it," Penny said.

Storm pointed. "There's the building you parachuted from."

He eyed the distance between the building and the nearest edge of the world. How had he ever managed to make it that far? He wished he could remember.

As Storm took the Harrier down, Faller watched the upturned faces, the shock and wide-eyed wonder of the people in the streets.

They set down at the foot of the skyscraper that had started all of this.

A rumble went through the gathering crowd as Faller stepped out. "Faller. It's Faller." It made him sad, that he didn't remember them.

"Does anyone know where I can find Daisy?" he called.

A teenaged boy broke away from the crowd and ran off.

"He's going to fetch her," an old man shouted.

They waited expectantly for him to say something.

"I guess you're surprised to see me back here."

Murmurs of assent rolled through the crowd.

"Well, I'm surprised to be here. I never expected to make it back. The important thing is, I'm bringing good news. From here on out, things are going to get better. There's going to be enough food. Plus medicine, and electricity. People to teach you how to plant crops—"

"*Faller!*" A young, brown-skinned girl pushed through the crowd, launched herself into his arms.

"Daisy." She was nothing but skin and bones. Not starving, but not far off.

She looked at him, eyes wide. "You died. I saw you."

"You saw me fall. I didn't die."

"Hello, Daisy," Storm said.

"This is Storm," Faller said.

"Hello, Storm." Daisy looked her up and down, eyes wide. "You're the woman in Faller's picture. You're so *clean*."

"Thanks." Storm laughed. "We're going to get you clean as well. Would that be okay?"

"Oh, *sure*."

Penny and two other crewmembers had begun unloading food and medicine. Over Daisy's shoulder, Faller spotted a bewildered-looking Asian woman at the edge of the crowd. She took an unsteady step forward.

"Hello, Kathleen."

"*Peter?*" One of her hands was moving frantically at her side.

"I'll answer to that name, but I prefer Faller."

Kathleen bolted toward him open-armed, and just about crushed his still-screaming ribs with a hug.

Ugo stepped out of the Harrier, his arms full of supplies. Kathleen shrieked, backpedaled half a dozen steps.

Ugo frowned, confused by her reaction.

"Don't worry about him," Faller said. "He's fine. Go ahead, Ugo."

"She startled me," Ugo grumbled as he set the boxes down and went back inside the Harrier for more.

"What's going on?" Kathleen said. "Is it safe now? How do you know my real name?"

"I don't know about *safe*. Definitely safer. And I know your name because I bumped into Melissa on my way down. She's back at our HQ. She says hi."

Kathleen lowered her voice. "What is *he* doing here?"

"Keep your friends close, and your enemies closer. Melissa told me that—I didn't come up with it myself."

Faller put an arm across Daisy's shoulder. "You want to take a ride with us, once we're finished here?"

"Oh, sure."

"You're going to live with me and Storm. Plus you have a brother and two sisters to keep you company." He looked at Kathleen. "You, too. We need your help. We're getting the band back together."

Faller looked up at the skyscraper. It made him dizzy and a little queasy to stare up that sheer, towering wall. He couldn't believe he'd actually jumped off it wearing a homemade parachute. But then again, he could.